"But do not take this responsibility lightly, my boy. The Gauntlet casts an ominous shadow."

—High Mancer, Council of Mages

the shadow of the gauntlet

by

casey caracciolo

illustrated by casey caracciolo

To CLAUDIA,
I HOPE YOU THINK
THE ADVENTURE
IS ENTIRELY
NARSH!

2/10/18

roundstone
PUBLISHING

Text copyright © 2011–2013 Casey Caracciolo
Illustration and design by Casey Caracciolo
© 2013 Roundstone Publishing
All related characters and elements of the Scargen series
are ™ of and © of Roundstone Publishing.
All rights reserved. Published by Roundstone Publishing.
The Shadow of the Gauntlet; book one of the Scargen series

No part of this publication can be reproduced or transmitted
in any form or by any means, electronic or mechanical, including
photocopying, recording, or by any information or
retrieval systems without written permission
from Roundstone Publishing.

For permission requests write to:
roundstone@scargen.com

Library of Congress Control Number:
2013906000

ISBN 10: 0615779204
ISBN 13: 978-0615779201

Printed in the U.S.A.
First Edition: September 2013
Edited by Joe Hansche, Christine Carbone, and Casey Caracciolo
Typesetting by Shanna Compton

Visit scargen.com

To Christine:

Without you,
I am nothing.

You are
my muse,
my rock,
my love,
and my heart.

You are a
damn fine editor
and
an extraordinary wife.

Words cannot express
how much you mean
to this book
and to me.

This is **our** achievement.

contents

prologue
perchance to dream

Old Egypt, the Future

Warning sirens sounded as several red lights flashed atop the floating platform on which Dr. Carl Scargen and his colleague Sigmund Jacobs were working. The platform hovered one hundred feet above the highest of the pyramids, the Pyramid of Khufu, the Great Pyramid of Giza. The massive sandstone cave housed all of the pyramids as well as the Sphinx and hundreds of newly unearthed tunnels, passageways, and tombs. The cautious howl of the warning siren echoed throughout the artificially lit cavern.

"Sig, what's the problem?" asked the doctor as he rushed over to his partner's control station.

"Let's have a look," said Sigmund, concentrating on the holoscreen directly in front of him. The two men resembled an old comedy duo. The doctor was tall and thin, while Sigmund was short, pudgy, and balding. The doctor looked at the holoscreens, peering over Sigmund's shoulder. Several holographic displays that normally relayed footage back to the platform were now blank.

"They're completely scrambled," said Dr. Carl Scargen, grabbing his ears. "That siren only goes off when something has potentially compromised the dig."

"I can't tell what's going on, Doc. The cameras on the diggerbot must have been fried."

"Did you see anything that could've done this?"

"There was a glowing light that originated from where Digger 211 was excavating. He found a container, and when he went to open it, there was a flash and the holoscreens all went kaput." The two men had spent the last ten years of their lives uncovering the past. Egypt had been buried under hundreds of feet of sand and sandstone, an event that started the Tech War. A terrorist act is what the Global Alliance had called it, but the data the diggerbots had collected did not support this idea. They had not found any evidence of weaponry being used that could have caused this type of damage. Egypt had simply and purposely been buried—by what or whom was still a mystery. Whatever Digger 211 had found could help answer some of these questions. The doctor looked down at his wristcom.

"It looks as if Digger 211's right forearm unit is malfunctioning." The doctor pushed a button on his wristcom. "211, return to the platform for repairs."

"As you wish, Dr. Scargen," said 211 in a pleasant male voice.

"Sig, try switching to 212's feed, and could you please turn off that damn siren." Sigmund moved a few icons on the holographic display and the alarm ceased. Seconds later, the screens were once again filled with holographic images.

"Looks like we're back in business," said Sigmund as he jiggled his finger in his ear.

"212, move in closer to that box," ordered the doctor. "Let's see what all the fuss is about." The camera angle adjusted as the Digger progressed forward. The robot's camera focused on the object. The box appeared to be made of sandstone and was cracked open. The diggerbot moved closer. The contents of the box were now clear on the display. Inside was a black stone. "212."

"Yes, Dr. Scargen," said the diggerbot.

"Retrieve the artifact and return to the platform."

"Affirmative, Dr. Scargen." The doctor moved away from the station and over to where Digger 211 had just appeared over the edge of the platform. The android's body was oval in shape. A small head extended from the middle of the torso. It resembled a pair of scuba goggles in shape with a solitary eye in the middle. This housed the camera and the robot's light source. The arms were long hoses connected to a bulky forearm that contained the Digger's tools. These made the robots more maneuverable in tight quarters. The Diggers, as they were aptly nicknamed, were the lifeblood of the operation. This type of controlled excavation would not have been possible without these artificial life forms, or artifs as they were commonly called. In total there were forty-four diggerbots sorting through the piles of debris and rock, carefully removing, cleaning, and cataloging pieces of time.

Dr. Carl Scargen surveyed the large egg-shaped robot that levitated in front of him. His bulky torso was tattooed with the number 211 in white. The artif's body was intact with limited scarring, but his right forearm had been demolished.

"Let me have a look at it." The robot lifted what was left of his arm. "You're going to need a full forearm replacement," said the doctor. He would know: he had created them all. He had designed and built thousands of artifs in his lifetime. "But I have no clue what could've done this."

"The big bossman of the most advanced robotics company in the world, for once, can't figure something out," said Sigmund. "I never thought I'd live to see the day." The man smiled at his colleague.

"I didn't say I couldn't figure it out. I simply said I don't know what did this." Dr. Carl Scargen had always been adept at figuring out how things worked, and he used this ability to build incredible pieces of machinery. Scargen Robotics was his brainchild. They designed, built, and serviced artifs of every kind, and they were largely considered the best in the field.

Digger 212 floated onto the platform. The doctor turned to see what had been found. Maybe this artifact would somehow explain the damage. "Okay, let's see what you got," said Sigmund. The artif's chest opened just below the 212 on his torso. Digger 212 grabbed the dark stone from his storage unit and placed it into Sigmund's hand.

Sigmund looked intently at the rock. "There are peculiar markings on the outer ring. I'm not sure what these symbols are. This could take some time."

Dr. Scargen moved over to the containers where he kept the spare parts for his artifs. "Well, you get started on figuring out what that thing is while I repair 211." The doctor punched several keys on the holographic keyboard floating above his wristcom. A holographic control interface emerged above the keyboard. He began to interact with the controls.

Two small toolbots rose out from the container carrying the new forearm for the injured artif. These were also the work of Carl Scargen. He used these smaller artifs to fix and maintain the larger ones. They flew towards the egg-shaped robot as the doctor lowered his safety goggles.

"Hey, Doc, I just thought of something," said Sigmund. "What if this stone is what the Global Alliance is trying to hide?"

"Oh, we're back to your crazy conspiracy theories. Were you always this suspicious?" asked Dr. Scargen. "And what exactly do you have against the GA? Without the work I've done for them, we wouldn't be able to afford to play in such a big sandbox."

"They aren't the only contracts you have," said Sigmund as he scanned the dark stone with his wristcom.

"Building and maintaining servicebots does not pay anywhere near as well as government contracts."

"You could always build sportsbots for one of the robotic sports leagues. I've heard Ricky Nones pays his engineers ridiculous credits, and he has his hands on teams in all of the major robotic sports: the NRFL, the NRHL, MRLB, the NRBA. If it's a sport with artifs in it, he's got a team."

"I could never work for a man that treats artifs the way he does," said the doctor as he continued operating with the toolbots. "I believe artifs should be afforded the same basic rights as any living creature and treated humanely. They shouldn't be exploited for entertainment, and that's exactly what Nones is doing."

"I'm just saying there are options, and you need to be careful when working with the Global Alliance," said Sigmund. "Not every-one shares your views when it comes to artifs."

"Scargen Robotics is doing just fine with our partnership with the GA. My contracts are very specific, Sig. Gideon and I are on the same page on this. All robotic designs are strictly for peaceful applications. No military . . . nonviolent only. I have made my stance very clear."

"I trust Gideon Upshaw about as much as I trust the GA."

"Without the Alliance, we would've never procured the rights to this excavation, and without Gideon running Scargen Robotics, I would never have the time to excavate anything." He looked over at Sigmund. "And why would they let us dig here if they had something to hide?" The tiny toolbots removed the android's mangled arm.

"I suppose you have a point there. It's just that I've read a lot of disconcerting things about the GA, and I just have a feeling about Upshaw. He seems a little too eager to agree sometimes. I just don't want to see my best friend get taken advantage of."

"You shouldn't worry so much, Sig. That's how you lose your hair."

"Too late for that," said Sigmund, scratching his head.

"Besides, my best work I keep close to home." He looked up at the diggerbot that was being repaired. "These Diggers are the best things I've ever created . . . well, besides Tom's artif LINC . . . and Tom, of course."

"How is the boy? It's been ages since I've seen the lad."

"Good, I guess." Dr. Scargen lifted up his safety goggles. The holographic interface vanished, but the toolbots continued to work on the Digger. "I called him about an hour ago. No answer. I guess he's out with those idiotic friends of his."

"There's something to be said about idiotic friends," said Sigmund as he winked at the Doc.

"We're just so different. I mean I loved school. He barely scratches by." He rubbed the back of his neck with his free hand. "If he spent half the time studying as he spends playing hologames or reading those silly fantasy books of his, he'd be the valedictorian." He turned to look at Sigmund. "For the life of me I don't understand why he insists on collecting actual books. People don't read actual books anymore. Holobooks yes, but not actual books."

"So he's obsessed with fantastical places and far away lands." Sigmund scratched his head. "And you say he collects remnants from a forgotten world." He massaged his chin. "I don't know, Doc. He sounds a lot like someone I work with." They shared a laugh.

"Thanks, Sig. I guess the apple landed a little closer to the tree than I'd thought." The doctor smiled as he returned to the injured artif. The toolbots had just finished attaching the new arm. He moved towards the Digger. "He graduates tomorrow, which is a small miracle in itself." He reached into the Digger's new forearm with both of his hands. "I can't wait to surprise him. I told him that I couldn't make it because of the dig, but nothing's going to stop me from seeing him grab that diploma. The ticket cost me a small fortune, but I should be back in New Salem just in time for the ceremony."

"The Diggers and I will miss you," said Sigmund. "Isn't that right, 211?"

"Yes, Dr. Scargen. Your absence will not be convenient," said Digger 211. The doctor again smiled.

"I'm just so proud of Tom, no matter how much he slacks off." He turned a switch inside the armpiece of the robot and slammed the panel shut. After wiping his hands with a towel, he threw it aside and turned his attention back to the Digger. The holographic interface again appeared above his wristcom. With a few movements of his hand, the toolbots flew back into the container. "I just have this gut feeling, Sig, like he's meant to do extraordinary things."

"He's a smart kid, Doc. I'm sure he'll figure it out sooner or later."

"I'm just hoping it's sooner rather than later," said Dr. Scargen as he looked back at his colleague and smirked. "And thanks, Sig."

"Ah, don't mention it, and besides, we can't all be naturals like you."

"I don't know if I'd call what I do natural," said the doctor as he laughed away the compliment and returned his attention back to the artif. "That should just about do it, 211. You should be as good as new." The doctor finished typing on the holographic keyboard.

"Thank you, Dr. Scargen," voiced Digger 211. The artif raised his new arm and moved his finger-like appendages.

"My pleasure, 211. Now back to work."

"Affirmative, Dr. Scargen." The artif raced back downward into the tombs of Ancient Egypt.

"What you do is a god damn miracle . . ." trailed off Sigmund, slowly laughing to himself. His eyes were fixed on the strange stone in his hand.

"It's almost like the way you read and decipher glyphs," said the doctor.

"Yeah, but something tells me that if you spent ten minutes looking at this thing you could figure it out your damn self."

"But Sigmund, think of how lonely I would be." The two men laughed. It must have been the hundredth time they went through the same lines, but to the two of them, it was always funny. Sigmund was probably right in his assumptions. Dr. Carl Scargen had several language degrees to go along with his seven in robotics and still four others in archeology. Good companionship, though, cannot be measured.

As Sigmund's laughter subsided, his attention was again drawn to the gem that rested in the center of his left palm. The artifact was salvaged from one of the deepest tombs that the Diggers had uncovered. It measured about four inches in diameter, hardly dangerous looking, but somehow opening its case had caused severe damage to 211's arm. "I have to say that I think I'm stumped. At first I thought it was part of an amulet worn by some snot-nosed brat of a pharaoh, who was undoubtedly stabbed or poisoned by a relative before he reached his twenties."

"I love your factless speculations." The doctor smiled.

"Thank you, but that's just it. I was way off. I mean centuries off." Sigmund's wristcom was scanning the artifact. An array of red beams washed across the dark jewel. "The grooves on the back clearly indicate that this stone, at some point, was set inside of something else."

"Like what?"

"My best guess is a rock of some sort." He flipped the dark stone over carefully. "The computer found tiny particulates on the back of the artifact, most likely left behind from whatever it was attached to, but it's having difficulty naming the actual substance."

"That's odd."

"I thought the same thing. One thing is certain. This thing, whatever it is, it's old—really old. The radiometric dating suggests that it easily predates Ancient Egypt." The Doc looked astonished. "That would explain why I'm having difficulty deciphering the glyphs. The computer has been no help either. Like I said, Doc, I'm stumped." Sigmund looked at his friend. "You might be useful after all."

"I guess I'll have to save your butt again. Let's see what my keen sense of language can decipher," remarked the doctor as he leaned over and extended his hand.

"Here ya go, Doc," said Sigmund, pretending to throw the priceless find. Instead, he smiled and began to move the rock carefully towards the doctor's hand. "If I remember correctly, the way you catch, I'd better just hand it to you."

As the artifact touched the doctor's hand, a high-pitched sound emanated from the rock, shortly followed by a huge pulse wave that sent Sigmund hurtling backward. He landed on his back.

The portly man quickly worked to stand back up. "Doc," said Sigmund as he cautiously rubbed his eyes. "I can't see a damn thing. The flash blinded me." The siren was ringing once more. The red lights through the black smoke were disorienting.

Two diggerbots were now hovering above the site of the explosion, no doubt a piece of clever programming by the doctor for disaster recovery. They were scanning the area with their sensors to evaluate the risk involved with the rescue and recovery of their human counterparts. "Are you okay, Doc?" asked Sigmund into the cloud of smoke.

No answer.

"Doc, where the hell are you? Carl, stop playing around."

No answer.

The artifs began to hover lower and lower and reached out and plucked Sigmund off of the pile of spare parts that he had landed on. The Diggers leveled off and lifted Sigmund by either arm like a prisoner. His feet could not touch the ground. A black mist, another result of the explosion, surrounded him. Then all of a sudden the artifs stopped.

"Diggers 211 and 214, put me down," said Sigmund.

"Negative, command invalid," said the artif.

"That's preposterous. I am authorized to—"

"Former authorization has been terminated," whistled 211.

"This is absurd, on whose authority?" demanded Sigmund, dropping the niceties of his last enquiry.

"Mine, of course, my dear Sigmund," echoed a voice from the black fog.

"Doc, is that you? Thank God, I thought you were . . ." Sigmund's voice trailed off as the mist seemed to swirl and form itself into a hooded figure that moved towards him. "Who the hell are you? Where is the Doc?" The hooded man raised his hands over his head as if to stretch, completely ignoring Sigmund's questioning.

"I'm afraid the good doctor is currently . . . unavailable," uttered the hooded figure, raising his right hand towards Sigmund. "I'll have to do." Embedded in his palm was the black stone he had handed to Dr. Scargen. A beam shot out from the stone towards Sigmund's shaking body. Sigmund cried in pain. The hooded man leaned over and whispered to the convulsing man. "I swear this will only hurt for a second, and then the pain will be gone . . . forever." Sigmund's body slowly became still, the last ounce of life being sucked out by the mysterious rock. The essence that was pulled into the dark artifact was being ingested by the hooded figure. Energy coursed through the mysterious figure's whole body as high-pitched laughter echoed endlessly throughout the enormous cavern.

the shadow of the gauntlet

1

the midnight meeting

"**D**ad!" screamed Thomas Scargen as his eyes flashed open. The boy jolted out of his sleep. His copy of *Dragon's Omen*, the third book in the *Dragon Fire Chronicles*, flew off of his chest and onto the bedroom floor. Thomas was nestled in the trench he had carved into his queen size bed over the almost seventeen years of his life. The boy's feet dangled slightly over the edge of the bed. His breathing was erratic, and sweat dripped from his hair.

Stella, Thomas's gray tabby cat, had flown from her resting place on the bed, startled by the boy's sudden movement. She leered at the boy. He was vaguely conscious of what was going on. Thomas's eyes slowly began to focus on the feline. He could now make out the embossed Scargen Robotics logo on the circular metallic tag that dangled from her collar. She had been a gift from his father.

Stella hopped back onto the bed and flopped down next to the boy. She nuzzled against his rib cage while stretching her white, paint-dipped paws as far forward as possible. Thomas's breathing began to slow.

Sweat covered his New Salem High School Ice Hockey tee, slightly darkening its light gray color. He pushed his dirty blond hair out of his eyes and tucked it behind his right ear. He noticed he had left the holovision on from the night before. It was stuck on the start screen of one of the hologames he was playing, *The Legend of Gar.* Thomas closed his eyes as his mouth stretched into a yawn. Extending his arms above his head, he turned to the right. When he reopened his eyes, an android was staring back at him. The boy jumped back. "LINC." The white exterior of the artif was easy for Thomas to make out in the dark. Red beams of light emanated from the robot's eyes, scanning the boy.

"Thomas Scargen, are you fully functional?" questioned LINC. The robot spoke in a high-pitched but distinctly male voice. His mouth glowed when he spoke. Two optical sensors resided on the artif's pill-shaped head. "Your heart rate is accelerated, and your brain functions are slightly irregular." The motherly robot was standing over the bed as the eleventh and twelfth chimes rang out from the clock downstairs.

"I'm fine, LINC." The boy sat up. "I'm a little thirsty." A hovering tray floated over to Thomas carrying a glass of water.

"I anticipated your requirement for rehydration upon awakening," said LINC, an acronym for Learning Intelligence Networked Companion. The boy grabbed the water and began to drink. LINC was Dr. Scargen's best invention and Thomas's best friend. The artif was built to serve, protect, and care for the boy.

Dr. Carl Scargen had also filled the home with additional artifs and inventions that were designed to predict the needs of the inhabitants. The machines did everything from household chores to tending to the sustainable farm that occupied part of the Scargen estate. Besides Stella, Thomas was the sole biological resident when the doctor was away. The boy finished the water and replaced it on the tray.

"You know that's a little creepy, hovering above me while I'm sleeping, scanning my brain and all. How many times have I asked you to stop doing that?" questioned Thomas.

"If you are counting this last instance, it has been approximately 357 times you have verbally requested that I cease this action," said the artif. "That, however, does not include the 263 instances that your facial expression has indicated the same. After years of observation, I have ascertained that you are extremely adept at nonverbal communication."

The boy's thoughts dwelled on his father and his nightmare. Dr. Carl Scargen was somewhere in Old Egypt, making history—or "finding history" as he called it.

Thomas looked down and remembered he had logged off and put his wristcom on silent to get some much-needed sleep. "Maybe Dad left me a message," said the boy to the artif as he raised his wrist up towards his mouth. "Computer, log on," commanded the boy.

"Request complete," said a voice originating from his wristcom.

"Status update."

"There have been twenty-three interactions since your last *Interface* log on," answered the wristcom.

"How many messages?"

"Your account currently shows thirteen unplayed messages," said the wristcom.

"Play them for me," said the boy. The holographic screen that floated above his wristcom transitioned into a three-dimensional image of a teenage boy. Thomas recognized his friend Stu.

"Hey, T, I guess you're sleepin' or somethin'. Me, Eric, and Garret were just makin' sure you were still goin' to the party tomorrow after graduation. It's gonna be so narsh man. Can you believe we're graduating? Especially you, ha, ha. Lates." The image morphed into a blond female.

"Hi, Thomas. It's Veronica. I was wondering if we were meeting at the party or if you were gonna pick me up." She tossed her hair back and rolled her blue eyes. "And Thomas, leave that machine of yours at home."

"Where are the female humanoid's manners?" said LINC. "I am more than a mere machine, I would have her know. I am a fully articulated artif with a superior artificial intelligence. No other artif in the world has a learning matrix as advanced as mine. *Machine* is an inadequate elucidation of my complex functionality."

"I know, LINC. I know," said the boy, still wiping the sleep out of his eyes.

"Hello again, baby. I was wondering why you haven't called me back yet, so I figured I'd call you instead." Veronica's image again floated above his wristcom. "What do you think you are going to wear, because I was thinking you could wear that nice blue button-up—"

"Computer, skip message," said Thomas. The wristcom skipped to the next message, and surprisingly enough, it was Veronica again. He skipped ahead again, but with the same result.

"Remind me again, why am I dating this girl? There's like another ten holomessages from her." Thomas was beginning to get annoyed. "Computer, skip all messages from Veronica Hollingsworth."

A different hologram appeared. This time it was his father Dr. Carl Scargen. "Look, LINC. Dad did call like an hour ago."

"Hi, Tom. It's Dad. I was just calling you to say congrats on the graduation thing. I know it was touch-and-go there for a while, but we both know you are smarter than that, Tom. Anyway, I am so proud of you." His father paused. "I just know you're going to do great things. Sig and I are about to go back in and see how the Diggers are doing. They are excavating in one of the deepest tombs. I sent you some pics if you're interested. Who knows what they might find down there." A holofile appeared next to the hologram of his father marked EGYPT PICS. "Anyway, say hi to LINC and Stella for me. Bye, Tom. I love you, Son. Your mom would've been so proud." This last statement annoyed Thomas. His father had raised Thomas by himself. The boy had never met his mother. She had left when he was just two years old. He had never known what happened to her and never really pushed the subject with his father. It had always been a sore spot in the doctor's past. Thomas had stopped caring about what had happened to Merelda Scargen. He had dealt with the pain early in his short life, or so he had rationalized. *Any mother that did not want to know her own son is no mother I want.*

It then occurred to Thomas that his father had mentioned calling him in his dream. This worried the boy. *Does that mean that it wasn't a dream?* he thought. "Call Dad," said Thomas into his wristcom.

No Signal. "Your father is currently not logged on, and his *Interface* status has not changed in three hours, seventeen minutes, twelve seconds. He made one phone call, one hour, five minutes, and twenty-three seconds ago. Would you like to leave a message for him?" asked his wristcom.

"No, I'll try again later. No reason to bother him over a stupid dream." His father being unreachable did not prove much. This would happen often when Sig and his father were on a dig. The ancient Egyptian cavern did not make for great reception, and his father was a busy man.

Thomas opened the folder with a movement of his hand and began to peruse the pics his father had sent. "Dad never sends pictures of digs. They really must be on to something." He zoomed through the pictures, and although the dig looked impressive in its scale, nothing grabbed Thomas's attention. He closed the folder with another hand gesture.

"It was another nocturnal disturbance, was it not, Thomas Scargen?" Thomas knew this was more than an assumption by the robot. "I have already done the necessary calculations after processing the relevant data that I gathered while scanning the room and your vital systems simultaneously during your nocturnal hibernation. My sensors had previously indicated your achievement of REM sleep. Therefore it is fair to extrapolate that you were indeed dreaming, and from your sporadic twitching and sudden yelping I can also conclude that you were most assuredly subjected to a nightmare. I cannot hypothesize on the subject of said nightmare without more valid information or psychiatric evaluation. Doing such would be mere conjecture."

"Yeah, another one about Dad . . . but this one seemed . . . I don't know . . . more real or something." Thomas knew it was impossible, but he could not help thinking that it was not a dream. It felt too intense, too hopeless, too overwhelmingly real. "I'm sure I'm over-reacting. It's just that, in the dream Dad was in serious trouble, and it just felt so damn rea—"

A loud ripping noise cut him off. It sounded like paper being torn in two, but much louder. Stella began to hiss and her ears collapsed onto her head. "It's all right, little monster," said Thomas as he caressed the head of the snarling feline.

"Reeeer!" the cat cried and then dashed away. Thomas looked at the artif.

"What the hell was that?" asked the boy. He grabbed his boots and rushed downstairs.

"I have searched my auditory database, and I have found no suitable match for the sonic disruption in question," said LINC as he followed Thomas down the stairs and out the back door. The inexplicable sound had originated from the back of the house.

The Scargen home could easily be described as secluded. The house was comfortably settled into the base of a small cliff, which jutted out over the roof. The ledge of the rock face had upon it a single tree. Farming artifs moved up and down the rows of sustainable crops that surrounded the cliff. The Scargens were self-sufficient.

Thomas and LINC hurried outside to meet the disturbance and found nothing. The boy put on his boots as they stood on the grass. The screen door slammed behind them. Beads of water pelted him and his companion. This struck Thomas as odd. Rain was rare in Massachusetts this time of year. He looked up and saw the raindrops grow in size as they made their way closer to his face. The sound of the drops hitting LINC reminded Thomas of the sound of the rain hitting the gutters. Thomas's T-shirt hung off him, now drenched in the precipitation, and his pajama bottoms were stained with specks of mud bouncing off the freshly mowed grass. There was no sound of thunder, which might have explained the previous noise, nor any sign of lightning.

A faint white glow projected from the cliff top. Then as quickly as the light appeared, it vanished.

"Did you see that?" asked Thomas.

"Yes, Thomas Scargen, my optical sensors did indeed register that luminescent emanation," answered LINC.

The boy and his artif raced to the raising platform his father had installed to easily navigate the cliff face. The view from the top was spectacular. It was a place that Thomas had spent many evenings in his childhood gazing into the night sky, dreaming of the wondrous adventures that awaited him. He would still go up there on clear nights and read by the moonlight. The cliff had always been magical to him.

When the platform reached the summit, it came to an abrupt stop, almost flinging Thomas over the rail. Thomas glanced across the cliff, and what he found was unexpected.

A Native American girl, about the same age as Thomas, stood on the edge of the cliff. She was tall for a woman but shorter than the boy and his artif. Thomas had grown six inches in his senior year, taking him to six foot three. LINC was exactly six feet tall.

The teenage girl was dressed in a short, brown, strapless dress made of animal skin. An armband made of the same hide adorned her upper right arm. Her black hair melted down both sides of her head into two long braids. She had few possessions, which struck Thomas as odd. The girl wore a wrist communicator on her left wrist and grasped a deadly looking bow in her left hand. An empty quiver hung from her back. *Why would someone carry a bow with no arrows?* wondered Thomas, but the thought passed quickly, replaced by more adolescent concerns. He found himself captivated by the girl. She was naturally beautiful, from her enchanting face to the curve of her form. *I guess staring at her might be a little creepy,* thought the boy. *Maybe I should say something.* The girl beat him to it.

"You're Thomas Scargen, the son of Dr. Carl Scargen?"

"Yeah, that's me. I'm Thomas Scargen." He smiled at her. She looked back, not sharing his enthusiasm. His smile faded. "But I think the better question is who the hell are you, and how the hell did you get up here?"

"I will explain later. You are running out of time, Thomas," said the girl. "*We* are running out of time."

"What do you mean running out of time? I'm sixteen. Seventeen in a few weeks, but still pretty young all things considered." He was taken aback by the fear in her voice. "I think I got plenty of time."

"Enough of this nonsense. They are coming. We need to get you out of here."

"Wait, who's we?" asked the boy.

A ghostly white figure appeared directly behind the girl, answering his inquiry. Thomas jumped backward and gasped. "What the hell's going on?" said the boy to himself. He stared at the odd apparition. The creature was half man, half fox. It had the face and tail of a fox but stood upright. It wore no shirt, but did have the hide of an animal as a loincloth. *It must be a he.* The size of the beast was astounding. He was taller than Thomas and twice as wide. The ghost carried a staff that was claw-shaped at the top. He should have been quite intimidating, but there was a pureness about the creature that was quietly reassuring.

"My lady, they approach from the north, at least a thousand of them in number," reported the ghostly fox in the deepest yet calmest of tones.

"Then we better get going, my friend," replied the girl as she turned towards the platform and firmly grabbed Thomas's wrist.

"I'm not going anywhere. I don't know who you are or what's approaching from the north." He ripped his arm away from the girl. "And what the hell is that?" He pointed at the fox creature. Thomas believed he was at least due an explanation, given the circumstances.

"Forgive me; I forgot you don't know who I am, because I have known of you for years now, Thomas Scargen. My name is Yareli Chula. I am a Spirit Summoner and a member of the Council of Mages. A Mage Warrior, to be specific, and this is my Spirit Ghost Warrior, Wiyaloo."

"Delighted." The words echoed from the large beast.

"Narsh," said Thomas to the Spirit Ghost Warrior, but he was still confused about the rest of Yareli's statement. He turned back to the girl. "What do you mean you have known of me for years? You some weirdo stalker witch or something?"

"I am no witch. I know this must be disorienting, but you have to trust me right now. I promise your questions will all be answered, but we must go. *They* will be here soon." Somehow he did trust her, but he still wanted answers.

"What exactly are *they*, and what are these things after anyway?" asked Thomas.

"I thought you'd be a bit smarter. These, *things*, as you call them, are after . . ."

Finally, we're getting somewhere, thought the boy.

"They're here for you," said Yareli. Thomas's mouth hung open.

What is going on? These two had come from who knows where to stop who knows what from getting to him for who knows why. It was all overwhelming, not to mention confusing.

"We have to leave now, Thomas, and you need to log off." She pointed to his wristcom. "They can track you that way." Yareli's voice had ceased being polite and bordered on frantic.

"Nobody can track me. My dad's just as paranoid as you seem to be. There's anti-tracking tech in my wristcom, and only Dad and LINC know how to get around it."

"Then how did they know where to find you?" She shook her head, annoyed with her own question. "It doesn't matter. We have to go," said Yareli.

"It is too late, my lady, they are upon us." Wiyaloo pointed towards the fields. Hundreds of tar-like creatures seeped out of the treeline and splashed towards the cliff, leaving rancid black smoke in their wake. The ground cracked open around the base of the cliff, and even more tar squirted out of the new fissures. These creatures moved in unison and were now hunting in packs. The blackness began to blot out the once-fertile ground.

"If my calculations are correct, there are approximately 1,327 of those unknown species moving directly towards this location." A three-dimensional representation of the surrounding area appeared on LINC's holodisplay. On the holomap there were 1,327 holographic representations of the tar-like entities that approached the cliff. "We are severely outnumbered, and we have no realistic means or chance of escape."

"But we didn't come to this party empty-handed, metal man," said Yareli as she reached back into her empty quiver. A single white arrow formed in the quiver. She reached and grabbed the glowing arrow and loaded it into the bow. "Wiyaloo, you need to buy us some time."

"Agreed," said Wiyaloo. At that instant, the white beast leapt off the cliff and plummeted towards the tar-like creatures. He landed with a thunderous thud, and before the dust could settle, he began mumbling enchantments. The spirit ghost began to illuminate as bursts of white energy flowed from his paws. The first pulse incinerated a dozen of the dark monsters, the subsequent pulses doing similar damage.

"Narsh," said Thomas. Still the monsters continued their assault, methodically advancing towards Wiyaloo and the cliff.

Yareli had finally chosen her target, a group of twenty or so trying to climb the south side of the cliff. Melting black goo moved slowly upward. She released the glowing arrow and shouted, "*Wan-blee!*" It sprung off of the bowstring with determination, a sight that startled Thomas. Right before it was to pierce the front of the oncoming pack, it expanded into a burning eagle that flew through and destroyed the entire group that was scaling the cliff side. The eagle let out a cry after it had carried out its task and landed alongside Yareli. The proud bird screamed one last time and extinguished into nothing.

"That's one hell of a party favor." Thomas could not believe that this was really happening. *Magic arrows, spirit creatures, gooey dark oily things.* It was a bit much for him to take in. "What the hell are those things?"

"They are known as the *Eerah*—or dark ones. They can only be summoned by highly skilled Necromancers."

"A necro-mincer?"

"Necro-*man*-cer. It's someone who practices dark magic," answered Yareli nonchalantly as she drew another magic arrow from her quiver, nocked it, and pointed it at a second group. "*Matto-ska!*" When this arrow was released, it formed into a great polar bear. The bear bounded down the cliff towards two dozen or so of the *Eerah*. The polar bear ripped through the attacking ooze, freezing them where they stood. "They will not stop until they get what they were summoned to retrieve." As she spun around to see Thomas face-to-face, another group of *Eerah* began ascending the cliff. The polar bear came to a rest beside Yareli, bowed its head with a groan, and then disappeared into the darkness.

Wiyaloo seemed to have his paws full on the ground as well. The dark ones had begun forming together and attacking en masse. The energy blasts were having less of an effect on them, and it was hard to tell whether they were getting stronger or Wiyaloo was getting weaker. Some had gotten in so close that the spirit ghost had torn them apart with his bare paws. Soon the blackness surrounded him, and just when it seemed like the beast had been bested, he would burst into energy, destroying the surrounding *Eerah*. He would then reappear in another place, and the cycle would begin anew.

"Does that hurt him?" asked Thomas.

"I'm pretty sure nothing hurts him, but if you are asking if he can keep up that pace forever, the answer is no." Yareli reached for another arrow, but like Wiyaloo it was getting increasingly difficult to keep the *Eerah* at bay. There were now several packs of them encroaching up every side of the cliff.

LINC's internal alarms began to sound. The blue lights that radiated from the artif all simultaneously turned red. "A new course of action will have to be implemented. Initiating protection sequence protocol." As the android spoke, his hands transformed and flipped backward into his forearm pieces, immediately replaced by two over-sized laser weapons.

"Totally narsh," said the boy, astounded by his robot's transformation. "That's new."

"I will ensure your safety, Thomas Scargen," said the artif in a deeper voice than usual.

"Dad always had a flair for the dramatic," said the boy. No doubt, he had programmed LINC to only use deadly force when the risk factor reached a certain threshold. The current situation seemed to merit just that. The robot leapt into the air and landed on the ledge opposite Yareli.

"Targeting sequence initiated," said LINC. "Commencing attack, threat level alpha." The forearm laser turrets on both his arms sprung to life. Bolts of concentrated light erupted from the artif's arm cannons, firing down into the black abyss. The lasers ripped through the approaching darkness, temporarily staving off another wave of the *Eerah*.

"Very effective, metal man . . . primitive, but effective!" shouted Yareli across the cliff top.

"Actually, Ms. Yareli Chula, I am made from a synthetic alloy, and I assure you my weapons systems are far from primitive," LINC fired back, turning his head completely around while continuing to shoot in the opposite direction.

Even with LINC entering the fight, the two were barely containing the situation on the cliff, and Wiyaloo below was noticeably slower. He was still holding down his position, but that would not continue for long. For every one he destroyed, four took its place. Thomas had tried to help, but between Yareli and LINC, he was continuously instructed to stay back from the ledge. Besides, what could he do? He did not have the weapons that the others possessed. He was the target of the attack, and he felt entirely helpless. His fate was in the hands of a girl he had just met, a fox ghost, and his normally docile artif. Fear began to replace his initial excitement and curiosity.

Yareli's brow was drenched in sweat. She had fired ten arrows, and the dark landscape had not changed. There was no end to the *Eerah*.

Wiyaloo appeared on top of the cliff. He slumped down on one knee. "I am sorry, my lady. I have failed you."

"You did well, Wiyaloo. Rest now, my friend." As Yareli said this, the *Eerah* had begun to reach the summit of the cliff. "I will teach these monsters a lesson." She turned and grabbed an arrow from the empty quiver and fired, all in one motion. "*Ta-tonka!*" A buffalo burst forth from the arrow and charged these *Eerah*. The buffalo disintegrated the *Eerah* instantly. "That bought us a little time."

Just as there seemed to be some cause for celebration, the sound of one of the artif's cannons became muffled. Thomas turned his head to see LINC drowning in *Eerah*. The robot had one cannon still free, firing blindly into the dark mass that was about to engulf him.

"LINC!" Thomas had caught Yareli's attention with his scream, and her focus turned towards the android. She reached for an arrow, but as she did her arm was grabbed by a tentacle-like formation coming from one of the black blobs. She was flung backwards, but before she hit the ground Wiyaloo caught her. He placed her down with a strong gentleness.

"I have rested long enough," said Wiyaloo as he jumped upon the attacking *Eerah*. Thomas had never seen anything fight with this kind of ferocity before. It was inspiring, but inspiration alone could not help them.

Wiyaloo ripped apart one tentacle, trying to free LINC, but another one grabbed hold of the artif. It was too late. LINC vanished into the darkness. The only thing that was holding Thomas back was Yareli. She had grabbed ahold of him with a viselike grip and was determined to not let his fate be that of LINC's. Thomas was losing his closest friend, and he was just supposed to watch him die. Wiyaloo's legs were suddenly knocked out from underneath him, and he too was dragged into the black. He and the robot were gone, lost somewhere in the dark ones.

Thomas finally broke Yareli's grip. Tears filled his face as he ran towards where LINC had disappeared. Before he could reach the artif, he heard Yareli let out a scream. Thomas pivoted to look behind him. *Eerah* surrounded Yareli and now Thomas. Thomas backed away and Yareli did the same until they were back to back. The *Eerah* pounced on to them. Blackness filled the landscape. Yareli and Thomas were completely enveloped by the dark ooze.

Thomas was blind. He could only see black. He could not breathe anymore, and he could not move. Desperation overwhelmed him. He felt helpless.

Darkness . . .

Emptiness . . .

Death . . .

Nothing . . .

A burning sensation started to fill his chest and began infesting his whole body, moving through him at an exponential rate. It would not be long now. The pain was intense, and the only thing Thomas could do was scream.

The noise erupted from inside the dark ocean that now covered the cliff top. At first it was a muffled moaning, but slowly the word could be heard. The dark layer began to crack, forming lines throughout the mass. A bright light began pouring out from these cracks, and the word now cut through the silent darkness, "Nooooooo!" The scream reverberated and shook the dark shell. The cracking mass exploded into a burst of blue light. At the epicenter of the chaos was one Thomas Scargen. Light continued out from its origin, destroying all of the *Eerah* in its wake. Thomas's body was illuminated by the energy expelling out of him. His eyes were on fire, and he was simply yelling "Nooooo!" Maybe it was the fear, or the sadness, or even anger that spawned this pouring forth of energy. Regardless of what had brought it on, it was effective. He was floating a few feet above a crater that had formed from the initial shockwave. The blackness had vanished, and his friends—old and new—were revealed to him.

He collapsed forward into the self-made crater and landed on his right arm. He heard the crack distinctly. Pain immediately filled his limb. He was too tired to scream, and what remained of his clothes had begun to smoke from his recent expenditure. The remaining *Eerah* slithered away into the night. Retreat was their only option.

"Thomas, but how did you . . . what I mean to say is . . . wow. I've never seen anything quite that . . . that . . . r-r-remarkable." Yareli spoke with a stutter of someone who has just witnessed a miracle.

"Remarkable?" said the beleaguered boy. "I feel like I'm gonna puke." The whole scene began to blur. Thomas felt exhausted and slumped over.

LINC sat up and pulled himself to a standing position. The artif was fine with the exception of a few dents. His cannons transformed back into hands. He ran quickly towards Thomas. "Thomas Scargen," buzzed LINC. His scans had already finished their diagnostic on the boy. "He appears to be in shock and has suffered a distal fracture of the radius in his right forearm with dorsal displacement of the wrist, sometimes referred to as a Colles fracture." He picked up the boy who was on the verge of passing out. The deep voice of the Spirit Warrior echoed through the boy.

"Give the boy to me," said Wiyaloo. The apparition accepted the boy's body from the robot. He kneeled with Thomas still in his arms and began to chant. His ghostly form began to glow blue. Thomas could feel a shock in his arm. Intense heat circulated through the injured bone. The pain began to slip and the queasy feeling all but subsided. The boy shot up in the beast's arms like he had just been given smelling salts. He could feel that his arm was completely healed.

"That is entirely narsh . . . but how . . . how is this possible?" asked Thomas as he stood on his own power, moving his arm and opening and closing his hand in disbelief.

"Wiyaloo is a practiced healer," answered Yareli.

"Well . . . thanks, Wiyaloo. The arm feels incredible." Thomas grabbed his head. "I was out of it there for a second."

"Your expression of gratitude is unwarranted, Thomas Scargen," responded Wiyaloo. "You saved Yareli when I could not. For that, I am forever grateful."

"That wasn't a dream? I did that . . . I really did that?" Thomas was gobsmacked. "I don't know what got into me." He was deathly afraid of what just happened. It was scary enough being around people who were doing magic, but to do it himself seemed amazing and frightening. He looked at his hands. "How did I do that?"

"I'm having a difficult time piecing it all together myself. There will be more answers where we are going." Yareli was quick to snap the group back to reality and the purpose of the midnight rendez-vous. "Speaking of which, where's our ride?" As she said this, Thomas noticed something large streak across the sky. The moonlight bounced off the unidentified flying object, making the light dance above the cliff.

In an instant, it had landed with more dexterity than its bulky size would suggest. The ground shook as the creature came to a halt in front of the boy. Thomas was petrified, staring at the over-sized monster.

The green, scaled beast was clad in armor and tech. It rocked its head back and forth as its enormous wings folded back. Puffs of smoke billowed out of the creature's nostrils. The boy could not trust what he was seeing. "A dragon? Really? A dragon?" He fell back into the crater, dumbfounded and tired. Thomas had no choice but to accept the unbelievable. "There's a dragon in my backyard."

2

dragons and such

The dragon stood up and lumbered in the direction of the boy and his new companions. Thomas's immediate reaction was to run, but he knew he would not get far. The boy was spent. Yareli made a move towards the towering monster with no hesitation. Thomas tensed, getting ready for another fight. LINC's defensive sequence initiated, and his hands once again transformed into cannons. *Apparently mythological creatures tilt the danger scale too*, thought the boy.

Yareli's pace began to quicken as she moved towards the massive beast. An attack seemed inevitable, but the dragon was still. This frightened Thomas even more. *Why isn't it moving?* Yareli stopped in front of the beast, made a fist, and punched the dragon on an unarmored part of its leg.

"Bloody 'ell. Now what cha go and do dat for?" cried the surprised behemoth with a strong English accent. The dragon was noticeably flustered from this unprovoked act of violence.

"You are late, Bartleby. Where in Spirit's name have you been?" asked Yareli. "*Eerah* were all over the place, and your flaming breath sure would have come in handy. If it hadn't been for Thomas, we all would be dead."

"Dat doesn't give you duh right to go and take a swing at me, now does it? Besides I 'ad my 'ands a bit full myself, now didn't I?

If you think dat I was duh only fing in duh sky tonight, you'd be sadly mistaken," snorted the dragon, two puffs of grey smoke leaving his nostrils.

Thomas let out a sigh of relief. *I guess the fighting is over for tonight*, thought the boy. He was relieved that the dragon was on their side, and now that the perceived threat had passed, Thomas could take a closer look at the dragon.

The boy immediately noticed that the dragon's right wing was completely artificial. The craftsmanship of this appendage was remarkable. He had seen similar tech used on artifs at Scargen Robotics, but not with this kind of application. *Cyborg dragons*, thought the boy. *The Dragon Fire Chronicles didn't say anything about that.*

Bartleby slowly turned towards him and began to speak. "And you, you must be Thomas Scargen. I've 'erd loads about you, I 'av, but where 'av my manners gone. My name's Bartleby . . . Bartleby Draige, teleport dragon for 'ire. Please ta make your acquaintance, Thomas Scargen." Bartleby bowed his head while finishing his sentence.

"Yeah, um . . . hi . . . Bartleby, was it? Pleased to uh . . . meet ya," said Thomas, still confused. The boy was intimidated by Bartleby but also intrigued. He had always been drawn to dragons in his books, and now he was talking to one. It was surreal. *First magic, now a freakin' dragon. This is so entirely narsh.* Thomas regrouped his thoughts. "Did you say teleport dragon?"

"Yes, he did," interrupted Yareli, "One of the best actually."

"Oh go on, you don't 'av to be so kind," said Bartleby.

"Especially when he is where he's supposed to be, when he's supposed to be there," finished Yareli. "And speaking of teleportation, can we get going? We are on a tight schedule."

"You mean there's more than one dragon?" asked Thomas, again surprised. One dragon was extraordinary, but the thought of several dragons seemed somehow more far-fetched.

"My dear boy, dere are more den one, but far less den many," said Bartleby. "Aw'right, everyone aboard, time being of duh essence and all." He gestured with his natural wing.

Thomas put his foot into the stirrup that hung from one side of the beast. He pulled himself up onto Bartleby and noticed that there was room for two, maybe three, people on the dragon. "Is LINC going to be too heavy? I'm not going anywhere without him."

"I will carry the one you call LINC." Wiyaloo had finally spoken. In all the commotion, Thomas had forgotten about this other remarkable creature. It had just occurred to him that Wiyaloo could teleport as well.

"You can teleport too, huh?"

"I cannot teleport, Thomas Scargen, not like this beast anyway. While in the Earth Realm, I can only exist in the area that my Spirit Summoner exists. Within relative proximity to her, I can phase in and out of this plane."

"That's still pretty narsh, Wiyaloo." Yareli began positioning herself behind Thomas on the large saddle as Wiyaloo lifted the artif by his two arms and took off into the night sky. The dragon was soon to follow. With two flaps of his wings, Bartleby was airborne.

Thomas could feel the night air slapping his face. Most people in this situation would have felt out of sorts. Thomas did not. He had flown before, with the help of an aeromobile or airship, but this was different. This felt natural, like something he was meant to do. It was exhilarating, and he knew instantly that he loved it. "Bartleby, this is amazing!" shouted Thomas over the whipping wind.

"You 'avn't seen nuffin' yet," Bartleby responded with a bit of smugness. "You'll love dis one."

"Bartleby, I have orders," said Yareli. "Open a teleportal and get us out of here." As the words left her mouth, the dragon dipped straight down into a barrel roll. "I'm not kidding, Bartleby. You said yourself that you were not alone."

"Calm down, Yareli, I chased 'im off. I'm just trying to give duh boy a frill," Bartleby pleaded. "I 'av my shields on maximum, and I assure you nuffin' is gonna 'it us. Stop being such a—" The red bolt of light that hit Wiyaloo ahead of them cut off his statement. The white ghost vanished as LINC plummeted towards the ground.

Thomas looked upward to see where the beam had originated.

He could make out three large bat-shaped creatures. Each of the massive creatures carried a rider strapped to its underbelly. "Umm . . . what are those things?" asked Thomas, beginning to realize that his theory that there'd be no more fighting was grossly premature.

"I guess dat one I chased away earlier wasn't alone, was it?" said Bartleby, questioning his previous findings.

"You, of all dragons, should know that Aringi Riders hunt in packs. What were you thinking?" said Yareli, sounding anxious.

"What the hell is an Aringi Rider?" yelled Thomas towards Yareli.

"Not now, Thomas," answered Yareli, still beside herself looking for any sighting of Wiyaloo.

"Why are they trying to kill LINC?"

"Thomas, dey ain't aimin' for 'im mate. Dey're aimin' for you," shouted Bartleby as he dove towards the flailing artif, trying desperately to catch the robot before impact. Thomas turned his head in horror, fearing the worst.

Seconds before impact, another self-preservation program engaged inside LINC. The bottom parts of his legs transformed, and his arms again turned into laser cannons. His legs were now turbines that quickly ignited and stopped his fall seconds before contact with the ground. LINC immediately changed direction and began climbing altitude, moving towards the mounted bats. He raced past Bartleby in the opposite direction, to the delight of Thomas. "Narsh!" shouted the boy. Bartleby flipped over and altered his course to match the trajectory of the robot.

LINC opened fire on the closest bat creature and shredded its oversized left wing, sending it into a spin towards the ground. The forest floor silenced the screams of the Rider and his mount. LINC immediately turned to confront the other two aringi, but they were already in attack formation, heading towards LINC. Bolts of red light erupted from the headpieces of both bats.

Bartleby flew in front of the artif, absorbing the first beam directly into his shielding device. The shield failed as the second bolt hit the dragon's armored chestplate. Electric current shocked the dragon. Bartleby was stunned, but still capable of flight. The dragon slowed down as one of the pursuing aringi moved along the left side of them.

Thomas could now see the enormous size of the bat. The beast was a twisted combination of genetics and tech. It rolled left to reveal the Rider strapped to its underbelly. The man wore body armor and a helmet with a dark visor. He moved his arm violently and what looked like a holographic rope extended from his forearm piece.

"Thomas, watch out!" yelled Yareli as the Rider flung the energy rope in the boy's direction. He dodged the attempt as the whip hit another part of Bartleby's tech. Sparks flew into Thomas's face as a small fire ignited where the whip had hit. The swirling air extinguished the flame just as quickly as it had started.

"That can't be good," said Thomas as he looked at the burnt piece of hardware. It was considerably damaged, and Bartleby was still struggling to gain speed after the first attack.

The aringi fought for better positioning. The creature crossed over top of Bartleby and now was on their right. "Snap out of it, Bartleby," said Yareli as the Rider pulled his arm back to attempt another strike.

"Sorry . . . 'old on," said the dragon as he shook his head back and forth. Bartleby accelerated as the energy rope again just missed Thomas. The dragon sped forward, leaving the attacker in his wake. LINC dropped in from above and kept pace with the dragon. "I fink we 'av overstayed our welcome," said Bartleby.

"I tend to agree with Mr. Draige. We are mathematically outnumbered, and from my sensors, there are four more of these creatures bearing down on our current loc—" said LINC as he was hit directly in the back by the incoming aringi. Thomas's wrist communicator rang in alarm, indicating the artif's power level was dangerously low. LINC's defenseless body fell towards the forest floor.

"Bartleby, you have to catch him, he has no power. He can't save himself," pleaded Thomas.

"One step ahead uv ya, Thomas," said Bartleby as he swooped towards the plummeting android. "It's like bleedin' *déjà vu* all over again, isn't it?" The dragon was desperately attempting to match the artif's speed. This time four Aringi Riders moved to intercept them.

"See what you can do about dem," said Bartleby to Yareli. "Dey look a bit put off, don't dey?" As the words left the beast, Yareli reached into her quiver and pulled out a spirit arrow.

"Just catch the artif. I'll worry about the aringi," answered Yareli, already releasing her arrow. "*Shumannytoo-tonka!*" The arrow erupted into a pack of wolves. The majestic canines ran across the dark sky directly at the aringi. The wolves attacked three of the Riders, ripping them from their hosts, but the final Rider still gained on Bartleby. The dragon spiraled to avoid the Rider's fire. "I'm out of arrows, and it will take some time to summon more," said Yareli. The sound of fear crept into her voice.

"Den I strongly suggest you 'old on ta somefin'," said Bartleby as he surprisingly picked up his speed. A teleportal formed as the dragon leveled out. He snatched LINC out of midair and sped through the tear in the night sky. The hole closed behind the dragon just as quickly as it had opened, severing the remaining Rider and his bat in two.

Bartleby and his passengers flew through the other end of the tele-portal. Thomas looked back just in time to see the bisected half of the aringi and the Rider drop into a vast body of water. *Water?* thought the boy. Thomas's eyes darted back and forth as he studied the noticeably different landscape. "We're not in New Salem anymore."

"Well-spotted, Thomas," said the dragon. "Nuffin' gets by you, does it, mate?"

"Where in Spirit's name are we, Bartleby? This is not where we agreed to be delivered," said Yareli.

"Dis, my luvly, is duh fardest I could teleport wif my amplification tech being fried," snorted Bartleby. "Dat bloody energy whip did it well in."

"Can it be fixed?" asked Yareli.

"I don't fink so. It's completely knackered, isn't it? It can be replaced, and as luck would 'av it, I know duh only people capable of doing such a procedure quickly and wif no questions." He paused for a second as if he were thinking. "Dey might even be able to fix up your robot too, Thomas."

"Can we trust these people?" asked Yareli.

"I 'ope so, dey are my roommates," said Bartleby, "And duh fact is, teleporting dat far really takes it out uv me. If I try it again, dere's no telling if I would make it, and dere'd be no way of knowing where we would end up—even if I did survive duh ordeal."

"I suggest we fix Bartleby's computer, and hopefully his friends can fix LINC," said Thomas, looking in Yareli's direction.

"It doesn't seem like we have a choice," said Yareli.

Wiyaloo reappeared in midair next to the dragon. Yareli nodded in his direction, and Wiyaloo returned the gesture. "I will carry the robot once more, dragon," said the foxlike apparition as he lifted LINC from Bartleby's talons.

"Fanks, mate. 'ee is a bit 'eavier den 'ee looks, isn't 'ee?" said the dragon as he stretched his arms.

"How far away are these friends of yours?" asked Yareli.

"About two 'undred kilometers, give or take, mum," answered Bartleby.

"How long will it take to get there?" wondered Yareli.

"We'll be dere in two shakes uvva lamb's tail," said Bartleby. "Mmm . . . lamb sounds good right about now, doesn't it? I'm bloody famished." The dragon flapped his wings as he moved upward. Bartleby craned his head backward. "I'd 'old on to somefin' if I was you." Thomas tightened his grip on the saddle's pommel, heeding the dragon's warning. The dragon turned his head forward and sped off towards the new destination.

3

consequences

The uniformed man stood on the precipice above the Scargen home. Looking around, the Captain of the Aringi Riders was befuddled by what had just transpired. He turned around and leaned down next to the crater that had been left by the unlikely energy expenditure. He did not understand how this had happened. Most of the *Eerah* had been eliminated, along with five of his Riders, and he did not know what he was going to report to the General. He would have to tell him the truth. Grayden Arkmalis was not a man to be trifled with, nor lied to. He would know if the Captain was not telling the complete story. This always made things more difficult. Still the Captain had to tend to his wounded and get them back to Grimm Tower, but mostly he needed some answers.

Captain Marcus Slade stood and turned to his Riders, who were awaiting orders. He moved to the first Rider. "I want you to trace the teleport signature, and tell me where that damn dragon went."

"Yes, Captain," said the Rider as a bat landed on top of him. The aringi flew off in the direction of the teleportal. Marcus addressed the next two Riders.

"I want you two to search the house and see if you can find anything," said the Captain.

"Yes, Captain," the two men said in unison. They too were picked off the cliff by their respective aringi. Marcus pivoted towards the next Rider.

"I need you to search the database and find me the name of the Native American girl and gather as much information about her as possible. I want you to know her favorite color by the time I get back. I'll expect a full report upon my return."

"Yes, Captain," said the Rider as he turned. His holographic display opened, and he began aggregating search criteria for the girl.

"The rest of you are going back with me to the Tower. Riders, mount up," said Marcus. The Riders lined up across the cliff. The aringi swooped down and systematically picked up the remaining Riders.

Marcus and his flying beast turned right through the night sky. "Riders, fall in." The men formed around the Captain. He looked down onto his wrist communicator embedded in his forearm armor. "Open rift, destination Grimm Tower." A beam shot from the headpiece of his bat. The beam formed a rip in the sky in front of him. Marcus commanded his Riders to follow him through the teleportal. He mentally ordered the aringi through the hole, and it complied. His men followed through the tear in space.

The sight on the other side was hauntingly breathtaking. A huge black tower jutted straight up out of the center of an active volcano. A river of magma surrounded the volcano. The searing red liquid tried as it would to spring forth from the mouth of the volcano, but the molten rock was stymied. Dark magic held back the lava flow and harnessed its energy. The energy was used to run the sprawling city in Grimm Tower. The side of the volcano was littered with other fortifications, living quarters for thousands of men and various types of beast and creature. Aringi circled the top of the Tower that rose straight through the dark clouds enveloping the structure.

The screeches of the bats filled the smoky air. The Captain and his remaining men began their descent towards the landing platform located near the top of the Tower. The torchlight flickered on their faces as they fell in unison. The Captain's creature was first to attach himself upside down on one of the landing poles. The Captain simultaneously released himself from the underbelly of the monstrous bat, landing on his feet with grace and precision.

Several lizard-like humanoids began corralling the aringi. The multicolored creatures wore sparse, tattered clothing. The Salamen were a peaceful amphibious race that had been enslaved decades ago by the Skinx, a warring clan. Small numbers of these newts, as they were commonly referred to, had been sold to the Tower by the Skinx in exchange for credits and tech.

The Salamen were responsible for maintenance of the aringi, a dirty job to say the least. "Treat them well, newt," said Marcus to one of the Salamen as he threw him a credit stick. The newt caught the stick between his slightly webbed hands. "They are going to need their strength in the coming days." The newt slave cowered and nodded, signifying he understood as he held up his reward.

"Yesss, my Captain," said the spotted Salamen as he fought to keep the credit stick away from the other newts.

The Captain had already turned and began walking towards the monstrous doors that led into the Tower. Lava trolls stood at attention on either side of the entrance holding oversized axes. They looked like massive statues made entirely of lava rock. Magma blazed orange from their eye sockets and open mouths. The lava trolls made up most of the Grimm Legion's ground forces.

"Good evening, Cap'n. 'ow goes duh search?" groaned Gibgot, one of the lava trolls. The Captain nodded his head in acknowledgement but did not respond to the pointless question. He proceeded through the right-side door that was being held open by Fronik, the other troll. "Cap'n looks like 'ee's in a right mood, don't 'ee?" said Gibgot when he thought the man no longer in earshot.

"Why don't you mind your own business for once," said Fronik looking at the other rock guard with one brow raised.

"I was just inquiring to duh status of duh aforementioned mission, dat's all," answered Gibgot, now leaning on his rock axe facing Fronik.

"Well stop. You fink duh Capt'n's got time for your stupid questions? I would say not. 'ee's got alotta better fings to be doin' than talkin' wif some dragon's rear-end uvva guard," argued Fronik. "And what were ya plannin' on sayin' if 'ee 'ad answered your question?"

"I didn't fink dat far ahead, now did I?" questioned Gibgot, retaking his position on the left side of the door. "'ee's only human isn't 'ee. 'ee's no better than you or I, when all is said and done, is 'ee?"

"Dis is not about the equal rights of the classes, so much as duh hierarchical intricacies of an army. Wiffout a proper hierarchy, mind you, dere is no order. Wiffout order, chaos ensues, and try to run an army in chaos. Ya can't do it now, can ya?" Fronik straightened himself up and returned to the right side of the door. "You'd be like 'hey you over dere, do dis,' and 'ee be all, 'no I'm not doin' dat, you can't tell me what to do, on whose afforaty?' Then you'd be like, 'I guess you're right, so let's go do chaos.' Circle goes round."

"I guess I 'ad'nt fought uv everyfing, now 'ad I? I was just trying to start a conversation, not destroy the embedded hierarchical system of our army," said the first guard, now slumping against the wall in disappointment.

"Dat's probably why I outrank you," said Fronik, trying to look as serious as possible.

"Fair enough, isn't it?" said Gibgot as he began to chuckle to himself. Before too long both lava trolls were hysterically laughing.

"I just 'erd you snort, you dodgy pebble-brained fool," laughed Fronik.

"I did not . . ." snickered Gibgot as he continued to snort. "Aw'right, maybe a bit." The two lava trolls were slumped over in amusement as the door slammed closed.

The main hallway that led to Grayden Arkmalis's chamber was full of activity. Guards and Riders moved this way and that through a sea of varied creatures. Marcus walked between the rows of columns, ignoring the commotion.

The supports that lined the main hallway were made up of various bones twisting and turning up through the pillars. The floor was composed of cobblestones made completely of skulls.

Captain Marcus Slade could still hear the echoes of the lava trolls' laughter. Under normal circumstances, the Captain might have laughed too, but these were not normal circumstances. The news he brought was no laughing matter. Captain Slade knew better than to enter his master's chamber without announcing his arrival. This formality gave him more time to compose his thoughts. A small imp hobbled towards Marcus. The imp wore a tan button-down shirt and a green vest—formal attire for an imp, seeing that imps did not normally wear clothing. The cloven-hoofed creature had been summoned from the Depths to serve the General. "Corbin, inform the General that I have returned and need to talk to him as soon as he's available." The imp said nothing and quickly turned back towards the imposing doors that lead to Grayden Arkmalis's chambers. He reached for the lower part of the right door. It opened to reveal a smaller imp-sized door. Corbin scurried through. His pointed tail followed.

"Captain," said a voice from behind Marcus. He turned around to see his Second and Rider Dalco Jakobsen, his third in command. "Didn't think we were gonna let you go in there alone, did ya?" said the Second as she smiled at Marcus.

Breathtaking, he thought.

His Second was named Evangeline. "Your problem is our problem, Captain. That's the Rider way. You taught me that, sir."

"Yes, I suppose I did . . . but I can handle this by myself. This will not be pleasant."

"You know I have had my fair share of unpleasantries, Captain." Marcus had found Evangeline some years ago on a covert mission during the Tech War. The girl was abandoned when she was five years old. He had taken pity on the child and brought her back to the Tower. "I can't tell you the last time I felt completely pleasant, to be honest."

The Second removed her sweat-drenched helmet. A long auburn

braid fell behind her. Marcus watched as the red tail swayed back and forth. "This is just something I should do alone." Marcus used all his discipline to act nonchalantly around the curvy Rider.

"Since when are you so concerned about my well-being? You couldn't even be bothered to give me a last name," she winked at the Captain. She had never had a surname—not one that she could remember—and he never had the heart to force one on her. She had only known her first name, Evangeline. As a child, Evangeline was often overlooked in the Tower. This was no longer the case. Now, everyone noticed the Second. "You going soft on me, Captain?"

"I just don't need to worry about any more of my men dying this evening," said Marcus. She was an adept Rider, both on and off an aringi, but the truth was, he did not want her in harm's way. He could not help how he felt. They had been through a lot together, but he was a soldier first. He would not let his emotions get the best of him. Besides, she was young—not even twenty years; he was far too old. Snow had settled on his beard years ago.

"We can handle ourselves, Captain," said Dalco Jakobsen, the other Rider. Jakobsen was a fine Rider in his own right. He had been with the Captain and a Rider for as long as Marcus could remember. The two men had been through the Depths and back. He was a man that Marcus could trust. "Besides, I haven't seen the General in years."

"There is no handling yourself when it comes to this man, Dalco." He caught himself getting upset. He did not want Evangeline in the same room as Arkmalis. "Even you, my dear Second, would be no match for the General."

"I hear he can eat a man's soul by just thinking it," said Jakobsen.

"Yes, but maybe not a woman's," said Evangeline with a smile that nearly melted the Captain. He collected his thoughts.

I am their leader first, and I will not let these urges get the better of me, Marcus rationalized. *She must never know how I feel.* His only consolation was that no other man dare court this woman. It was said amongst the ranks of the Riders that your first mistake would be to try and mess with the Second. Her only friends were the aringi.

"I heard he killed a High Demon when he was a kid," said the Second. This awoke Marcus from his pondering. "That's why he wears that creepy mask."

If she only knew, thought Marcus. "That's preposterous. Everyone knows you cannot kill a High Demon." He was not the best liar, but the point seemed to be settled. He had seen Grayden Arkmalis destroy the demon. Jakobsen had also been there, but had not seen the fight. He had been busy dealing with other matters. Evangeline was there too, but she was unconscious during the battle. One thing was certain—a lot of Riders had died that day. The General was only twelve at the time. The Captain would never forget what the boy had done. *It is not every day you see a demon die, let alone a High Demon.* He had never spoken of it to anyone. Arkmalis's actions had saved them all, but the boy from that day no longer existed. The man Marcus was about to see was different, colder, unforgiving. Something happened that day that had changed Grayden Arkmalis forever.

"We are going in there with you," said Evangeline, pulling Marcus back to the present.

"I appreciate the sentiment, but there is no need," said the Captain as he faced his Riders.

"It's the least we can do, sir," remarked Jakobsen.

"Thank you, old friend." The Captain knew there was no stopping them. He had trained them and knew their resolve. "Who am I to argue with such a generous display of loyalty as this one?"

Corbin poked his head through the small door. "His eminence will see you now." The imp's deep voice echoed in the hallway as he turned and vanished, the small door closing behind him. A booming noise sounded as the two colossal doors slowly opened.

"Whatever you do, do not, I repeat, do not say a word," commanded Captain Slade.

"But—" said Jakobsen.

"Not a word. That is an order. Trust me on this. You dare not interrupt Grayden Arkmalis, or that may be the last mistake you ever get a chance to make." These were Marcus's last words before Corbin reemerged. The imp's pupilless eyes glowed yellow through the shadows. The light that escaped from his eyes reflected off of his gray-blue skin. The imp gestured to the Captain and his men to follow. The Captain led his men into the revealed darkness.

It seemed like they had been walking forever before Marcus's eyes began to adjust to the sparse lighting. He could now distinguish the two gigantic full-bodied portraits on the far wall. A single window divided them. He began to make out figures moving on either side of him and could hear music. He could see that these figures were women of all shapes, sizes, and species dancing, writhing in the darkness. Some naked, others close enough, all moving to the erotic beats that were coming from what looked like a band that was made up of scantily clad females. Jakobsen's gaze began to wander around the chamber. The Captain remained focused. Evangeline the Second was even enthralled with this display. She too seemed engrossed by the spectacle. Captain Slade was still rehearsing in his head the message he was planning on giving to Grayden Arkmalis. This was a daunting task and quieted his carnal cravings. "Eyes forward. We are not here to play. We are here to deliver bad news," said Marcus, trying to regain the attention of his Riders.

"What was that, Marcus?" A cold voice bellowed from the direction of a mound of moving flesh. The sound froze the Captain. He had heard this voice thousands of times, and it always had the same paralyzing effect. The flesh mound systematically parted. Standing there, bathed in the moonlight pouring in from the chamber's solitary window, was the masked man from one of the portraits. This was General Grayden Arkmalis. "You were saying something about bad news, were you not?" This last statement was not a question, and the look on the Riders' faces made that fact obvious. "Now come, Marcus . . . come tell me the news that you so graciously have decided to ruin one of my few moments of frivolity with." General Arkmalis walked towards the Riders. He was a tall, fit, muscular man, half nude himself. His head was covered by long, straight black hair. The imp feverishly began to dress the General as he sauntered in the direction of Marcus. His pale complexion was contrasted by the black symbols and magical glyphs that were tattooed across his skin. The detail was astounding. The demon mask adorned the top half of his head. It looked like a skull of some unknown creature. The bottom of the mask ended with two large fang-like teeth that flanked the sides of his mouth. The man's fierce red eyes contained no pupils and glowed like the fiery pits of the Depths. The man known as Grayden Arkmalis, now fully dressed in uniform, stood in front of Marcus and the Riders. "That is all, Corbin," the man looked directly at his imp servant.

"My life is but to serve you, my master," said Corbin as he genuflected, then promptly scurried off.

Arkmalis turned back towards the Captain. "Now let's hear the news, Marcus . . . but first let's play a game, shall we? Do you like riddles, Captain?" Marcus nodded his head yes, still unable to utter a word. "I love riddles. I truly cannot get enough of them. Do you want to try and guess my riddle? And Captain, feel free to verbally answer this time," said Arkmalis, giving no doubt that he had noticed Marcus's muteness. The General was now calmly pacing in front of the men.

"Yes, General, whatever pleases you pleases me," said Marcus. The fear began to soak his clothes.

"What would please me would be you trying to guess the answer to my riddle. The riddle is . . ." The General paused and in an instant was face to face, not but an inch away from Marcus, his hollow crimson eyes fixed upon the Captain. Arkmalis now eerily lowered his voice to a whisper. "My riddle is . . ." The General moved in even closer, now grabbing the hair of Marcus and tilting his head back. "What happens to a captain of my guard who does not do what he is told to do?"

"General . . . there were . . . extenuating circumstances," replied Marcus.

General Arkmalis's grip tightened on Marcus's hair. "Excuse me, did I not explain myself fully, that I was after an answer to my riddle, Marcus?" The look on Marcus's face had grown even more dire. "Now let us try this again, shall we? What happens to a captain of my guard—now this is the bit you might not have been paying attention to the first time, and I would suggest that this time you focus. What happens to a captain of my guard who does not do what he is told to do? And if it has not yet become clear to you Marcus, I am indeed losing my patience."

"The boy was not alone, General," said Dalco Jakobsen, defending his captain. The words hung in the air for a long, uneasy ten seconds before Grayden Arkmalis showed the Rider the consequences of his interruption. Arkmalis's stare held on Marcus as his eyes began to glow red. While still holding the Captain in his right hand, the General raised his left, and a stream of red energy poured from his palm. Like magma spouting forth from the open crater of a volcano, but this eruption was focused. The energy blast incinerated Jakobsen. Marcus turned away.

Cries of horror escaped from the General's harem. The Captain looked back to where his old friend had stood. The only evidence of this man's existence that remained was the stench of his disintegrated flesh and a pile of scorched, smoking bones that just three seconds earlier had held up Dalco Jakobsen. Evangeline's eyes settled on Marcus. She began to open her mouth, but the look from Slade made her catch herself. Evangeline's lips trembled while she struggled to keep calm. Corbin hustled from seemingly nowhere and collected the smoldering bones. The remains, no doubt, were to be added to the Tower's decor.

"Damn him to Narg. He ruined my riddle." The General sounded disappointed, but the act of killing seemed to relax him. "That, Marcus, is what normally happens when someone fails to do what I have asked of them. Luckily for you, your Rider could not follow even the simplest of your orders. Insubordination will not be tolerated, Captain. Now . . ." Marcus was released and fell to the floor. "Tell me more about this help your Rider had the audacity to interrupt my riddle with."

Marcus tried to compose himself, knowing that he had just dodged a proverbial bullet. The Captain stood. "There was a Native American girl. We have encountered her in the past, but we do not know as of yet who she is. My men are working on identifying her.

She was there with a spirit ghost. They must have been sent to retrieve the boy."

"I had called upon enough *Eerah* to take down three Mage Warriors; you are not telling me the full story. The *Eerah* were scared by whatever happened on that cliff. Anyone with such powers could sense that. *Eerah* do not get scared, do they Marcus? So what really happened to the boy?" Arkmalis had gone from irate to inquisitive.

"I am afraid he eluded capture, General. The boy had an artif protecting him as well. It proved particularly bothersome, but I believe it to be no longer operational." Marcus already knew that his explanation was not good enough.

"You *believe it to be.* That's odd. I asked you to retrieve a boy, and you regale me with stories of incapacitating a silly machine?"

"There was also a teleport dragon. He was the reason for their escape. I believe his tech was severely damaged in the battle. He could not have gotten far." Marcus continued with the story, "But there is more."

"Please do go on, so far as I can tell there is no explanation how my best Riders and an army of *Eerah* could have failed so miserably in the simplest of tasks. I am eager to hear something that could possibly explain this phenomenon," said Arkmalis as he turned away from the Captain. "Please, Marcus, continue with this fantastical tale."

"Well, General, we believe—that is, I believe the boy was responsible for the *Eerah*'s destruction and subsequent retreat."

"That is inconceivable. A boy that age could not have that kind of power." The thought slowly weighed on Arkmalis's face. "I was extremely powerful at that age, but I am a rarity, and I also had been training for years. The boy has not. There has to be another explanation."

"There was an extreme power surge seconds before the destruction of the *Eerah* army. A surge that had, according to our sensors, originated from the exact position of the boy," said Marcus. The words did not seem plausible even to him.

"I had felt an extreme energy shift, but I just assumed it was from the *Eerah* retreating in fear, not the actual cause of their retreat." The General paused. "What about the girl? Could it have been her?"

"That is highly unlikely, General. She has never shown such skill in our previous encounters." Marcus had already weighed all possibilities. His hesitance was based on Arkmalis's responses, not his own certainty. Marcus knew without a doubt that the epicenter of that energy was Thomas Scargen.

"You are certain of this, Marcus. That much I can sense. This makes your failure even more disappointing," said Arkmalis as he silently debated his next move.

"I cannot change the past, General, but I can promise you I will find the boy—whatever means necessary," said the Captain, now standing at attention. "I have my men tracing the dragon's teleport signature as we speak. It will not be long before we discover his destination."

"Very well, Marcus. It appears that you are not entirely useless. You will get your chance at redemption. But, Marcus, do not fail me again," echoed Arkmalis's words as he looked piercingly at the Captain. "We must get to Scargen before *he* does. Corbin will consult the Seer on the whereabouts of the boy. I have more pressing matters to attend to. There's an old friend I must converse with, and I do not want to be interrupted by any more of your failures."

"Yes, General," said Marcus as he and the Second saluted the General, then turned and walked towards the exit. The imp waddled behind.

"Corbin, awaken the Seer," commanded Grayden Arkmalis as he returned to his bacchanal.

"As you wish, my liege," said the imp servant as he closed the doors behind the Riders.

Old friend? Marcus pondered the General's words as the slamming of the door echoed through the hall. As far as he knew, Arkmalis had no friends. *Who is he meeting with?*

4

a dragon's lair

The teleport dragon sped across a stretch of water unknown to Thomas. The spirit ghost matched Bartleby in altitude and speed, still carrying the lifeless robot.

The wind combed the boy's hair as goosebumps rolled down his arms. Thomas looked down and could just make out his reflection atop the flying beast, creating the illusion of a mirror that spanned miles in several directions across the water. Thomas felt alive—more alive than he had ever felt in his almost-seventeen-year existence.

He was not sure where they were heading, but moments ago they had soared over Paris. Thomas had seen the Eiffel Tower and the lights of the Louvre passing underneath as the sun began to rise. He had been to the City of Light when he was a child, but this was different. "Thanks, Bartleby. It's not every day you get a dragon tour of Paris," said Thomas with a grin on his face.

"You are most welcome, Thomas. It may not be duh fastest way to my gaff, but it is duh most breaftakin', isn't it?" Bartleby paused. "Now don't get me wrong. I'd take London over it any day uv duh week, but I do love ol' Pairee's sparkle. And don't get me started on duh food, mate. *C'est magnifique.*" The beast laughed as he glided right. Thomas could not help but think of a dragon-sized croissant, and he too began to laugh.

"How much longer?" asked Yareli, interrupting the merriment.

"My flat is just up a'ed." Thomas looked out on the water. "Now 'old on you two."

Just up ahead? Nothing's up ahead, he thought.

His confusion subsided when he saw the massive white wall jutting out of the water. He knew for certain they were flying above the English Channel. Thomas could not help but stare at this natural work of art as they approached the White Cliffs of Dover. Bartleby slowed his speed and rolled left. With the sudden heading change he appeared to be flying straight for the cliff face.

"Bartleby, we're gonna smack right into that wall if you don't pull up," exclaimed Thomas, grabbing tightly on the pommel.

"No worries, mate. I'd never 'urt you, Thomas," snorted the dragon, now bearing down on the cliff face. "And besides, I 'avn't gotten paid yet, 'av I?"

"Are credits all you ever think about?" asked Yareli, sounding as if she already knew the answer.

"No, it's not all I fink about. Sometimes, I fink about spending dem." The dragon picked up speed. It now seemed certain that they were going to hit the rock wall.

"Bartleby!" screamed Thomas and Yareli in unison. The dragon stayed the course. There was nothing the boy could do. Thomas's muscles tensed as he braced for impact. Right before the imminent collision, the white rock face phased out and they flew right through the stone facade.

Behind the cliff face was a bustling hangar. Bartleby, with wings extended, landed and with a bounce came to a complete stop inside the confines of this secret cave. "What the hell was that?" asked Thomas, still grasping the pommel.

" 'olographic wall, mate. Can't 'av everyone knowin' where I live, can I?" said the dragon.

"How about a little warning next time," said Thomas as he let himself breathe again. The boy looked around and could see several crews of tiny, big-eared, goggled creatures hurrying this way and that. He leaned over to Yareli, whose hair had been blown out by the flight. "Weird roommates."

"I've seen weirder," said Yareli as she rolled her eyes. Thomas turned back to get a better look at the little workers.

Their heights varied from about a foot to a foot and a half. All of them had a yellowish tinge to them, but the boy could hardly tell because most of them were covered in grease and dirt. Thomas could barely make out their true color without their goggles lifted. The goggles had kept their eyes clean from the debris and formed small yellow circles, much like when one wears sunglasses in the sun too long. Other creatures' faces were covered with soot from welding, and their uniforms were decorated with scorch marks.

Almost rhythmically the different teams began to attach various diagnostic equipment and scaffolding to the beast's electronic regions. A symphony of tools began to whirl in Thomas's brain. Welding, hammering, screwing, wrenching, and a murmur of conversations on the status of Bartleby's armor and tech were all that could be heard.

One of these creatures in particular stood out among the others. *He must be the foreman*, thought Thomas. He walked up and down the various platforms, barking orders this way and that—but this foreman did his fair share of the manual labor. It was a sight to behold. These little mechanics, welders, and electricians were already well on their way to fixing every dent, seam, or computer malfunction that the dragon's tech had sustained over the past few hours.

A landing platform had automatically sensed passengers on Bartleby's back and now descended towards the docked dragon. They walked onto the platform as Wiyaloo landed beside them, still holding the lifeless artif.

"I'll meet you in the grand room when dey finish takin' off my armor. My mate 'awforne is eager to meet you. 'ee's a big fan uv your dad's," said Bartleby, who was now covered by the small workers. The sound of two large automatic doors opening garnered the attention of the dragon, and his eyes darted towards the direction of the noise. "Oh, 'ere 'ee is now. Everyone, dis is my best mate, Franklin 'awforne."

A dark-haired, bearded man stood in front of them. He was dressed in a white lab coat that looked like an oilcan had attacked it. A stretcher flanked by two of the small creatures hovered behind him. Hawthorne was wearing a magnifying eyepiece. Thomas had seen one just like it worn by his father when he worked on LINC.

Where are you, Dad?

"Greetings." Hawthorne spoke with a surprisingly American accent. "I suppose you are Yareli Chula, and this ghostly apparition to my left must be Wiyaloo. You can place the artif down, and I'll have some of the boys take a look at what's ailing him." Wiyaloo placed LINC down on the floating stretcher. The little creatures pushed the platform through the door.

I hope he's all right, thought the boy.

"And you must be Thomas Scargen." This statement refocused the boy. He turned back from watching the stretcher and looked at Hawthorne. "You must be pretty damn important. Well if what they're paying Bartleby means anything. But where are my manners? You are guests here at Draige Manor. I shouldn't be talking about business. Who's hungry?" Thomas knew he was. He had been since the cliff.

"I could eat," said the boy smiling over at Yareli.

"It has been quite some time since I last ate as well," said the Native American girl.

"Then it's settled," said Hawthorne. "Let's eat."

"You better not start dinner wiffout me, Franklin," said the dragon in a joking manner. "I could eat a whole cow right now."

"I'll have some of the little buggers fetch one from the freezer then, and you know as well as I do, we never eat dinner without you . . . well hardly ever," answered Franklin, turning to Thomas. "One thing ya gotta know about dragons is, they have very large freezers, young man, and stomachs to match."

"Not to mention their mouths," chimed in Yareli. "Their very large mouths." She formed a half-cocked smile. Thomas noticed her expression, and he immediately thought it a better face for smiles than the usual frown.

"How long 'av you been waitin' to let dat one loose? Dat 'urts a bit," said Bartleby as he locked his stare onto Yareli. "And you said you were out uv arrows. Well I guess you were saving one, weren't you?"

They entered a long hall through the large doors. The ceilings were exceptionally high, and the hallway was just as wide. "This place is huge," said Thomas.

"Don't forget: a dragon lives here," said Hawthorne.

"Trust me, as long as I live, I won't forget that," said the boy.

Franklin Hawthorne smiled as he walked in front of them like a museum tour guide. Playing the role, he began to describe some of the items and massive paintings that lined the hallway. "This is Draige Hall. As you can see, Bartleby has saved a lot of stuff over the years. Most of it, however, has been handed down from Draige to Draige for thousands of years." The looming walls were littered with incredible paintings of various dragons from various ages. A plaque levitated above a stand in front of each painting. When Thomas passed one of these stands, he could see that the plaques were actually holoscreen panels. The screens were menus. On top was the title of each painting and below that were options for ARTIST BIOGRAPHY, EXPLANATION OF PAINTING, and SUBJECT BIOGRAPHY.

Thomas looked up at this particular painting. The subject was DELONIUS DRAIGE, Bartleby's father. The resemblance was staggering, though Delonius had a more worn look on his face. Costly wisdom had burdened his features. When Thomas reached to touch the screen, he was startled by a holographic image that leapt from the panel. Thomas regained his composure and looked at the image that was now in front of him. It was an extremely beautiful, life-sized woman. She had flowing blonde hair and round spectacles. She stood with both hands behind her back and began to speak.

"Hello, how are you today?" the holographic woman asked almost too politely with her proper English accent.

"Fine, I guess. You kinda startled me," answered Thomas, trying to catch his breath.

"I am most sorry, Thomas Scargen. Let me properly introduce

myself. I am the artificial intelligence that runs this facility, but I am referred to by most as ELAIN, or Electronic Learning Artificial Intelligence Network. I am servant, defense, daily maintenance, and curator of this complex. If you require anything, you need but ask," said ELAIN with what sounded like a hint of flirtation.

"It can get lonely in this big drafty place," murmured Franklin under his breath. "I created her in the image of my choosing, and well, I thought this place could use a woman's touch."

"Yeah, but for some reason I don't think it was only the place that needed the woman's touch," joked Thomas while quietly admiring Franklin's creation.

"Boys and their toys," Yareli said half to herself. "Men only think about one thing."

"Agreed," said Wiyaloo straight-faced as he stood perfectly still behind Yareli.

"Franklin's and my relationship is strictly platonic, and I assure you, Ms. Chula, I am no toy," interjected ELAIN, ending the conversation abruptly.

"I did not mean to suggest otherwise," replied Yareli, a little embarrassed.

"ELAIN, can I ask you something important?" asked the boy.

"Thomas, your robotic companion is currently being diagnosed by my systems, and from what information I have already obtained, the damage seems reversible, but it is going to take some time to perform the repairs," said ELAIN.

"How did you know I was—"

"Part of my functionality is to anticipate the needs of all inhabitants of Draige Manor. Your artif has been damaged, and your most logical inquiry would concern his current condition."

Thomas was amazed. The sophistication of ELAIN's artificial intelligence reminded Thomas of his father. He had thought for a long time now that his father was the only person capable of such miracles of programming and technology. Questions started to creep back into Thomas's head. *Is he dead somewhere in Egypt?* Thomas could not shake the reality of his nightmare, but he knew he was powerless to change his current situation. Thomas was not safe and needed to deal with that reality first. He would try to contact his father soon, but not until he had a better grasp on his current predicament. If there was one thing his father would expect from Thomas, it would be for him to keep his wits about him and not jump to conclusions without any hard data to back them up. There was no use worrying about something that, in all likelihood, was only a bad dream.

Thomas's thoughts began to settle. He wished he could say the same for his stomach, which now grumbled aloud. The power expenditure during the *Eerah* battle had rendered him physically useless and hungry. He could not wait to eat, but the painting intrigued Thomas.

The piece of artwork consisted of Delonius Draige leaning up against a bomber plane from World War II. He and the plane were surrounded by tiny creatures just like the ones in the hangar and several Royal Air Force pilots. He might not know the fate of his own father, but he was intrigued to learn about Bartleby's. "ELAIN?"

"Yes, Thomas Scargen," replied the hologram.

"Can you tell me about this painting—and Delonius Draige?"

"It would be my pleasure to tell his tale, but be warned: this story does not end happily." Thomas's curiosity was piqued. He was a sucker for a good story, especially one about a dragon. "This is an oil painting by Martin F. Jesop." A holographic picture of the artist suddenly appeared in front of the onlookers. "It is said that he was deathly afraid of dragons . . . but also terribly fascinated by them."

"Understandable," said the boy.

"He was borderline obsessed with their anatomy and design. Critics consider this his finest piece of work. The subject of said painting is, as you know, Delonius Draige, true hero to England and First Warrior Teleport Dragon of the Second World War. His exploits during the war are still unknown to most, but that does not make them any less heroic or historically necessary. In the composition you see Delonius leaning against an Avro Lancaster Bomber, considered by most historians to be the most proficient bomber of World War II." The artist's head morphed into old footage of these planes in formation performing a bombing run, and suddenly the gliding green body of Delonius Draige entered the holographic projection. "The dragons were primarily used in tandem with the bomber squadrons during night raids in Germany. Other dragons were rumored to be used in other theatres of the war, but they had their biggest impact in Europe.

"The dragons would only fight during the night for fear of discovery by the Germans, but that was no problem for creatures with night vision. In addition to Delonius, there were five other dragons flying alongside him. There are five complementary paintings of each dragon in Delonius's squadron. These were also painted by Martin F. Jesop." A three-dimensional image of the six of them replaced the footage from World War II.

Thomas was surprised by the different colors of the beasts. *This is way cooler than anything in The Dragon Fire Chronicles*, he thought. The first dragon became highlighted as ELAIN continued.

"There was Delonius's brother—Bartleby's uncle—Pascal Draige." Pascal was also green. The highlight moved over to a red dragon. "Delonius's love and Bartleby's mother, Desdemona." The highlight now moved to a dragon that appeared to be made of ice. "This is Aldrich Baldemar, the youngest of the six." The cursor jumped to a blue dragon with no wings slithering across the sky. "Ilyana Ragnor." The highlight moved to the final dragon. He was black, "and Larson Ragnor." Thomas noticed an uneasy look on Larson's face. "Pascal's portrait you have already passed in the hall, and Desdemona's is located directly across from this one on the opposing wall. Paintings of Aldrich and Ilyana can be found back closer to the hall's entrance. The painting of Larson Ragnor was believed to be destroyed during the War." ELAIN paused as the three-dimensional representation of the group transformed into actual footage of the dragon squadron.

"Delonius was their leader of course, but Larson was by far the most—for lack of a better word—aggressive of the group. The team proved most effective at any mission that was their charge. That is until the bombing of Dresden. Pascal Draige and Ilyana Ragnor were both casualties of this engagement. This siege would be the last for this group, and its outcome would ensure the exclusion of such squadrons f-f-from subs-s-s-sequent w-wars." ELAIN paused as her image flickered. The hologram quickly focused and turned towards the boy, who waited on her next words with clear anticipation. "I'm sorry that I cannot complete your request, Thomas. The necessary files cannot be located at this time."

Thomas stood there with a look of disappointment on his face. "It was just getting interesting, I—"

"Huh . . . well . . . Sorry, Thomas. I guess I'll have to fix that," interrupted Franklin. "But we can discuss the tales of yore later. Who's up for some grub?"

Intrigued as he was by the story, Thomas's stomach quickly reminded him of more pressing needs. "Lead the way, Mr. Hawthorne. I'm starving."

"Please, call me Franklin. ELAIN, let's get this show on the road. It's not every day this place has guests."

"Everything is ready as requested, Franklin Hawthorne." ELAIN moved towards the next room and phased through the wall. The huge doors opened in front of them to reveal a vast dragon-sized dining room with dozens of the phenomenal small creatures hustling this way and that, getting ready for the impromptu dinner.

Franklin sat down at the foot of the absurdly long dining table. A massive chair resided at the opposite head of the table. *That must be Bartleby's,* thought Thomas.

"Where are my manners?" Franklin sprung to his feet and pulled out the chair to the right of him and motioned towards Yareli. "Pardon me, I don't know the last time a real woman has blessed us with her presence."

"Am I not considered real?" said ELAIN. "I am not an illusion. I do exist."

"I didn't mean anything by it, ELAIN. I was just saying that we sure haven't had one eat with us in a long time, that's all," said Franklin, trying to avert an ensuing argument.

"An explanation is not required. I am needed elsewhere. I have an injured artif to attend to, and adjustments need to be made to

Bartleby's armor. Enjoy your food gentlemen . . . and lady," said ELAIN as she vanished.

Yareli sat in the chair that Franklin had pulled out for her. "Thank you, Mr. Hawthorne."

"Please, Thomas, Wiyaloo, sit." Franklin waved his arm, inviting the two over to his end of the table.

"I will stand," rumbled Wiyaloo as he took his usual position behind Yareli.

"You are too big to argue with," laughed Franklin.

Thomas looked around the room. The walls were made of the natural stone of the cliffs. There were two sets of mechanical doors and several bulky wooden supports. The dark supports were intricately carved with striking detail.

The table that was the centerpiece of the room was made of stone, but it was not the same material as the walls. The legs were chiseled works of art that any museum would have proudly displayed. They consisted of several different dragons in varying positions holding up the tabletop. The sheer amount of work it must have taken to move the sculptured monstrosity alone was enough to make one take notice. The amount and variety of food already atop the table was just as remarkable. "Being a teleport dragon must pay well," said Thomas.

"That it does," said Hawthorne. "But feeding a small army and a dragon takes a lot of credits."

"I can only imagine," said Thomas as he stared at the food. His stomach growled once more. He wanted to reach out and just start eating, but he did not want to begin the meal before their host arrived. The other set of doors slid open. An oversized floating serving tray hovered out to the far end of the table accompanied by a group of tiny servers. *That must lead to the kitchen.* The cow that had been promised to Bartleby was laid out on top of the first tray. More serving trays of reasonably sized food followed and lowered themselves onto the table. The small servers grabbed pitchers of what looked like green milk and began to fill everyone's glasses. This disturbed Thomas, but he did not want to be rude. He grinned at the small server as she poured the oddly colored liquid into his glass. The doors that led back to Draige Hall whooshed open. Thomas turned to see Bartleby entering the dining hall.

The dragon and several more of the little creatures made their way to the table. Bartleby wore a large dress shirt with a red-and-green plaid vest. Thomas thought it was funny that he wore no pants. His sleeves were rolled up, and a smoking pipe hung in his left claw. He lit the pipe with a fire blast from his left nostril and raised the device in the direction of his mouth, but before he could take a drag, the dragon was attacked by a dreadfully excited black Labrador. The dog ran up his lowered right arm and began licking the dragon's snout.

" 'ello Webster, dat's a good boy. I told ya I'd be back. Yes I did . . . yes I did," said Bartleby while rubbing his snout against the dog. " 'ey Webby, what do I 'av in my pocket?" The dragon's free right claw dug into his vest pocket and emerged with a red round ball that looked miniscule in his hand. Bartleby threw the ball down the length of the table. Webster dashed after the toy, promptly grabbed it with his teeth, and bounded back proudly to his master.

"Ruff," barked the dog as he placed the ball back in Bartleby's claw.

"Aw'right . . . aw'right . . . I'll frow it again." The beast continued to play fetch with the dog, as he smoked his pipe. "Dat's a good dog."

The tiny creatures had also dressed and cleaned in a way more-suiting dinner. It had now become easier to discern between the males and females. The females were curvier—not as stocky as the males. Thomas could tell they were one big family. Various groups formed and couples paired off as they found their places at the large table. Once they sat, their chairs rose to the height of the table. Thomas could not tell if this was a mechanical or magical accomplishment, but either way it was impressive. Bartleby and company looked as hungry as Thomas felt. "Why does everyone look like they are starving?" asked the boy.

"There is a lot of time and attention to detail that goes into Bart's return, docking, and repair of the dragon and his tech," said Franklin. "Sometimes that means dinner becomes second priority. Besides, it has almost become tradition to wait for the founder of the feast. It only seems fitting. Sometimes Bartleby's gone for days, sometimes, weeks on end, but the late dinners are pretty much a staple. It seemed to suit the little fellows' internal clocks, truth be told, and I've always been a night owl."

"What exactly are these creatures?" asked Thomas.

"They are technically called gremlings, Thomas," answered Franklin, turning towards the boy. His voice turned purposely lower. "But they are more commonly known as gremlins."

"Which do they prefer?" asked Thomas.

"Well I suppose I'd prefer to be called by my name an that," one of the gremlins sitting next to him murmured under his breath. Immediately Thomas recognized him as the foreman from the hangar. "It's just we *are* bloody gremlings, not gremlins. It does my 'ed in to fink about it. You might as well call me a bloody midget or a dwarf. Alls I'm sayin' is, it's a matter of simple decency, innit, to call somefing by its rightful name? But ja know what I mean?"

"I didn't mean anything by it. I was just wondering—that's all. I'm sorry if I insulted you," said Thomas in a genuine tone.

"Aw'right," said the gremlin boss while quickly finishing off his glass of green milk. The gremlin wiped off his emerald milk mustache. "My name is Fargus, Fargus Hexelby." He extended his petite hand towards Thomas.

"Thomas, Thomas Scargen," the boy offered as he shook Fargus's hand. He was caught off guard by the gremlin's strength, but before he could comment on it Fargus had returned to the fish he had been devouring. It seemed that the gremlin had waited long enough to eat.

"Don't take it personally. They can be pretty abrasive sometimes. It's part of their charm. Anyway, I guess somewhere along the way *gremlings* turned into *gremlins*. Most of them can't be bothered by the distinction and actually prefer being called gremlins, but Fargus is not like most of them. He's a big fan of small details." He looked at the boy. "They are good folks though, and damn brilliant when it comes to technology. It's hard to believe that when they were first found they were a bunch of troublemakers."

"How do you mean?" asked Thomas, puzzled.

"They originally were a pretty big thorn in the side of the Royal

Air Force. These guys were responsible for millions of dollars in damaged RAF airplanes during the beginning years of World War II."

"Wait, you mean, *those* gremlins?" Thomas was finally starting to catch on to the scope of the whole thing. "I thought that was a myth, a pilot's tale."

"Yes, Thomas, *those* gremlins, and as you can see, it's not a myth. They were initially upset with the RAF for destroying all their homes and their way of life. The Royal Air Force had built an airstrip right on top of their sacred homes, and to the gremlins it seemed like vengeance was the only course of action. These little guys have been around since the early days of Britain—well not these particular gremlins, but their families for sure. They were entitled to that land and were angry when it was taken from them. It took some time, but the gremlins began to understand that what the RAF was doing was for the greater good, and a truce was declared, but not until after a lot of damage was done."

"What kind of damage?" asked the boy.

"They had sabotaged hundreds of planes, and there were several casualties."

"What happened after the truce?" wondered the boy.

"Well, Thomas, they began to use their natural talents for destruction to severely cripple the Luftwaffe, and at the same time hastily learned how to repair and improve the Allied planes. This is when my great-great-grandfather first met the gremlins . . . or was it my great-great-great-grandfather—I can never remember. It was so long ago. Anyway, his name was Alfred Hawthorne . . . no, wait . . . it might have been Clifford Hawthorne?" He looked away and then back over to Thomas. "No . . . it was Alfred—it was definitely Alfred." Thomas lifted his eyebrow. "I'm like eighty-six percent sure his name was Alfred." The two laughed as Franklin continued. "*Alfred* had come from America to help improve the design and functionality of the Allied planes. He worked directly with the gremlins and quickly befriended the little guys. Come to think of it, that's where he met Bart's pop too."

"Delonius Draige?" Thomas thought about the corrupted file.

"Now can you tell me what happened to him and the dragon squadrons?" He was certain Franklin would have some answers.

"The only thing I know for certain is that after the war, the gremlins were relocated as part of the truce, and they moved in with my family. Our families have lived together ever since. They tried to keep in touch with the Draiges, but the correspondence with Delonius and Desdemona ended abruptly. Several decades later, as the story goes, Bartleby just showed up, and came to live with my parents and the gremlin families. I myself had been living in the States for most of my life, and after getting my degrees in robotic engineering and artificial intelligence, I moved back here. That's how I've come to be such good friends with Bart, but he never has spoken of the subject of what happened to his family. I know what you know for the most part. I have known the old dragon for years now, but I haven't the heart to directly ask what happened to his uncle, or to his father and mother. My dad would always say to me 'If a man—well, dragon in this case—wants to talk to you about something, he will. Otherwise it ain't none of your damn business.' Pop always had a way with words. I gotta give the old man that." Franklin and the boy laughed again.

"But do me a favor, Thomas: the subject of Bartleby's father is . . . well it's sort of a sore subject around here. What I mean to say is, could you not bring it up to Bart or the little guys. Some of the gremlins have heard these stories from their ancestors, like Fargus, and they seem content with never talking about it."

"Quite content actually," added Fargus. "At duh end uv duh day, it's none uv me business, is it—or yours, come ta fink about it. It's best just left alone. No need to poke duh bloody dragon, is there?" Thomas looked at the gremlin with surprise, not realizing he was listening. Fargus just kept eating, not even looking at the boy. Thomas slowly turned his head back to Franklin. "None uv us know duh whole bloody tale anyway, do we?"

"I've known that old dragon for decades now, and I still haven't gotten the whole thing out of him," said Franklin.

"So he erased the information from the computer," surmised Thomas.

"I don't have any proof, but I believe so, and like I said, it wasn't the whole tale to begin with," said Franklin, reiterating his ignorance of the whole subject. Franklin's gaze turned from Thomas, and he began staring down the other end of the table as Bartleby clumsily sat in his gigantic dragon-sized chair, eating and laughing.

"That won't be a problem, Mr. Hawthorne. We all have our bad family stories, I suppose," said Thomas as he covered up his own pain in this area with a grin.

"That we do, Thomas . . . that we do, and please, call me Franklin. Mr. Hawthorne married my mother." Franklin turned his head back towards Thomas. "I suppose we can start eating now that the big man has finally arrived, and when we are done here, I'll show you where we are keeping LINC."

The dragon stood and tapped on his large goblet. It appeared to be filled with red wine. "I would like to propose a toast . . . to new friends! May our friendships always be . . . profitable." Everyone raised his or her glasses. Thomas clanged his green concoction against Franklin's, Fargus's, and Yareli's glasses, and, before realizing it, took a swig. His mouth contorted when he realized what he had done. He coughed but swallowed the alien elixir.

"That's not half bad," said Thomas, as if this revelation was the most surprising thing that had happened that evening. He took a larger gulp. "Not bad at all."

5

diagnosis

*A*fter the late dinner, the dragon and his dog retired to his bedroom in need of sleep. Thomas could not tell whether Webster or Bartleby was more exhausted. Yareli also went to her newly designated room to lie down. Thomas figured that she had fallen asleep when Wiyaloo vanished. Franklin led the boy down a series of corridors. The two made a right down a particularly long corridor. "So your pop's *the* Dr. Carl Scargen . . . of Scargen Robotics? That Carl Scargen?"

"Yeah," said the boy. "Bartleby mentioned you were a fan."

"A huge fan actually. I'm almost ashamed of how much I know about your father." Hawthorne smiled as if remembering something. "When I was growing up, I had a Scargen Robotics poster hanging over my bed. I used to stare at that thing for hours, reciting the motto over and over again." Hawthorne cleared his throat. "*Scargen Robotics—building the artifs of tomorrow, today.*"

"I know it all too well. You know how many Scargen Robotics T-shirts I've owned over the years?" said Thomas. He thought about his father and where he might be and why he had still not gotten back to the boy. Part of him wanted to tell this man he hardly knew about his dream, but something stopped him.

"He's a genius," said Franklin, interrupting the boy's thoughts.

"That's what they say," said Thomas. He was desperate to change the subject.

"He's done more for robotics than any ten of his peers. He's basically the architect of the modern artif. He's my measuring stick for success."

"We've got something in common." He felt guilty instantly for having said such a thing. "Anyway, from what I've seen you are doing a great job. I bet my dad would love to see your work." Hawthorne smiled.

"There was something else I was wondering . . ." Hawthorne's face slightly changed. "Is your father a technic?"

"A what?"

"A technic. It's what they call technopaths."

Thomas shook his head no, still confused. "I'm sorry. I still don't get it."

"It's someone who is naturally adept at fixing computers and tech. Some can even do it with a simple touch or a thought. I just assumed your dad must be one."

"Just by touching? That's completely narsh, and would explain a lot, but I'm not sure." He had never thought of his father's abilities as a power. The concept stunned him for a few seconds. "He does do some crazy things with tech, but he's never told me anything like that. I'm not sure he even knew that this was a thing. Why do you want to know?"

"Because I'm one, Thomas. When I touch any tech, it's like I can immediately understand it. Fargus is one too, but he'd tell ya differently." Thomas smiled. "When I developed ELAIN, it was like I could see everything just moving into its necessary spot. It just came to me, ya know?"

"I guess." *Is Dad a technic? I guess it's possible.* From what Thomas had seen in the last few hours, anything seemed possible.

"Here we are, as promised," said Hawthorne, interrupting Thomas's thoughts.

They had made their way to another set of grand sliding doors with a flashing red light and a sign that read DIAGNOSTIC CENTER.

This must be the place they're keeping LINC, thought Thomas. He would not sleep until he was certain of LINC's well-being. Franklin raised his hand and a holographic screen appeared, scanning his hand.

"Handprint accepted," said ELAIN's voice out of the computer. Franklin leaned his head towards the holographic screen as it morphed into a retinal scanner. Franklin then placed his eye into the scanner as if he had done it an absurd number of times.

"Hawthorne, Franklin," said Franklin. The light located above the doors now blinked green.

"Retinal and vocal scans confirmed. Access granted," said the voice of ELAIN.

"I guess whoever designed the security is a little paranoid, huh?" joked Thomas.

"Yes Thomas, I can be quite paranoid," said Franklin as he drew a smile. The doors slid open.

Thomas was taken aback by the vast amount of tech in the room. There were dozens of holographic displays simultaneously collecting information from the incapacitated artif. Hawthorne reached down on his wristcom and more screens activated. LINC was flat on his back on a floating table in the center of the room. Thomas moved over to the artif and placed his hand on top of LINC's chest. Franklin studied the displays.

"How's he doing?" asked the boy. "He doesn't look so good."

"According to these readouts, he's actually fine, Thomas. Look, I'll show you," said Hawthorne as he started moving his fingers across the holographic display that faced the table. He then turned his attention to his wristcom. Two orbs floated out of his wristcom and over to the artif's body. Red beams washed across the exterior of LINC. A holographic representation of the artif's interior arose in front of Hawthorne's display.

"It's been a few years since I've seen his insides. I always forget how—"

"Amazing it is?" finished Hawthorne. "Your father is a damn genius." The two stared quietly at the display for a few seconds.

"I'm gonna go with a big yeah on the whole my-dad's-a-technic thing," said Thomas.

"After seeing this, I totally agree," said Hawthorne. He moved his hand across the holographic controls. The image of LINC began to rotate. "Let's see what's ailing your artif." He paused the rotation. "That's interesting."

"What is it?"

"Well, according to this LINC should be fine." The boy sighed in relief.

"That's good to hear, but why isn't he moving?" A red circle flashed on the hologram. It seemed to indicate the artif's damaged area. The display zoomed in. A tiny component was highlighted in red.

"That's why." He pointed at the hologram. "His articulix is malfunctioning," said Hawthorne.

"I think I've heard Dad mention one of those before."

"Well that would make sense, considering he invented it," said Hawthorne.

"Of course he did." The boy paused for a few seconds. "What exactly does an articulix do?" asked Thomas staring at the holographic screen.

"It enables him to move. It basically controls all of his mechanical processes. LINC is wired fine. He's just got a busted articulix."

"Can he hear us?"

"It's hard to say. There isn't really a human equivalent for the state he's in right now. He's in a kind of hibernation, like a deep sleep. That's the best way I can explain it."

"Oh." The boy again walked over to LINC. He picked up his cold hand and placed it in his. "Hang in there, buddy. Hawthorne here tells me you are going to be just fine, and don't worry. These guys seem to know what they're doing. They'll fix you. I promise you that." He turned back to Hawthorne. "It can be fixed, right?"

"I'm afraid not. It looks like he needs a completely new—"

"Articulix," interrupted ELAIN as she appeared next to the artif. "Hello, Franklin. Hello, Thomas. I guess you have come to see what progress has been made on your mechanical friend. As you can see,

I am afraid he is still not quite functional. With a fully operational articulix and some patience, your robotic cohort should be up and running shortly. We have repaired most of the internal as well as external damages, but the articulix is completely liquidated and cannot be salvaged."

"That's no good," said Thomas.

"Precisely. I was trying to locate an articulix, but we do not currently have one in our stock. I then began to explore other possibilities."

"Other possibilities?"

"That is what I said. We also need a tech enhancer to complete Bartleby's repair. I have the specifics downloading to your wristcom, Thomas, as well as the coordinates of our tech dealer. His name is Ronald Hosselfot. Someone will have to go to the city to retrieve it." The hologram looked at Thomas. "He will be expecting you and Ms. Chula in the morning."

"Wait a second. Slow down. Why are me and Yareli going at all?" asked Thomas, completely confused by the suggestion.

"I wanted to just send Ms. Chula, but she insisted that you are her responsibility, and if she has to go retrieve the needed material, you would have to accompany her. She said, and I quote, 'If I go, he goes.' I need Franklin's unique abilities to get the artif prepared for the operation or he would have gone. You can take one of the aeromobiles located in the garage," said ELAIN.

"Just do not touch the black Toyunda. That one is mine, and it's my baby."

"I guess that's why Yareli went right to bed," said Thomas, wondering why he was just being told this information.

"I told her the circumstances and details as soon as I understood the dire need for these resources. I then spoke with Mr. Hosselfot about your pending meeting and subsequent purchase of said goods. I then appeared here just a few minutes ago to update you on these decisions, Thomas Scargen. Like I previously stated, I did not originally factor you into the plan and only did at the insistence of Ms. Chula. If I had, I would have informed you at an earlier time," said the beautiful hologram.

"I'm sorry, ELAIN. I am a little tired and cranky. It's been a long night, and I am exhausted," said Thomas.

"Your apology is not required, but accepted," responded ELAIN. "My scans of your body indicate that you are in need of REM sleep cycles."

"Well I guess that's my cue to show you to your room. Sounds like you have a long day ahead of you tomorrow," said Franklin, sounding a bit tired himself.

"If it's all the same, Franklin,"—the boy yawned—"I'd rather sleep here with LINC." Thomas pulled up one of the chairs next to LINC's floating table. Once more Thomas grabbed the artif's hand.

"I completely understand," said Hawthorne as he looked down at LINC. He placed his hand on the artif. "Your father's work is simply remarkable." Light flickered in LINC's optics for a second. Hawthorne lifted his hand off of the artif. He looked over at Thomas. "Sorry, that happens sometimes when I touch things."

"The *technic* thing?"

"Yup. Well, good night, Thomas."

"Good night, Franklin and ELAIN." ELAIN dissipated, and Hawthorne made his way to the exit. "Good night to you too, LINC. I hope you're dreaming of electric sheep." He again yawned, and before the doors slid shut behind Franklin, the sounds of snoring echoed in the Diagnostic Center.

6

planes, trains, and aeromobiles

Morning came sooner than Thomas wanted. He was abruptly awakened by the whoosh sound from the doors opening. He was lying on the artif's arm. A line of spit dangled from the corner of his mouth. Yareli stood in the doorway looking rested and ready to go. The large foxlike beast stood at her side. "Good morning, Thomas," said Yareli. "Looks like you had a good night's sleep."

"So it wasn't a dream?" said Thomas jokingly. He was still in a bit of shock over the events of the last twelve hours, but he knew for certain that it was not a dream. There was something unequivocally real awakening in him. "So is there somewhere I can take a shower?"

"I'm sure Bart won't mind if you use his. He won't be needing it anytime soon." The boy jumped, startled by Hawthorne's voice.

"Hi . . . Franklin. I didn't see you there."

"Sorry, Thomas. Just trying to get a head start on LINC's procedure." The man's hands moved with precise skill across the numerous holographic interfaces.

"What did you mean by Bart not needing a shower?" asked the boy.

"Well he's asleep."

Thomas looked down at his wristcom. "It's almost 10:00 AM. He might get up soon."

Hawthorne heartily laughed and stopped his interaction with the computer. "That's a good one, Thomas." He turned towards the boy. "There's something you need to know about dragons—Bart especially." The boy listened intently. Dragons had fascinated him long before meeting one, and so far *The Dragon Fire Chronicles* had been way off. "You see, they like to sleep—"

"That is a gross understatement." ELAIN appeared once more. She was wearing a black dress. "The dragon is an innately slothful creature. So much so that if the existence of dragons were widely known, the term might be dragonful to depict lethargic behavior, rather than slothful." The hologram smiled. "It is not uncommon for a fully mature dragon to sleep for periods of forty-eight to seventy-two hours at a time. This propensity is intensified after teleportations of great distances."

"Like I said Thomas, he won't be needing the shower," said Hawthorne.

The shower system was as ingenious as it was massive. There was a large shelf twenty feet above the boy from which water rained down. The water settled in a basin that resembled a pond. The boy was currently wading in two feet of water. Bartleby was fast asleep as Hawthorne had explained.

The room was carved right out of the cave, and according to Hawthorne, the water flowed from a natural spring that was controlled by a series of aqueducts. The liquid stream felt great on Thomas's skin, and his thoughts again turned towards his father's whereabouts. He had attempted to contact him again before his shower. He still could not shake the thought that his dream had been something more. Part of him felt guilty that he was feeling so relaxed in this natural shower, but Thomas knew that there was nothing he could do about his father right now. He had to focus on the task at hand. They needed the articulix to fix LINC. Thomas's best chance to find his father would start with LINC, and this was his priority. Thomas was determined to figure out his current predicament and do what he could to figure out what, if anything, had happened to his father. He had thousands of questions for Yareli, and he planned on asking them today when they would be alone.

Thomas finished his shower and changed into the clothes Franklin had laid out. He could not go to London in his pajamas. The clothes were loose but overall not a bad fit. He wore a green T-shirt with an owl logo on it and a navy blue jacket. A pair of jeans covered the tops of his boots that he had thrown on before running outside the night before. He felt great, but wanted to see how he looked. There were no mirrors in this bathroom. Thomas thought that was odd. *I guess dragons aren't vain*, he thought.

He was also given a pair of sunglasses. Thomas thought they must be to help disguise him. The glasses looked more like goggles. He pulled the black specs down and was surprised by how well he could see in the dimly lit room. He lifted the goggles and stepped out into the hallway that led to Bartleby's room. This was the only way in or out of the bathroom.

Thomas slinked passed the enormous bed that held Bartleby's snoring body, trying his best not to stir the dragon. The scaled creature was dressed in light blue pajamas and matching nightcap. The bulk of his body was covered by his blanket, which appeared to be ten or so regular-sized blankets sewn together. Every time he snored, a little puff of smoke would release into the air. When it was a particularly strong exhale, flames could be seen. This explained the scorch marks all over the room.

Thomas was so preoccupied with watching the monster rest that he did not see the lamp he walked into. He grabbed at the shaking lamppost, trying to prevent it from falling, when the dragon shot up in his bed still asleep. "Did someone say credits?" Bartleby snorted and then dropped back into the bed and continued with his snoring. Thomas let out a sigh of relief and straightened the lamp's position. He then hurried towards the doors.

When he walked out of Bartleby's room, Thomas nearly knocked over the female gremlin. She was standing next to a seated Webster, Bartleby's black Labrador. " 'ello Thomas, my name is Lenore, Lenore Bugden," squeaked the little woman. "I 'av been sent to take you to the garage. This place can get a bit confusing if you don't 'av your bearings about you, as I'm sure you might 'av noticed." She had what looked like some sort of pastry on a tiny tray in her hands accompanied by another glass of the green milk. "I also brought you some breakfast. It's not much, is it, but you should always start off duh day with somefing in your stomach." The dog barked in agreement and blinked while his tongue oscillated in and out of his smiling mouth.

"It's a pleasure to meet you, Lenore Bugden, and hello again, Webster," said Thomas, still relaxed and a bit out of it from his dragon-sized waterfall shower. He had gorged himself the evening before, but he was still hungry. Thomas reached down and devoured the baked morsel, and then without hesitation, proceeded to chug the jade milk as they began to walk. "Now, let's get this show in the air." Lenore let out what sounded like a polite laugh then turned, obviously not amused with Thomas's attempt at a joke. She began to walk down the hallway, presumably in the direction of the garage. She whistled at the dog, and Webster immediately sat up and walked to her side. Lenore grabbed the side of the dog and slung herself onto Webster's back like she was getting on a horse.

"What is this stuff anyway?" Thomas lifted the green milk to his lips and drank. "It's incredible, don't get me wrong, but I've never seen or tasted anything like it."

"It's an old family recipe, isn't it? Passed down from generation to generation. We call it Gloop, named after duh family dat makes it. I don't fink I can tell you what's in it dough, on duh account uv duh fact dat I don't 'av a clue what's in it meeself. It's a big secret, isn't it? Dere's actually only duh one family dat 'as dat classified information, Thomas, and uv dem only one knows duh recipe at any given time. You 'avn't met 'er yet, 'av you? 'er name is Verona Gloop. She's duh 'ed chef, she is. Cooking, as you could imagine, is very important to us, well second only to eatin'. I guess it is important to ev'ry being wif a bit uv a 'ed on dere shoulders, isn't it? Well anyway, she is duh only one dat knows duh bloody recipe. But I know one fing dough, dere is a bit uv 'ealin' magic in it. What I mean is, it 'elps wif recovery or somefing. It also is duh reason we 'av such beautiful yellow skin," said Lenore with a grin.

"What happens if, heaven forbid, Verona passes away before passing on the secret formula?" questioned Thomas, trying to find holes in this strange gremlin family tradition.

"It's almost 'appened before, 'asn't it? Luckily, dere is a ravver intricate ceremony for duh passin' uv duh Gloop recipe. Rest assured it's very detailed and foolproof."

"Oh, so you know the ceremony?" asked the boy.

"Nope, dat is also a Gloop family secret," said Lenore with a straight face.

The answer caught Thomas off guard, and he almost choked on the Gloop he was drinking. He cleared his throat and let out a final sigh of amusement. Thomas reached down and grabbed the smallest of crumbs he had left on the serving tray and threw it into the back of his mouth. "Thank you, Lenore. I needed that."

"Don't mention it," giggled the gremlin. "Very proud family, dose Gloops—a bit untrustin' I would say, but proud nonedaless."

"Well, whatever's in this Gloop, it's entirely narsh . . . and delicious. I feel like I could take on another army of *Eerah*." Thomas guzzled the last of the green milk as they turned a corner.

They walked down the new hallway that looked identical to the one they had just turned from. "I see what you mean about losing your bearings down here: All these passageways look the same. Who built this place? It must've taken forever."

"Dese burrows 'av been 'ere since the Middle Ages. Dey 'av been used various times in almost every war since, minus the Tech War, mind ya. Dey 'ad been well vacated when we moved in. Now it makes for a perfect 'ideaway for a dragon and a couple 'undred of me lot." She looked back as she bounced on the back of Webster. "One could easily get lost and never found in dis vast system of tunnels, if one was so inclined . . . more so if someone wasn't so inclined . . . come to fink uv it." She looked back at the boy. "I don't suppose Franklin told you what else dose glasses of yours can do, did 'ee?" asked Lenore.

"No. He just gave them to me with the rest of the clothes."

"The goggles are intuitive, some uv duh most advanced tech actually. They will anticipate your needs and automatically adjust to environmental conditions."

"So if it's dark out they'll change to night vision?"

"Precisely," said Lenore. Thomas lowered the goggles and the dark hallway was illuminated in front of him.

"Narsh," said Thomas as he lifted the glasses.

"And dat's just for starters."

Thomas followed the mounted gremlin through a never-ending maze of passageways. The journey was disorienting, and he could not imagine having to remember how to get back. He kept walking as Lenore continued to clarify the goggle's functionality.

They came to a door marked GARAGE. "Well, we're 'ere. I 'ope dat gives you a bit more information on dem goggles."

"Thanks, Lenore, and here I just thought they were narsh shades." Lenore and Webster walked through the door as it automatically opened. Thomas followed the gremlin and her steed and was met with an astounding sight. The garage was enormous—like everything else in Draige Manor. There were hundreds of parking slots, all filled with various types of cars, trucks, trains, planes, and hovering vehicles from different periods of time. Most of these were antiques, but they looked practically new.

"It's unbelievable, isn't it?" said Lenore.

"That is an understatement," responded Thomas. "Who did all of this?

"Well, we did . . . and by we, I mean Franklin and the rest of us. It started as a hobby, and well it just kept building, didn't it? There can be a lot of downtime between jobs for Bartleby, and it gives us somefing to do. If you 'avn't noticed, we do enjoy our work."

Thomas spotted Yareli across the room. She was sitting in a black Toyunda. He was pretty sure it was the one Franklin had gone on about so fervently the evening prior.

"Well this is where Webster and I leave you," squeaked Lenore.

"It's been a pleasure, Lenore. Thank you for your help," said Thomas, looking down at his new gremlin friend.

"Don't mention it, Thomas, and if anyone asks you about duh Gloop recipe, don't tell 'im I said anyfing to you, and don't forget what I said about dem glasses," she said with a wink.

"I can handle that, Lenore," responded Thomas, "And bye-bye, Webby. You're such a good boy." Thomas leaned down and pet the dog on his head and behind his ears, much to the pleasure of Webster.

"Ruff," barked the black dog as if to say goodbye. The dog turned around, and he and Lenore left via the door they had entered through.

Thomas turned and walked towards the black Toyunda with his head on a swivel. He was having a hard time absorbing the striking mechanical history contained in this garage. Yareli, as usual, had a very serious look adorning her face. "What took you so long?" she inquired, sounding impatient.

"I was taking a shower, remember? Are you always this way?" asked Thomas, finally feeling more like himself after the luxury of a decent bath and some magical elixir.

"And what way is that?" pondered Yareli.

"So serious all the time," replied Thomas. "Don't you ever loosen up?"

"My mission, Thomas, is to get you back unharmed. I swore an oath to do so to someone who I hold in the highest regard. That means I don't have the luxury of *loosening* up."

"I didn't mean anything by it. I just figured if we are going to spend the whole day together . . ." Thomas paused. "Well I don't know, but I do know one thing."

"And what would that be?" asked Yareli.

"We can't take this one, as much as I want to. It's Franklin's pride and joy, and I sort of promised him we wouldn't touch it," replied Thomas. "But he did say we could take any other one."

"I suppose it would do us no good to upset Franklin, being his guests and all." She got out of the black aeromobile and began looking around for another one. "It has to be a convertible."

After some bickering on models and make, the two agreed on a red aeromobile, the Volatilis 827, which was also a convertible. The vehicle was sandwiched between an early twentieth-century Aston Martin and a 1925 Baldwin steam locomotive. Yareli jumped into the driver's seat and before Thomas could sit in the passenger's seat, Wiyaloo appeared in it.

"What is the term you humans use? An old weapon, I believe. Oh yes: *shotgun*. I call shotgun," bellowed the spirit with inadvertent humor. Thomas slinked into the back seat of the craft mumbling something to himself, distinctly sour in tone.

Yareli looked at the boy with a mocking smirk, "You should try loosening up, Thomas." She turned her head back towards the controls and giggled a bit. With a wave of her hand the flying car started. They rose straight into the air, and when the vehicle reached a suitable height, the thrusters engaged and the aeromobile shot into one of the departure tunnels. The Volatilis sped through total darkness. Thomas could not see his own hands that were tightly gripping onto the upholstery.

White light seeped through an opening hatch, tearing through the darkness around them. Birds flew off in every direction. Thomas felt something wet hit him on top of the head. He reached his hand up to confirm his suspicions. "That stupid seagull just shit on me," said Thomas, wiping off his head.

"They're actually black-legged kittiwakes," said Yareli with a straight face.

"How do you even know crap like that?" asked Thomas. "Actually, on second thought, I don't want to know. I've got more pressing matters." The boy held out the hand he had wiped his head with.

"They say that's good luck," said Yareli, smiling from ear to ear.

"You know who said that? The first guy that ever got shit on," said Thomas as he laughed. The Volatilis sped upward over the Channel. The aeromobile made a sharp turn and stopped.

"Would you like me to download the destination from your wristcom, Thomas Scargen?" asked the computer. The voice was distinctly male and obviously English.

"Yes, computer, that would be fine," responded Thomas, feeling more important now, considering he was the one with whom ELAIN had entrusted the destination, as well as the name and appearance of the tech dealer. The aeromobile's computer downloaded the information. A holomap appeared on the windshield.

"This is a three-dimensional representation of your journey to London. This is where one Ronald Hosselfot can be found." A three-dimensional image of the man appeared in the right bottom corner of the map. "He is the only dealer of such goods in the whole of England," the computer echoed. "Would you like to engage autopilot or manually fly to this destination?"

"What kind of choice is that?" asked Yareli. "Switch to manual override."

"Manual override initiated," said the computer. The hovering craft dipped when Yareli was given full control.

"Now let's see what this baby can do," said Yareli.

Thomas was situated directly between Yareli and Wiyaloo, but in the back seat. He lowered his goggles to cover his eyes. "This should be fun. I've never been to London," said the boy as the aeromobile sped away.

7

seer no evil

The spiral staircase twisted down the dark tower's innards. The imp servant hurried down the creaking stairs. Corbin was eager to accomplish his master's orders—eager to be done with them, to be more precise. He was to awaken the Seer to try to locate the Scargen boy. "Dis is by far duh worst part of my job," said the imp. Years ago, Corbin had been summoned to serve Grayden Arkmalis. Since then, the sole purpose of his existence was to serve his master. "I guess job's not really duh proper word, is it? I mean it's not like dere was an application process, was dere? I never 'ad a bloody choice. One minute I'm in the Depths scavenging for food on duh outskirts of duh Wastelands wif my mates, the next minute I'm being told what to do by some pale, tattooed top-worlder. Before I can even voice an opinion on duh matter, I'm forced into servitude for duh ungrateful git . . . not to mention dese bloody clothes I 'av to wear. It's not right to make an imp wear cloving, is it? I'd be duh laughing stock of my peers if dey saw me in dese rags." Corbin grabbed his shirt as he looked down. "But I do look bloody marvelous, if I do say so myself." The imp realized he was talking to himself. "Oh dat's just great. Now, I'm goin' bloody mental." He continued downward.

Corbin disliked awakening the Seer because it was a nasty and disgusting process. The Seer resided in the lowest level of the castle, hidden away in the bowels of Grimm Tower. The location of the Seer was one of Grayden's biggest secrets. This kind of intuitive power was a commodity that plenty of people would kill to have. The only two the General trusted with this secret was Corbin and Captain Slade. Unfortunately for Corbin, that meant he was responsible for awakening the clairvoyant beast.

The imp reached the bottom of the stairway and walked down the narrow hallway. The Seer's cell was only accessible through a locked metal hatch on the floor. Corbin twisted the wheel to open the rusted door. "I can't believe dat I always get stuck doing dis. 'Corbin, awaken duh Seer.' 'Corbin, fetch me some food.' 'Corbin, dress me.' A grown man dat can't dress 'is bloody self. It's mental. Dis way of life is humiliating enough wiffout 'avin to be subjugated to dis nonsense." Corbin again caught himself speaking aloud.

He finished spinning the metal circle and could hear the air pressure escaping from the sides, accompanied by a wrenching stench. The smell was rancid, and it knocked the imp backward. He gathered his composure and began his descent down the metal ladder to the platform, trying to avoid the infesting spiderwebs.

The Seer's cell was enormous and dark, resembling a swamp. This made the task of finding the prophetic monster difficult. The darkness was the first obstacle. Corbin hit a combination of buttons on his wristcom. A tiny glowing orb floated out of the bottom of his wrist device and lowered down into the chamber. The orb erupted with incandescent light. Corbin could now see where he was going.

The humidity in the room was palpable, causing the imp to sweat. He was relieved when he reached the hanging platform. He straightened out his vest and wiped off the webs that were sticking to him. He looked across the platform. At one end was a large horn that dangled off the railing. Corbin scurried to the instrument. With a flick of his wrist, several more light spheres shot out of his wristcom and began flitting about the cavernous room. The orbs raced around, illuminating the massive dungeon. The light unveiled the bubbling swamp to the imp, but he could still not see the far end of the chamber.

He focused his attention on the horn. Corbin had to jump to reach the mouthpiece of the instrument. He grabbed onto the mouthpiece and lowered the horn to his lips. It had been a while since the last awakening, and he had to remember the song he was to perform. If the melody was even slightly off, the Seer would not emerge. It would be days before he could try again. That was not an option considering the consequences that Grayden Arkmalis imposed for failure.

Fear jogged the imp's memory. He grabbed the horn and pursed his lips. Right before he blew into the instrument he heard a distinct croaking noise. The imp tilted the horn forward and a frog slipped out of the top of the apparatus. The amphibian landed with a splash below the platform.

The imp tried once more to blow into the horn. This time Corbin began playing a complicated selection. The melody was beautiful and uncharacteristically soothing for something that was meant as a wake up call. The imp finished the tune and rested his lips. The chamber reverberated with the final echoes of the song.

The swamp was silent. Corbin searched the water. There were no signs of any movement. The imp contemplated his possible fail-ure—and more importantly, his punishment. He lowered his head and turned towards the ladder in defeat. He was about to recall the orbs and surrender to his fate when a barely audible bubbling sound drifted from the water.

Corbin's head spun around, and he grabbed onto the railing. His eyes darted back and forth, excited at the prospect of not dying today. The ugliest of grins formed on the face of the diminutive imp. Corbin jumped up and down twice while still grasping the bar, cir-cled around, and began dancing what resembled an Irish jig. "The Seer has awakened!" shrieked Corbin with glee. "The Seer has awak-ened." The water gurgled and splashed as the bubbling intensified. The luminescent orbs moved around in unison, adjusting to where the Seer would appear, but still no sign of the creature. The mystery was settled with an eruption of water that manifested from the center of the swamp.

A mountain of algae, toadstools, and swamp grass sprang forth from the green liquid. The top of the formation was different from the rest. It was coconut in shape and about seven and a half feet tall and almost as wide. Arms sprouted out from the sides of the olive-colored, oblong sphere and began to stretch as algae and fungi flew off of its coarse fur. Seconds later, two eyes slowly opened and began to blink from the center of the monstrosity. They focused on the imp. A small mouth opened to a yawn as the orbs settled into an advantageous lighting position above their subject. There was no indication of legs on this beast, just the mountain of swamp that it seemed to grow out of. The Seer had risen from the depths of the marsh.

Although the task of locating and waking the Seer was a nasty, undesirable job, Corbin was always awestruck when he finally surfaced. The monster lurched forward, approaching the platform, and stopped three feet short of the imp. "Hello, Corbin, imp servant to Arkmalis General. I've been expecting your arrival. Your arrival was most expected," said the Seer in a deep yet peaceful voice. "The location of the innocent Scargen boy is what the Arkmalis General desires, correct? Is it not so?"

"You know dat's why I've come, Orac," said the imp with little concern for the proximity of the Seer. "You always know why I'm 'ere. Dat's why we come to you, innit, because you know fings well before dey 'appen."

"What if I refuse to help you find this innocent, the one named Scargen . . . yes, Scargen the innocent one?" asked Orac. The imp was sure the Seer knew the answer to his question, but he answered anyway.

"Well den General Arkmalis will be most disappointed," answered Corbin. "And I believe you are rather familiar wif what 'appens if duh good General gets angry, aren't ya, Orac? His temper often gets duh best of 'im, and well, I 'av been assured dat if I cannot secure your cooperation, den grave and terrible fings will befall your—"

"Family, my kin . . . the ones I love," finished the Seer as he settled back into his original position. He seemed to lament on his predicament that he had had an ample amount of time to come to terms with. Grayden Arkmalis relied on the fact that Orac would never betray his own family. If the bog they inhabited were ever to be disturbed, it would mean the destruction of his kind. "I will tell you where you can find innocent Scargen, Corbin imp servant, but first I need the awful Arkmalis General's promise, his assurance of my family's complete and utter safety. Yes . . . yes . . . they must be safe." The Seer closed his eyes in meditation and waited patiently for a response from Corbin.

"I cannot speak for 'im uv course. I must contact my master for an answer," replied the imp, sounding like he was saying something he had repeated thousands of times before. "It will take but a moment." Corbin held down the button that powered his wrist-com. The imp cleared his throat. "Master, this is your humble servant Corbin reporting on the status of your request, please respond."

The holographic bust of Grayden Arkmalis emanated from the wrist communication device. "This better be good, Corbin. I do not enjoy being interrupted, let alone twice in one day. What do you have to report?"

"The Seer is willing and able to help us . . . I mean you, help you. There is just one caveat, however, a request," squeaked the imp in a tone befitting groveling.

"Come now, Corbin. I have no time for this nonsense. Did you tell that overgrown lily pad what will happen if he does not help us?"

"Of course, Your Majesty," replied the imp. "I told him exactly what you had instructed me to say. He just wants your word . . . on the safety of his . . . family."

"Tell Orac the Seer that I cannot guarantee the safety of the ones he cares for if I do not have the location of the boy," said Grayden, growing more annoyed.

"There is no need to speak through Corbin the imp servant, Arkmalis General . . . General of the Grimm Legions. Imp servant Corbin has already spoken the Arkmalis General's need. I can hear you, hear you quite fine," interjected Orac while reopening his eyes.

"Very well then, first of all I am not asking for your help, beast. I do not make requests, and I do not bluff. I will destroy the bog that your kind calls home with no remorse. I will then single-handedly annihilate everything you have ever loved and will make you watch me do it." The General paused. "That is obviously the hard way, Orac. But since we have a—how would you put it—a special relationship, I will give you my word that no harm will befall your kind if the information you give me is indeed accurate and leads me to Thomas Scargen. I assure you the boy is what I desire. There is no need for any more accidental casualties, now is there?"

"I will find the innocent Scargen," said the Seer. He then curled inward and submerged into the water, creating a wave and an enormous rippling effect. Orac had gone down into the swamp to prepare for the reading. *I suppose dere's a certain amount of acceptable theatrics dat comes wif such an undertaking*, thought Corbin.

"Corbin, report back to me once you have the boy's location," said the General as his holographic representation vanished.

"Yes, my lord."

Orac pierced the surface of the marsh for a second time, with his arms extended at his sides, palms up. His eyes reopened, and his pupils were nowhere to be found. The Seer began to chant, repeating the same mantra over and over again. "*Astra divinato, prostremo, divinato, divinato, Astra . . .*" Corbin heard a second gurgling coming from the bottom of the man-made swamp. Both of the Seer's hands now glowed with purple electricity, still turned palms up. His arms slowly began to rise. The higher his arms gradually climbed, the louder the noise grew. The bubbling was muted by a carved rock that pierced the surface of the water. This was an ancient artifact with peculiar symbols adorning its rock face. The artifact elevated out of the water, surrounded by the same type of purple energy that surrounded Orac. The artifact levitated above the head of the Seer.

"*Astra divinato, prostremo, divinato, divinato, Astra!*" The chant rang out, echoing in the swamp chamber. The artifact began to spin in its place, and as the chant grew faster, so did the spinning. Then with no warning, the rotating ceased. The Seer's empty eyes grew even wider and more vacant. The chanting stopped, and the only sound that could be heard was the crackling of the violet electricity that encircled the stone and the Seer. The spherical center of the artifact opened like an eye. The rock lids opened to reveal a glowing purple gem. The ancient eye blinked while the Seer's own eyes remained open. The creature and the stone had become one.

Dis is my favorite part, thought the imp. Beams of energy shot out of the Seer's empty eyes and flew straight into the artifact, completing the connection. The energy that encircled Orac and the stone began to sputter out now that the link was established. The old stone eye blinked one last time then remained opened. A light projected out of the purple gem and began to morph into an image of a boy. The detail of the image was slowly taking form. It was clear enough to see now that it was not a still image. It looked more like a poorly edited movie. The moving images seemed to be a jumble of moments from Thomas Scargen's memories. The Seer was trying to make a mental union with the boy.

The memories slowed and began to gain focus. A representation of an ambiguous woman rocking a baby unfolded in front of the imp. The child was presumably Thomas.

Suddenly the scene changed. A man was talking to Thomas. The boy could not have been older than five. The two were in a robotics lab. The man held what looked like the arm of an archeologic artif. There was a large holographic projection of the artif's plans emanating from the center of the table. The boy looked up at his father with a quizzical look.

"Dad . . . ummmm . . . I miss Mom," admitted the boy.

"Me too, Thomas . . . me too," said the man with an uncomfortable smile.

"Dad?"

"Yes, Thomas."

"Is she ever coming back?" asked the boy. Before the question could be answered, the image shifted once more. Thomas was now about nine years old. He was reading in his bedroom. A book titled *The Dragon Wars* sat in his lap. Thomas turned one of the pages and laughed out loud.

The vision changed to a celebration of the now-twelve-year-old Thomas's birthday. The father instructed the boy to open his eyes.

As the boy complied, the guests all yelled *surprise*. Standing there before him was a brand new artif. "I call him LINC, and he's all yours, Tom."

"I am most satisfied to make your acquaintance, Thomas Scargen. I look forward to sharing common proximity with you for the remainder of my existence," said the artif. As the boy smiled, the picture faded into Thomas dancing with an attractive young lady at a school dance.

Subsequently the mental projection altered into Thomas Scargen erupting with energy and incinerating the *Eerah* army. "Noooooooo!" howled Thomas as the dark tar receded.

The imp looked on in disbelief. "I've never seen someone—well, besides the General—wif dat kind uv power."

There was another stutter in the psychic connection, and when it refocused, the image was of an aeromobile convertible. In the front driver's seat was a Native American girl, and across from her in the passenger's seat was a spectral fox. Thomas Scargen was in the backseat.

"Are we there yet? I am getting bored back here," whined Thomas.

"We are approximately 57.2926 kilometers or 35.6 miles outside of London," answered the car's computer. "At our current speed and altitude, we will arrive at the chosen destination in fifteen minutes, thirty-six seconds."

"Thank you, computer," said Yareli as she looked back at Thomas. The boy was about to respond as the mental transmission failed. The energy beams that had connected the stone eye to Orac dissipated. The artifact plummeted back into the depths of the marsh. The Seer's eyes closed and shot back open, and in an instant the swamp was silent once more.

"What are you doing, Orac? Dey weren't done talking. Why are dey in London? What are dey doing wif Scargen?" asked the imp. "What if duh General asks me dese fings?"

Orac sagged and hunched over. He looked considerably exhausted from the events that had just taken place, but he spoke nonetheless. "I gave you what you asked for . . . what you asked for I gave you . . . no more . . . no less. More now . . . you know . . . the innocent Scargen's destination, his whereabouts, where he is going. Now please, leave me, let me be, leave me alone . . . so all alone. I did what you asked . . . no more . . . no less."

"Well, ya don't 'av to be so literal," said Corbin. He touched a few keys on his wristcom and the General reappeared.

"Where is the Scargen boy?" asked Arkmalis.

"He's in London, my master. He's with the girl and her spirit ghost."

"Report what you know to Captain Slade and return to my chamber for debriefing." The hologram of General Arkmalis dissipated. Corbin was relieved the General had not pressed him for more information. The imp recalled the light orbs back to his wristcom as he toddled towards the ladder. He could faintly make out what Orac was mumbling.

"Sorry, innocent Scargen . . . forgive me . . . forgive my selfishness, my self-centeredness. I couldn't let him hurt them. No . . . no . . . I could not," said the Seer as he slowly slunk into the murky water.

The imp began his long journey upward through the darkness. The sound of his tiny feet drumming on the metal rungs echoed in the chamber. The loud crash and pressurization of the prison's circular seal brought complete silence.

8

hunted

Thomas adjusted his goggles. The specs were pointing out and cataloging life signatures that crossed within Thomas's vision. He was viewing miles ahead of where they were cruising. There had been a few aeromobiles and a couple cargo ships on the way, but that had been some time ago. There was little traffic where they were currently traveling. This struck Thomas as odd considering how close they were to London. The thought passed, and the boy began pondering thousands of questions to ask the young lady that just last evening had swept him away from everything he had ever known. *I can't believe I'm going to miss graduation today*, thought the boy. But everything had changed.

Thomas was on his way to London to pick up parts for his artif and a dragon—a talking, flying, fire-breathing dragon. He had seen spirit ghosts and metamorphosing spirit arrows. He had been chased by massive bat creatures shooting lasers from their heads while carrying men on their underbellies. He rode on the back of a dragon and teleported through space. He witnessed people using magic and had done some magic of his own. And as if that were not enough, he could not get a hold of his father. It was a lot for any sixteen-year-old to deal with. He had some questions that needed answering, but there was one thing in particular he could not get out of his head. He kept coming back to something Yareli had blurted out earlier in haste. The boy thought it the best place to start. Thomas leaned forward. "So . . . who were you talking about before, in the garage?"

"I don't know what you are asking," said Yareli, trying to avoid the subject.

"You were saying you swore an oath to someone to protect me, somebody you hold in high regard. You promised this person you would bring me back safely. Who is that person?" asked the boy, now being a bit more direct with his line of questioning.

"It's not my place to say, Thomas," responded Yareli. "Just trust in the fact that we are trying to help you."

"I think I have trusted you enough up to this point. I deserve to know what's going on, and why I'm such a hot commodity."

"Well I think it has something to do with your energy output back on the cliff," said Yareli. "I really can't tell you much more."

"Well the way I see it, I saved your life . . . right?" said Thomas. He was not holding anything back. "So I think you owe me some answers."

"You arrogant little—"

"Thomas Scargen is correct, my lady," interjected Wiyaloo. "If it were not for him, we would not be here."

"As always, I respect your counsel, Wiyaloo, but this is not your concern," said Yareli as she jerked the Volatilis 827 harshly to the left.

"Yes, my lady."

"Thomas, I will tell you what you want when the time is right. We have other things that we need to deal with right now. The artif and Bartleby's tech are the priority."

Thomas felt a sudden twist of guilt. Yareli was right. LINC was the priority right now. "I'm sorry. I'm just a little out of it. This is a lot to process. Between the powers, and the mythological creatures, and my dad missing—"

"What was that?" interrupted Yareli.

"It's a little overwhelming is all I'm saying." Thomas looked down in introspection.

"No, about your father, you said he is missing. Is this true?" asked the young lady.

"Yeah, I guess. I'm actually not one hundred percent on that one. That's one of the reasons I need LINC back online. I've tried several times to reach him on my wristcom, but he's excavating in Egypt, and sometimes he's in places that don't get the best reception. I've been trying not to freak out about it, but I had this crazy dream last night. It's actually why I was awake when you two showed up."

"What exactly does your dream have to do with your father's whereabouts?" asked Yareli.

"Well if you would stop interrupting me," Thomas said half jokingly. "In the dream, my dad was . . ." this was hard for Thomas to say. "He was missing, and his colleague Sigmund was murdered by some guy in a hood who was definitely using some sort of magic stone." Thomas was a bit relieved getting that off of his chest.

"I cannot believe you did not bring this up sooner. I will have to report this as soon as possible, but there is no time right now. We are here." The aeromobile slowed as the landing thrusters began to fire.

"Report? Report to whom? Is my father all right? It's just a dream, right? Just a stupid dream." Thomas was worried about his father. He had almost talked himself into believing that it was merely a dream, but Yareli's response had squashed that hypothesis.

"Thomas, I will help you get to the bottom of this, but I need you to calm down and focus on what we are about to do. We will be dealing with some very questionable people in about fifteen minutes, so I need you here. You will be no good to anybody if you get yourself killed down there. I promise you as soon as we are done here, I will make it my priority to personally locate your father and his colleague." Yareli's tone was soothing and reassuring to the boy.

Thomas began to compose himself and think about the reason they were there. LINC was the priority now, and he needed to keep reminding himself of that. "Thank you, Yareli. I appreciate that." Thomas was still on edge about his father, but now he had a powerful ally in the matter—and a promise. His rescue was proof that she clearly kept her promises. "Let's go buy us an articulix."

The Volatilis 827 landed on the rooftop parking spot as gently as it took off. Wiyaloo disappeared. "I guess we can't have a seven foot fox roaming the streets of London," joked Thomas while still making a fair point.

"There is more to it than that. Let us just say there are others that do not take kindly to users of magic," said Yareli.

"Others?" questioned the boy, eager to learn this new world's rules and players.

"All in due time, Thomas," said Yareli. "Just keep your eyes open for suspicious characters."

"Oh, right . . . suspicious characters. I'm sure we won't find any of them in London." Thomas's words were bathed in sarcasm. "Let's hope we don't need me to explode again, cause I'm still having trouble duplicating that little trick."

"Do not worry, Thomas Scargen. I may be invisible, but I am indeed still here and more than capable of protecting the two of you," growled Wiyaloo. The invisible beast startled the boy, who instinctively flinched when he heard the rumbling voice.

"That was totally uncalled for," said Thomas holding his palm on his chest.

"My apologies, Thomas Scargen."

"I'm just saying . . . next time . . . give me a little warning." Thomas took a second to compose himself. "I appreciate you having our backs."

"I appreciate the offer too, but I'm capable of protecting myself," said Yareli.

The craft had come to a complete stop, and the companions disembarked from the vehicle as the roof of the aeromobile engaged. "When you have further need of my services, you can call on me by using your wrist communicator, Thomas Scargen," instructed the computer as the aeromobile cloaked itself.

"I guess Wiyaloo's not the only one that can hide," said Thomas with a smile. The spirit ghost did not laugh, but Yareli managed a smirk.

"The address we are supposed to go to is three blocks over, in Canary Wharf," said Yareli, looking down at her wristcom and then at Thomas. "I do not want you to appear until I say so, Wiyaloo. You are the only element of surprise that we have."

"Yes, my lady. As you wish," grumbled the spirit.

"I'm pretty sure Hosselfot is friends with Franklin. I don't know if we need to be all stealth," suggested the boy.

"Listen, Thomas, I'm in charge, and we'll do it my way, understand?" Yareli looked straight into his eyes. "We have no idea what we are walking into, and we need to exercise caution. There are more variables than you are aware of, and I have no intention of failing."

"All right, all right . . . I get it."

"So here is your first lesson. Your energy level is fairly strong, as you now know, so this should be relatively simple once you get the hang of it. We're going to jump down to the street." Yareli turned towards the boy. Thomas was scared. He did not realize there would be a test so soon.

"That's ridiculous. It's like a hundred-foot drop," said Thomas, backing away from the ledge.

"I'll go first and show you how it's done," said Yareli. "First, you must believe you can do it. I know this sounds obvious, but it's the hardest part. Second, you jump. Pretty easy so far, huh? Then before impact you want to focus your energy in the balls of your feet and use the energy to push back. This dampens the impact for landing. Try it where you stand."

"Okay, here goes nothing," answered Thomas, while jumping in place. He tried three times and felt nothing. "I don't think I'm doing it right."

"You just jumped right into it without thinking about it. Remember, you have to believe it first," said Yareli, questioning Thomas's listening abilities. "Try thinking about the *Eerah* and what you did to them. That should help you trust your capability."

"Believe . . . believe," mumbled Thomas to himself. He leaped in the air and landed like usual. "Believe, Thomas . . ." He jumped one last time and before he hit, he could feel the dampening effect take hold. "I did it. That was totally Narsh. I think I'm ready to try the big one." Thomas—in all of his excitement—leapt over the ledge.

"Thomas, no!" screamed Yareli. She was too late.

Somewhere between the ledge and the alley below, Thomas's belief turned into doubt, and he began to flip forward. "Ahhhhhhh!" yelled Thomas as the concrete came into focus. He closed his eyes. The thought that he would never see his father again rushed to his head.

Right before Thomas hit the ground he was stopped in mid-air by the arms of the spirit ghost. He opened his eyes just in time to see Yareli perform the stunt that he had just failed. When she landed, the alley floor cracked, and a small impact crater formed beneath her. Wiyaloo put the boy down. "Thanks, Wiyaloo." The boy was trying to breathe normally. "I'd be a stain . . . in an alley in London . . . if it wasn't . . . for you."

"Just returning the favor, Thomas Scargen," responded Wiyaloo.

"I guess that was less . . . than a success," said Thomas, trying to shake away his fifth near-death experience in less than twenty-four hours.

"I would say so," critiqued Yareli. "You stopped believing, and that is why you fell."

"Well . . . no harm, no foul," said Thomas as he brushed himself off. "Better luck next time." The boy smirked.

"Is everything a joke to you?" asked Yareli.

"No, no it's not," said Thomas, turning and looking directly at the girl. "I just don't take everything so seriously, unlike someone I know." He stepped towards Yareli.

"Well maybe it's time you start," said Yareli in a motherly tone, moving closer to the boy.

"My sense of humor is part of my charm," said the boy, trying to break the girl's icy demeanor. Now, only a couple feet separated the two.

"You have a lot to learn about being charming." Their two faces were now inches apart.

"Really, are you giving lessons any time soon? Cause I wanna make sure I sign up now, before the class fills up," said Thomas, trying to get a rise out of the girl.

"Enough!" interjected Wiyaloo. The spirit ghost snapped the two of them out of their argument. Thomas had gotten so caught up in their fighting that he had forgotten the presence of the invisible Wiyaloo.

"Ooh, you are impossible," said Yareli. The comment was definitely directed at Thomas. "You would be wise to follow." She turned and began walking away.

"Whatever you say, Your Majesty," retorted Thomas, still trying to get under the girl's skin. The boy jogged to catch up to Yareli.

They reached the building five minutes before the agreed time, and by the looks of it, they were certainly not in the best part of London. They were to meet on the roof of the Bayford Financial building in the middle of Canary Wharf at precisely 11:15 AM. The money had already been dealt with. Franklin had set up the credit transfer with Ronald Hosselfot earlier that morning. The plan was to meet up with Hosselfot, collect the parts they required, complete the credit transfer, and return to Draige Manor.

But there was an obstacle they had not counted on. The building was boarded up and seemed abandoned. Yareli walked up to the front door and raised her hand. "*Ta-tai*," she whispered. The air began to swirl, and the door was blown inward by what looked like a focused push of the wind.

"Did wind just shoot out of your hands?" asked a stunned Thomas.

"Not exactly," answered Yareli, now walking cautiously into the bottom floor. "It's more like I moved the air that was already there. I sort of pushed it."

"Why didn't you use that little trick when we were fighting the *Eerah*?" asked Thomas. He followed her into the building.

"I'm still learning how to control it. I would've had to build up the energy needed to destroy an *Eerah*, and if I didn't control it properly, I would've killed us both." Yareli continued to the staircase.

"Good safety tip," said Thomas, ascending the unstable staircase.

"So, why are we meeting a man on the roof just to buy an articulix anyway?"

"The sale of the tech we need for the dragon is looked down upon in certain circles," answered Yareli.

"Certain circles?" Thomas pushed the issue.

"It is not exactly legal," said the young lady.

"No wonder you are being so damn cautious," said Thomas. He finally understood the reason for all the sneaking around. *That was probably the reason we'd parked so far away*, thought Thomas. He started looking around more cautiously with this newfound knowledge. He had broken the law before. Once when he was twelve years old, he had been caught shoplifting baseball cards at the Q-Mart in town. The look on his father's face when he found out was enough for Thomas never to break the law again. This was different though. This was necessary to help his best friend and his new favorite dragon, Bartleby.

"Four more flights to go," said Yareli as she picked up her pace. Thomas followed. "And when we get to the roof, do not so much as open your mouth. I will do all the talking. I do not know this Ronald Hosselfot."

"This should be no big deal, Yareli. This guy is a buddy of Franklin's," said Thomas trying to calm her.

"I don't care if this man is Franklin's brother. These people are not to be trusted." Yareli leered at the boy.

"*People?* You think there will be more than one?" asked the boy, sounding a bit uneasy.

"Did I come alone?"

"I see your point," said Thomas as they reached the end of the stairs. They stood approximately eight feet from the entrance to the roof.

"One last thing, Thomas, before I open this door: if you do accidentally say something, do not mention our powers to these men." Yareli opened the door before Thomas could ask any more questions.

"I will be right behind you, my Lady," rumbled Wiyaloo.

"I never doubted that for a second, friend," said Yareli as they now found themselves on the roof of the Bayford Financial Building.

There was no sign of Ronald Hosselfot or his possible men. "Spread out, and keep your eyes open," ordered the girl.

The view from the top was limited. Most of the neighboring buildings had been built upward over the years, concealing the roof from the outside world.

"No wonder they picked this place. You can't see in or out," said the boy. "If I were going to do something illegal, this is where I'd do it." He turned his head and looked up. "Come to think of it, I am doing something illegal, and this is where I'm doing it."

"I said not a word, Thomas," reminded Yareli as she continued to scan the roof's surface.

"There's no one here. What could I possibly say to nobody that's gonna screw things up?"

"Things are not always what they seem, Thomas Scargen," whispered Wiyaloo directly behind the boy. Thomas stumbled two feet forward in surprise.

"Point proven," said Thomas. "You would make a good teacher, Wiyaloo." Yareli stared at the boy. "My bad, shutting up." Thomas reached up and pulled down his goggles in shame.

The specs' display sprang to life. He could now make out five figures about twenty paces in front of Yareli. The men were outlined in red on his display. Thomas recognized the man in the lead from the hologram he had seen earlier on the computer. *Ronald Hosselfot,* thought the boy.

There was another man next to Hosselfot fiddling with a hand-held device. He was followed by three others carrying weapons. The goggles outlined the weapons in blue and identified them as LAWLER 349 ENERGY RIFLES. The gun's full technical specifications were listed off to the right side of the goggles' interface. "Yareli," said the boy. The interface quickly flashed to an X-ray view, and Thomas could see the men's skeletal structures. The five figures changed from red to green outlines through the specs. He lifted the goggles to find the five men were now visible.

"Thomas, what is it?" the young girl said under her breath, so only the boy could hear.

"Never mind," said Thomas, realizing his newfound information had instantly become common knowledge. The five men walked towards Thomas and Yareli. Ronald Hosselfot held a backpack in his hands, presumably housing the articulix and the dragon tech. The other man was still preoccupied with his apparatus. *That must be the device they used to cloak*, thought Thomas.

Hosselfot spoke first. " 'ello my sweet. My name is Ronald 'osselfot, but you can call me Ronny if you so wish. And you must be Yareli, but 'oo, might I ask, is dat?"

"He is nobody, Mr. Hosselfot. Do you have the merchandise?" said the girl, cutting the introductions short.

Nobody? thought Thomas.

"Well, well . . . you are all about business, aren't you? I like dat. I can relate to dat. I was just sayin' dee uvver day to my geezer here, I was like, aye we should be a bit more businesslike during our uvver-wise illegal transactions, shouldn't we? After all, time is money, isn't it? Oh, I'm sorry. Where are my manners at? Dis is my business associate, Girard Lesinge. 'ee's a Frenchman, yeah, being born in France and all, but don't 'old dat against 'im. 'ee can't 'elp where 'ee was born, can 'ee?" Hosselfot moved his left hand towards the man holding the cloaking mechanism.

"*Bonjour*," said Lesinge without looking at Yareli or Thomas. His attention was focused on the device.

"Hello. Now can we have what we came for?" asked Yareli.

"Yeah sure, 'eer ya go." Hosselfot opened the bag to expose a metallic package. "I ain't got a bloody dragon, do I? What could I do wif it anyway?" Hosselfot threw the bagged box at Thomas. "Don't say much, does 'ee?"

"Quite the opposite actually," said Yareli. Thomas put on the backpack and lowered his goggles once more, trying to hide himself from further embarrassment. "Here's your credits." Yareli punched a few keys on her wristcom. She looked more comfortable with the tech now in their hands.

"Fanks," said Hosselfot, looking down at his own wristcom. It's ben a pleasure doin' business wif you."

"So your full name would not be Yareli Chula, would it *mon amour?*" asked Lesinge, still not looking up.

"How does he know your last name?" blurted out Thomas as he looked over at the girl. Thomas noticed several more cloaked life form readings all around them in the neighboring buildings. There were new purple indicators on his optic display. *Apparently purple means artif,* thought Thomas. The X-ray view confirmed this. Thomas could now see the robotic mechanisms inside the large, heavily armed robots. He lifted the goggles and could see nothing. He then wiped his eyes and replaced the specs. They were surrounded.

"*Merci.* Dat beet of eenformation ees very useful *mon amie.*" Lesinge smiled and finally looked up at Thomas. He then turned to Yareli. "I 'ad to be sure, Madame Chula, you understand."

"Yareli!" cried Thomas.

"Not right now, Thomas, you have said plenty for one afternoon. Yes, Monsieur Lesinge, I am Yareli Chula."

"*Mon dieu*, you are so young and quite attracteeve. When I saw 'ow mooch your bounty was worth, I 'ad just feegured you would be a leettle more, 'ow do you say, oold," laughed the Frenchman as the three men with the rifles now pointed them at Yareli and Thomas. "I 'av dabbled een bounty 'unting for quite some time, so I frequently keep myself up to dat weef wanted eendividuals like yourself. Eet's just zat zees job, eet pays so well. Eet's not usually worth eet." The man smiled. "But ween I saw your name on zee manifest eet cleecked in my 'ed. I weent back and double chacked just to be sure I 'adn't eemagined eet. Eet's just the name Yareli, eet's not zat common. I was positeeve eet wasn't a coincidence, and zee amount of credeets you are worth ees just . . . *magnifique.*"

"What are you whingin' on about, Girard? Bounty from 'oo? I must admit, you do look a bit knackered, yeah. Do you need to take a nap or somefing, cause I'm pretty sure we are all done 'ere. Yeah, we 'av given dem duh merchandise, and dey 'av given us duh credits in return. Dat's duh way it works, isn't it? It's called capitalism, mate. Credits are exchanged for goods and or services. It's bloody brilliant, isn't it?" Ronald Hosselfot turned to look at the Frenchman, but his eyes quickly were diverted. "Wait a tick, just 'oo are they pointin' dose guns at?"

"I believe Monsieur Lesinge here has been promised a large sum of credits in exchange for me, Mr. Hosselfot. He seems to think that three gunmen will be enough firepower to take me captive. Is that fair to say, Monsieur Lesinge?"

"I could not 'av said eet better myself, *mon chere*."

"Uh, Yareli, there's something you should know," pleaded the boy. He could now see two large hovering crafts squeezing through the alleyways of the surrounding buildings.

"Not now, Thomas. I am busy at the moment with Monsieur Lesinge and his three unarmed associates. *Ta-tai!*" The words erupted as she pointed both of her palms at the three gunmen and pushed them back, separating them from their weapons.

"Well done, Madame Chula." The Frenchman was now clapping. He abruptly stopped. "But I deed not breeng a knife to a gun faht," said Lesinge with confusing confidence.

The signals were forming around them in all the buildings, and more life forms were descending from two hovering personnel carriers. "Yareli, listen to me damn it. That French moron isn't bluffing." Thomas was done being polite. "There are a lot of things all around us that don't look very friendly." Yareli looked back at the Frenchman.

"Monsieur Lesinge, could you be so kind to put your hands where I can see them?" Lesinge lifted his arms above his head.

"The boy, 'ee's not as dumb as 'ee looks," said the Frenchman, still smirking.

"What are you talking about, Thomas?" asked Yareli finally.

"You see . . . Franklin gave me these goggles . . . and I can see things that are not there," rambled the boy in fear.

"What?" asked Yareli with a look of total confusion.

"Sorry, we are surrounded by a bunch of soldiers and artifs with all these crazy weapons, well mostly artifs. I'm talking big—really big—robots. I can see them through these goggles," explained Thomas.

"Hunters," said Yareli as the small army revealed itself.

9

the game is afoot

Ronald Hosselfot turned and punched Girard Lesinge straight in his unprotected mouth. "You sold me out, you tosser. I can't believe we were evva mates. My uvva mates kept saying, 'oh don't trust 'im. 'ee's a bit off.' But I said, 'no 'ee's aw'right. 'ee just talks a bit funny'."

"So you had nothing to do with this?" asked Yareli as she crouched in a fight-or-flight stance. Thomas tensed up as well.

"I might be a criminal, mum, but I do 'av me morals, now don't I?" answered Hosselfot. "You two betta get goin' before dose 'unters get any closer." It was already too late.

"Hunters? What the hell is a Hunter?" asked Thomas as he raised his goggles. *They keep saying it as if it's something I should already know.* Energy blasts began raining down from all directions. Yareli's eyes glowed white then returned to normal as she raised her hand.

The laser fire began deflecting all around them, bouncing off of a force field that surrounded Yareli and Thomas. "Narsh. Can you teach me that trick, if we survive this I mean? I realize we're kinda in the middle of some—What's a Hunter?"

"Remember when I told you that there are others that do not take kindly to users of magic?" asked Yareli.

"Yes."

"Well that's them," shouted Yareli as another energy blast deflected off of the shield. She pulled Thomas behind her, ducking behind a large climate control unit at the far end of the roof.

"Who's *them*?"

"They are Hunters."

"What do they hunt?"

"That's a stupid question at this point."

"Fair enough, but why are they hunting us?"

"Cause of our abilities."

"Well they could at least have the decency to wait till I could use mine properly."

"Can you be quiet for one second? Do you have any idea the concentration it takes to maintain this shield?"

"No . . . I mean yes . . . I can be quiet, and no, I have no idea." Thomas saw Hosselfot grab Lesinge and drag him through the door Thomas and Yareli had entered from.

"Shall I prepare for battle, my lady?" inquired Wiyaloo. Thomas spun around, startled by the spirit ghost.

"No, do not reveal yourself. We are severely outnumbered. Flight is the only viable option. We just have to bide our time until an opportunity presents itself." Yareli moved along the edge of the unit to get a better look at what they were up against. She saw an advancing group of massive robots.

"There are close to twenty collectorbots out there," informed Yareli.

"Collectorbots? Well I guess that one's kind of self-explanatory, huh?" said Thomas, joking to mask his intense fear. He could not help but stare at the artifs. Their designs looked familiar.

"These artifs are used to corral rogue artifs, but they have been reprogrammed to hunt and track down magic users. They can sense our energy output when we use our powers." Suddenly, the energy storm quieted. The two looked at each other simultaneously and slowly peered over the top of the climate control unit.

Thomas studied the insignias on the collectorbot's arms. *Scargen Robotics . . . there's no way.* Thomas wondered how this was possible.

Dad would've never approved this. He'd never use artifs in this way. There's only one other person with the power to do this. Thomas had found his answer. *Gideon Upshaw.* This was the man his father had hired to run Scargen Robotics. Thomas had never trusted Upshaw since the day he had met him six months ago, and it now seemed as though his instincts were correct. The new CEO had been busy the last few months while his father was away. Thomas's speculations were cut short by an amplified sound of a man clearing his throat.

"Yareli Chula, you are hereby under arrest for direct violation of Section 419 of the Code of Hunters: The explicit and unlawful use of magic. Put down your bow and come out quietly, and you have my word no one will be hurt." Thomas looked around to see who was speaking. The boy quickly found him. A tall, bald black man stood facing them, wearing a green military uniform with an orange armband wrapped around his upper right arm. The man's left eye was robotic, and a heavy cannon-shaped weapon resided where his right forearm should have been. His voice was being amplified by tech.

"I know what your word is worth, Thatcher Wikkaden," said Yareli.

"I suppose you of all people do." The man paused. "Have you missed me, dear?" Yareli did not answer. "You should really make this easy on yourself and your new friend. I presume he's a filthy Defect, like yourself."

"Defect?" asked Thomas.

"I heard you were dead," said Yareli, ignoring Thomas's question.

"Obviously an inaccurate assessment of my health," said Wikkaden.

"That's a shame," said Yareli. "What has it been . . . two years?"

"Three years, but who's counting. I didn't believe the Frenchman when he said you would be here today. I couldn't pass up the chance, though, even if it was only that. It's the best five hundred thousand credits I've spent in a long time," said Wikkaden.

"Are the other two here as well?" asked Yareli, trying to buy some time to think of their next move.

"Yes, Pekora and Okland are here."

"Pekora," said Yareli under her breath.

"Hello, Yareli," said a woman's voice. "Who's the boy? He's cute." She lifted her sunglasses. "Not to mention his energy readings are off the charts." She tucked the glasses into her short blonde hair. "You two make a cute couple, but I don't hear wedding bells in your future," said the female Hunter, shifting her shapely form.

"Pekora, you're still slumming it with those two? I thought you would have seen the hypocrisy of helping these men by now, or doesn't your ability to gauge power levels count as magic?

"Darling, there's no hypocrisy in trying to make a few credits. You should try it you know. You might find it as enjoyable as I do."

"I will never find any joy in the taking of another's life," responded Yareli. "Speaking of murderers, where's the fat man hiding?"

"Oh, Okland, he's on the top of that building." Pekora pointed to the glass tower to her right. "He has a rather accurate photon sniper pointed right at your friend's head."

Thomas shuttered and caught his breath. *Six and counting on the near-death experiences. I'm almost getting used to this,* he thought, *almost.* "So what's our move here, Yar?" Thomas desperately awaited a great answer.

"I'm still working on that," she answered under her breath. "Try contacting the aeromobile."

"Something's interfering with the signal." Thomas pantomimed his last effort to do so, raising his left wrist slightly.

"Yes, I should have told you. Your wristcoms will do you no good," interrupted Wikkaden. "Okland is jamming all communications on the Wharf. So, you see, there is no use. There is no escape. Surrender now, and I promise we will dispose of you quickly."

"Wiyaloo, we must take care of this problem first," said Yareli.

"Agreed," said Wiyaloo as the invisible spirit presumably took off in the direction of Okland.

"What's he going to do?" asked Thomas.

"Just be ready," said Yareli.

"We might be old friends, my dear, but my patience is waning. You can't hold that shield forever," said Wikkaden. "You have until the count of five before I give Okland the order to fire and send the collectorbots to finish the job."

"I hope you know what you're doing," said Thomas to the girl. "I'm just starting to get used to you."

"One . . ."

"Two . . ."

"Thr—" The sound of the photon sniper rifle crashing at Wikkaden's feet ended the ominous count. The monocled man looked skyward in the direction of the dropped weapon. Okland was approaching the platform face first, hysterically flailing. He had fallen—or been thrown—from his perch. Wikkaden raised his weaponed arm, and an electronic net shot out in the direction of Okland. The electronet trapped the obese marksman against the building from which he had just plummeted. Wikkaden spun back to his primary targets.

Wiyaloo appeared in front of a stunned Thatcher Wikkaden, his paw against the man's chest. "Five," bellowed the spirit ghost, finishing the countdown. The blast knocked the man backwards, destroying three collectorbots.

"Now, Thomas," commanded Yareli. The boy hurdled over the climate control unit and ran towards the door. She leapt from her hiding spot and drew a spirit arrow from her quiver. "*Ma-toe!*" she yelled as she pulled back the arrow and fired. The arrow turned into a grizzly bear. The beast growled and rushed at the artifs, promptly mauling five collectorbots that were closing in on Thomas's location. The bear returned and bowed its head to Yareli before dissipating. "This wa—" Her words were cut off by a targeted blast from Okland's pistol. He had managed to wedge it out of its holster and fire from his net prison. The blast hit Yareli in her right shoulder and twisted the girl around.

"Yareli!" screamed Thomas as he sped in her direction. He caught her injured body before it hit the roof. Without thinking, Thomas leapt off of the Bayford Financial building with Yareli held securely in his arms. *Believe, believe, believe.* He felt awkward with the extra weight of the girl. *Concentrate and focus.* "Haaaaaaaa!" cried Thomas at the approaching street. Energy thrust from both of his feet. A crater twelve feet in diameter and three feet in depth surrounded the two on impact. An asphalt wave rolled from the epicenter. The foundations of the adjacent structures quivered. Thomas slowly stood from his crouch, the girl secured in his arms. The reality of his feat dawned on him.

"What was that? That was completely narsh. Did you see that?" Thomas emerged from the hole. "I can't believe I just did that."

"I have to admit, that was impressive," said Yareli as she looked up at Thomas, "but if it's all the same, I will walk the rest of the way." The boy lowered her to the ground. "Oww," she grabbed her shoulder. Yareli's arm hung limp. The smell of burnt flesh was palpable.

"Everything's gonna to be fine. We'll find Wiyaloo, and he'll fix you right up." They began to run down the devastated street.

"I'm fine. Wiyaloo will not be able to occupy them forever. We need to get moving."

The London afternoon was interrupted by rain. The loud thunderclap resonated in the boy's ears. Thomas craned his head down the street perpendicular to them. The roads were empty aside from the large droplets that pounded the street. "Where is everybody?" asked Thomas as they ran down the new avenue.

"I'd assume the area has been evacuated," said Yareli as if Canary Wharf being emptied was a normal occurrence.

"Why'd they do that?"

"Hunting down magic users is only half their job," said Yareli, again grabbing her right shoulder.

"What's the other half?"

"They're also responsible for limiting the public knowledge of magic's very existence."

"*They're* the reason I'm just finding out about this shit?"

"Yes," said Yareli as she slowed down and cut across to Cabot Square.

"Why don't they want people to know?" Thomas had finally caught up to the girl.

"The Global Alliance is afraid of our abilities because they

can't control us. To them, control is power, and power is everything."
She stopped and turned towards Thomas. "They believe their only
recourse is to hunt us down and make it seem like we never existed."

"So . . . these guys . . . they're everywhere?" asked Thomas, trying
to catch his breath.

"For the most part, yes, but not where we're going."

"You mean . . . the place with the guy . . . you won't . . . you won't
tell me about?"

"Yes," Yareli looked around to get her bearings.

"You think . . . we lost them?" asked Thomas, panting heavily
now, with his hands on his knees.

"Wiyaloo managed to give us a good head start, but this is not
over. Are you all right?"

"This? I'm fine. Just . . . catching . . . my breath. I mean I got the
stuff . . . on my back . . . which is surprisingly . . . heavy . . . otherwise . . .
I'd be . . . I'd be fine."

"I suppose so," said Yareli, almost smiling. "Try contacting the aeromobile again. Wiyaloo should've taken care of the jamming device."

"Computer, we are in . . ." A map of the immediate area floated
above his wristcom. He examined where they were located on the
map. "Cabot Square. Come get us fa—"

Thomas's command was interrupted by a deafening shriek. Both
of them turned. Something was moving towards them. Another
shriek. Thomas dropped his goggles down. The specs zoomed in
automatically. A hideous monstrosity of tangled flesh and metal was
running directly at them. *That thing is definitely part human, or at
least it used to be,* thought Thomas. "What the hell is that?"

"That is what happens to us if the Hunters catch us, if they don't
just kill us first. They are called Re-psyches. Thatcher is most likely
controlling it. That means we have to deal with this Re-psyche now.
They'll be here shortly. If it can see us, then Thatcher can."

"Well push it away, or hit it with a freakin' spirit arrow or
something," pleaded the boy. The thing screeched once more as it
gained speed.

"Thomas, I can't do anything with my arm like this. "The

Re-psyche raised its hands and a ball of fire steamed forward through the downpour. Yareli dove to avoid the impact.

"Yareli!" screamed Thomas. She somersaulted and rolled forward to a standing position. The Re-psyche pushed forward.

"It's up to you, Thomas. Remember: believe, focus, and push," said Yareli.

"Believe, focus, push," said Thomas to himself. "You make it sound so easy." He turned and pulled his hands towards his side and then pushed his palms towards the metallic monster.

Nothing happened.

The Re-psyche jumped up onto an adjacent wall and directed another fireball, this time at Thomas. He turned his head as the glowing orange sphere flew by his nose. "Okay, that was close," said the boy. He had no time to react as a third ball of fire shot out and crumbled the wall where Yareli was slumped. The rubble from the blast covered the girl. Thomas could not see her through the debris.

"Yareli!" shouted the boy.

No reply.

Intense fear coursed through Thomas. His fear quickly turned to anger, and his anger found a focus. Thomas planted his feet. The Re-psyche wailed aloud and bounded towards the boy. It was now thirty feet away and closing. The rain poured down the boy's face as his eyes burned. Thomas again moved his hands inward then quickly outward with palms open and screamed, "Haaaaaaaaa!"

10

a solid lead

His wristcom alerted him that he had an incoming message. Captain Marcus Slade looked down to see that it was Corbin, the General's imp. His men had been surveying the scene of the *Eerah* massacre for hours and had answered a few questions, but they still had no concrete leads. They had ascertained the name of the Native American girl. One of his men had hacked the Hunters database years ago without detection. They had cataloged thousands of magic users over the years. After a quick search, he had found the desired file: YARELI CHULA. Though talented in her own right, the information contained inside confirmed that she was incapable of the energy release that destroyed the *Eerah* They had also managed to obtain the teleport signature of the dragon, but there was no sign of the beast, the girl, or the Scargen boy. One of the Riders had managed to find a few pieces of the artif that Marcus had thought destroyed. The incessant beeping continued from his wrist as the Captain looked down from the cliff above the Scargen's home. *Maybe this is good news.*

"Yes, Corbin, what is it?" inquired the Captain.

"I need a word regarding the Scargen boy," answered the imp as his hologram appeared from the wristcom.

"I hope it's good, because we have yet to discover anything here," said Marcus. "We have flipped the house and followed the teleport signature and still nothing."

"Our most incredible leader, General Grayden Arkmalis, has asked me to inform you that we have obtained information pertinent to the successful completion of the task at hand," informed Corbin.

"You can cut the fearless leader routine, Corbin," said Marcus. "I know that's not how you normally speak."

"Fank you, Cap'n. That can get a bit tiresome," replied the imp.

"What is this information you spoke of?"

"We know the location of the boy."

"Out with it, imp, where is he?"

"Well 'ee's in London, sir, but I'm afraid dat's all we know."

"That makes sense if that robot of his is damaged. The dragon had to have taken some hits as well," said Marcus as his mind turned. "They will need parts and tech."

"You know where 'ee is, don't ya?"

"Just a hunch, Corbin, nothing more. Thank you for the information," said Marcus, looking upward into the skies overhead.

"My pleasure, Cap'n," grunted the imp servant as his hologram faded.

Marcus hailed to his Second who was flying above. She swooped down and detached from the aringi. She did a forward flip and landed next to the Captain. Marcus could not help but notice the natural grace in Evangeline. She had been riding this same beast since the age of eight—a first in Rider circles. She was a natural.

"What is it, Captain?" asked the Second. "You look a lot happier than you should right now, I'd say."

"Corbin just delivered us some good news," answered Marcus, knowing full well that was not the only reason he was smiling.

"Well go on, what is it? We could use some good news," inquired the Second.

"The boy is in London, and I think I know why."

"Shall I gather the men?" asked Evangeline.

"Yes, a small team of five Riders, including you and me. This mission is to be handled discreetly."

"I understand." The Second nodded her head. "Why is he in London, Captain?"

"To fix his artif." Marcus turned away from her and began typing onto the holographic keyboard that leapt from his wristcom. "He presumably needs some sort of part for his artif, and from our own reports, the dragon's tech was also heavily damaged. There can only be a handful of people in London who can help him with both." He turned back to show her the holographic map of London that floated above his wrist. "If we can find the tech dealer, we should find Thomas Scargen."

"Is there anything else, Captain?"

This question caught Marcus off guard. *Is there anything else? If only I had the nerve.* "No, Second . . . that will be all." *I cannot let my feelings interfere with my duty.*

"I will collect the three best Riders we have and report back, sir," said Evangeline as her aringi landed on top of her. With the subtlest motion, the Second attached herself to the beast's underbelly.

Marcus paced back and forth on the clifftop. He pecked away at the virtual interface, vigorously searching for the tech dealer in the vast database. The pictures began to slow as he narrowed his search parameters. *He or she would have to sell artif parts as well as dragon tech, not your normal specialty,* he thought. "Computer, cross reference artif and dragon tech dealers in London."

"One match has been found," said the computer. The holographic representations settled. Instantly the suspect's entire biography appeared beside the three-dimensional image.

It's been a long time since I've seen that name, thought Marcus. An unflattering representation of Ronald J. Hosselfot floated above the Captain's wristcom. *The Scargen boy must be at Canary Wharf.*

11

power corrupts

The blast poured from his hands. Light blue streams of pure energy exploded from his palms. The boy shook as he continued to scream out loud. "Haaaaaaaaa!" He turned his back foot to gain more balance and pushed harder. The anger and fear started somewhere in his heart and now encompassed his whole body. The sensation was intoxicating.

The Re-psyche was blown backward. It landed face down forty-five yards away, bounced once, and tried to regain its footing. Thomas did not let up. He twisted in the direction the Re-psyche had gone, tracking the monster. He continued the powerful onslaught. When the blast reconnected, it blew off most of the robotics of the Re-psyche.

Wiyaloo appeared next to Thomas. He lifted the rocks off of where his master had been with one motion of his paw. The floating rocks were flung to the left and exposed a battered Yareli. "My lady, are you all right?"

"Y-y-yess," said the girl as she winced. The spirit noticed the injury and picked up Yareli. Wiyaloo cradled her. His normal white glow transitioned to a blue color.

"I have healed your wound," said Wiyaloo, placing her feet back on the ground.

It took her a second to regain her thoughts as the spirit ghost's color settled back to white. She looked at Thomas who was bathed in the same glowing light blue color as the energy pouring from his hands. Yareli saw Thomas's target. "Thomas!" yelled Yareli.

He heard her voice cry out but did not stop. The anger had grown to a level of vengeance. *This thing will pay for what it did. I will make sure of that.* Thomas began to smile. The rush of adrenaline was like nothing he had ever felt. He did not want to stop. He liked what he was doing. The intensity of the blast increased once more as Yareli broke away from her healer.

She tackled him from the side. The surprise woke him from his fury. The energy stream bounced off the street and extinguished. He lay there on the road panting. The glow in his eyes disappeared as he grabbed his now aching head. "What—what happened?"

"You almost killed that poor creature. What is wrong with you?" screamed Yareli while staring at the boy.

"What is wrong with me? Poor creature? That poor creature almost killed you. I was just trying to save our asses," said Thomas, defending his actions.

"That Re-psyche has no clue what it's doing. Wikkaden is controlling it." She shook him. "It's a puppet being played with by a madman."

"I didn't—I didn't know," sighed the boy. "I was in control, and then it felt so good. I thought—I thought it killed you. I was so angry. I . . . just wanted to destroy it, to make it pay." Thomas slumped down on the puddle-covered street. There was an uncomfortable silence as the rain splashed around him.

"I'm sorry I yelled at you. It would've killed me if given the chance. It's just—" She looked directly at Thomas. Tears swelled and dropped from her eyes. "I was really young when they came."

"When who came?"

"The Hunters. It's really a blurred memory."

"They came for you?" asked the boy.

"At the time I didn't know what they were after." Thomas did not know what to say. "I just don't want to think that her life ended that w—"

"Whose life? What are you saying?" asked the boy. He was scared to hear the answer.

"She had locked me away in a small hidden compartment in the basement, seconds before they kicked in the door. My powers hadn't completely manifested yet, but if not for her, I suppose I'd have been taken as well. My father must have put up too much of a fight, so they killed him, but Mom wasn't as lucky. They took her."

"Why would they do that?" He knew the answer as soon as he had asked.

"They turned my mother into one of those . . . things. They stole her humanity and turned her into a—a damn weapon." The tears fell faster now. Thomas's mouth hung open, but no words crossed his lips. He wanted to hold her and tell her that everything was going to be all right, but instead he did nothing. "She never hurt a soul in her life, and the only thing I could think of when I saw you attacking that thing was maybe it never meant to hurt anyone either."

He felt ashamed. "I'm sorry Yarel—"

"Thomas, Yareli, come here," interrupted Wiyaloo, standing by the now-moving body of the Re-psyche. His apology would have to wait. Thomas tried to stand, but fell back down. Yareli made it to the spot as the boy tried again to lift himself.

Thomas reached the body of the fallen Re-psyche and could not believe the damage he had done. He could tell now that it was a male. Wiyaloo kneeled by the man, waving his paw over the fallen man's ravished body. Yareli held the Re-psyche's head in her lap. Her tears dripped onto the already soaked rags the man was wearing. The appearance of his tattered clothes suggested he had been wearing them since his hideous transformation. No working robotics remained on the Re-psyche. They had been blown off or melted by Thomas's blast. The metal areas were still steaming. "K-kill m-m-mee, p-please," requested the dying man. The boy turned his head. He could not look at what he did.

"Do not turn away, Thomas," said Wiyaloo. "This will be for nothing if you do not watch and learn." The beast was not lecturing.

He said it with a calm that made Thomas understand the importance of this lesson.

"Kill me," the Re-psyche's voice grew more desperate. "Please . . . I will not . . . do his . . . bidding . . . anymore." The man coughed aloud.

"You can leave him to me," said Wiyaloo. Yareli sobbed and rested the man's head on what was left of the road. She stepped back then turned and walked away.

"Are you gonna heal him?" asked the boy.

"No, Thomas." Wiyaloo looked directly at the boy. "I will do what he requests." The white beast left Thomas with those words. Wiyaloo opened his paws downward over the suffering man. He lowered them as a pale blue light released from his palms. The man's eyes slowly closed as he accepted his end. A faint smile of relief remained on the deceased's face. "Life is something that needs to be cherished, no matter what form that life takes." The beast paused. "He asked me to thank you before he crossed. In a way, you helped this man. His name was Nicolas Gorter." The spirit ghost rose and was instantaneously next to the boy in one fluid motion. "There is something you need to see." The ghost reached over and touched Thomas's head. There was a flash of white light.

A rush of cold energy flowed into his brain. His mind was confused by what he was seeing at first. He was no longer on the street in London. He was spinning through a lifetime of memories—Nicolas Gorter's memories. The images settled as Thomas's mind disappeared into Nicolas's.

Nicolas was just five years old. He was playing soccer with his father. Thomas could hear, see, and feel everything the little boy could, but he could not alter the boy's actions. It was more like reliving something that had already happened. For all intents and purposes, Thomas was Nicolas Gorter.

"Kick it to me, Nicky," said the boy's father. The boy giggled as he made contact with the ball. Nicolas radiated happiness. His sheer joy of life was incredible. The boy unconditionally loved his father.

flash

The memory shifted to Nicolas as a teen. Several older kids were kicking him while he was on the ground of the high school's parking lot. The pain in his abdomen was intense and pulsated. Nicolas spit out blood as the boys ran off. He laid there for what seemed like hours, grasping his stomach.

A young girl knelt down to help him. "It's going to be okay, Nic," said the girl. "I'll make sure of that." The two locked eyes longer than two people normally do. "I should go get the nurse."

"Don't go, Pam." Nicolas felt absolute love for her. It consumed his whole body.

"I'm not going anywhere." Despite the blood and the pain, Nicolas Gorter could not have been happier.

flash

Nicolas was now in his twenties. The same girl that had come to him when he was down was standing next to him on the beach in Cape May, New Jersey. They had come here every year they had known each other. She held his hand as they watched the sun set over the ocean. Nicolas was incredibly nervous as he turned to face her. He then bent down on one knee. "Pamela Elizabeth Jenkins . . . I love you more than I ever thought possible to love another human being. I cherish every tiny second I get the honor of sharing with you. You make me want to be the best man I could ever be." He paused for a second and cleared his throat. "I'm just going to shut up before I say something stupid." He produced a box from his pocket. Nicolas's anxiety began to build. He opened the container, and there in the middle of the box was a diamond ring. "Will you share your life with me?" She jumped back in surprise.

"Nicolas, nothing would make me happier." She leaped into his arms and kissed him as both of them fell to the sand. They both giggled.

flash

He was now in the middle of a delivery room. Pamela was holding a newborn baby. Nicolas stood next to her. Complete joy embraced him. The feeling of pride was overwhelming. "Say hello to Eric Gorter," said Pamela covered in sweat.

"Hello, my boy."

flash

Nicolas lay on the floor. The room was dark. A one-year-old Eric rested on his chest. "You can do anything you put your mind to," said Nicolas to the boy. Eric smiled at his father. "I didn't believe in miracles until you came along. I bet you didn't know that. You are truly amazing." The boy burped and then smiled again. "And I'm the luckiest man alive, but I'm sure your mother has told you that one before. Yes she has . . . yes she has." The two Gorters laughed at one another. Nicolas stared into his son's eyes. "I promise you, Eric Felix Gorter, I will never let anyone ever hurt you. No, I won't . . . no, I won't."

flash

Nicolas was standing in front of a burning warehouse. He was the one sweating now. He could not believe what he had just done. Fire had materialized from his hands. Nicolas could not control it and he had inadvertently set this place on fire. Guilt coursed through him. "What have I done?" He fell to his knees.

flash

"I don't have time to explain, Pam, but they're coming. You need to grab Eric and get the hell out of here."

"But . . . aren't you coming with us?"

"There's no time. I have to hold them off." The two kissed each other for the last time. "I love you." He picked up his son and squeezed him as hard as he could.

"What's a matter, Daddy?"

"Nothing, Eric. You and your mother are going on a trip."

"Why aren't you coming?"

"I can't just yet. I have a promise I have to keep. I will see you soon though, okay?"

"I love you, Daddy."

"I love you too, little man." He kissed his son on his forehead. Pamela grabbed the bag that had been packed and dragged a now four-year-old Eric out of the house. Nicolas could hear the aeromobile start and take off into the night sky. He was washed with relief. His family was safe.

flash

The tall black man with one eye stood above him with a photon pistol in his hand. It was Thatcher Wikkaden. "You are to come with me in accordance with the Global Alliance." Nicolas felt anger. He would not be taken without a fight. He focused all of his power at the gun. Flames shot from his hand. The dark man's arm caught on fire. He screamed in agony. Two others subdued Nicolas. The man had put out his arm, but it had been severely burned. "We always have to do this the hard way." He blacked out.

flash

He was now strapped to an operating table. The dark man stood at the end of the table. A cannon had replaced his burned arm. "Thank you for volunteering, Nicolas Gorter."

"Volunteering?" He looked down and could see that half of his body had been replaced by metal. "What have you done to me?" There was no response. A man in a lab coat wielded a drill and moved closer to Nicolas. The sound of the drill was overbearing.

"Brace yourself, Defect. It's about to start hurting," said Wikkaden as he leaned over. Electricity surged through Nicolas's body. The pain was like nothing he had ever felt. His screams were muted by Wikkaden's laughter.

flash

Nicolas awoke. The only thing he could see was a bright light that was pointed at his face. He was lying down, restrained. He tried to talk, but no words could be heard. He tried to move, to struggle, but he could not. Nicolas's fear and anxiety smothered him.

Thatcher Wikkaden appeared above Gorter. "He's awake. It's good to see you again, Nic. I can call you Nic now, right? I mean we have been spending so much time together." He again tried to speak, but his mouth did not move. "You might be noticing a few changes since we last spoke. We've implanted a small device into your cerebral cortex. We are in control now, Nic." Nicolas tried to scream—to reach out and strangle this man that took away his wife, his son, his beautiful existence. "We had to make sure there would be no more accidents like the warehouse. You understand, don't you, Nic?" Somewhere in his thoughts, Nicolas believed he deserved this torture for what he had done. "Don't look so sad. We have a lot of work to do. I want you to meet your fellow Re-psyches." Someone was controlling his movements, forcing him to sit up. He could now see five others just like him, more machine than man, not in control. "Welcome to your new family." Nicolas slowly gave in to the transformation. His last thought was of a picture of Pam and his son Eric that he had kept in his office . . . then . . . nothing. Nicolas Gorter's mind was lost.

flash

Nicolas was hunting a boy. The target's name was Jetra Klin. He had cornered the boy in an abandoned hospital and was moving in for the kill. Klin shot a few energy bursts back at him, but Nicolas easily dodged these. Hate rushed through Nicolas. He was just a tool now, powered by anger. He increased his speed and shot out an enormous fireball. The ball bore down on the seemingly helpless child.

flash

Nicolas was now in front of a house that was burning to the ground. "Well done, Nic." The voice belonged to Wikkaden. "Once again, you have served me well." He boiled inside. The flames rippled as the man that used to be Nicolas Gorter watched his handiwork.

flash

Nicolas landed on the street in London. He ran at his designated target. There was a female and a male, both magic users, both dangerous. One was known: Yareli Chula, Spirit Summoner. The other was unknown, but his energy readings were unusually high. Nicolas let out a scream and advanced.

flash

A large pulse of energy was coming right for him. Nicolas could do nothing. The force of the blast knocked him backwards, destroying most of the metal parts that had been secured to him. Nicolas felt hope for the first time in a long time.

Nicolas was sure he would finally get to rest.

flash

Nicolas was looking at the boy that had defeated him. He felt pure relief. The torture of being controlled and used was over. No more anger. No more hate. This boy had done the impossible. He had freed him from Wikkaden and his Hunters.

flash

Thomas was back on the street in London again. The boy reeled backwards and drew in a deep breath. He instantly felt sick. The sensation of seeing a man's life unfold was disorienting, to say the least. He wanted to laugh, cry, and scream at the same time, but nothing came out.

"Life is a gift, Thomas. You mustn't forget that," said the spirit ghost. "Your spirit is strong. Your control is not. You must address this." Wiyaloo turned and looked at Thomas. "Thank you again for saving her." The spirit ghost faded away.

Thomas now stood there alone, staring at the results of his hastiness. He began to talk to the lifeless man. "Nicolas Gorter, I'm— I'm . . . sorry. I swear to you I'll never forget this. I'm glad that you are freed, but that doesn't change what I did. I swear to you I'll make this right, maybe not today, but someday." He turned to join his friends. "Rest in peace, Nicolas." A tear slipped down the curve of Thomas's cheek. He lowered his specs to hide his emotions from the others.

The impromptu eulogy was quickly interrupted. Blue and red outlines were reappearing in every direction through Thomas's goggles. The Hunters were on the hunt again. "Computer, how long until you get here?" Thomas screamed into his wristcom. The boy raced towards his companions. Wiyaloo's large paw held the back of the girl's head as she continued weeping. Her head was buried in the beast's side as she hugged him. "They're here," said Thomas.

Yareli spun around to see three collectorbots fall in behind the boy. They had no legs but were capable of flight. They flew towards Thomas as he ran to Yareli. "I am triangulating your position now." informed the computer's voice. "Estimated time of arrival is approximately eleven seconds."

Yareli reached into her empty quiver, pulled out an arrow, and nocked it. "*Ick-toe-mee!*" shouted Yareli as she loosed the spirit arrow. Wiyaloo had also made his first move. He planted his feet and shot a pure white energy blast aimed center-mass at the middle artif. A large hole bore through the collectorbot as it stopped midflight and exploded.

The spirit arrow erupted into six spiders, each the size of an aerocycle. The arachnids moved swiftly along the walls and leapt upon the artifs. They webbed the two remaining collectorbots together and squeezed the machines until they exploded.

The Volatilis 827 shot out of the sky towards their current location. "Computer, lower the convertible roof!" yelled Thomas, using every ounce of his remaining power to run to the hovering vehicle.

"That is a most unusual request, Thomas Scargen," questioned the computer. "The inclement weather would suggest tha—"

"Damn it, just do it," the boy shouted as he drew nearer to the vehicle. The aeromobile now hovered at street level as its roof lowered. Thomas jumped over the door and into the driver's seat. "Disengage autopilot."

"Autopilot disabled," said the Volatilis 827.

Thomas assumed control of the craft and with a quick hand gesture turned back towards Yareli's position. He had flown an aeromobile before but never while being chased. He zoomed in her direction and stopped the craft in front of her. "Get in."

Yareli jumped into the passenger seat, and Thomas took off into the sky. He knew Wiyaloo would appear in the backseat momentarily. Where Yareli went, Wiyaloo followed. The boy accelerated.

"Well done, Thomas," the spirit ghost echoed as he appeared in the back seat. A plasma bullet flew through the ghost, and the windshield shattered, throwing glass shards in multiple directions. The two in the front seat covered their faces.

"We're not out of the mouse trap just yet," said Yareli as she saw the three Hunters approaching, each on their own flying platform. Thatcher Wikkaden lead the three.

Thomas pulled back on the controls and the Volatilis 827 began to ascend. "I'm gonna need a little help here," said the boy.

"Agreed." Wiyaloo stood and dove out of the back of the climbing craft. His target had already been picked. Okland had the farthest range and was therefore their biggest threat. The beast landed on the platform's railing and pushed his paws against the chest of the overweight Hunter. A white force pushed the fat man off of his platform.

"Ha, ha, ha, ha . . ." Okland laughed hysterically as he fell. A parachute deployed as the fat man slowly lowered to the streets of London.

"Why is he laughing?" asked Thomas.

"Because he's a deranged psychopath," answered Yareli as a blast from Pekora's pistol shot across the aeromobile. Thomas steered the Volatilis to the left to avoid a second blast.

"Yar, grab the controls," commanded Thomas. "I can help."

"You've helped enough this evening. You can't keep up that kind of energy expenditure. You'll burn out." He looked at her curiously. "Just keep your eyes on the sky," said Yareli as she reached again into her quiver. "This is my last arrow, so let's hope this works." She placed the feathered end onto the bowstring between her thumb and index finger and tugged. "It's not the strongest one I've ever created, but it should do the trick. *Ee-tawn-kalla!*" The arrow rushed towards Pekora, and before impact, transformed into a horde of mice. The tiny creatures overwhelmed the woman, and all that she could do was screech as she jerked the platform hard to the right. Pekora's platform knocked into Wikkaden's as he let out a premature pulse from his arm cannon. The female Hunter lost control of her hovercraft and veered off course. "Never got over that fear of mice, I guess," said Yareli, amused by the odd spectacle. Still Thatcher Wikkaden gained.

Wikkaden's second shot hit the Volatilis 827 in the side and jarred the vehicle to the left. Thomas circled around and stopped the craft. The boy took a deep breath as he engaged the accelerator. The aeromobile rocketed towards the Hunter's leader. *Okay, you can do this. Just control the shot.* Thomas stood up and pointed both palms at Thatcher Wikkaden and yelled, "Haaaaaa!"

A blue orb soared out of his hands and flew at the Hunter's hoverplatform. The sphere collided with the floating base, causing an explosion that knocked Wikkaden backward. The Hunter swerved away from the aeromobile, trying to regain control, but the platform was now on fire. The tall, dark man quickly surveyed his options and abandoned the platform seconds before it exploded. His parachute opened as he tried once more to fire on the aeromobile but missed. Thatcher Wikkaden's muffled cursing could be heard as he drifted towards the ground.

The boy let out a sigh of relief. "Not exactly what I had in . . . mind." Thomas reached for his head as the world began to spin.

"See what I mean about burning out, Thomas. I hate to say I told you s—" His body collapsed into the seat, and darkness eclipsed his pupils. Thomas Scargen was unconscious.

12

better late

The sky ripped open above London, England. Five massive bat creatures emerged from the teleportal. Captain Slade was the first one through the event horizon. The Second and three other men followed him. Marcus had tasked Evangeline with picking the team to track the Scargen boy. She had chosen three diverse yet capable men: Nolan Taunt, Brett Jurdik, and Gamil Farod.

She has again exceeded my expectations, thought Marcus as he assessed the assembled crew. The wind whistled in his ear as Captain Slade and his Riders veered in formation towards Canary Wharf. Marcus's thoughts began to dwell on his squad as they swooped in closer to their destination. The first Rider's holofile appeared on his optical display. The file name read GAMIL FAROD. A three dimensional image of a Middle Eastern man stood next to the Rider's pertinent statistics and history.

Gamil Farod was an advanced Healer—as good a medical doctor as a magical one. His father, Dr. Khalid Farod, had brought him to the Tower when he was barely one year old. Khalid was a single parent when Marcus had met him for the second time. His wife had been a skilled Necromancer who specialized in magical artifacts. She had died a year prior to the boy's and his father's arrival at the Tower. A dragon attacked her during one of the doctor's more gruesome contracted genetic experiments. Her wounds proved fatal, and Gamil's mother bled to death. He was just four months old. This infuriated Khalid, and he decided to seek revenge on the dragons the only way he knew how—genetics. His previous experiments with dragons had given him an idea: Khalid would create a creature capable of fighting the dragons. To do that, he would need access to dragon DNA and unlimited credits. The man was an accomplished geneticist, but genetics did not pay well. That is why he came to the Tower. Here he would have the resources needed to accomplish his goal. The Tower would afford him his revenge.

After two years of experimenting, he had successfully crossed the DNA of a Dracavea dragon with a flying fox bat—the only creature whose DNA was found to be compatible. The resulting creature could fly faster than the dragon, but still maintained their ability to teleport. This made it a formidable opponent for the dragons. With the use of tech, the rider could control the creatures telepathically. Dr. Khalid Farod had created a new species—it just needed a name. He decided to name these beasts after his late wife, Aringi.

Marcus had been one of the original test pilots and could still vividly remember his first flight. *I was so young and stupid*, thought Marcus as he looked over at Gamil. That day had changed his life. *I was born to ride the aringi, and if not for this man's father, that wouldn't be possible. There would be no Riders.*

Gamil Farod had begun flying and treating the aringi by the age of twelve, but for the most part, without his father. Khalid had become so obsessed with his revenge that he had missed his son growing up. By this time, word had spread within the dragon community of the nature of his father's experiments, and some of the beasts took it personally. Three years after Gamil began to fly the beasts his father had created, a wingless black dragon killed Dr. Khalid Farod. His son watched the horrific event unfold, helpless. Some reports suggested that the dragon had been one of the test subjects, and that the creature was exacting revenge. This was never substantiated, but it did not matter. From that day on, Gamil had adopted his father's obsession with destroying the dragons. He threw himself into his father's work. He began to familiarize himself with his father's findings, improving on some of Khalid's research. In the process, Gamil had become an adept medic for both the Riders and the aringi. Marcus had also seen him in battle and knew Gamil could handle himself in a skirmish. He could trust this Rider with his life. Gamil Farod had nowhere else to go.

The Captain's optical display switched to the next Rider's holofile: BRETT JURDIK. The image of a stout, bald black man floated on the display. Jurdik was a marksman and had once been a soldier in the Global Alliance. He had left after realizing he had telekinesis. His patrol had been caught in an ambush, and without thinking, he had saved his men by hurling a tank with his mind at a group of advancing insurgents. Although he had been a hero, that was his last mission with the Global Alliance. Jurdik knew word would spread of his powers, and the Alliance had a zero-tolerance policy when it came to magic users.

Marcus had found him six years prior, competing in underground Mage fighting. The square-jawed man had been unassuming as he waited quietly for the start of his match. The crowd discounted Jurdik because of his size, but Marcus knew better. The man's build and strength more than made up for his stature, but his control of his telekinesis was his real talent. Jurdik won his match handily in front of the silent crowd. Marcus recruited him on the spot. His telekinesis had proven helpful in the past, and he was proficient with any weapon he touched. Jurdik could shoot the hair off of a gorgol's head from three kilometers.

The optical display in the Captain's helmet changed once more to the next Rider's holofile: NOLAN TAUNT. Nolan Taunt was a thirty-nine-year-old technic. He had spent most of his life in a poorly lit office before becoming a Rider, and his complexion suggested as much. He had developed and produced military tech and weapons systems for Lawler Technologies. Their biggest contract was the Global Alliance. Taunt had accidentally stumbled upon the Riders while trying to hack into an Alliance server. The holofile was marked CLASSIFIED, which naturally meant Taunt had to break the encryption. He found the information in a file named HUNTERS. He could not believe what he was reading. There was a world of magic out there that he had known nothing about, but the section on the Riders caught his attention. He became mesmerized by the idea of being a Rider, and he quit his job the next morning. Taunt spent the next year training and transformed his scrawny, frail self into a toned, athletic man. When he believed he was ready, he found Marcus. After hearing the man's tale, the Captain was impressed with his dedication. He began training that day.

Taunt was the finest technic Marcus had ever seen. *If it has a computer in it, Taunt can fix it*, he thought. Since becoming a Rider, he had streamlined the aringi's tech and used his knowledge to design the forearm weapons systems that were now standard-issue for all Riders. The current model was the Taunter 27—T27 for short. The man had named the weapon after himself. This did not surprise Marcus, considering Taunt's complete lack of modesty. His skills and tech proved useful in the field and almost made up for Taunt's constant rambling. The pale man had been a Rider for some time, and due to the untimely death of Dalco Jakobsen, he was now third in the chain of command, behind Evangeline and the Captain. *And if not for that database of his, we would have never known the identity of Yareli Chula.*

Marcus's thoughts shifted back to the task at hand as they approached the target. "Riders, check your coordinates. We will be landing on the Bayford Financial Building, weapons at the ready. There's no telling what we are walking into," commanded Marcus. The team flew in unison towards the roof. They flung themselves from their beasts and landed on the top of the building. The five stood up simultaneously and armed their Taunters.

"Looks like something crazy went down here—something really crazy," said Taunt. He scanned the area with his wristcom. "I hate to say it, but it looks like the work of Hunters. That's the last thing I want to deal with right now."

Marcus's nod confirmed that this was most likely the case. There were discarded robotic corpses everywhere, and rifle blast burns covered the roof. "Taunt, scan the interior of the building," ordered Captain Slade.

"I'm already on it, Captain," said Taunt, studying the building's holoschematics. "There are two life forms three floors down."

"Let's move. Jurdik, take point," instructed Marcus. The aringi circled overhead in the dark rain clouds as the five entered the door on the roof. The door itself was grasping onto its last hinge, another casualty of the day's events.

The narrow stairway creaked aloud as Jurdik vigilantly descended. He was half a flight ahead of the other Riders. Blood splatter painted the walls of the stairways like a Jackson Pollock piece. *Someone is injured and fleeing,* thought Marcus.

"The readings indicate movement one floor down," said Taunt.

"Send in a recon orb," ordered Marcus.

"Yes, Captain," said Taunt. He lifted the T27 and a tiny sphere escaped out of a newly opened hatch. The orb pushed ahead of the men. A holographic display appeared above Taunt's embedded wristcom.

"Listen up, Riders. We have two Mages on the floor below us," began Marcus. "The boy is the primary objective, but the girl must be taken down first. She is the experienced one. Yareli Chula is an advanced Spirit Summoner. She also has a spirit ghost that accompanies her. He is a formidable opponent, and the two are inseparable. If Chula is there, so is he." He rubbed his snowy beard. "That's not to say that the Scargen boy is not dangerous. As explained in your mission brief, our newest intel suggests that Scargen is a skilled and practiced Mage. This is contrary to what we previously thought, but we now have reason to believe that he was responsible for the *Eerah* slaughter."

The Riders looked back and forth at one another. Jurdik signaled to stop. "I still think that's impossible, sir," Jurdik whispered. "I mean that had to be the work of someone a little more . . . ya know . . . experienced. I've been at this a while, Captain, is all I'm saying, and I've never seen a power expenditure like that, especially from someone . . . well . . . so young."

"The facts say differently, Jurdik. I've gone over Taunt's data myself. The boy was definitely the origin of the power surge," interrupted Evangeline. "We need to be extremely cautious with him."

The Captain nodded in agreement. "When we breach this door, I want Taunt and the Second to take the girl, and I want Farod and Jurdik to help me with Scargen. The girl is expendable, but we need the Scargen boy alive. Taunt, I need you to tell me as soon as possible which one is which."

"Won't be long now, Captain. We are almost in range," answered Taunt as they descended the last group of steps.

They were now standing in front of the fifth floor door, two Riders on each side. The door was locked. The recon orb flitted around the door handle.

"I can rip it off its hinges," suggested Jurdik.

"I do not think that course of action would be very wise, considering the element of surprise we are attempting to utilize," said Farod in a calm and even tone.

"I got this," said Taunt as he kneeled down to the door's handle. An extension came out from his forearm piece, and in seconds, he had opened the door. "Smarts–1, Telekinesis–0." The comment was directed at Jurdik. The two men shared an odd rivalry.

"That's enough, Taunt. We go on three," commanded Marcus into the microphone imbedded in his helmet. "One . . ." Compartments reopened on all their forearms, exposing a trio of lasers on each arm-piece. "Two . . ." Marcus grabbed the handle on the door. "Three." Marcus turned the handle and moved forward. He stepped through the doorway and pushed up against the wall to the right. The recon orb raced straight down the hallway.

Evangeline and Taunt moved next from the right of the door and proceeded down the corridor on the left hand side. Jurdik and Farod did the opposite. Captain Slade turned and now covered the rear.

"Clear," whispered Taunt into his headset as he and the Second exited the first room on the left.

"Clear," echoed Jurdik from the right. The group slowly made their way down the hall, systematically clearing all the rooms as they went. There were no signs of the targets in these rooms. The sound of music came from the open area at the end of the corridor.

"The two signals are dead ahead, Captain," said Taunt, now

situated behind Evangeline, looking at the display. "Still no indication of who's who though. There seems to be some interference with some of the sensors—the recon orb has stopped transmitting."

"We go in blind." Marcus gestured to the Riders. They moved instinctively into position. "Go," he commanded.

"Freeze!" yelled Jurdik as he saw the two silhouettes on the far side of the room. "Down on the floor!" Only one listened. The other dangled in the air. The five Riders now advanced in formation. "I said get down on the floor." Jurdik shot the music device that was located on the floor next to the person who had heeded the warning. The song abruptly stopped.

"What did you do that for? I liked that song," said Taunt, never taking his eye off of the target.

The poorly lit room made it difficult to discern what exactly was going on. *Why haven't they attempted to use their magic?* wondered Marcus. *Why aren't they fighting back?* The closer they approached, the odder the scene became. The figure on the right was chained to an exposed rafter in the ceiling, hanging limp. The other was on the floor laughing. *Something is not right here*, thought the Captain. "Riders, hold." Marcus lurched forward.

"It looks like you've got the wrong men, 'avn't ya?" laughed a prone Ronald Hosselfot. "I fink someone might 'av beat ya to it anyways. Dose 'unters don't exactly play fair, do dey? Not to say you lot do eiver." The man looked directly at the Captain. "So 'ow 'av you been, Marcus?"

"Can't complain." Marcus lowered his arm shamefully as the T27 transformed back into its unarmed status. "Tell me, Hosselfot: who's your disheveled friend?" The Captain pointed at the beaten and chained man.

"Oh, Lesinge 'ere. Well 'ee fought it be funny if 'ee betrayed 'is employer to some 'unters. You probably saw some of dere carnage on your way in. Yeah, so I've just been tendorizin' 'im a bit. And besides, 'ee's a Frenchman in jolly ol' England. No one will miss 'im if 'ee don't show up for 'is bloody morning crepes, will dey?"

"You can sit up now, Ronald." Hosselfot jumped up to his feet.

The sudden movement garnered the attention of the Riders. They armed their Taunters and pointed the weapons at the man.

"Keep it in your pants, please," answered Hosselfot as he lit a freshly rolled cigarette that he produced from his front jacket pocket. "I 'av no beef wif you people. If you want to spend your lives dangling from duh belly of a large bat, flying around God knows where, 'oo em I to say no? Live and let live is what I say, isn't it? I'm just trying to puff a fag dats all. I don't want any trouble wif you lot."

"Stand down, Riders." The Riders disarmed their weapons as Marcus moved closer to the man. "A real cigarette. I haven't seen one of those in . . . well, what's it been, thirty years—outside of the Tower anyway. Where were you able to find the tobacco? It's scarce, to say the least."

"If you 'av duh credits, you can 'av anything you like, can't ya? I've got a mate of mine who grows it 'imself in a 'uge ware'ouse in duh middle uv Paris uv all places." Hosselfot took in a soothing drag. "Don't ever tell a Frenchman 'ee can't 'av a smoke now and again. 'ee'd go mental, wouldn't 'ee?" The man again indulged in the nicotine-infused treat as he chuckled to himself. " 'ee's a nice enough bloke, but got no 'ed for capitalism. 'ee could be makin' a bloody fortune if 'ee so desired wif dis stuff. But 'ee don't for some reason. It's none uv my business now, is it? Like I said dough, nice enough bloke, crap businessman."

Marcus stared at the man for a few seconds, unable to comprehend half of Hosselfot's diatribe. "I need something from you, Ronald."

"Dat's all you 'ad to say, mate, isn't it? We go way back, Marcus, you and I, don't we? Anyfing for an old mate. What can I do for you guys? You need some tech then? Perhaps a new 'ed unit for one uv you chaps or for one uv your ravver large bat friends you guys are always flyin' around wif," inquired Hosselfot.

"No, Ronald. I need information on your last transaction," said Marcus. "Possibly artif circuitry . . . or maybe even . . . something along the lines of . . . dragon tech."

"Now you and I bofe know dat's illegal Capt'n, now don't we? I would never sell such goods to no one. Dat girl was buying a piece to fix her dogbot wif, I swear," said Hosselfot, raising his hand.

"Come now, Ronald. You and I both know that that is far from the truth. I know for certain that a Ms. Yareli Chula and a boy were recently in the market for dragon tech and artif parts somewhere in this very city." The Captain walked closer to the man. "And you being the sole proprietor of such merchandise in the whole of London must have sold these goods to them." Marcus smiled gently. He turned and stared at Ronald Hosselfot.

"Let's just suppose dat maybe I did do somefing uv dat nature. What is in it for me?"

"I could make it worth your while."

"I would like to 'elp you, really I would, but I 'av a very strict policy on not divulging my customers' personal information. It just wouldn't be cricket, would it? You can understand why wif duh nature of my business being against duh law and all. Dat being said, I do 'av dis very fine scrambler 'ere for sale, guaranteed to disrupt most electrical devices in a certain radius."

"I don't think you understand, Ronald. I am not asking you. The way I see it is, cooperate with us, or end up like Monsieur Lesinge over there. The choice is yours," said Marcus.

"If I could 'elp you, Capt'n, I would. But like I said, my 'ands are tied, in duh figurative sense of course."

"I guess you leave me no choice. Second, see what this man knows."

"Yes, Captain." The young lady slowly moved towards the Englishman.

"Aren't you a pretty little fing?" said Ronald as she approached.

"You won't be thinking that in about five seconds," replied Marcus. "She is not as docile as her looks would suggest."

"Well, Mr. Hosselfot, is there any way I could change your mind?" asked Evangeline peacefully.

"No, I don't suppose dere is. Policy is policy, Ms. . . . Evangeline, was it?"

She stopped in front of the man and grabbed the top of Hosselfot's head. "I would prefer to be called the Second." An orange energy burst dissipated from the young lady's hand and shocked Ronald's brain. The man went limp and fell out of her palm.

"Franklin Hawthorne is the man who set up this deal, Captain Slade," said Evangeline with calm certainty.

"Did you happen to get who, and where, this Franklin Hawthorne might be?" questioned Marcus.

"No, he passed out before I could get that far."

"You need to learn control. We need to know how this man connects with the Scargen boy and Chula, and Ronald Hosselfot can't tell us that unconscious."

"*Bonjour*, Captain Slade. Perhaps I could asseest you with your current, uh, predeecament," uttered the bloodied Lesinge. "Eef you scratch my back, I will, uh, how do you say, scratch yours."

"What do you know, Frenchy?" Evangeline rushed over to Girard Lesinge and hovered above the man.

"For say, 100,000 credeets I could give you this eenformation."

The Second clawed the head of Girard Lesinge. "Say the word, Captain, and I'll get the info we need."

"Stand down, Second. Look where that approach got us with Hosselfot." Marcus turned towards the Frenchman. "Now, Lesinge, you can have your 100,000 credits, but this better be good."

"I assure you, *mon amie*, it is beeter than goood. I know where Hosselfot and Hawthorne dreenk in Dover. They would meet at Hawthorne's favoreete poob. Hosselfot took me along a few times. He thought eet was a nice place, but I thought it was a sheet hole. It ees magic-friendly, however, so wee conducted a lot of businees there."

"Spare me the details. Just give me the name of the place, Lesinge," said Marcus with eager impatience.

"*Je m'excuse, mon amie.* Zee place ees called the Dodgy Toadstool. They meet there every other Wednesday for dreenks. Hawthorne is our biggeest buyer of dragon tech. I can take you there if you'd like." The Frenchman began to stand up.

"I don't think that will be necessary," said the Captain.

"Then I weel take my credeets and be going," announced Lesinge. The Captain began to giggle to himself. "What ees so funny?"

"It's just a certain phrase springs to mind with your request, and it makes me laugh." Marcus reached into his pocket and pulled out a credit stick.

"And wheech phrase ees that, Captain Slade?" asked the grinning Frenchman.

"*You can't take it with you,*" said Marcus as he lifted his left hand. Yellow electricity flowed from his fingertips, instantaneously stopping the heart of Girard Lesinge. The Captain flung the credit stick at the charred corpse. "That's for calling the Hunters." Marcus spun to look at his Riders. "Let's mount up before the Hunters come back. They're the last thing we need to be dealing with right now."

13
rebooted

The hooded man's laughter bellowed in his ears as he looked towards the desperate man. Power poured from his palms as he sucked the soul out of a tortured Sigmund Jacobs. Jacobs screamed, "Help me, Thomas . . . help me . . ."

The boy's eyelids flapped open. "Thomas . . . Thomas," the artif's voice stopped abruptly. Thomas sat up, startled by his dream. "Thomas, you have achieved consciousness," chimed LINC. "I was diligently monitoring your life signs and—" The boy interrupted the artif with an embrace.

"What did I tell you about the creepy hovering thing while I'm asleep?" joked Thomas as he tightened his hug.

"It is my prime directive to ensure your safety at all times."

"I wouldn't have it any other way." Thomas untangled himself from the artif's synthetic frame. The boy began to notice his surroundings. He was in what looked like a recovery room, and from the looks of the rock walls, he was safe within Draige Manor. Yareli was sitting in a chair across from LINC and Thomas.

"How was your nap?" asked Yareli, still fumbling with her wristcom.

"What happened to me? Last thing I remember we were being chased by Wikkaden and then nothing." Thomas now had one hand on his head, looking at the girl. His ears were ringing, and he had a terrible headache. The room was spinning.

"You knocked him from his hover platform and passed out," answered Yareli. "I tried to warn you about overdoing it, but to my surprise . . . you didn't listen."

"How long have I been out?" Thomas rubbed his eyes and yawned. The rotation of the room had lessened, but he was still disoriented.

"Three days."

"Three days?"

"Did I stutter?"

"Hello, Thomas Scargen," echoed Wiyaloo as he materialized in front of him. "It pleases me that you are finally conscious."

"Yeah, kid, I wasn't sure when you were gonna wake up," said Franklin Hawthorne as he drank a glass of Gloop. "The boys had a pool going."

"I 'ad you pegged for a coma meeself. I saw dis show on the holly duh uvver day about comas and it looked very similar to your predicament, didn't it?" said Fargus as he appeared next to the boy. "I was sure Bartleby would wake up before you."

"Wait . . . what?" Thomas was confused.

"I 'ad guessed you'd be out for free months, cuz dey said dat most short term comas last four months an that. You seem like a quick learner. So I fought, oh, he'd probably heal a bit faster."

"No, not that. Did you just teleport? Can gremlins teleport?" asked Thomas, astonished by the feat.

"We can't exactly teleport can we? We can turn invisible, right and then move and then like reappear an that. Ja know what I mean?" Fargus pointed at the boy. "And can ya stop callin' me a bloody gremlin. I've asked ya nicely now, haven't I?"

"I'm sorry, Fargus. You just startled me."

"I was just takin' the piss out uv ya, Thomas. It's good to 'av you back amongst the living, an that." Fargus jumped down off the boy and onto the floor. "I will see you guys in duh 'angar later den. I gotta go wake duh sleepin' giant now, don't I? Den get 'im ready to fly, an that. It could take a bit of time." The gremlin walked out the doors, whistling.

"Yeah we have to get going as soon as you feel up to it," added Yareli. "Your artif insisted that we not attempt to move you until you were stabilized, but we are wasting time here."

"I simply did not see the logic in possibly causing additional emotional and physical damage by prematurely subjecting your feeble human frame to travel of any nature," said the robot.

"Thank you, LINC. I honestly feel amazing—an apparent perk to hibernation. I'm one quick shower away from being ready to go wherever it is we are going," said Thomas as he sat up in his bed.

"There's some more clothes for you at the foot of the bed. I guess I should go help Fargus wake that damn dragon up. I think he's had enough beauty sleep," added Franklin, winking at Thomas.

Bartleby lumbered into the large hangar, yawning small flames. "So, we are finally ready to get dis show on duh road, are we? Splendid then, I can't wait to count all uv dose credits I tell ya. I'm going to buy myself a nice new pipe." Teams of gremlins swarmed the dragon and began placing armor and tech onto Bartleby.

"I can't believe it took me forty-five bleedin' minutes to wake you up. Like I don't 'av anyfing better ta do. Franklin quit ten minutes in. It's completely mental," said Fargus as he noticed Thomas. A look of revelation crossed the gremlin's face. "I almost forgot. If you'll excuse me." The gremlin disappeared.

"Well, Thomas, I'm gonna miss you," said Franklin as he hugged the boy. Thomas almost dropped the last bit of toast he had been eating. Lenore had made him what she called a "proper English brekkie." He drew the boy out at arm's length and looked at him. "Don't be a stranger, Thomas. You are always welcome here."

"Thank you. That's very kind. I'm sure we'll see each other

soon enough, Mr. Hawthorne," mumbled Thomas as he swallowed the last piece, desperately trying to get the jam off the roof of his mouth.

"Please, Thomas, call me Franklin."

"Sure, Mr. Hawthor—I mean, Franklin."

Fargus appeared in front of the two men holding a case of Gloop above his head. "Well if duh two uv you are finished, we 'av a schedule ta keep, and I intend to keep it. Besides, if I'm to be taggin' along, I'd like to get goin' as soon as possible. The sooner I bloody leave, the sooner I can get back 'ere." The gremlin whistled as he walked towards the partially suited dragon. "Come on, ya lazy bums. It shouldn't take dis long to dress Mr. Draige, now should it?" His words faded as he ambled farther away.

"I would like to thank you, Franklin Hawthorne, for replacing my malfunctioning articulix," chimed LINC. "I did not think it possible that anyone other than my maker, Dr. Carl Scargen, possessed the required intelligence and relevant experience to perform such a complex and intricate procedure."

"Don't mention it, LINC. The pleasure was all mine. I got to see inside a genius's masterpiece. That is a treat unto itself."

"I suppose that is an accurate assessment," responded LINC as he turned and walked away.

Yareli was twenty paces away, talking with Wiyaloo. The boy approached them and they immediately stopped their conversation. *They must have been talking about me*, thought Thomas.

"Are you ready?" asked Yareli, trying to cut off any question Thomas was pondering. "Actually before we get going . . . I just wanted to say . . . thank you for saving my life."

"But what I did . . . it still hurts. That man . . . Nicolas Gorter . . . his face."

"You are supposed to hurt, Thomas," interjected Wiyaloo as he stood like a totem pole behind the girl. "It is what makes you different from them."

Thomas had experienced a man's life in seconds, and this had changed him. He was different from the Hunters. He would never let hate determine his fate. Once had been enough. "Thank you, Wiyaloo," said the boy as he looked up to the apparition.

"Something else, Thomas: I contacted our friend and told him about the situation with your father." Thomas's gaze focused on the girl. "We sent a team to Egypt to your father's last known whereabouts."

"And?" wondered the boy.

"Well . . . nothing . . . there was nothing. There was no sign of him or Sigmund Jacobs." Yareli's face looked worried.

"Are you saying Dad and Sig *have* gone missing?"

"We don't know for certain. There are still a lot of possible explanations. He wants to ask you more questions about your dream when we arrive."

"We should go look for my father!" cried Thomas. It had all been a dream up until then. He was upset and angry. "I don't want to waste any more time talking."

"I assure you, everything that *can* be done *is* being done to find your father and Mr. Jacobs. We have some of our best Mages trying to track them." Yareli checked her wristcom. "Some of them are currently on their way back to your house to see if they have returned and, if not, to look for any clues to their whereabouts." Yareli looked up at the boy.

"Do you think those bat people did this?" asked Thomas. He was more worried now than he had ever been about his father. *He's really missing.*

"The Aringi Riders? Possibly, but if they have, there will be evidence of such, and these Mages will find it."

"What if my dream was true and that hooded man is responsible?"

"That's why we need to get you to our friend. If there's anyone that can figure this out, it's him." Yareli moved closer to the boy. "He will get to the bottom of this, one way or another, but he needs to talk to you directly, and like I said before, you're not safe, Thomas. Those Hunters are nothing compared to the Aringi Riders and the man these Riders answer to."

"I think I handled myself pretty well against the *Eerah*," said the boy.

"Yes, Thomas, but we can't rely on that happening again, and trust me when I tell you, this time they will be prepared, and Spirit forbid if Grayden Arkmalis himself comes for you."

"Who is Grayman Arkmolemoose?" asked the boy.

"Grayden Arkmalis," corrected Yareli. "He's who the Riders answer to, and he is not someone you want to run into."

"How powerful can one man be?" inquired the boy.

"You've never seen Grayden Arkmalis," replied Yareli. "His power is unmatched." The girl glanced at Thomas. "There are few that could dream to battle this man and survive. It remains to be seen if you might have such power."

"What's that supposed to mean?" asked the boy.

"I promise you, all of your questions will be answered."

"By the guy I don't know yet? In the place I'm not allowed to know about?"

"Exactly," said Yareli.

"Okay, just checking," said Thomas. A whistling noise came from the artif.

"I am fairly certain that the diminutive creature that prefers to be referenced as a *gremling* is currently trying to gain our attention," interrupted LINC.

"Well just don't sit there. Let's get those arses movin'. I don't 'av all night, do I?" Fargus sat, goggles down, perched on Bartleby's headpiece like a pilot, his tiny arms folded across his chest. "This flight will take off wif or wiffout its passengers."

Yareli and Thomas hurried over to the platform and then lowered themselves into the dragon's saddle.

"I will see you when we get there, my lady," said Wiyaloo before disappearing.

"LINC, just follow us through the teleportal," instructed Thomas.

"Well 'old on, everyone. Fank you for flying Draige Airlines. Please put your tray tables up, and do make sure your seat is in an upright position. In case uv an emergency, emergency exits are located . . . well, everywhere, quite frankly." The magnificent creature leaned over as Webster ran over to him with Lenore on his back.

"Rufff." The dog licked the dragon's face.

"We won't be long, Webby. I promise you dat. We're just dropping off dese fine people, collecting some credits, and den we will be back straight away." Bartleby smiled with each new stroke of the dog's tongue. "Who's a good pup?"

"Rufff," barked Webster in response. "Ruff," and then another for goodbye.

"It was a pleasure meetin' ya, Thomas Scargen," said Lenore. "I'm glad dose goggles came in 'andy for ya against dose nasty 'unters."

"Likewise, Lenore, and thanks again," replied the boy as he leaned over and whispered to the female gremlin, "And I haven't told anyone about the you-know-what."

"I appreciate dat, Mr. Scargen. I really do."

Bartleby craned his head back and giggled like one does after being licked by a dog in the face. "Let's go get my credits." The dragon flapped his wings twice, and with that, they were airborne. The beast turned in midair and darted towards the faux cliff wall, LINC following in his wake. The boy still clenched his eyes even though he knew the wall's secret.

The sun was shimmering off the Channel, so Thomas lowered his specs. "I will never get used to this!" screamed the boy. The dragon gained speed, and the robot kept pace. The two were racing ten feet above the Channel's waters.

"Entering the destination's coordinates into the navcom . . . and 'ere we go," said the dragon as he punched the keys on his arm piece. An electric hole tore open in front of them as Yareli and Thomas held on for dear life. "Next stop . . . Africa." The dragon and the artif vanished into the teleportal.

14

sirati

The dragon poured through the rip in the atmosphere. The robot followed suit. After the still-unfamiliar effect of teleportation began to wear off, Thomas Scargen looked around. He could not believe his eyes. He was flying above a lush green landscape of trees. The sounds of the jungle were deafening yet orchestral. Thomas just breathed it all in as nature's symphony played in his ears. It was a sight that few ever saw and even fewer experienced. "Africa is so completely narsh!" yelled Thomas over the cacophony of the wildlife.

"You 'avn't seen anyfing yet," said Bartleby as they rose above the tree line, exposing a jungle city in the crux of two mountains.

Thomas looked down to see the city hidden in the valley below. He slowly lifted his goggles; he had to see this with his own eyes. The city was immense, but it did not look out of place. On the contrary, it looked as if it had always been there. "This is where you are taking me?" asked Thomas.

"Welcome to Sirati," answered Yareli as the dragon slowed his approach. As they got closer, Thomas could see that there was a force field that surrounded the entire metropolis. Large trees jutted out of the valley floor on each side of the city. At the tops of these trees were hoop-shaped branches that appeared to be entrances. A man stood on a platform next to each of these circles. Bartleby was flying towards the closest one of these gates.

"What's that?" asked Thomas.

"That is how we get in," replied Yareli. Bartleby pulled up and hovered in front of the opening.

"Why can't we just teleport right through it?" asked Thomas.

"That would be unwise," said Yareli.

"Why?"

"We would all be fried, Thomas," said Bartleby. "It wouldn't be too safe of a place if aringi could just teleport right in, now would it?"

"You have a point," said Thomas.

"There is a great deal of defensive magic that protects Sirati," added Yareli.

"Like those guys?" The boy took a closer look at the guard as the dragon proceeded closer to the gate. He was amazed at what he noticed as they approached. The guard was no man. It was a spotted jungle cat standing on its hind legs. He was dressed in a uniform and holding an energy axe that extended to the base of the platform. "Am I seeing things?" asked the boy.

"No, Thomas, you are not seeing things," said Yareli. "But you have to stop staring."

"I can't help it. I've never seen anything like it before. He looks so . . . so—"

"Human?" said Yareli.

"Yeah, that's exactly what it is," responded the boy.

"He's a Leopard," said Yareli.

"Well, I figured as much."

"No, Thomas. That is his tribe's name, not just his species. He is a Leopard—one of the many Felid tribes."

"*A Leopard*," repeated Thomas as he looked at the guard. "Felids are the cats, right?"

"Correct, Thomas."

"How is this even possible?"

"The same magic that created Sirati transformed the Animals as well."

"You mean there's more of them—not just Cats?"

"Felids, Thomas, but yes. There are a lot more. At least half of Sirati's population is made up of Animals."

"Can they use magic?"

"Some of them, yes. The Felids are naturally adept at it, but there have been others from the other tribes."

"You think he can?"

"Most likely if he's on border detail," said Yareli.

Thomas thought of the possibilities of this wondrous place. Bartleby moved toward the gate's force field.

"Name?" inquired the Leopard on the platform.

"Bartleby Draige."

The guard typed into the holographic keyboard above his wrist-com. "What is your business in Sirati?" Beams scanned the dragon and his passengers.

"I am collecting my payment for services rendered and delivering Thomas Scargen." The boy waved.

"That explains the heightened security," said the Leopard as the sensors ceased their scan.

"Identities confirmed." The statement came from the Leopard's wristcom.

"Proceed," said the guard in a monotone voice as the force field dissipated only where the hoop was located. Bartleby zipped through and the field raised before LINC could follow. "Name?" asked the Leopard.

"My full name is Learning Intelligence Networked Companion. Most humans prefer using the acronym of LINC," said the artif. The Leopard again checked his wristcom as the robot was also scanned.

"What is your business here, artif?" asked the guard.

"I was designed by Dr. Carl Scargen to ensure the safety of Thomas Scargen." The Leopard looked at LINC with a confused look on his face.

"He's with us," said Yareli. The scans stopped.

"Proceed."

"Thank you, *Panthera pardus.*" The artif's leg turbines fired, and he too passed through the circle. The force field returned instantly.

"That's some security system," remarked Thomas.

"Each guard's specific voice needs to be used to give the PROCEED order. The guard's body needs to be in close proximity for retinal, paw, and heartbeat scans, all from a wristcom," added Yareli proudly.

"I guess you weren't kidding about me being safe here," said Thomas.

"I have already told you: I do not kid," answered Yareli.

"You're to land at platform 16 over by the waterfalls," said the guard matter-of-factly. "Anson Warwick is waiting for you there." Bartleby and the artif turned in unison and darted off towards the waterfalls.

"Is Anson the one that sent you?" asked Thomas.

"No, he's not, but he's an ally," answered Yareli. Bartleby proceeded to the platform marked 16. He slowed his speed as they approached the landing area. The dragon landed, bounced twice, and then abruptly stopped, throwing his passengers forward.

"So sorry," snorted Bartleby. LINC landed while his turbines transformed back into mechanical legs and feet. The platform was a flat rock jutting out of the cliff above an enormous waterfall. The energetic water was relaxing to Thomas. Yareli and the boy dismounted the dragon.

A man approached them from the far end of the rock that extended from an opening in the cliff. *This must be Anson*, thought the boy. He walked in a poised, confident manner with both hands behind his back, slightly tilted forward. The man was well-groomed from head to foot, from his maintained short, black hair to his polished shoes. He was young—somewhere in his mid twenties. He wore round spectacles, which struck Thomas as odd. Most people opted for optical implants. The only thing more peculiar was the man's yellowish-orange eye color. *That's not normal*, thought the boy. He drew his right hand out to adjust his glasses and stopped in front of the group. He produced a handkerchief with his left hand and proceeded to wipe his spectacles. He replaced the glasses and leaned over to Thomas.

"The evil that men do lives after them, the good is oft interred with their bones," said the man in a sophisticated English accent as he extended his right hand. "Words to live by." The boy reached out and shook the man's hand.

"Act III, Scene ii, line 75, from *The Tragedy of Julius Caesar*, or more commonly and mistakenly referred to as *Julius Caesar*, written by William Shakespeare. First published in 1623, but thought by historians to be performed as early as 1599, the play depicts the 44 BC conspiracy against, and brutal homicide of, the Roman dictator Gaius Julius Caesar and the ultimate defeat of his conspirators at the Battle of Philippi by the armies of Mark Antony and Octavius, Caesar's adopted son," interrupted LINC. "The line is designated to the character of Mark Antony during his addresses to the Romans directly following the assassination of the emperor Caesar. This fictional discourse is a classic example of subtle political rhetoric."

"Well said, artif. I believe the first performance was September of 1599, if my memory serves me. What a remarkable piece of machinery. Most impressive," said the man as he turned back towards Thomas. "Introductions are in order. My name is Anson Warwick, Mage Knight, and member of the Council of Mages."

"It's nice to meet you, Mr. Warwick."

"Please, Thomas, call me Anson."

"How do you know my name?"

"We have known of you for quite some time, Thomas. I had just imagined Yareli had told you. I—well *we* know a lot more about you than just your name," informed Anson. "But we have plenty of time for these conversations." Anson sniffed the air. "Eggs . . . bacon . . . and I believe . . . grilled tomatoes . . . is that English Breakfast I smell? Most peculiar."

Thomas put his hand in front of his face and blew on it to check his breath. *I don't smell anything*, thought the boy.

"Where is your brother?" asked Yareli.

"He'll be meeting us shortly," said Anson.

"Just as well, I don't need to deal with his attitude at the moment. There is much to talk about."

"Malcolm can be a bit . . . overwhelming, to say the least," said Anson. "He's meeting us at the pub. We can talk on the way."

"I am a bit thirsty," said Bartleby.

"I could 'av a go at a pint or free meeself," added Fargus.

"I too require a lubricant replacement," said LINC.

"Come gentlemen, I hope we shall drink down all unkindness." Anson turned and began walking back towards the cliff. The rest of the group followed, including the dragon.

"It would probably be easier if you just flew straight down, Bartleby. We can meet you at the bar at the base of the falls," said Yareli.

"Is dis place dragon friendly?" asked the beast.

"The friendliest. It's just behind the falls." Before she could finish her instructions, Bartleby flew off the platform and raced downward. The rest of them walked towards the opening in the cliff face. Two large doors slid open as they entered the cliff.

The inside of the cliff was not what Thomas had expected. The walls were tall and smooth with thousands of pieces of artwork. Thomas looked out at the people walking around. Yareli was right: about half of them were Animals standing like men and walking among the humans.

"These creatures are most peculiar, Thomas Scargen." The artif scanned every creature that passed him. "They are almost genetically identical to their quadrupedal counterparts with minor exceptions. These minor exceptions, however, would account for the ability for bipedal movement and higher brain function. I can find no evidence of these species existing in my databanks or on *Interface*."

"I hear ya, buddy. It's all a little crazy." Thomas's head pivoted back and forth. He saw two Vultures discussing what sounded like politics as they passed. He looked over and saw a Zebra talking with three Chimpanzees and a human woman. A Hippo waddled by talking to someone on her wristcom, and a Giraffe was craning his neck talking to another Leopard guard. A Rhinoceros dressed in formal robes shuffled in the opposite direction with a tattered leather-bound book tucked under his arm. Two Warthogs, four Baboons, and an Ostrich followed the Rhino, all dressed in similar robes and carrying similar books. Under normal circumstances, the books would have garnered more of the boy's attention, but these were far from normal circumstances. *Amazing*, thought Thomas. There were so many types of Animals and humans all interacting with one another that the boy's eyes could not fully interpret what they were seeing.

They walked past a giant window, and the boy glanced out of it. The sight froze him. He stopped while the rest of the group moved on, including LINC who continued to catalog every new Animal he crossed.

The boy stared out above the jungle. Colossal waterfalls framed the city of trees. Natural walkways connected the tree buildings. Inhabitants—Animal and human alike—filled the living city. It was stunning, and Thomas felt a sense of comfort and serenity that was unexplainable.

"Thomas!" yelled Yareli from the end of the hall. He was awakened from his daydreaming and looked down at the girl who was waving him towards her.

"I'm coming," said Thomas as he took one last look at the view.

The group waited for the boy near a pair of tall elevator doors. Anson and Yareli were finishing a conversation as Thomas approached. The wall was made of glass, and the elevators resided inside the waterfall. The group entered the elevator and disappeared into the water.

The doors opened with a chime. They exited the elevator and walked through a glass tube that lead them into the sparsely lit bar. Bartleby flew through the waterfall and landed right next to Thomas. He shook off the water that remained on his body, inadvertently soaking the boy. "Sorry, Thomas."

"Welcome to Warwick's," said Anson as he made a beeline to the bar. "It is not much, mind you, but it is mine—well, ours. Truth be told, there wasn't a place to unwind here before my brother and I had this idea, and not having a local pub is simply uncivilized."

"Quite right," praised Bartleby.

The bar was made of dark wood and oval in shape. It had the appearance that it was not *made* so much as *found* there. The centerpiece was a bulky tree. Cubbyholes and indentions of the tree served as shelves and cabinets. Various bottles of liquor and elixirs decorated the natural shelves. Tables made of the cave's stone circled the bar, and booths were carved out of the cavern wall. Patrons were strewn about the pub: some at the tables, others at the bar. He noticed two Jackals in a corner booth. He could hear their continuous laughter as he surveyed the bar. The smell of fermenting beer slightly eclipsed the scent of freshly running water that surrounded half of the pub.

Behind the bar was a Silverback Gorilla, apparently the bartender. The Gorilla was hanging from one of the tree's branches scratching its head and watching robotic soccer on the holovision. "Get down from there would you, Sinclair. We have guests."

"Sorry, Anson. I was just watchin' duh football match."

"A talking gorilla bartender . . ." said Thomas as he sat down at the bar. He had never seen an uncaged gorilla before, let alone one with an English accent. Thomas thought of everything he had witnessed since they landed. "I guess that's par for the course at this point."

"What indication is there that the Silverback is a golfer?" asked LINC. Thomas looked at the artif and smiled. Anson approached the bar.

"I wasn't sleepin' on duh job or nuffin', boss. I swear," said Sinclair to Anson. "I just got a lot of credits ridin' on dis game, but don't say anyfing too loudly. I don't want my ladies to hear ya. Dey'd kill me if dey knew I was gamblin' again, especially on bloody artifs."

"Give thy thoughts no tongue," insisted Anson. "You know I normally couldn't care less what you do, but my friends and I need a drink, and as such, I need your undivided attention. The Botspurs just scored."

"Bloody 'ell . . . I can't win one bleedin' match, can I?" said Sinclair.

Thomas scanned the bar and noticed other Gorillas were wiping down tables, and some seemed to be serving cocktails to other patrons. From what Thomas could discern, most were female, but there were a few younger males. "Did he say ladies?" asked the boy.

"I have postulated that the Silverback is referring to the female Gorillas currently in the vicinity. It is not uncommon for a dominant silverback to have several mates and be in charge of groups ranging from five to thirty gorillas."

"Warwick's is completely family-owned and family-run," said Anson with a grin on his face.

"It's just 'is family owns it, and my family runs it. Ain't dat right, boss?" said Sinclair. Anson nodded and the two exchanged a laugh.

Thomas leaned over to LINC. "What I don't understand is why does Sinclair keep saying he's watching football? I looked at all the holovisions. Four of them have robotic soccer on them, and the other two are playing the news. I don't see a football game anywhere."

Sinclair began to laugh. " 'ee's barkin' mate," said the Ape to Anson, and then turned towards Thomas. "Sock-errr, is what you Americans erroneously call the beautiful game." The Ape swung over to the android. "But make no mistake, the rest uv duh world calls it football."

"You learn something new every day," said the boy.

"I actually learn something new every 1.5 milliseconds when utilizing my central processors to their maximum capacity," said the artif. "The Silverback was accurate in his assertion that *soccer* is known as *football*, however, his contention that the word *soccer* is a colloquialism distinct to America is invalid."

"In what way?" asked the Gorilla.

"Ironically, the derivation of the word *soccer* originated in England. Football is also identified as *soccer* in New Zealand, Canada, Australia, and several regions of Ireland."

"And 'ere I fought only Americans were ignorant," said Sinclair as he winked at Thomas.

Fargus materialized next to the boy. He wasted no time with his order. "I'll 'av duh Warwick Lager," said Fargus. The bartender zipped from branch to branch, grabbed a pint glass with his foot, and began pouring the beer. "I must admit, I've never seen a talking gorilla before. I gotta say, it's pretty all right. I mean, I've 'erd uv duh one gorilla before, right, who did that talking wif 'er hands.

You know, sign language, I fink dey call it, but dis is unbelievable. I mean who taught 'im how to speak and that. It's not as if dere's like a human-to-gorilla dictionary, is dere?" He paused and looked directly at Thomas. "I couldn't see meeself talkin wif me hands. It's just not right, is it? I mean how do ya get anyfing done? Your hands are always busy talkin' and that. How do ya go about your chores? Ya can't, can ya? Impractical." The Gorilla let the head settle, topped off the beer, and then slid it to the gremlin. "Cheers, mate." Fargus focused on his pint. The glass looked oversized in his hands.

"What can I get you?" Sinclair asked the boy.

"I'll have the same," answered Thomas. He had had beers before with his dad but never in a Gorilla bar.

"Do you think that's wise?" inquired Yareli.

"Yes, I think I could use one of these right now, actually . . . and last time I checked, you're not my mother." Thomas grinned at her and sipped his beverage.

"Well, I know when I'm not wanted," said Yareli. "I need to catch the big man up on some of the events that have occurred anyway."

"Come on, I was just joking. Have a drink," pleaded the boy.

"I don't drink."

"Now there's a surprise," said Thomas. He raised the pint glass to his lips.

"I will see you soon enough." Yareli walked off towards the waterfall.

"I'll 'av a keg uv duh Warwick Pale Ale," instructed the dragon. Sinclair whirled around the bar branches to the other side. He returned with a half-keg under his arm. He swung and tossed the barrel to Bartleby. The dragon caught the keg in his right claw, popped the top like a can with one of his talons, and began to chug. "Cheers."

"Put their drinks on my tab, Sinclair." Anson pointed to himself. "Would your artif care for anything? We cater to artificial life forms as well."

"I currently require approximately 46.431 centiliters of articulation lubricant, Anson Warwick." LINC caught the can as the ape tossed it to him. "Thank you, Silverback."

Another dragon flew through the waterfall and landed with a thud, shaking the hanging glassware behind the bar. The black dragon quickly worked its way to the bar. Thomas stared at the beast. *Two dragons . . . narsh*, thought the boy.

"This would be a good place to open a bar," commented the dark dragon in a feminine voice.

"Are you suggestin' that I'm not a top bartender?" asked Sinclair as he swung over to her.

"I would never say such things," said the dragon as she smiled at the Ape.

"The usual, Talya?" Sinclair hung from his feet, already grabbing another keg.

"Yes, Sinclair. That sounds perfect." Talya turned and looked at Bartleby. "Oh, look what we have here. I've never seen you around before."

"I don't get down 'ere much, to be 'onest wif you," snorted Bartleby. "Just doing a job to make a few credits I am."

"Would you leave the poor dragon alone, Talya?" insisted Anson.

"Sorry, boss. It's just not every day I get to see another dragon, let alone one of the opposite sex. Looks like he's ready for battle. Is there something I should know?" countered Talya.

"She 'as a point, don't she?" interjected Bartleby. "Dis stuff is merely precautionary, my dear. Always be prepared and all. Many a time it 'as saved my dragon arse dough." He looked down and gathered his strength. "Fancy a story over a keg or seven, love?"

"I'm a sucker for a good story." She exhaled noisily, and a small flame escaped from her nostril.

"Let's go somewhere a bit more private den, shall we?"

"My name is Talya Grenfald." She extended her claw.

"Bartleby Draige, at your service, mum." He took her claw and kissed it. She giggled out loud. He picked up her keg and motioned with his head, and the two waddled away towards the waterfall.

"Love is a smoke made with the fumes of sighs," said Anson.

"Who is she?" asked Thomas.

"That, my dear boy, is my transport." Anson returned to his

own beer. "Just as well. The two of us can sit down and have a proper chat then."

"Good, finally some answers." The boy turned to Anson. *Let's start with the basics.* "Where exactly are we?"

"This is Sirati—a living hybrid of nature and technology working together as one. There is no other city like this in the entire world." Anson paused and looked at the boy. "Sirati is much more though. I cannot talk on it too much, but you will learn and do feats here that will simply dumbfound you—if you choose to stay, of course. Thomas, you have the potential to change everything."

"How can you be so certain?" asked the boy as he placed his empty pint glass onto the bar.

"It is not I who has to be certain, Thomas. This above all; to thine own self be true. Think about what you have already been through. You single-handedly destroyed an army of *Eerah*—"

"Technically, Anson Warwick, I destroyed precisely two hundred and thirty-seven myself," interrupted LINC as a drop of lubricant rolled down his steely chin.

"Not now, buddy. We all know you more than helped that day, but let Anson finish," said Thomas.

"Like I was saying, you destroyed an army of *Eerah*, escaped the Hunters, and then defended yourself, as well as Yareli, against a Re-psyche—a feat that not many of the most advanced Mages have accomplished. You then proceeded to defeat the oft-feared Thatcher Wikkaden."

"I just did what I had to."

"And that's what makes you special. Do you think a normal boy your age would have been able to deal with such events and decisions?" Anson waited for his response.

"No . . . I guess not," replied the boy.

"You have little fear in you, when most in your situation would simply be cowering in the corner." Anson sniffed the air nonchalantly. "Trust me when I say this, Thomas; I can smell fear in men, and you are clean, my friend."

"Sinclair, can I 'av another beer while dey hash dis out?" asked

Fargus, lifting the glass that was almost as big as himself. "These pints are the perfect size for me." The gremlin began to whistle to himself, content with his alcoholic nectar.

"I didn't do those things by myself. Without Yareli and Wiyaloo, who knows what would have happened." LINC looked directly at the boy. "And you too, buddy." LINC whistled with delight.

"Humble, too?"

"You sound like my dad," remarked Thomas. His face quickly saddened when he remembered his missing father.

"I want you to know, Thomas: we are working on finding him. You can be sure that we have some of our finest on the job. Our second team has reached your home and is still performing a sweep of the area and trying to locate your father and Sigmund Jacobs. I'll keep you posted as new information comes to light."

"I appreciate what you guys are trying to do, I really do, and I don't want to sound ungrateful . . . but from what I gather, there's only one guy that can help me, and I haven't seen hide nor hair of him yet."

"In due time, Thomas, but first we need to square up with Mr. Draige over—" Anson's words were disrupted by a sudden splash from the top of the waterfall. Thomas turned and his pupils met what looked like a gargoyle from far away. It was definitely human-oid, but winged. The creature soared towards them at a ridiculous speed. Thomas leapt from his stool and pulled back both hands, sensing imminent trouble. His hands glowed the now-familiar light blue color as the monster swiftly approached. LINC, following his master's lead, unfurled his arm-cannons as well. Both were poised for battle as the unknown creature still advanced. The boy moved his hands back and pushed forward. The flow of energy emanated from his palms and shot out directly to the being.

"Thomas, No!" screamed Anson Warwick, but it was too late.

15

a bat and a wolf walk into a bar

The blue stream of electric light sought out the flying beast. The words of Anson Warwick still hung in the air. The beam was just about to strike the creature when it made a quick movement with his hand and deflected the energy into the waterfall where it dissipated into white steam. "Wow, mate, dat really was impressive," said the winged being as it landed. The beast was no beast at all; he was a man. Long black hair framed his chalky face. His crimson eyes burned against the paleness of his skin. His leathery wings settled behind the man, blowing back the hair from his face. He wore a long black coat, a blood-red button up shirt with black pants, and a pair of black boots. His wings seemingly folded into the man's back through slits in the trench coat. He calmly sat down at the bar and lit a cigarette. He inhaled as if it were the only thing that gave him joy. The pale man smiled, exposing his protruding fangs. Thomas could now see that, despite the obvious differences, this man was the spitting image of Anson.

"Thomas, meet my brother, Malcolm Warwick." Anson placed his hand onto his head, knowing that a disaster had just been avoided. Malcolm nodded at the boy.

"You're—you're a-a . . . a . . . you're a . . ." Thomas stuttered.

"Come on, out wif it, boy. You almost 'av it," teased Malcolm.

"You're a vampire."

"Strong *and* insightful. You're gonna make some lady very 'appy one day, mate." Malcolm inhaled his cigarette.

"But, if you're a vampire . . . how did you just come from outside? I thought sun was a no-no for you guys—or is that just a myth."

"No, dat one's pretty true . . . for most vamps." He smiled at the boy. "But I'm not most vamps, now am I? Let's just say I've got a really high SPF on and leave it at dat, aw'right?"

"I didn't mean anything. I was just wondering . . ." Thomas dropped the subject.

"Oi, Sinclair, give us a pint uv duh red stuff," said Malcolm as he winked at the Gorilla. "So I guess you're duh one dat all duh fuss is about."

"Yes, Malcolm, this is Thomas Scargen," said Anson.

"Hello, Mr. Warwick." The boy extended his sweat-filled hand.

"Pleasure . . . and, Tommy, Mr. Warwick died centuries ago. 'ee's buried next to our muvver. Call me Malcolm." He reached out to shake Thomas's hand. When the boy reached out, the vampire grabbed his hand tightly. Thomas felt a chill run up his spine from the man's icy touch. "Ooh, you smell good, Tommy," laughed Malcolm Warwick. "What are you, B negative?"

"I don't know." Thomas was a little frightened by Malcolm's question. "I've . . . never needed to know." LINC's optics settled on the vampire.

"Well, if anyone asks, you're B negative," said Malcolm nonchalantly while dropping Thomas's hand. "What's the Tin Man staring at?" asked the vampire as he drank down his red ale.

"I can only assume you are referring to me. You must be referencing *The Wonderful Wizard of Oz*, written in 1900 by Lyman Frank Baum—the heartless character of the Tin Man, or Tin Woodman, to be more precise, first portrayed in 1939 by Jack Haley, under the direction of Victor Flemming, in the popular archaic film reel *The Wizard of Oz*." The artif stepped closer to Malcolm. "I assure you, vampire, I have no need of an organ as poorly constructed and rudimentary as the human heart."

"Dere's somefin' we agree on then, isn't dere, Tin Man? I fink I like you."

"My calculations suggest that there is a 97.623 percent probability that I will not benefit in any manner from your close proximity, vampire, therefore approval is difficult for me to ascertain at this time," said the artif. "These types of calculations can never be exact, mind you, and are always fluctuating due to unforeseen variables, such as acts of service or subtle changes in one's attitude. Perhaps it will be best if I forgo judgment until a later date."

"You just love to 'ear yourself talk, don't ya?" said Malcolm.

"What are you wearing a coat for?" asked Thomas as he wiped his brow, trying to change the subject. "It's like ninety-five degrees in here."

"It's actually 98.3 degrees Fahrenheit or 36.83333 degrees Celsius," said LINC as his optics fluttered.

"You're just full uv questions, aren't ya, Tommy? I wear duh jacket because it looks bloody wicked for one," said Malcolm. "And because I've got no body 'eat, mate. Vampire blood runs cold, doesn't it?"

"Okay, that explains how ridiculously cold your hand was, but there's still one thing I don't get," said Thomas. He looked over at Anson and then back to Malcolm.

"Get on wif it," said Malcolm as he puffed away on his cigarette.

"If you are immortal and have been around for centuries, how is your twin brother still alive?" asked the boy. "Is Anson a vampire too?"

"Uh . . . not exactly," said Anson. "There are more things in heaven and earth, Thomas, than are dreamt of in your philosophy."

"I can't believe you 'avn't told 'im yet. What is wrong wif you?" asked Malcolm as he turned and looked at Anson.

"It's not quite something that comes up in normal conversation, now, is it?" Anson tried to defend himself.

"Tell me what?" The boy was facing the twin brothers, arms crossed.

Anson adjusted his vest. "All right, well I suppose there's something I should tell you." He grabbed the corner of his glasses and raised them slightly. "I am what the French call a *loup-garou*, or as the Spanish say, *hombre lobo*. The Russians use the term *oboroten*, and the Greeks refer to us as *lycanthropos*. In Latin . . . *Daemonium lupum*. Old Norse . . . *hamrammr*. The term you would probably associate me with would be—"

" 'ee's a freakin' werewolf, Tommy, bayin' at the moon, scratchin' for fleas, silver bullet-dodgin', werewolf," interrupted Malcolm as he puffed out a solitary smoke ring. "Well go on, ya can't just drop a bombshell like dat and not show duh boy, can ya?"

"I did not drop the bombshell, Malcolm, you did."

"You can control it?" asked Thomas. "In all the books I've read, werewolves never can control it."

"Which texts have you studied? *A Werewolf Field Guide* by Professor Joseph William Bevy or *The Unknown World of Werewolves* by Dr. Dawn Moriens?" asked Anson. "Both great introductory works, mind you, but if you want a more serious look at werewolves you should read *The Immortal Wolf* by Robert Girmscheid or Pack Life by Anita Wrislar."

"I was talking more along the lines of *The Werewolf King Saga* by K.C. Rowlkien," said Thomas. "I read all ten of them." He smiled.

Anson looked at the boy with a confused look. "Being able to control one's transformation is in fact uncommon, Thomas, I assure you. Over these many years I have learned to use my powers to suppress my metamorphosis, as well as unleash it when needed. Full moons can still give me a bit of trouble, but for the most part, I'm in complete control."

"Dat's all well and good," said Malcolm as he turned and looked at his brother. "But seeing is believing. Let's get on wif duh show, Anson. Tommy 'ere is growing impatient. I'd wager 'ee's never seen a werewolf before, 'av ya Tommy?" Malcolm winked at him. "Duh boy should see it, shouldn't 'ee? It's not like all werewolves are as cordial as you, Bruvver, and 'ee should see 'ow it works."

"Surprisingly enough, you make a fair point. All right, in the name of education, I will do this." Anson removed his jacket as he moved to an open area. "This is so embarrassing." He began unbuttoning his vest and then his shirt underneath. He flicked his shoes at Malcolm and placed his glasses on the bar. "Okay, here goes nothing, but be wary Thomas. He's mad that trusts in the tameness of a wolf."

Anson at first began to twitch. His eyes then rolled back into his head, and his body started violently convulsing. His hands jutted out and his fingernails began to grow into claws. Screams coincided with the restructuring of his spinal column as it twisted and cracked into its new state.

"Dat bit looks bloody painful, doesn't it, Tommy?" interjected Malcolm as he turned away.

Anson dropped to his newly metamorphosing knees. The front of his face stretched outward as his neck elongated. Fur infected his skin. It covered him at an astounding rate. His pants slightly tore as his leg muscles grew and his feet and legs turned into hind-quarters. Anson's front paws pushed down onto the ground as he stood on his new legs. His teeth ripped through his gums as his head arched upward. Anson panted, standing hunched in front of them. His wristcom miraculously survived the transformation. The were-wolf's hair was predominantly black with a white patch on the end of his tail. He raised one of his extended arms and touched the tip of his snout. His head quickly pivoted towards the boy. "Be honest, Thomas, does my nose look big to you?"

"That is freakin' totally narsh," said the boy as he laughed aloud.

"I fink you look like a tosser," joked Malcolm. "An overgrown, furry tosser."

"You have transformed your human form into a hybrid of *Canis lupis* and *Homo sapiens*—a most impressive metamorphosis, Anson Warwick," whistled LINC.

"Thank you," growled the werewolf. "At least someone appreciates me." Anson grabbed his beer off the bar and began drinking it. He slowly changed back into his human form as he finished his beverage. "I spend more money on pants than I care to admit," he said as he buttoned his shirt. "And I am constantly losing my glasses." Anson rested the specs back on his nose. "That's better." He reached down and slipped on his shoes as well. He looked ridiculous with his half-torn pants. Thomas began to laugh. "You having a laugh at my expense?" Anson knew the answer to this question as soon as he looked down. "I guess I do look a bit odd, don't I?"

"So, wait a second." Thomas thought of his books. "Now correct me if I'm wrong, but werewolves and vampires aren't exactly supposed to get along. Aren't you guys pretty much mortal enemies?" asked Thomas.

"I'll field dis one, Anson, if you don't mind."

"By all means, Brother, continue."

"Well, Tommy, ya see, dat is a good question, and I fink it's best answered simply wif a yes, but bruvverly love, ya see, supersedes the age-old battle between our two distinctly opposed species," said Malcolm as he inhaled another toxic draw. "Now dat being said, neiver one of us is exactly what one would call *accepted* by our own kind. So we don't 'av much uv a choice on duh matter, do we, Tommy?"

"I suppose not," said the boy.

"I'll 'av one more barkeep," said Fargus, ignoring the festivities all together.

"What duh 'ell is dat?" wondered the vampire. He was next to the gremlin instantly. "You're an odd little bugger, aren't you?" This got Bartleby's attention, and the dragon moved back towards the bar. Talya followed.

"That's my best mechanic," chimed in Bartleby.

"I've read of such creatures. The stories suggested that they helped us win the Second World War," said Anson. "I didn't think they actually existed until I saw him with my own eyes." Thomas chuckled to himself. He found it rather amusing that a werewolf would question such things. "They call your kind gremlins, correct?" Up until that moment, it would have been impossible to tell that Fargus had been listening at all.

"Can you please not call me dat? I wouldn't call you a *dog*, would I? That wouldn't be right would it? Gremlin is a human term. It's not like I can't be fed after a designated time or take baffs, is it?" He looked at the vampire and then the werewolf. "If you need to call me somefin', call me Fargus." The gremlin returned to his drink. The two brothers were silent. Malcolm still stared at him intently. It appeared that the vampire was also smelling the air. Fargus turned to him as if he could feel his stare. "Can I 'elp you wif somefin'?"

"It's just dat I can't smell you, and I can smell everyfing, and I mean everyfing. My senses traditionally don't miss much, do dey? But, you, I can't get a read on." He turned his ear to him now. "I can't even 'ear your 'artbeat."

"My heightened senses are also currently failing me," said Anson. "That makes you rather unique."

"I don't know about Anson 'ere, but I've never run into dis type of problem before." Fargus turned to speak to Malcolm.

"Well . . . what good would becoming invisible be if fanged blokes like yourself or bloody wolfies like your bruvver could just like sniff the air and be like oh dere 'ee is, mystery solved. I found 'im."

"What?" replied Malcolm.

"I mean, what I'm tryin' to say is, at the end of the day, if I was like invisible in duh same room you were in right, and all you 'ad to do is like smell the air or like listen to me 'artbeat or whatever it is dat your lot does"—the gremlin's eyes rolled upward like he was piecing his argument together on the fly—"it would like defeat the purpose of being able to turn invisible, wouldn't it?"

"You can turn invisible?" Malcolm's face lit up.

"Right, so?"

"Let's see."

"I'm not some pet you can just 'av a go at and den like expect me to play fetch when you ask me to."

"Pleeeeease?" pleaded the vampire. It dawned on Thomas that being immortal, Malcolm probably did not often experience new things. He seemed genuinely excited.

"No," said Fargus as he sipped again from his oversized beer.

"Oh come on, Fargus." Bartleby momentarily looked away from Talya. "Show duh man your little trick already."

Fargus disappeared and then quickly reappeared. "Right . . . 'ow's that for ya?"

"Amazing," the twins said in unison.

"Now, if ya don't mind, I'd like to be getting back to me beer."

Anson's wristcom began to beep. He looked down at the display. "It appears he's ready for us. It is about time we get going, Thomas. Talya, it's time." The werewolf raised his voice so the dragon could hear him over the sounds in the bar.

"I'm kinda busy if ya haven't been paying attention," the female dragon retorted out of the corner of her mouth.

"I pay you enough not to be busy."

"The wolfman has a point," whispered Talya to her new dragon suitor.

"It's aw'right. I believe I might be stayin' a bit longer than originally anticipated, so no worries. We will 'av plenty a time ta get ta know one anuvver." Bartleby grabbed her claw and bent over to kiss it.

"How chivalrous."

"You 'avn't seen nuffin' yet, my lady," rumbled Bartleby. "Besides, I believe someone owes me a fair amount of credits, don't they?" They looked down at the motley group. "Fargus, looks like we'll be stayin' 'ere for a bit longer. I kinda like dis place I fink."

"I bet you do," said Fargus as he glanced at Talya. "Can I get one more ta go, barkeep? Maybe a bit smaller, so I can carry it." Sinclair slid him another beer, this one was in a shot glass. "Cheers, mate." The gremlin placed some credits on the bar. "Dat's for one for yourself." He whistled to himself as he got down from his barstool.

Talya walked over to Anson and lowered her shoulder so he could climb onto her. "Come on, Thomas. We mustn't keep the old man waiting."

"Yeah, even I don't mess wif dat old geezer," said Malcolm as he extinguished his cigarette in his hand and proceeded to finish his drink.

Thomas mounted Bartleby. He sat in the saddle as the tiny gremlin friend appeared on top of the dragon's head. "Izza good fing I'm not . . . drivin'." Fargus was visibly intoxicated. He began to whistle, but this time the tune was occasionally interrupted by a hiccup. This did not impede his progress on the tiny Warwick Lager that resided in his hand.

The vampire turned to LINC. "So I get stuck babysittin' the bleedin' Tin Man then?" Malcolm's wings sprouted out of his back, and he took flight. The android's legs burst into turbines and he hovered alongside the vampire.

"I am not an infant, Malcolm Warwick. I was brought online 5 years, 3 months, 27 days, and approximately 6 hours and 42 minutes ago."

"Dat's impressive. I only got ya beat by six centuries or so, give or take." The vampire laughed as he flew away. " 'I'm not an infant,' 'ee said . . . priceless." His words faded as he passed through the wall of water. LINC, still hovering, rotated his head towards the Gorilla, who was again preoccupied with the robotic football on the holovision.

"Thank you for your hospitality, Sinclair."

"Don't mention it." The Ape did not turn his head away from the match. LINC's jets fired as he followed the vampire. The dragons had yet to take off.

"Just follow me, Bartleby, and try to keep up." Talya looked back at the beast and batted her eyes.

"I don't foresee dat as a problem, love." Bartleby had toddled his way beside her now.

"I'm actually starting to feel nervous," Thomas said as he felt his stomach drop. "What if I'm not what this man expects? What if I am totally the wrong guy? I don't know . . ." He looked at Anson, looking for guidance and a bit of reassurance.

"Be not afraid of greatness, Thomas: some are born great, some achieve greatness, and some have greatness thrust upon them." As his sentence ended, Talya Grenfald streaked off into the waterfall. Bartleby and his companions crossed the liquid barrier soon after. Thomas held on for dear life as he tried to absorb the werewolf's last statement.

16

home

Talya was the first dragon to land; Bartleby was close behind. They landed in a clearing in front of a baobab tree. *That is the biggest tree I have ever seen*, thought Thomas. His mouth hung open as he stared up into the green canopy. "That tree is bigger than a freakin' redwood," said Thomas aloud to no one in particular. His father had taken him to the Mariposa Grove in Yosemite National Park when he was eight years old.

"It *is* bigger den a redwood. What I mean to say, an that, is what's a redwood?" asked Fargus.

"It's a big tree," said the boy.

"But not as big as dis one?"

"No, definitely not as big as this one."

"Aw'right," said Fargus as he turned back around to look at the tree once more. Thomas did the same. The immense scale of the baobab suggested that it had been there for some time. It rested on top of a huge plateau of rock and vegetation that jutted out of the jungle's floor. It was connected to the rest of Sirati by various natural walkways that broke off from the plateau.

The giant doors that were embedded into the tree swung open. Yareli appeared. As she got closer, Thomas could see she was carrying a credit stick and walking towards them. "I believe this belongs to you, Mr. Draige," the girl said as she held out the stick for

Fargus to grab. Thomas dismounted the dragon. "250,000 credits, as we agreed."

"Fank you, my lady. It's a pleasure doin' business wif you." Bartleby dropped his head. The dragon then looked back up. "If one was inclined to stay anuvver night or so, where would one inquire to find proper lodgings for duh evening?" The dragon smiled, "And it goes wiffout sayin' dat credits are no object."

"Well, Bartleby, I might be a bit biased, but Warwick's has dragon suites currently vacant." Anson jumped off his dragon. "Talya can take care of all the arrangements."

"Fank you, mate. I am a bit knackered from the long teleport and all." He glanced at Talya and winked. "We probably should take care uv duh arrangements straightaway then, love, shouldn't we?" His fake yawn was almost saved by the tiny flames that escaped his nostrils.

"I guess I'll go ahead and stay wif dese guys den, Bart. If you don't mind." Fargus winked at his dragon friend. He drank his beer and burped.

"Can we get on wif dis? I mean just because duh sun don't kill me don't mean it doesn't still bloody 'urt." The vampire lifted his trench coat over his head and sped through the doors.

"I guess this is it," said the boy, nervous as ever.

"Thomas, you have nothing to worry about," said Yareli. "You are extremely capable. You've saved my life at least twice, not to mention you've displayed a definite natural talent."

"Wow. That almost sounded like a compliment." Thomas smiled at the girl. "I could not have done any of it without you and Wiyaloo."

The spirit ghost appeared behind Yareli as if summoned. "It is we that could not have achieved our goals without you, Thomas Scargen."

"I was wondering when you were gonna join us." Thomas smiled. "Where've ya been?"

"I was traversing the Spirit Realm," said Wiyaloo.

"The Spirit Realm?" questioned Thomas.

"It's where one's spirit may ascend to when and if it successfully sheds its corporeal form," said the spirit ghost.

"Oh . . ." The boy was confused, but thought better of asking for an explanation. He did not want to seem stupid, especially not in front of Yareli. "What were you doing there?"

"I was looking for answers to your father's disappearance."

"Did you find anything?" asked Thomas.

"No, I did not."

"Thanks, Wiyaloo. I appreciate the effort. It means a lot to me."

"But my effort has not helped you," said Wiyaloo.

"Yes it has. You not finding him in the Spirit Realm gives me hope that he's not dead, and I should be getting some answers soon."

The fox nodded. "Agreed."

"Speaking of which," interrupted Anson. "We do not want to keep him waiting, now do we?" Anson extended his arm toward the doors his brother had disappeared behind. "After you, Thomas."

The boy walked to the opening in the base of the mammoth tree with his robotic counterpart at his side. "My sensors indicate that there is no viable data to suggest that we should trust the cantankerous vampire, Thomas."

"Lighten up, LINC, he seems harmless to me."

"Malcolm Warwick displays various character traits that make several of my subroutines glitch." The artif's eyes fluttered. "I assure you I will be keeping an optic fixed on his general vicinity," responded the artif.

Fargus appeared next to Thomas. His sudden appearance startled the boy. " 'ee seems aw'right to me," said the gremlin as he raised the empty glass to take a sip. "Well, for a blood-sucking, undead creature uv duh night anyway," said Fargus, trying to free the last drop of his beverage. "The most civilized fanged bloke I've evva met. Only fanged bloke I've evva met, mind you, but civilized nonetheless." Fargus placed the shot glass on the ground and stared at it for a second. He then turned and reached up to the boy. "Can you give us a lift den, Thomas?" The boy grabbed the gremlin and slung him on his shoulder. "Fanks, mate. If I 'ad to walk duh rest uv duh way, I fink I'd go mental." He began to whistle.

As Yareli approached the doors, they opened. Thomas was still taken aback over the sheer size of the tree as they crossed the threshold. "Welcome to Maktaba," said Yareli. "You'll find the knowledge of the ages contained inside, and the answers you seek as well."

"I hope so," said the boy as he walked into the bottom floor of the tree. No sooner had he passed through the doorway than the elaborate wood doors slammed behind him. This startled Thomas as well as the gremlin.

"Dat was a bit uncalled for," said Fargus, momentarily interrupting his whistling. "Maybe a bit of fair warning next time."

The inside of Maktaba was even more astounding than the outside and much cooler in temperature. The interior was a vast open space that was simply and elegantly hollowed out. There were tiers upon tiers that climbed to the apex of the tree. The bark walls were littered with natural bookshelves. Millions of written tomes filled these shelves. The place was bustling with various species of Animals intermingling with their human peers. Some of them were reading, some conversing. Teachers taught classes, and there were guards standing at attention at every entrance. Most of these guards were Felids. They were dressed similarly to the Leopard Thomas had met when they arrived, but with one small difference. There was a different insignia on their armor.

The tree itself was alive. Vines hung from the ceiling—some draped all the way down to the floor. These vines were the tree's arms and hands. Some of the vines were arranging and cataloging the manuscripts. Others were finding books for people. The dance of the dangling foliage was hypnotic in its scale and simplicity of movement. It was magical.

"I've never seen so many books . . . let alone in one place," whispered the boy to the gremlin. Thomas looked upward while he slowly turned. He was completely gobsmacked by the sight. The boy sniffed the air; he could smell books—real books.

The volumes contained in this tree were remarkable. He remembered what his father had said about libraries: *They're antiquated Thomas . . . remnants of a fleeting time in history when man had no choice but to use such primitive forms of communicating ideas.* Now every written work that had ever been published could be accessed wirelessly through one's wristcom. This did not stop Thomas from seeking out actual books. They were more tactile, more real. He rejoiced in turning the pages with childlike hope and reckless wonder. There was a certain promise of adventure that did not come across by simply paging down a screen. Holding an author's work in his hands had made him feel more a part of the story. This place made him feel at ease.

He looked back down and saw that the rest of the group had continued on without him. The group walked towards an elevator. "Hey, wait up." Thomas hurried to catch up.

The common pillar that housed the elevator shot up from the ground and continued straight up to the ceiling. Multiple floors broke off of this central tube. Each floor was connected by thick vines that formed twisted natural stairways. At the base of the cylinder was a set of elevator doors. They slid open to reveal a sharply dressed Pachyderm standing upright, though crouching a little. *An elephant man?* thought Thomas. *Narsh.*

The Elephant seemed to barely fit inside the spacious elevator. "This way, my friends," said the Elephant as his trunk held back the persistent doors. Thomas did his best not to stare, but the creature was amazing. Everyone crowded into the already overstuffed elevator.

Wiyaloo stayed outside. "I shall take the stairs." The ghost vanished in a whirl of smoke.

"Is this him, Anson . . . is this Thomas Scargen?" the Elephant eagerly asked.

"Yes, Onjamba, it is."

"Pleasure to meet you, Thomas." The Elephant extended his trunk, and the boy paused for a moment, confused. The Elephant studied LINC for a few seconds. "Simply remarkable."

"You're a talking elephant," said Thomas as he looked up at the Pachyderm.

"Nothing gets by you," said Yareli as she rolled her eyes.

Thomas reached out his hand and shook the tip of the Elephant's trunk like a hand. The doors glided shut. "It's nice to meet you . . . Onjamba."

"At your service. If you need anything, don't hesitate to ask." Without warning, the Elephant's trunk pushed the uppermost button on the holographic controls on the elevator. "Next stop: the penthouse." The tightly packed capsule rocketed skyward. It abruptly stopped, and the doors opened. Everyone seemed jarred except Onjamba who had not moved. "Top floor." The Elephant pried himself out of the compartment first. The rest of them filed out.

They had reached the top of the baobab. The level was enormous. The bookshelves at this height were swollen with the most ancient of volumes. Several of the guards stood at the opening of the elevator, still as marble—energy axes in hand. If not for the slight rise and fall of their chests, Thomas would mistake these soldiers for statues. Their uniforms were slightly different from the guards on the ground level, and they had yet another different emblem on their armor

"More Leopards," said Thomas to Yareli.

"Actually, Thomas, they are Cheetahs," said Yareli.

"You shouldn't judge people," said the boy with a smile on his face. She turned away. "Come on, how can you tell the difference?"

"A cheetah has a taller, more slender build and has solid black spots. It is also the fastest animal in the world," said LINC. "A leopard, on the other hand, is a smaller and stronger felid whose spots are in a rosette pattern. The major difference is the black tear marks that extend down the cheetah's face. The leopard has no such lines."

"Oh, that does make it pretty easy to tell them apart," said Thomas. The artif looked at the boy, and his optics blinked.

The Elephant parted the sea of protection, and the others followed. Each member of the guard eyed up the boy as he walked in the Elephant's wake.

"What are they looking at?" the boy asked. "They look hungry."

"Pay no attention to the Sentry Mages, Thomas. It's their job to be suspicious. Don't take it personally," said Yareli as she passed on his left. Wiyaloo materialized next to her as she moved forward.

"Well if you ask me, Tommy, dere all a bunch of tossers anyway." Malcolm made a sudden movement towards one and was instantly next to the Cheetah, fangs extended. The Sentry did not so much as blink. "Bloody good at their jobs dough." He patted Thomas on his right shoulder as he walked by.

Anson grabbed his left shoulder. "Are you ready?"

"I don't know . . . I mean those things I did were by accident . . . mostly, and the others more than helped . . . I didn't do anything really."

"Modest doubt is called the beacon for the wise." Anson smiled and then proceeded to join the others who had sat themselves down at a large, circular wood table at one end of the grand floor. A massive round door was situated directly behind the head of the table. The strange symbol that adorned the armor of the Cheetahs was inset in the middle of the door. Two rather sizeable Sentry Mages were posted on either side of the peculiar entry. The same strange symbol appeared on their armor. They too were Cheetahs.

A loud knocking erupted from behind the odd door, interrupting the boy's ponderings. The Sentry Mages did not budge, but Thomas jumped back, and Fargus nearly fell off his shoulder. "Did you hear that?" asked Thomas to Fargus.

"Hear what? I can't hear a bloody fing."

"You don't hear that constant knocking noise?"

"I fink you've gone daft," said Fargus.

"That wouldn't surprise me at this point," said Thomas.

The boy, the gremlin, and the robot stood at the front of the intimidating assembly.

Three people sat at the far end of the table that Thomas did not recognize. There was a large Lion standing behind them. *He looks scary*, thought the boy. He was dressed similarly to the guards on this floor, but his demeanor and the large sword sheathed on his back suggested a higher rank.

Seated to the left was a tall, thin man with a pointy nose that curved slightly downward. His skin was chalk-white and distinct dark circles surrounded his eyes. His long fingers were intertwined in front of his upright form. His expression suggested that he was not amused.

To the right was a plump woman who was fumbling with a small statue between her sausage-like fingers. She was Hawaiian from what

Thomas could tell. She seemed childlike to the boy—the polar opposite of the pale, gaunt man.

In the center was an old black man covered in brilliant green robes. The little hair he had remaining was pure white. His right arm was hidden underneath the folds of his clothing, and he held a knotty wooden walking stick in his left. The top of this staff housed a green gem. Thomas knew immediately that this was the man who had sent for him.

"Thomas Scargen of New Salem . . ." The dark man's voice echoed soothingly as he stood with a push off of the stick. The rapping noise coming from behind him immediately ceased. "I am High Mancer Ziza Bebami. I am the leader of the Council of Mages. Welcome to Sirati: my vision, my dream, and my home—in time maybe yours as well." Ziza walked over to the boy. "Introductions are in order." He pointed to the pale man with the elongated nose. "This is Mancer Elgin Neficus. He specializes in dark magic."

"Hello, Elgin," said Thomas. The scrawny man stood, and the boy followed his example.

"Pleasure," said Neficus as he looked away from the boy. "I guess we are on a first-name basis already."

"Leave him alone, Elgin," said the pudgy woman. "He hasn't even been here for an hour yet."

"I told you, Ziza, that he is not the one," said Neficus, ignoring the woman's words. "He is just a boy."

"I believe that has yet to be determined," said Ziza. Neficus lowered himself back into his chair. "This is Kekoa Lolani. She is also a Mancer." The boy sat up almost at attention.

"Hello, Mancer Lolani."

"Welcome, Thomas. Your light is beautiful."

The boy didn't quite know how to respond to that statement. "Thank you?" said Thomas to the large woman.

Ziza motioned to the Lion standing behind the old man. "This is Emfalmay. He is a Mage Knight and the voice of the Animals here in Sirati. He is also my personal bodyguard—not that I need protecting. I can manage by myself." The wrinkled man smiled.

"I know, High Mancer," said Emfalmay. He looked at Thomas and nodded his head. Thomas returned the gesture.

"And last but not least, my busy friend here, Flora." A vine shot down next to Thomas and extended itself like a hand waiting for a handshake. The boy shook the plant's appendage. When he let go of the vine, it shot straight back up and continued its duties. "She helps me keep all of this in order." Ziza motioned to the immense volumes of books that lined the interior of the tree. "I believe you have met the rest." Thomas scanned the room and the unlikely companions he had acquired over the last few days.

"Now I'm sure you are wondering why you are here. We will get to that shortly, I assure you, but first, Thomas, tell me about this dream of yours."

17

flatmates

"Your dream is perplexing," said Ziza as he paced. "There are only two conceivable possibilities that come to mind." He cupped his chin with his hand. "The first is that it is just a dream, and your father's lack of communication is easily explained. His wristcom might be damaged or destroyed. He could be somewhere without reception, but I am sure you must have already considered these things.

"The second is more distressing, and I'm afraid it is my first inclination considering your father's disappearance." He looked Thomas in the eyes. "Your dream was a premonition—or a seeing of events."

"Is that common?" asked Thomas. That is what it had felt like to the boy, but he had dismissed it as an impossibility.

"Not common, but not unheard of," said the High Mancer. "But you are not common, Thomas Scargen." Ziza smiled. "I cannot be certain of your father's fate without further introspection. I will have to think on this longer." He walked back towards his chair. "One thing is for certain: we must discover who this hooded man is." The look on the old man's face was one of sincere concern.

"Do you think my father's all right?"

"It is hard to say." He paced using his staff. "I believe the answer will emerge if we exercise patience."

"I'm not here for patience. I'm here to find my father, and I was told you were the guy that could help me."

"I can help you, Thomas, but I fear your eagerness to act may be detrimental to your goal."

"In what way?" asked Thomas.

"You are not ready to face the man from your dreams."

"But you said you weren't sure if it was a dream or not."

"No, it was definitely a dream, Thomas, but that does not mean it did not really happen, and if it did in fact happen, then you are not capable of handling a Necromancer of that level."

"Remind me again: what's a Necromancer?"

"A Necromancer is a high level Dark Mage."

"Like a bad version of you guys?"

"Not always, Thomas. There are always exceptions. Mancer Neficus is a Necromancer."

Why does that not surprise me? thought the boy.

"The kind of magic you described can only be harnessed by uncommonly powerful men, and there are not too many of us." The fact that Ziza Bebami grouped himself with this man was unnerving to Thomas. "The hooded figure in your dream sounds like a possible associate of Grayden Arkmalis. From every indication, he is a Necromancer. It is possible that he had prior knowledge of this artifact your father had found and was waiting for his chance to steal the black stone." He walked over to Thomas once again. "We do know that Arkmalis has been recruiting agents. For what end, we are not certain. He has spent the last several years strengthening his fleet of Riders, and now seeks support from other Necromancers and magic potentials."

"Magic potentials?" questioned Thomas.

"Untapped potential that he can manipulate, like yourself, Thomas." The old man stared into Thomas's eyes. "We believe that is why he wants you so desperately. He needs you to accomplish his plan, whatever that may be." Ziza continued to pace, leaning on the gnarled staff. "Which brings us to why you are here. Whatever Arkmalis's plans are, we are going to need your help fighting him.

But as it stands now, you are not equipped to face this hooded man, let alone Arkmalis." The old man paused. "But if you were to stay here and train, I promise you, we can help you, and in turn you could help us."

"Train?"

"What you have done is only the beginning, Thomas. You have great abilities you have not even begun to imagine. These abilities will take some time and persistence to mature. We can help you awaken these powers and show you how to use them properly."

"If I say yes, will you do everything you can to help me find my father?"

"Of course, Thomas. I will help you even if you do not say yes. I fear that without this training, your father's whereabouts would matter little. Like I said before, there seem to be powerful men involved."

"Count me in," said Thomas. Ziza smiled, as did everyone, with the exception of Elgin Neficus. The boy wondered if this man had ever smiled.

"So . . . what now?" asked Thomas.

"You should get some sleep," answered Ziza.

"Why? I'm not even tired," said the boy. "It's like middle of the afternoon, and I just got to frickin' Magic Town. I want to see everything."

"In due time, my boy . . . in due time. Now you need to get some rest. Onjamba will show you to your new home. I think you will find the accommodations comfortable."

"Yeah, but why can't I do that later?"

"Your training starts tonight, Thomas." The boy's eyes met the old man's. "And vampires are stronger in the evening. You are going to want to be at your best." His eyes shifted to Malcolm's.

"We're gonna see if you can catch me, Tommy, aren't we?" said the smiling vampire. The boy's grin reversed. "Don't look so glum, mate. You got till dawn." Thomas turned back to Ziza.

"Your power is great, there is no denying that, but you are still slow, and the reports of the Nicolas Gorter incident suggest a lack of control." The boy thought of Gorter's life that he had lived in an instant. He still felt so much pain and guilt for what he had done. He felt like he had to defend himself.

"I don't know . . . I outran those Hunters," argued Thomas.

"You will be facing things far more powerful and faster than mere Hunters, my boy."

"Trust me. Do what he says." Yareli had a serious look on her face. Her words were wrapped in experience. He looked at Anson for a second opinion.

"Sleep that knits up the ravelled sleave of care, the death of each day's life, sore labour's bath, balm of hurt minds, great nature's second course, chief nourisher in life's feast," said the werewolf.

"I guess that means I should take a nap?"

"In a word, Thomas . . . yes." Anson smirked and then patted the boy on the back. "Welcome aboard. You are officially a Cadet Mage." Everyone stood up from the table and began to applaud.

"Cadet Mage?" asked Thomas.

"It's the first rank for a Mage in training," answered Yareli. "Don't worry. I'm sure you'll be a Mage Warrior like Malcolm and me in no time. That's if you don't kill yourself first."

"Thanks . . . I think."

"It's time, Thomas," said Ziza. "I will see you later in the evening for your first training session. Meet me behind Maktaba at precisely 3:30 AM. There is a clearing a few hundred feet into the jungle." Ziza walked away from the circular table. The boy took a deep breath as Onjamba motioned to follow him. The Elephant was holding a plant in his arm as the two of them walked towards the elevator. Thomas could not help but feel a little nervous as the elevator doors shut.

The Elephant and the boy had been walking for some time through the streets and pathways of Sirati. Onjamba walked upright, lumbering next to Thomas, holding the odd-looking potted plant. LINC trailed slightly behind. The city was amazing to the boy. It was the perfect mix of nature and tech, but at the moment Thomas could not appreciate it. He was preoccupied with a particular phrase he had heard at Maktaba, and it was gnawing at his brain. He decided to take the Elephant up on his offer of helping him with whatever he needed. "So, Onjamba, what did Neficus mean when he called me *the one?*"

"If my sensors were working properly—and they always are—I am fairly certain that Mancer Elgin Neficus actually said, 'I told you, Ziza, that he is not the one.'" His head rotated in the boy's direction. "'He's just a boy,'" said LINC, sounding exactly like Neficus.

"Thanks, LINC. That was very helpful," said Thomas.

"You are quite welcome, Thomas Scargen," said LINC.

"What I was trying to say is: what's *the one* thing all about, Onjamba?"

"Well, Thomas, it's simple really. He thinks you can make a difference—the High Mancer, I mean. Ziza began to sense your power a few years ago."

"A few years ago? How's that even possible?"

"The High Mancer is strangely attuned to potential power levels. He is incredibly adept at it actually, and your readings were unbelievable."

"Narsh. So why didn't I get my acceptance letter sooner?"

"When I said your power level is unbelievable, I meant just that. We would have contacted you sooner, but there was a difference of opinion among the Council. Some questioned your readiness—and Ziza's reading."

"Neficus," said Thomas.

"It wasn't just him; there were others. But I wouldn't take it personally. It's rare when someone your age is as powerful as you are. Your energy had not manifested itself, and there were some who doubted Ziza's word. If there's one thing I know about Ziza, though, it's that he's right an awful lot more than he's wrong." Onjamba plucked what looked like a dead leaf off of the strange plant with his trunk.

"Am I the first?"

Onjamba laughed so hard he almost dropped his shrub. "That's very funny, Thomas." The Elephant caught his breath. "Ziza has been searching a long time for someone with your potential. All the people here have been handpicked by High Mancer Bebami to live in peace with the Animals. Some of the inhabitants here are truly exceptional, like you, Yareli, the twins. Others have no where else to go, and still others' families have lived here for many years before we were transformed and Sirati was created. But everyone belongs here; everyone has a purpose in Sirati."

"Yeah, how did that happen?"

"It was Ziza's will and his unusual capacity to wield his power."

"He's more powerful than he looks, huh?" asked Thomas. The Elephant nodded.

"That's one way of putting it," said Onjamba. They crossed a wooden bridge over a gurgling creek. Like all the architecture in the city, the bridge seemed to be a part of the natural landscape. "But enough of that. The High Mancer likes to let his students find their own way before he explains things in full. It's his sink-or-swim method, I believe he calls it. I have already said too much, but I figured we're going to be flatmates so I should let you in on some things."

Flatmates? thought Thomas.

The stone path they were walking on led directly to a tree grove. The trees were large, but not as big as Maktaba. Large vines connected the trees, doubling as walkways and staircases interconnecting the copse. People and Animals were moving along the walkways and stairs, in and out of the baobabs. The trees were houses, shops, and restaurants. Together they formed a remarkable natural community.

They approached one of the trees on the edge of the forest. As they got closer, Thomas could see a huge door embedded into the base of the trunk. The door had a circular window at eye level. "Here we are," proclaimed Onjamba. The boy and the Pachyderm stopped in front of the entrance. Thomas looked up to see a balcony on the second floor of the massive treehouse.

"Where's here?"

"My sensors are incapable of ascertaining our current latitude and longitude."

"LINC, that's not what I was asking." LINC's optics fluttered. Thomas turned back to the Elephant. "I mean what is this place?"

"The Grove, Thomas. We're home," answered Onjamba.

"I get to live in a treehouse," said Thomas as he looked straight up into the leaved canopy. "That is entirely narsh."

Onjamba searched his pockets with his trunk. His face indicated that he could not find what he was looking for. "Hold this, will ya?" He shoved the plant into the boy's abdomen. "Ahh." He pulled the keys out of his front right vest pocket. "Here they are." The plant chomped in Thomas's direction.

"You want your bush back now? I don't think it likes me."

"Nope. It's your bush now. It's a housewarming gift."

"Thanks . . . Onjamba." Thomas pushed the plant away as it tried to bite him again, and he handed off the shrub to LINC.

"Don't mention it, roomy." He unlocked the door with the keys that were nestled in his trunk's hand.

"What a peculiar specimen," said the artif, analyzing the plant as it attempted to take a bite out of him.

"It's a hybrid I created: half Venus Flytrap, half lily. I call it a Saber-toothed Lily. It's like a Tiger Lily with a bit more bite."

"Well it's beautiful, Onjamba," said Thomas. The Elephant opened the door.

"Welcome." His trunk invited Thomas into the home with a cordial sweeping motion. The boy walked through the threshold and was immediately greeted by an unexpected friend.

"Meow," said Stella. His cat had somehow made her way to Africa. The feline rubbed up on Thomas's leg. The boy leaned over and picked her up. She purred in his arms as he nuzzled her.

"The team Ziza had sent to your house to investigate found her," said Onjamba.

"Investigate?" asked Thomas.

"To study or observe by close examination and systematic inquiry," said LINC.

"I know what it means," said the boy as he turned towards the artif. "Are these the guys trying to find my father?" asked Thomas.

"Yes, but they did not find much. The Riders had tossed the place, but most things were still in good working order. They found Stella hiding under your bed. She obviously had been frightened. You poor thing."

"Don't encourage her." Onjamba petted her with his trunk, but after a few seconds, Stella had had enough. She clawed Thomas, so he put the furry beast on the ground.

"I miss you too. You're a little monster, you know that?" Thomas stood back up and got a good look at the first floor. Everything was appropriately oversized, considering Onjamba's bulk. It was stunning and immaculate as well, and there was a generous amount of vegetation for the interior of a house.

"I love cats, I must tell you," said the Elephant.

"Really?"

"Yes, we share a common enemy." This statement intrigued Thomas.

"And that would be?"

"Mice, Thomas. Stupid little rodents. We are both, in fact, natural mice haters. Isn't that right, Stella?"

"Meoow." The feline answered promptly as she lapped out of her water bowl made from a coconut.

"I thought that was a myth. I mean look at the size of you."

"Don't let their size fool you, Thomas."

"Come on, Onjamba, you're like eight feet tall."

"He is approximately seven feet, ten inches," interrupted LINC. "Considerably undersized for a male pachyderm, actually."

"Does he always do that?" asked Onjamba as he turned and pointed at the artif.

"I'm afraid so, but don't try to change the subject."

"There just so . . . icky . . . I don't know, I just hate them, ew." They both laughed. It was the funniest thing he had heard in a long time. "Seriously though, I hate them."

"Can I ask you something kind of serious?"

"Shoot."

"What happened to Ziza's arm?"

"I am definitely not allowed to talk about that, but let's just say he fought a formidable but mad Necromancer. It was an extraordinary battle, but it did not have a happy ending for either man. Both paid a great price that day . . . but that's all I can tell you, Thomas."

"Come on, Onjamba. That's not fair. You have to tell me more than that."

"I may be the Sirati historian, but it is not my tale to tell. Rest assured, Ziza will tell you himself in due time."

"I get it."

"I'm glad you understand. You should be getting some sleep anyway. Let me show you your room."

They walked up the spiraling staircase to the next floor. They reached a landing that opened up into a large bedroom. "Lights on," said the Elephant. The lights in the room turned on. "This is your room." Onjamba motioned with his trunk.

"It's huge." He surveyed his room. One side of the room was made up of large, natural windows. There appeared to be no glass in the openings, but Thomas knew a force field when he saw one.

"What's with the force field?" asked the boy.

"It's mostly to keep the bugs out, but it can also help with the noise at night."

"Sound dampeners, that's ingenious."

"This place is more than just magical, Thomas."

Between the windows a door opened up to a large balcony that wrapped around half of the tree. He moved over to the windows and looked out at the jungle view. The tree's natural awning shaded the balcony and most of The Grove.

Stella rubbed against Thomas's leg and jumped up on the bed. She nestled into the sheets. He immediately recognized the bed as the one from his house. He began to look around and noticed that most of his stuff had been moved here. The boy smiled as he looked at the Pachyderm. "It's perfect, Onjamba."

"Stella wasn't the only thing we rescued. We thought if you had some of your things it might make the transition a little . . . easier." Thomas ran over and grabbed his hockey stick.

"I never thought I would see this again." He rolled the stick in his fist and pantomimed a shot. "He scores." Thomas raised his hands like he was celebrating a goal. He could almost smell the ice. He leaned the stick against the wall and plopped on the bed. Stella meowed in protest. The cat came back around and nuzzled next to the boy. He looked over at the nightstand and his copy of *Dragon's Omen* stared back at him. He grabbed it and paged through it. He stopped at the bookmarked page where he had stopped reading the night this all began. He looked at Onjamba. "It almost seems silly now."

"There is nothing silly about losing yourself in a good book."

"I suppose you have a point." He smiled at the Pachyderm.

"Well, you should be getting some rest," said Onjamba as he backed out of the doorway, pulling the door shut.

"Thanks, Onjamba . . . for everything." The Elephant popped his head back into the room.

"You're quite welcome, Thomas." He shut the door behind him. Thomas could hear his heavy footsteps going down the stairs.

"I guess I should try and take a nap."

"That is the course of action the elderly man had suggested earlier," chimed the artif as he placed the odd plant on the bedside table. The plant made a move towards Stella, and the cat batted at the opened mouth of the Saber-toothed Lily.

"You two play nice," said the boy as he lay down into his groove on the bed. "Good night, LINC."

"Thomas, it is only 4:35 PM." The boy laughed out loud and rolled on his side. He did not even want to try and explain this figure of speech.

"Good afternoon then, LINC." He felt Stella purring next to him as he formed his pillow. He scratched the cat's head behind her ears. This place was already beginning to feel like home. For a moment, everything in the world was perfect. The only thing that was missing was his father. He lifted his wristcom and hit a few keys on the virtual interface. Thomas gestured with his hand, and the pictures his father had sent him spread out around him. *Where are you, Dad?* The question haunted the boy. He stared at them for a few minutes, looking for an answer. Nothing. He closed the folder. *Wherever you are, Dad, I hope you're okay.* "Lights off." The room darkened as much as it could for midafternoon. A gentle wind touched his face as the boy closed his eyes and slowly succumbed to slumber.

18

to catch a predator

Thomas woke to a rapping noise. His new room was deep-space black except for the glowing lights on LINC. The usual nightly scans were still running as the artif hibernated. Stella purred next to Thomas. The cat seemed happy to have her human pillow back. The boy yawned and blinked his eyes, adjusting to the darkness. He heard the noise again. LINC whistled to life, brandishing his turrets as a precaution. The sounds of gears and moving parts filled the room. Stella jumped off the bed and hid. "Are you in danger, Thomas Scargen?"

"No, LINC, I am fine. Please put those away." The artif's arms collapsed into hands again.

"As you wish, Thomas Scargen. I was merely responding to a perceived threat. After further evaluation, it seems the threat has passed." There was another knock. The boy and the artif turned towards the noise. Thomas could now discern where the noise originated. Fargus was perched on Bartleby's snout, knocking on his balcony door.

Thomas walked out onto the balcony. The dragon was lying on the ground with his head extended even with the balcony. "Hey, Bart, how are you? What's up?"

"I'm good, Thomas. My . . . business took less time than I originally fought it would. I'm about to 'ed 'ome actually, and I just wanted to stop and say goodbye."

"You didn't have to do that."

"I beg to differ."

"Well thanks, Bart."

"My pleasure, Thomas. I also just wanted to say dat I'm proud of what I done 'ere, getting you to Ziza. Don't tell dem, but I might 'av done it for nuffin' if dey 'ad asked." The dragon smiled proudly. "Dese people are good, Thomas, and dey can 'elp you. You are goin' to do amazing fings. Somefing is special about you."

"I don't know about that, Bart. Thanks for all you've done, and make sure you tell Hawthorne I said hi, and hopefully we'll meet again soon."

"I would like dat, Thomas Scargen. I would like dat." The dragon's eyes crossed as he looked at the gremlin. "Say goodbye, Fargus."

"Goodbye, Fargus," said the gremlin. He started to whistle as he played with his little device. "Good luck an that. In the end, you were quite aw'right, actually."

"Goodbye, Thomas, and knock 'em dead."

"See you guys," said the boy as the dragon took off into the night sky. Bartleby streaked through the checkpoint and through a tear in the atmosphere. The boy looked at his wristcom. It read 2:45 AM. "Bed's all yours, Stella. I gotta get ready to chase a vampire." He stretched his arms above his head as he yawned and walked back into his room. The absurdity of his last statement made him laugh.

"Meeeow," answered Stella as she blinked and rubbed her mid-section against his legs. She hopped back into bed.

It took the boy longer to reach Maktaba than he had remembered. Even with the lighted orbs that lined the pathways of Sirati, he had found it difficult to find his way back. *Everything looks the same this time of night in a jungle.* He found the path Ziza had spoken of and continued down it. His stomach began to feel the weight of what was about to happen. He took a deep breath and looked through the dense foliage. The boy could see a clearing ahead.

Ziza was standing in a ring surrounded by unlit torches. "Hello, Thomas." His words reverberated in Thomas's head. With a lift of his staff, the torches ignited with magical fire.

"Hello, High Mancer. Where's Malcolm?"

"I 'ope you are ready for dis, Tommy," asked Malcolm. The bushes were still swaying from where he had made his speedy entrance.

"Ready as I'll ever be." The words sounded more confident than the boy felt.

"Good, well go on den."

"What?" asked the boy, bewildered.

"Try and catch me."

"That's it?"

"You make it sound so easy, Tommy."

"So all I have to do is touch you?"

"It's simple, isn't it?" Thomas lunged at the vampire, but before he could make contact, Malcolm had moved. He reappeared ten feet away, lighting a cigarette. "You got to be kidding me, Tommy. Ya gonna 'av to move a bit quicker den dat to catch a vampire, son, especially one as old—and I might add, incredibly handsome—as me." Malcolm took a drag from his cigarette. "Unlike you blood bags, we tend ta get a bit stronger wif age."

"Try pushing yourself forward, similarly to when you landed from the roof, but project that energy behind you," instructed Ziza.

"Oh, okay . . . let's try this again." Thomas collected his thoughts.

"I'm ready whenever you are." The vampire giggled as he inhaled again. Thomas pushed himself the way Ziza explained, but he fell over onto the ground.

I can do this, thought Thomas as he dusted himself off.

"Remember, he has another advantage over you, Thomas. It is important to always know your enemy's strengths—sometimes more than your own." Thomas thought hard on what Ziza meant, and then it came to him.

"He can see in the dark, right?"

"Correct." Thomas lowered his goggles. They automatically switched to night vision.

Thanks, Lenore, he thought to himself. He gazed around him and finally read the cold signature of the vampire. He was puffing away on his cigarette.

"Here goes nothing." This time Thomas propelled himself perfectly at Malcolm. The vampire stepped out of the way at the last second. The boy could not stop, and he crashed into a tree. "I think I got this now." The boy was rubbing his red nose. A blur passed in front of his face, and he took off after Malcolm. He could feel himself gaining on the vampire. He pushed even harder. Thomas was moving on instinct now, and his instincts were impressive.

"You are fast for a 'uman, Tommy." Thomas was a mere five feet behind Malcolm.

"Why are you smiling if you know I'm gonna catch you?"

"I, unlike you, 'av not used magic yet, 'av I?" The vampire took off into the night. Thomas focused and released. He was now rocketing at unpredictable speeds, nearly colliding with every tree and rock. He focused harder on keeping his balance. Again the boy accelerated, one blur chasing another blur.

Hours passed and Thomas found himself no closer to catching the vampire. He started to think that tagging Malcolm might be impossible. His body began to ache. Thomas could not keep up this pace. The boy stopped running. His breath was exaggerated, panting like a dog.

Ziza appeared next to him. The old man lifted up Thomas's head and pushed in his stomach with the staff, forcing him to stand up straight. "Now . . . try controlling your breath. In through your nostrils as your belly goes out, then out through your nose as it retracts." Thomas did as he said and his breathing slowed. He felt instantly refreshed. "It is something everyone does, but few do properly. Many go their whole lives forgetting how we were meant to breathe. I have made it easier for you for tonight, but without practice and patience, your body will forget." Thomas's body flowed with new energy.

"Thank you, High Mancer."

"Please, call me Ziza. Now how do you plan to catch Malcolm? Dawn swiftly approaches."

"I don't know. He's fast."

"You have matched him at his strengths, but this will take more. Malcolm has but one true weakness, Thomas." The old man paused. "Know your enemy's weaknesses. They, too, can become your strength." Before the boy could ask what weakness he spoke of, the old man vanished in a swirl of leaves.

He stood there, alone amongst the trees. For the first time during the chase, Thomas could hear the sounds of the jungle. He pondered what Ziza had told him, but could only think of the traditional weaknesses of vampires. *I can't stake him. I don't have garlic or a crucifix. I'm totally screwed.* Malcolm zipped by the boy.

"Come on, Tommy, I 'avn't got all bloody night, do I?" said Malcolm.

Thomas took off after the swift vampire. The breathing technique Ziza had shown him gave him a new burst of energy. He was reaching astonishing speeds, but it seemed whenever the boy caught up to Malcolm, he would bank in a different direction and avoid the boy's tag. Thomas would adjust his course, but at these speeds, he would lose valuable time and would have to waste more energy trying to catch up. The boy realized that this was not going to work. The sun was on the verge of peeking over the horizon, and the test would be over soon. *I can't fail on my first test. Think, Thomas, think. What is his weakness?* He stopped abruptly, digging slightly into the forest floor. "I got it," said the boy.

He ran in the general direction of Malcolm, but not at full speed. *It's so simple. I can't believe I didn't think of it sooner.* He was swiftly approaching a thicket of thorn bushes he had remembered seeing earlier. Thomas extended his right hand and pricked the top of his index finger. He felt a slight stabbing pain in his fingertip. The boy stumbled and rolled on the ground. Thomas grabbed his injured hand. The boy writhed in pain.

Malcolm stopped running and was now only fifty feet away from Thomas. The boy panted and acted as though he was exhausted. The look of total need occupied the vampire's bloodthirsty eyes as he instinctively made a move towards the hemorrhaging boy. Malcolm could not seem to control himself and lunged at the boy. Thomas smiled. *Human blood is his weakness*, he thought. The boy side-stepped the advancing vampire and placed his left hand on Malcolm's right shoulder. "Got ya." The realization of Thomas's ploy washed over the vampire's pale face.

"You little—" said Malcolm. "You're a clever little git, aren't you?"

"I just exploited . . . your . . . weakness?" Thomas held his injured hand as the light from the sun's first beam whispered on the horizon.

"Well done, Tommy," said Malcolm. His eyes darted back and forth from Thomas's eyes to his bleeding hand. "But I gotta get out of 'ere before I act on my . . . animalistic urges. Ziza is waiting for you at Maktaba." Malcolm winked and disappeared into a blur. The boy began walking back to the oversized baobab tree. He had done enough running for one night. Thomas grinned. He had done it. He had caught his first vampire and passed his first test.

19

spellbound

T homas made his way back to Maktaba. He took the elevator to the top floor. The doors opened up to an empty hallway. The same two Sentry Mages stood at attention next
to the odd door at the head of the table. The conference table was
empty. The same faint sound began to ring from behind the circular
door. The boy stared at the opening. *What is that?* he wondered. The
arrival of Onjamba interrupted his thoughts. He appeared in front of
Thomas holding a serving tray. "Hello, Thomas."

"Hi, Onjamba."

"I thought you might be hungry after your first night of training." The Elephant lowered the covered tray in his hand. Thomas
could see a distorted version of himself in its metallic reflection.
Onjamba lifted the cover with his trunk. There was a meticulously
made triple-tiered peanut butter and banana sandwich on a palm
leave at the center of the silver serving platter. The boy grabbed the
stacked sandwich.

"Thanks, Onjamba . . . I'm starving." Thomas took a huge bite
and began to chew. He paused before he swallowed. "This is freakin'
delicious. Are there Chef Mages here too?" asked Thomas with a smile.

"Actually, I made it—never forget a recipe." The Elephant's trunk
tapped his head.

"Is there anything you are not good at?"

"I'll have to get back to you on that." The pounding echoed from the circular door once again.

"Do you hear that noise?" the boy wondered aloud.

"Hear what?"

"That loud pounding noise."

"I don't hear anything, and if I can't hear it . . ." He lifted his oversized ears. "Then it's not making a sound."

Am I going crazy? thought Thomas. "I guess I'm just exhausted."

"The High Mancer will see you now. He's just up the staircase in his study."

"Thanks, Onjamba," said Thomas as he took another bite of his sandwich and began to walk up the stairs.

"Hide-and-seek," said the Elephant abruptly.

"What was that?"

"Something I'm not terribly good at, Thomas, hide-and-seek. Yes, apparently being a massive mammal with huge ears makes it hard for one to find places suitable for hiding oneself." He shrugged his shoulders. "Bye, Thomas." The Pachyderm smiled as he turned towards the elevator.

"See ya later, Onjamba," said the boy as he laughed. He then pulled himself up to the next step. The railings—like all of Sirati's architecture—looked like a natural part of the tree. He once again heard a faint sound coming from the mysterious circular door. Thomas could not help but wonder what was being concealed.

Thomas reached the top of the root staircase. It opened up to the middle of a large open-aired branch landing. Above the boy, the wind rushed through the great branches. Thomas looked over to the extending branch and saw a knothole the size of a door, but there was no way to get up there. He moved closer and looked down at the distant ground. "Good thing I'm not afraid of heights," said the boy as he took another bite from his sandwich. The branch began to move as another large vine moved to form a natural stairway leading up to the knothole. As he cautiously walked up the stairs, he looked out over Sirati and could see the sun rise. Thomas saw colors he had never seen before as the sun found its way up into the morning sky. It was breathtaking. He reached the knothole doorway and entered.

Emfalmay was walking towards the boy. Thomas nodded, but the Lion passed him without any response. *I guess he's not in the mood for conversation*, thought the boy. Thomas continued into the room.

This room, like the main one, was filled with books. There were stacked books and others carefully arranged in bookshelves along the walls. The study was lit solely by candles. They produced the perfect amount of reading light. Ancient artifacts accompanied the books on the shelves, along with various jars filled with strange specimens. The old man was standing behind a podium that was topped by an enormous book. He was intently reading. The book glowed green, as did Ziza's eyes. The pages turned without him touching them. *I can't wait to learn that trick*, thought Thomas. This place amazed him. The boy clearing his throat broke Ziza's trance.

"Hello, Thomas Scargen of New Salem. Welcome to my study and private library. What you see here are some of the oldest tomes on Earth. The information contained in them is precious, to say the least. You are probably wondering why I have called you here."

"The question had crossed my mind," said Thomas as he looked up at the old man.

"You did well this evening with your training." Thomas smiled at the compliment. Ziza looked directly at the boy. "It is time for you to begin your studies."

Studies? thought Thomas. *What did I sign up for?* He hated studying. It bored him. It's one of the reasons he did so poorly at school. Thomas loved reading out of curiosity, but he did not like being told what to read or think.

"Your studies will be a daily activity and will complement your physical training."

"I thought I was going to be trained so I can find my father. I don't have time for studying. I want to get right into it."

"You will be trained, Thomas, but without understanding your powers and the new world you have entered, physical training will mean little. You must mentally train as well." He motioned with his staff at the surrounding manuscripts. "Books, Thomas, are not just for escaping into magical realms. They are a window to the past. Without them, the knowledge and wisdom of our ancestors would be lost." Ziza continued to read as he spoke. "Knowledge is power, Thomas, and wisdom is an efficient weapon. The more you know, the better prepared you are for when reading is not enough."

"When you put it that way . . ." Thomas took a bite from his sandwich, and Ziza smiled.

"I see your appetite is healthy."

"I'm starving," said the boy while taking another bite. "It's like I haven't eaten for days."

"That's from your energy expenditure. The more power you use, the more fuel you will need."

"I guess that makes sense."

"What did you learn tonight?" The old man looked at Thomas.

"Not to race a vampire, that's for sure." Ziza lifted the corners of his mouth.

"I was referring to how you ultimately caught Malcolm."

"Oh, the blood thing. It just kind of popped into my head," said the boy.

"Like the situation with your father, it benefited you to stop and remove yourself from the chase. You then assessed the situation and developed an effective solution. Sometimes stopping and thinking prevails. You used his weakness as your strength." Ziza turned back to his book. "How's your hand?"

"It hasn't stopped bleeding yet, but it feels fine." The boy moved towards the podium. "What are you reading?"

"The contents of this tome are of no consequence to you."

"Is it one of those boring whodunnits? I can't stand those."

"This is no normal book. You are not ready to read this." Ziza remained focused on his book. "But I have a book for you." One of Flora's vines lowered, clutching a small text. She handed the book to the boy. He looked down at the title etched into the ancient leather book: MAGIC FOR IDIOTS.

"Really?" The boy put the book down on a nearby wooden

table and moved towards Ziza. A vine shot down and halted the boy's advance. A second vine picked up the book Thomas had just put down. The vine in front of him waved as if it was a shaking finger.

"Start with this one," reiterated Ziza. The second vine shoved the book into Thomas's midsection.

"I get it. I get it . . . patience and all." Ziza smiled, but his emerald gaze did not divert from the book on the lit stand. Thomas looked down at the book, and the title had disappeared. Thomas was intrigued. He moved away to a private corner. He sat down in a pillowed, curved booth and made himself comfortable.

He slowly opened his new textbook. The book sprung to life. "Hello, Thomas Scargen," said a voice that originated from the book. The boy jumped backward and slammed the book shut.

"Is there a problem, Thomas?" asked Ziza.

"You didn't hear that?"

"Hear what?"

"The book . . . it-it—it . . . spoke."

"Come now, Thomas."

"It did. It said, 'Hello, Thomas Scargen.'"

"Well it is your book."

"I was just trying to be polite." The book's opening flapped as the words escaped from the pages. The bookmark moved like a tongue. "Most books start with *Introductions* you know."

"Sorry, I'm sort of new."

"Really?" The books sarcasm washed over the boy. "So let's try this again, shall we, provided you don't slam me shut again. You nearly broke my spine."

"I promise." Thomas picked up the book again, and a new title emerged: **THE REPOSITORY OF MAGIC**.

The words were printed in the middle of the cover.

"I thought this might suit you better."

"Yes, thank you."

"Now let's start at the beginning. *Introduction:* I am, for lack of a better title, your spellbook. Any new power, trick, tip, thought, or any bit of information pertaining to the use of magic will be automatically recorded into my pages. This process will happen every time there is physical contact between you and my cover. There are also explanations of certain powers and interesting tidbits of information about the magical world contained on my pages. The number and difficulty of your powers will increase as you develop. As you grow, I grow."

"You mean the better I get, the better you get?"

"Precisely."

This is going to be way cooler than studying. "Let's get started."

"Not so fast. First you must pledge your allegiance to me. It is a ritual that binds us together. And, yes, the puns are always intended."

"Okay, what do I need to do?"

"Your blood seals the deal."

This seemed extreme to Thomas. "I don't know about this . . ."

"It's not as if I have asked you to perform a human sacrifice or to deliver the soul of a demon. I didn't ask you to bring me the eyes of ten dragons like some books would have. I only ask for but a single drop of your blood."

"Some books ask for the other things?"

"Of course . . . well not the soul of a demon thing. Everybody knows demons don't have souls. But you shouldn't concern yourself with these other types of books. They are extremely dangerous, Thomas. Dark things happen when you walk that path, my boy."

"I get it. So what do I need to do?"

"Do you see the hole in the top left corner on the front of me?"

"Yes." Thomas stared at the beveled opening.

"Drip one droplet of your blood into the hole."

"Okay." Thomas pondered for a second before it came to him. He began unraveling the bandage that covered his right index finger. The self-inflicted wound still had not clotted from his race with Malcolm. He squeezed the finger to awaken the cut and turned his finger over the hole. A single drop clung to the top of his pointer finger. The scarlet liquid paused for a split second before losing to gravity. The blood fell through the air and found its target.

The book shook in his hand and fell onto the table in front of him. The cover now glowed in a similar way to Ziza's book but Thomas's color—light blue.

The light radiated inward quickly and began forming a word on the cover of the text. A brand new word now rose from the leather. Thomas edged closer. He felt connected to this book like no other before. The illumination made him squint as he raised his right hand to block the intensity. The glow diminished as the boy looked down onto the book cover. The title now read: SCARGEN'S REPOSITORY OF MAGIC.

"That is enough for one evening, Thomas," said the High Mancer. The man stood in front of the boy with his staff in his left hand. His deformed appendage was hidden in his robes as usual.

"But I was just getting started."

"There will be plenty of time for you to read later." Flora reached down and extended her vine. The boy begrudgingly put the book into her leafy hand.

"Don't worry, Thomas, I bookmarked where we left off," said the book as Flora retreated upward into the shelves.

"Go home and get some well-earned rest. Your next training session will not be so easy."

"Tonight was easy?"

"In the grand scheme of what's to come? I would say yes." The old man smiled. "I too need some rest, my boy. These old bones are not used to all this commotion." Ziza made his way over towards what looked like his bedroom. "I want you to practice what you have learned tonight over the next few days. Remember what we have discussed: patience, breathing, and control. Someone will be in touch with you to continue your training, but until then, I expect to see you here studying every night. Goodbye, Thomas." Ziza moved aside the cloth doorway and vanished into the adjoining room.

"Bye, Ziza." Thomas turned and moved towards the exit. He walked down the large branch and saw Emfalmay looking out over Sirati. He walked towards him. The Lion's tail wriggled behind him. The sun dangled low in the morning sky.

"It's incredible, isn't it?" asked Emfalmay. The boy stood next to the Lion and looked out from Maktaba.

"It's unbelievable. I'm still not sure how any of this is possible."

"This is Ziza's dream come true: nature and humans peacefully coexisting. He used his power to create something that some said was impossible." Thomas turned towards the Lion.

"If you don't mind me asking, how exactly are you possible?"

"We were the key to Ziza's plan. His hope was that in our new forms, it would be easier for man to accept us—to understand that we are the same as them. You see, Scargen, our survival is directly tied to your survival. Life is life, no matter what form it takes, whether it's a baobab tree, a human boy, or a stubborn Lion. It is a precious gift that should never be squandered—a fleeting gift, but the greatest gift there is. That is what Ziza has shown me."

"He seems like a great man," said Thomas.

"He is a great man." The Lion stopped staring out over the jungle and looked at the boy. "Do not waste his time if you are not ready. Appearance aside, he is a very powerful man, but he is over five hundred years old. Another disappointment could kill him."

"I don't intend to disappoint anyone." Thomas paused and thought about how old Ziza was and all the things he had lived through. "You really care for the old man."

"We all do. He freed us." Emfalmay looked back out towards the jungle. "He is my father. Everything I am is because of this man. Without him, Sirati doesn't exist. We don't exist. My pride doesn't exist."

"Your *pride?*" The Lion pointed upward into the canopy of leaves. Thomas looked up and could not see anything. He remembered his goggles and lowered them and immediately saw what Emfalmay was pointing at.

"This is my pride, Scargen, my family." There were fourteen Lions on several tree branches above them. Thomas could discern that most of the Lions were female, with the exception of two younger cubs that seemed to be play-fighting. "They make up Sirati's Elite Guard. We swore an oath some time ago to defend this beautiful city."

"No offense to your family, but isn't that a big job for four-teen Lions."

"There is no offense taken to a good observation. There are more than fourteen of us. My son Emkoo and several of my brothers are running Sirati's perimeter as we speak." He looked up at his pride and his eyes began to glow green, a noticeably lighter green than Ziza. "We are also all adept Mages." As he said this the other Lion's eyes began to glow the same color as Emfalmay's. Thomas lifted up his goggles to see the spectacle with his own eyes. Emfalmay looked at Thomas and his eyes returned to their natural green color. "We have the help of the humans and the other Felid tribes as well. The Cheetahs and Leopards make up most of our Sentry Mages, but there are others."

"This place just gets *more* and *more* amazing." The boy yawned. "Sorry, it's been a long day—or night, depending on what way you look at it."

"You should get some rest." Emfalmay leapt to a higher branch. "You need to be here tomorrow morning to begin your conditioning."

"Conditioning?"

"You will run with my son in the mornings, if you can keep up with him. You need to work on your stamina."

"When do I get to do the cool magic?"

"Hard to say, but if I know Ziza, he's going to be keeping you busy as well. You should sleep whenever time permits." He turned and looked down at the boy. "Until tomorrow, Scargen."

"Goodbye, Emfalmay and Emfalmay's family."

The pride was eerily quiet as Thomas walked towards the confer-ence room. He could hear the faint pounding sound coming from the circular door on his way to the elevator. The two Cheetahs still had not moved an inch. *They are good at their job*, thought Thomas as he entered the elevator. He pushed the ground floor button on the holographic display.

The doors of the elevator shut. He yawned again as he descended to the ground floor. Thomas thought of his day and everything that had happened. It all seemed surreal to him, but one thing had become abundantly clear: he could not wait to get to his bed.

20

the dodgy toadstool

Hawthorne sat across from Lenore at the corner booth of the Dodgy Toadstool. The Toadstool was not the only bar in Dover that was magic friendly, but it was definitely the best one. The place was overflowing. The booth they sat in was situated in the back of the pub. The secluded area was where they always met Ronald Hosselfot.

Lenore stood on the booth's seat leaning up against the table with her hands holding up her head. A straw extended from her lips to a small glass in front of her. She took a sip of her almost empty drink as she surveyed the bar.

Lenore looked over at the bouncers that flanked the entryway. Two gigantic creatures stood guard as people entered the bar. "Somefin's a bit off wif dose two, isn't it?" said Lenore. Both of the creatures were different shades of green, and their arms reached to the ground and dragged behind when they lumbered around the pub. It was hard to tell where their heads ended and their torsos began.

"If you haven't noticed, there are quite a few oddballs in the pub tonight," commented Hawthorne.

"Dey just seem like dey are expecting something. Ja know what I mean?"

"You mean because they keep talking to themselves?"

"No, dat's to be expected from grumblings. I mean, the way dere eyes keep darting around all suspicious like."

"That's their job, Lenore."

"Yeah, I'll be keepin' an eye on dem is all I'm sayin'."

"You do that." Hawthorne looked at the door again and then down at his wristcom. "Hosselfot's gonna be here soon. We're going to do this like usual."

"Why do I always 'av to 'ide before 'ee gets 'ere?" asked the female gremlin. "It's kinda demeaning, isn't it?"

"Well I can't turn invisible, or we could try it that way. I told you before; it always helps to have an ace up your sleeve."

"I fought dat's why I was recording the whole fing." The tiny recon orb flew out of the handheld device she was playing with. The sphere floated over to Hawthorne.

"Ronny and I go way back, but after what happened with Thomas and Yareli . . . I just want to be careful, that's all. And besides, an ace up both sleeves can't hurt." Lenore smirked at Franklin.

"Is it wurf it? I mean 'ee might not uv known about duh 'unters, but 'ee's been compromised now, 'asn't 'ee?" said Lenore.

"Is that what you're all freaked out about?" asked Hawthorne.

"Well, can 'ee be trusted? "

"I hear what you're saying, and part of the reason we are here is to hear Ronny's side of the story. Besides, Thomas and Yareli both said it wasn't him. It was the Frenchman."

"Who I never liked, by the way."

"I know, Lenore."

"I just 'av a bad feeling is all I'm trying to say," said the gremlin. "You know I 'av a sixth sense."

"There's only one problem. He's the only guy in England that can get his hands on the dragon tech we need." He looked away from Lenore and then back. "He also has the best prices," admitted Hawthorne as he winked at her.

"I get it. I get it." She finished the remnants of her beverage. "Dat's me done. You want another?" She placed the device back into its holster. The orb continued to flit around Franklin's head.

"That's a dumb question." Hawthorne drank from his glass. "I'll be done this before you get back."

"I suppose you will." She hopped down onto the slate floor and began her tiny-stepped walk to the bar. She squinted her eyes, staring at the grumblings as she passed. One of them grinned at her. She scowled in disgust and moved towards the bar.

The bar area was busy. Strange creatures were interspersed with a dozen humans in the smoky pub. Conversations riddled the air while several people fought for optimal position to get the bartender's attention. A goblin band played off to the left. They were playing a slow, rhythmic tune with bizarre instruments. The band members were covered with caked-on mud. *Bog goblins*, she thought as she reached the bar. Lenore walked up the narrow stairway that had been provided for the smaller patrons. When she reached the top, she deposited the empties on the bar. She nearly knocked over a leprechaun who was smoking a curved pipe that smelled suspiciously like Bartleby's dragonweed. She fanned the smoke aside as she moved down the bar top. She looked back at the table, and Hawthorne waved. *I 'ate being invisible for dese meetings, but I do fancy the Toadstool.* She turned back around and motioned to the bartender.

The bartender was an artif—a bottender. It was made to do one thing: serve drinks as fast as possible. *This robot gots nuffin' on LINC*, she thought. Still, the design was brilliant. *Definitely a Scargen.* If gremlins appreciated anything, it was fine craftsmanship. The multi-armed android was making five different cocktails. One of the drinks was served in a tall, thin glass. Fumes emanated from the liquid's surface. The bottender placed the drink on the rail that circled its body. The artif poured something out of one of its fingers that opened up and garnished the smoking concoction with a piece of orange tropical fruit that Lenore was unfamiliar with. It grabbed the boiling beverage and placed it in front of a woman holding a pilot's helmet. One long red ponytail swung behind her. She was dressed in a military-style uniform and was incredibly fit. She definitely was not the usual clientele that this place attracted. With another arm, the bottender placed a rocks glass full of brown liquid in front of the leprechaun next to Lenore.

"Tanks," said the leprechaun as he picked up what Lenore guessed was whiskey.

"15 credits," commanded the bottender.

"Oh . . . I still 'avn't found me potta gold. Can ya just pootit on me tab?" He raised his glass to the bottender. "*Sláinte*." The tiny red-headed man guzzled the liquor but spilled a bit on his emerald vest. He ignored the mistake and continued smoking his pipe.

The robot's head pivoted in the direction of the female gremlin who still stared at the leprechaun. "Whacha 'avin love?" asked the bottender.

"I'll 'av a Toadstool IPA and anuvver Screamin' Banshee," said Lenore. "Put it on 'awforne's tab." She looked around the bar as she waited for her drinks to be made. Her eyes focused on the door as four others dressed similarly to the strange woman entered the bar.

The man in front was older than the rest. *'ee 'as to be their leader.* Experience wrinkled his bearded face. The striking young lady now walked in the direction to meet this man. Three others were behind the oldest man. *Somefing's wrong*, Lenore thought. *Could dey be 'unters?* The music seemed to get louder and faster. The team of uniformed men made their way over to Hawthorne. Lenore immediately made herself invisible and hurried to get closer to the table. *Dey're not 'unters*, thought Lenore. *Dey're bloody Aringi Riders.*

The bar continued to thrive. The only people who stirred besides Lenore were the two grumblings. They seemed to be expecting something. Lenore got close to the table, remaining at a safe distance. The woman leaned over the booth. "Hello, Mr. Hawthorne. I'm afraid Ronald won't be able to join you this evening. He sends his regards. My name is Evangeline, Second Rider of the Grimm armies. This is my commander, Captain Slade."

"Hello, Mr. Hawthorne," said the Captain as he sat across from Hawthorne.

"Pleasure . . ." said Franklin. "Thanks for the heads up, dear. I hope Ronny's all right."

"Your friend is fine. I assure you," said the Captain as he leaned in a little closer. "I do not wish to waste your time, Mr. Hawthorne. We have a situation that I think you can help us with, and time is of the essence."

"If there's anything I can do to help you fine gentlemen . . ." Evangeline's eyes pierced Franklin. "And lady," finished Hawthorne.

"We are searching for a boy," started the Captain as a holographic image of Thomas Scargen appeared above his wristcom. "The boy's name is Thomas Scargen. We believe you may have had contact with him and may know his whereabouts." The Captain produced a credit stick from his forearm armor. "We are prepared to pay a large sum for this information."

Hawthorne smiled and leaned back in the booth. "I wish I could help you, but I've never seen this boy before. I'm afraid you must have me confused with someone else." He reached down and grabbed his empty glass. "As you can see, I need a drink. If you'll excuse me," said Hawthorne with a grin on his face. Evangeline grabbed him by his shirt and yanked him out of the booth. In a blur of motion, the two grumblings sped towards the table. They came up behind the Riders. The music still echoed in the old tavern.

"Take it outside," said the shorter of the two grumblings. The creature was still over seven feet tall. The Riders spun to meet the voice.

"And what if we don't?" asked the smallest of the Riders. The two grumblings looked at each other and laughed.

"I knew dere was gonna be trouble when we let the girl in. Riders . . . Well then, shorty . . ." said the other grumbling in a much deeper voice. He was easily eight feet tall. "We'll makes ya." Evangeline moved with beautiful precision and flew at the larger grumbling. With a quick motion of her leg, she snapped the creature's head to the right. He fell to the floor. The second grumbling swung at her. His arm was met with the open hand of the older man. He caught the larger grumbling's arm, spun the beast around, and produced a red transparent energy blade from the top of his forearm armor. The glowing blade was pressed against the incapacitated grumbling's throat.

"It would be unwise for you to continue this," said the older gentlemen. He twisted the grumbling's arm back.

"Please don't kill me, I 'av a wife and seventeen bugh-iffull children. Dis is just my job, mate. You understand, don't ya? I promise ya, you can do what ya want wif dis bloke," said the grumbling, the blade almost touching his large neck.

"That is a wise decision. Now give us a minute to talk to the man, and we will leave here quietly."

"O-o-okay," the grumbling squealed in agreement. The large creature that had been kicked lay unconscious on the ground. The Captain let go of the grumbling's arm and extinguished his blade. The conscious grumbling scooped up his comrade, and they disappeared into the silent crowd. Hawthorne brandished his weapon, but before he could fire, the pistol flew from his hand into the Captain's.

"Evangeline, continue your questioning," said the Captain.

"Where's the kid?" she asked.

"Who are you talking about?"

"Thomas Scargen . . . where is he?"

"Never heard of him." She picked him up and threw him into a support beam. He laughed as he got back up to his feet.

Evangeline kicked out Hawthorne's legs and palmed his head. "If you won't tell me, then I guess I'll look for myself." The woman's eyes went blank, and energy flowed down her arm into his head. He appeared to remain unharmed. This seemed to confuse Evangeline. "What is going on? I can't read anything."

"That magic crap don't work on me." Her pupils returned as she ended the attempt.

"What do you mean?"

"My mind cannot be read with your stupid tricks. That only works on less intelligent folk with no control over their thoughts."

"We will see about that, mechanic." A redwood of a man was now standing in front of Lenore. Lenore did not recall him entering the building. A bony mask covered his face. An oversized scythe rested on his back, and a small imp accompanied him. It had been years since Lenore had seen an imp. The large man's stare froze the patrons of the Dodgy Toadstool. The scythe was peculiar as well. It appeared to be made of two large bones. She could not tell from where she was if it was human bone or not, but the interlocking bones made for a horrifying weapon.

"General Arkmalis . . . I was not informed of your arrival," said the Captain.

"Come, Marcus, I wasn't aware I had to keep you informed of my whereabouts."

"I didn't mean . . ." The Captain hastily tried to explain.

"What happened to your sense of humor, Captain? Corbin and I are here on a fact-finding mission, and I thought that it might be time to get my hands a little dirty." The man reached down and grabbed Hawthorne by the front of his shirt, directly under his chin, and lifted him off his feet. Hawthorne wriggled and twirled in his hands. The sight was too much for Lenore, but she forced herself to watch.

"Where is the boy?"

"I'll tell you what I told her. I don't have a clue what you're talking about." As the sentence ended, Arkmalis moved his arm slightly and Hawthorne was sent flying through the stained glass window that adorned the front of the Dodgy Toadstool. Glass shattered outward and littered the sidewalk in front of the pub.

Lenore fought through the crowd to reach Hawthorne. The patrons funneled out the door, following Arkmalis and his Riders. Arkmalis grabbed Hawthorne.

"You are trying my patience, mechanic. I will only ask you one more time. Where is the Scargen boy?"

"I already told you I don't know who you are talking about." Hawthorne giggled.

"It's nice to see that *someone* has not lost their sense of humor. You could learn something from this man, Marcus." Arkmalis turned to look at the Captain. "Let's see if you've heard this one before." He lifted Hawthorne higher until they were eye to eye. Arkmalis's eyes went blank as he turned and stared at Hawthorne. "Where is the Scargen boy?"

Hawthorne's eyes rolled back into his head as he began to spasm. The man's body convulsed in midair. Hawthorne was desperately trying to keep his mouth shut. He screamed out an indistinguishable word. "Just tell me where he is, and this all ends."

Hawthorne clenched his teeth harder. The light coming from the man's hand intensified. "Have it your way, mechanic." A single scarlet drip ran out his nose and over the arch of his lip.

Lenore cried silently. Hawthorne's eyes were now completely white. Pain was all that was left on his face. *No man should suffer like this*, she thought.

Tears flowed from both of his lifeless eyes as he opened his mouth and whispered, "Sir-r-rati." Hawthorne's eyes returned to normal, and he hung limp in the air.

"You see, mechanic, was that so hard?" He dropped the man. "Ziza was wise to hide him there. I should have known that's where he'd take him. Clever little man."

"You bastard." Hawthorne wiped the blood from his nose as he clumsily stood. "At least I have the satisfaction of knowing that you'll never find him. You're too late, and there's nothing you can do."

"That's where you are wrong, mechanic." The General spun and drew his scythe. It was over in an instant. The blazing blade flashed before the gremlin's eyes. The headless body of Franklin Hawthorne stood on his feet, defying death for only a second. The body dropped. A glow rose out of Hawthorne's corpse and flew into the night air. A sigh was the last thing she heard as the light vanished. Lenore almost passed out. She was about to vomit. The gremlin shook with tears.

"I do hope you have some sort of plan for drawing out the boy," said Arkmalis. "We both know the futility in searching for Sirati."

"He cannot stay there forever," said the Captain.

"And when he leaves, Captain, you better be waiting for him." Arkmalis turned and sliced his scythe through the air, ripping open a teleportal. He looked back at the imp. "Corbin." The masked general replaced the bloodstained weapon on his back.

"Yes, Your Grace." Arkmalis crossed through the slice and was followed by his cowering servant. The cut healed behind the General.

The bearded man shook his head. "This death was avoidable." He looked down at Hawthorne's lifeless body. He looked back at his men. "Riders," said the Captain. In seconds, large bat-like beasts flew down and picked them off the ground. As fast as they had come, they were gone. The onlookers began to talk amongst themselves.

The gremlin slowly reappeared. Lenore stood in the ever-expanding puddle of blood, hugging herself as she shook. Tears streamed down her face. *'ee's . . . gone.*

21

a light jog

Thomas moved with incalculable speed. He had listened to Emfalmay and had been going for runs in the morning. Sometimes he ran the perimeter with Emfalmay's son Emkoo and the other male Lions. On these runs, he practiced his breathing techniques. He could tell that he was getting faster and had more control. He was starting to keep pace with the Lions.

In the evenings he would meet Ziza at Maktaba and read his spellbook. He had stopped into Warwick's and spoke with Anson a few times, but he had not seen Yareli or Malcolm since his first night of training. Despite this, Thomas was settling into life in Sirati.

Today he was alone on a short fifteen-mile run down his favorite part of the jungle. He was listening to *Movement* by Distracted Youth, one of his more upbeat music selections, through his earbs. It had been nine days since his first training session, and although he was getting faster and learning more everyday, he was eager to continue his *real* lessons. Sweat drenched his clothes as he turned to follow the colossal river that slashed through Sirati.

A blur of white suddenly cut in front of Thomas, interrupting his run. Whatever had done this was just as fast as him, if not faster. The blur came to a complete stop about half a mile in front of Thomas. It was Yareli. The boy applied the brakes. A dust cloud emerged from where his feet had come to rest. "Hey . . . long time no see." He was inexplicably happy to see her. Her mouth moved, but he could not hear the words over the music. He hit a button on the display on his wrist. The earbs vacated his ears and returned to the wristcom. "Sorry, what did you say?"

"I was asking you why you were yelling at me, but that explains it." She looked up and then back at the boy. "Hello, Thomas."

"Hi, Yar. I haven't seen ya around." Thomas looked upward. "Not that I've been looking or anything. Where've ya been hiding?"

"I was in Egypt conducting my own investigation on your father's disappearance, like I promised I would."

"And?" inquired the boy. He was terrified to hear the news.

"I'm afraid there wasn't much to go by. There was no sign of your father, your father's friend, or the diggerbots."

Thomas had hoped that it was a dream, but the evidence was mounting up against this. The boy was worried. "You found nothing?"

"Nothing. If it weren't for the large cavern, I would have never guessed anyone had been there in quite some time. It look-ed abandoned."

The thought of it was unnerving. He could not help but think that his father was in danger. He felt powerless. And although it was hard to come to terms with, the only way he could save him was to continue training. "I appreciate you coming out here to tell me."

"That's not why I'm here."

Thomas was confused. "Then why *are* you here?"

"It's time for your second lesson."

Finally, he thought. "Where's the High Mancer?"

"He will be meeting us later."

"Thank you, Yareli." He looked down and scratched his head. "I mean it. Thank you for going to Egypt."

"I promised you I would help," she said as she took off down the riverbank.

"Here we go." Thomas followed her. They ran through a long stretch of jungle that was unfamiliar to Thomas. He struggled to catch up. "Where are we going?"

"You'll see soon enough." She rushed through the branches and shrubbery, and Thomas lost sight of her, but her trail was easy to follow. She had left plenty of trampled leaves and broken twigs in her wake. The boy increased his speed.

I'll be damned if I'm gonna let her outrun me. Thomas closed his eyes as he pushed himself harder. He was moving faster than he ever had. As soon as he hit his top speed, he opened his eyes. The jungle stopped. He had only two seconds to slow down before the ravine started. Thomas caught himself on the edge of the canyon. "Whoa, whoa, whoooooooa!" screamed the boy as he waved his arms. He stared across an abyss that extended for miles. Rock platforms jutted out of the top of the massive hole. The boy looked down. He could not see the bottom. He quickly looked up. The sky above was perfectly calm. He was not. His breath quickened as he backed away from the drop off. "I could've died, Yareli." He turned and looked at her. She was smirking with one eyebrow up. Wiyaloo stood next to her.

"Stop being so dramatic. You're fine," she insisted as she walked by him.

"What is this place?"

"It is called *Kuzimu Shimo.*"

"What's that mean?" asked Thomas.

"Bottomless hole," said Yareli. "This is where we will begin your second lesson."

"What exactly am I supposed to do?"

"You are supposed to get to the other side."

"Like the chicken?" asked Thomas.

"Amusing," interjected Wiyaloo.

"I can't even see the other side," said the boy.

"I know," said Yareli, still smiling. "There's one other thing."

"What's that?"

"You are going to need to learn some defensive powers."

"Like the shield you made when we were fighting the Hunters? My book mentioned shields, but they seemed pretty advanced."

"If you haven't noticed, Thomas, you're taking the accelerated course," she said as she looked at him, squinting with a smirk. "As I was saying, you need to learn some defensive skills. I will show you how to focus your energy into a shield." Yareli walked about twenty feet away from him. "I want you to hurl one of those energy spheres at me."

"I don't want to hurt you, Yar."

"You will not hurt her, Thomas Scargen," said Wiyaloo. "I will not let that happen."

"Okay, I get it. I will not hurt her."

"Agreed," confirmed the spirit ghost.

"Here goes nothing." The boy set his feet. He began to draw back his arms. He threw his arms forward and yelled, "Haaaaaaaaaa!" The energy shot out of his palms and formed a blue sphere. He hurled the sphere at Yareli.

She turned towards the sphere and put her hands palms out, shoulder length apart. Her eyes turned solid white. A shield broadened out from her palms. A wall of white energy was now in front of her. The sphere hit the shield and deflected to the right side, but the force of the blast knocked the girl backward. She flew into Wiyaloo's arms before she could hit the ground.

"Thanks," said Yareli as Wiyaloo placed her down. She brushed herself off.

"She remains unharmed, Thomas Scargen."

"I can see that, Wiyaloo."

"Now it's your turn," said Yareli.

"What do you mean?"

"Well, Thomas, I didn't bring you out here for a quick shield lesson. I feel a more practical approach is needed. So you're going to run across that canyon from rock to rock while I fire my spirit arrows at you. Knowing how to form a shield will be necessary if you hope to survive this test. It's not always about offense."

"So let me get this straight. I'm basically learning on the fly?"

"Exactly. You have shown that your powers seem to manifest quicker when your adrenaline gets going."

"When do we start?" He looked back at her, and she was reaching back into her quiver. Yareli nocked the spirit arrow. "Okay . . . I guess that answers that question." She fired directly at him. He rolled to the left and jumped to the first rock. It swayed from side to side and felt like it was about to fall apart. The spirit arrow turned into a mountain lion. It landed one rock over from the boy. The lion roared and leapt at Thomas. He jumped to the next rock as the former one crumbled into the bottomless pit. The boulders were unstable. "That's good to know." The animal did not cease its attack. The boy threw an energy blast at the charging beast, incinerating it. "You're gonna have to do better than that, Yar." Thomas began to hop from rock to rock.

"I was just letting you warm up," said Yareli as she followed Thomas onto one of the floating boulders. She reached back and grabbed two arrows this time and loosed them in Thomas's direction. "Try fending off two at the same time." The arrows danced around each other, darting towards their target. The first arrow transformed into a grizzly bear as it ran across the sky. The second turned into a pack of wolves that intently began their hunt. Yareli followed her creations from afar, deftly traversing the rock formations.

Thomas turned to see the new threats just in time. The grizzly took a swipe at him as he rolled to his left and leapt across to another boulder. The wolves were upon him quickly. Three of them landed on one side of him and three behind him. The grizzly had recovered and now was also making a move at Thomas. He quickly turned in the direction of his objective. "Let's see how you like this. Haaaaaaaaaaa!" A blast of energy destroyed one of the wolves as he ran at the newly vacated position. He jumped over the other two as both tried frantically to bite him. He began hopping from rock to rock, trying desperately to outmaneuver the pack and the bear. The rock formations moved and slid as the boy ran across them—some swaying, others falling into the abyss. *I can't keep this up forever*, the boy thought. The wolves were gaining, and if he stopped, the grizzly would catch him. *If I knew I was going to be fighting Yareli and her freakin' spirit animals, I probably wouldn't have gone for that run.* It was at that exact moment that Wiyaloo opened fire on him from the sky. *You gotta be kiddin' me. Not him too.*

Thomas put his hands out as he ran and tried to focus his energy. At first energy flickered from his fingertips as one of the spirit ghost's white blasts whizzed by him. He tried once more. *Come on, Thomas, concentrate.* A small sphere began to grow from his hands, but it too failed. Wiyaloo stopped in the air and was now generating a huge energy attack. He held his staff in the air as particles spun around it. The spirit ghost surged with white energy.

Thomas ran as fast as he could. It was too late for him to turn and face the fox, and if he could not make a shield, then running was his best defense. The animals continued their attack. *You gotta do this.* Wiyaloo's white energy sphere grew even larger.

The white fox released the collected force down in the direction of the boy. Thomas turned to see his incoming fate. He could run no more. *It's now or never.* He turned to face the massive glowing pulse. He stuck his palms out. "Haaaaaaaaaaaaaaaaaa!"

A light blue field formed around the boy. It looked as if he were in a bubble. *I did it . . . I freakin' did it.* The energy collided with the shield. The force of the blast instantly destroyed the base of the rock, as well as the remaining wolves. He was completely protected within the shield, but he was now falling off of the rock face. The rock formations on all sides began to fall apart as well. Thomas acted quickly.

The shield faded as he ran up the falling rock. When he reached the end of the formation, he jumped as high and as far as he could to the next piece of plummeting earth. He ran up the new formation and leapt diagonally to another gravity-stricken boulder. From where he was, it was hard for him to see if he was making any progress. He looked down, and the bear still followed. *Stubborn little grizzly spirit.* He jumped one last time and reached out and held onto the cliff. He had gotten his head back above water. He struggled to pull himself up. He could see the other side now. What seemed like an impossibility was now within reach. If only he were not being chased by an enchanted bear and a fox spirit.

Wiyaloo had been waiting for Thomas to resurface. He released another attack. The boy threw himself upward at the exact time that the bear pounced. Thomas jumped up and over several balancing rocks and landed thirty feet away from the ravine's north side. Wiyaloo's attack incinerated the bear spirit on contact.

Thomas landed on the other side just as Yareli had caught up. She stood on the last balancing stone. He waved and smiled. She smirked back at him. He turned around and was about to celebrate when he almost ran into Ziza. Thomas was sure he was not there before. "Where did you come from?"

"Ah, the eternal question," joked Ziza. "I was waiting here the whole time."

"I didn't see you."

"There is a lot you do not see. We will correct that." Yareli joined them, and Wiyaloo appeared next to her. "That was an impressive showing of control. There was no point where you overreacted or became flustered. Even in the worst moments, you still held your composure. You've done well. Remember, Thomas, physical control will beget emotional control. Yareli." Thomas looked at the girl. "I would appreciate it if you could accompany Thomas back to Maktaba for his study session. I have some matters to attend to."

Thomas turned back to the High Mancer. "What are you gonna d—" Ziza had vanished before Thomas had turned around. He looked at Yareli, but she just shrugged her shoulders.

Yareli had not said anything to him while they made their way back across the canyon, and Wiyaloo was his normal taciturn self. He had chalked it up to ego for having beaten her, but he could not take the silence anymore. He desperately wanted to know what her problem was with him. "Why do you hate me so much?" Thomas just blurted out the words without thinking. Yareli looked at him, surprised by the outburst.

"I will leave you two," said Wiyaloo.

"Don't you dare, Wiya—" said Yareli, but it was too late. The spirit ghost had vanished. She looked back at the boy. "I don't hate you, Thomas."

"Sorry . . . why do you *dislike* me so much? Is that better?"

"Ahhh! You are impossible. Do you really want to know?"

"I just asked, didn't I?" said Thomas.

"I *was* you . . . I was the prodigy—before they found you, I mean. I was supposed to do great things, but I messed up big time. Do you have any idea how that feels? One minute everyone is looking to you for everything, and then the next minute you're just another Mage." She looked away. "Then you come along to save the day, and now everyone loves you." Her head lowered, and then her eyes met his. "I wanted to hate you, but . . ." Thomas moved closer to her.

"But what?"

"But I don't—hate you, I mean. I can't hate you. How could I? You've saved my life, twice, and you are definitely something."

"Something, eh?" said Thomas with a huge grin on his face.

"Don't let it go to your head."

"I just don't get why we can't both . . . well . . . you know . . . work together."

"We can, Thomas, but you're not getting it . . ."

"I do understand. You think there's only room for one of us."

"That's not it, at all. Trust me. You'll understand in time."

"Don't treat me like a boy."

"Stop acting like one." She turned and walked away. "Good night, Thomas." Thomas felt a sudden flash of anger and sadness.

"So, that's it? You're done talking, so we're done talking?" She didn't answer and kept walking. His shoulders slumped in defeat as he turned towards Maktaba.

I wish I understood.

When he entered the meeting room, he was greeted by the pounding noise. Thomas did his best to ignore it as he made his way to Ziza's study. Emfalmay was not at his normal station. *That's odd,*

thought the boy. None of the Lions were present. Thomas walked up the branch to the knothole door.

He found the High Mancer staring wide-eyed into the glowing green book. Ziza nodded in the boy's general direction, but said nothing. This had become comfortable for the boy. These study sessions were not like the ones at New Salem High. These were exciting, and Thomas began to understand that the more he knew, the better suited he would be to help his father. He looked forward to these sessions all day.

Flora was replacing books when she noticed Thomas. She shot up in the air and grabbed *Scargen's Repository of Magic* from the high shelf, handing it to the boy. He had grown tired of not knowing what to call the book, so he named him Booker Spells. Thomas still laughed at the clever name. "Thanks, Flora." The vine waved and continued slotting the towering stacked books.

He was eager to begin his lesson, but besides a nod, Ziza had given him little in the way of direction. Thomas quietly sat down. Spells broke the silence. "How was your day, Thomas?"

"Good—for the most part." Thomas thought of Yareli and their misunderstanding. "So what's this evening's lesson gonna be?"

"Well, Ziza was thinking you could choose tonight's topic."

"What?"

"He said tonight you could pick what it is you want to learn." He looked over at Ziza who simply smiled. This was odd. He had never gotten to pick before. There were so many weird things he had witnessed and so many questions swirling in his head, but there had been one thing that had fascinated him more than most. He knew immediately.

"Dragons," blurted Thomas. "I want to know as much as I can about dragons." The boy smiled.

"Sounds good to me," said Spells as he opened up and began to glow the familiar light blue color. Thomas was excited. He had always loved dragons, and he had been enthralled by Bartleby and his kind since their initial meeting, but not until he met Talya did it even register that the world was still full of these amazing creatures. This intrigued him. The pages turned swiftly until they settled on a chapter beginning. "Dragons," announced Spells. Thomas pushed the book slowly down to the desk and began to read.

DRAGONS

Dragons are rather large scaled creatures that are capable of flight. Reptilian in appearance, these creatures covet treasure above all else with the possible exception of a good four-day sleep.

That explains the long naps and his obsession with credits. The boy thought of Bartleby. Thomas paged through the general description. He wanted specifics. He stopped at the section on dragon races.

DRAGON RACES

There are six known dragon races. Each one exhibits distinct markers and colors that distinguish it from the others. They are as follows:

AEQUOS (SEA DRAGON): These dragons originate from Asia and are traditionally varying shades of blue. Unlike other dragons, they have no wings, but are still capable of flight. They have snakelike bodies with four legs. This sleek design makes them the fastest of the dragon races. The Aequos, however, prefers water to air. Some have the ability to shapeshift—assuming a human form for short periods of time. They are fire breathers.

SILVAS (FOREST DRAGON): Silvas are varying shades of green and brown and are the most intelligent of the dragon races. Originally forest dwellers, this species has adapted and has been seen in various climates and environments. They have four legs and long, strong tails. These dragons have large wingspans, and their horns begin to resemble tree branches as they get older. Silvas are fire breathers.

That must be what Bart is, thought Thomas.

GLACIAS (ICE DRAGON): Predominantly white in color, the Glacias's skin mimics the arctic environments to which they are indigenous. Do not take their seemingly fragile appearance lightly. They are just as lethal as any other dragon race. Glacias are impervious to cold, and instead of fire, they breathe out freezing winds.

INCENDIAS (FIRE DRAGON): Their colors range from bright orange to dark red and are at home in any form of fire—often inhabiting active volcanoes. They have only two legs, using their wings in place of front legs when walking. Because of this, they have the largest wingspan of any other dragon race. These dragons are also fire breathers.

FIMUS (DESERT DRAGON): Fimus are varying shades of yellow. They can go months without water, and they have the smallest wingspan of all dragons. Their small wings make them more apt for flying low to the ground. They are distinguishable by their multiple sets of eyelids, with an inner set that is transparent. This protected vision is useful during sandstorms and when burrowing in the sand. Fimus do not breathe fire. They can shoot concentrated gusts of wind out of their mouths, making it easier for them to handle desert conditions.

DRACAVEA (CAVE DRAGON): Dracavea are black in color and typically the strongest of all dragons. They have multiple sets of horns for protection, and a keen sense of smell for hunting. Dracavea are often solitary, leaving their mothers as soon as they are physically capable. They dwell in dark caves where they hoard their treasures. They are another fire-breathing race.

He read the book intently. He had to keep reminding himself to blink. Thomas read all he could about the different races: from technical data on the speeds of the creatures to environmental details of their natural habitats. He paged through to the ANATOMY section. This section dealt with each race's anatomical makeup—complete with detailed illustrations. He continued to read.

Dragons are older than man. How much older is still up for debate. They have survived for millennia because of their durability and physical makeup. Dragon bone is the hardest substance ever discovered. Silvas in particular have the strongest bone density of all of the dragon races. The dragon's skin is protected by a hard outer shell of scales that make a natural suit of armor. Ancient accounts have been discovered that suggest an adult dragon's blood may possess magical properties, but these have yet to be substantiated due to the difficulty of collecting and testing blood samples of the different dragon races. Dragons are not cooperative by nature, and their dwindling numbers make it increasingly difficult to perform studies necessary to confirm these accounts.

The boy paged ahead once more, completely enthralled, trying to take it all in.

ARINGI & DRAGONS

Narsh, he thought. *I was wondering about the bats.*

There is only one creature that has the natural ability to teleport—*Draco teleportare*, more commonly known as the dragon. Not all dragons have the innate ability to teleport, but all have the capacity to learn the skill with time and practice. The species' lethargic tendencies seem to curtail the latter.

The aringi's teleportation abilities, in contrast, are man-made. These monsters are genetically created and altered by tech to achieve this goal. It is a dark and twisted abomination of nature, the aringi, but much like the dragon, its teleportation ability can be augmented and amplified by tech. The biggest difference between the aringi and the dragon is that the bat-like creatures cannot work without their human counterparts. They share a psychic bond that allows the Rider to control the aringi. This skill takes years of practice to master, and only someone with strong mental capacity can perform the feat.

"That is enough for tonight, Thomas." The old man's voice caught the boy off guard. He had been concentrating on the pages and lost track of time. "I have something for Anson, if you do not mind delivering it for me." A box floated over to Thomas. He grabbed the package. "I would like him to have the package as soon as possible. If you leave now you could get a shower before promptly meeting him at 9:00 PM at Warwick's." Thomas nodded his head in agreement. His thoughts were still focused on dragons. *I wonder how old Bart is.*

He had been thinking about going to Warwick's anyway, but he did need a shower after today's exercises. Flora reached down and grabbed his book off of the cluttered desk.

"See ya later, Thomas," said Spells.

"Good night, Spells . . . Ziza," said Thomas as he made his way down the massive branch. The old man said nothing. His face was still stuck in his book. Thomas walked down the stairs and made his way to the elevator. The elevator opened up, and there stood Malcolm. The vampire walked towards Thomas. His movements were graceful and precise. He wasted no effort. The vampire was striding in the direction of Ziza's study.

" 'ello, Tommy," said Malcolm as he smiled at the boy. "I would love to stop and chat, but I've got business to attend to, don't I?" The vampire climbed the stairway to Ziza's study. Thomas watched him with a smile on his face as he disappeared. *Why didn't he just give the package to Malcolm?* wondered Thomas as the elevator door closed.

22

cry wolf

Thomas walked into Warwick's with his head down and the box he was instructed to give to Anson tucked neatly under his arm. The shower and the fresh clothes felt great, but he was still exhausted from training. He finally got the strength to look up as the elevator doors whooshed open.

"Surprise!" The words were shouted by everyone in the pub. Thomas was taken aback. *My birthday? I can't believe I'd forgotten.* He had been so preoccupied with his father and his training that he had forgotten it was the eighteenth of July.

"Happy birthday, Thomas," was all that could be heard for a good five minutes as Thomas methodically made his way to the bar. When he finally got there, he sat down. Sinclair swung over.

"What will it be, birthday boy?" the Simian asked as he polished a glass.

"I'll try the Warwick Amber, Sinclair." The Gorilla reached out his arm and placed the glass under the pour spout. He filled the glass and slid it down the bar. It skidded to a halt directly in front of the birthday boy. "Thanks, what do I owe you?"

"I got dat one, Sin." Thomas turned to the right to see Malcolm smiling at him. "You should've seen duh look on your face when everyone yelled surprise. You looked completely astonished, didn't ya, Tommy?"

"You guys got me good," said the boy.

"So 'ow's it feel ta be seventeen?" The vampire took a long drag off his cigarette.

"To be honest, I didn't remember it was my birthday until I walked through the doors." Thomas took a sip of his beer. "How did you guys know?"

"The Tin Man spilled duh beans, actually."

"LINC," said Thomas. "Well thanks for the beer."

"Cheers, mate." The two clinked glasses. "I wanted ta make sure I saw ya before I shot off."

"Where ya going? The party has just started."

"I've got a few fings to attend to before I take off tonight. I got some business outside of our fair city—boring stuff actually."

"It wouldn't have anything to do with that little business you had with Ziza earlier, would it?"

"It just might, Tommy, it just might. Nuffin' gets by you, does it?

"Well there are a few things that I have yet to piece together. I thought you probably could help."

" 'av at it. It being your special day and all."

"The first thing is actually a question about your brother. I was wondering . . . what I mean to ask is . . . "

"Go on already, would ya? I don't bite, Tommy. Well . . . anymore."

"Okay . . ." Thomas looked at Malcolm. "What's up with your brother and his obsession with quoting you-know-who all the time?"

"A little respect, mate. We are talkin about duh Bard. I mean 'ee was a bloody knight, Tommy, wasn't 'ee? And a pretty decent writer if I'm not mistaken."

"I'm familiar with him. Mrs. Hughes spent half the year on him."

" 'oo's Mrs. 'ughes?"

"My eleventh grade English Lit teach—doesn't matter. Why does he do it?"

"Do what?"

"Quote you-know-who."

"What did I just get done sayin'?"

"Sorry, Sir William Shakespeare."

"Dat's better, Tommy. What's it to you anyway?"

"Nothing really. It's just . . . he seems to be somewhere else every time he does it." A look of understanding settled on the vampire's pale face.

"He, well, sort uv knew 'im. We sort uv knew 'im, I guess, although I never liked 'im much. 'ee was always whingin' away about something, eloquent git. My bruvver, however, was 'is best mate. I guess some time after 'ee passed—Shakespeare I mean—'ee began quotin' dose plays . . . poor bastard."

"Really?" It had never dawned on Thomas all the things the two brothers must have done and seen, let alone the people they had known. "He was really best friends with Shakespeare?"

"Na, I'm just takin' the piss mate—windin' you up a bit on your birfday. He just reads a lot. Shakespeare's 'is favorite. 'ee can't get enough uv 'im. I 'ad you goin' for a minute." Malcolm began laughing. "How old do you fink we are, Tommy?" Malcolm got up. "Well, 'appy birfday, mate."

"There's another thing I was wondering, but this one's about you."

"I will allow it, but dis is the last one."

"How do you walk around in the daylight?"

"Cut right to the chase, don't ya, Tommy? I like dat." He lifted his right hand and extended his ring finger. A dark gray metal ring rested there. He pulled the ring off and handed it to Thomas. "Dis is my sunscreen." The boy examined the circular artifact. There were several carvings of different moon shapes and alien markings engraved on the inside. "It's called da Lunalus."

"How's it work?" asked the boy.

"I don't know exactly. I just know it forms a shield dat shades me from duh sun—very powerful magic, very rare. Most vampires don't even know it exists. In fact, you, Ziza, and Anson are the only free people dat know I 'av it. Yareli 'as 'er suspicions, but doesn't know for sure. I want to tell 'er, but Ziza doesn't want me to tell anyone about it, seeing it's kind uv a weakness and all. Obviously, people around 'ere are a bit wary of the day-walking vamp, but no one knows how I do it."

"Why did you tell me then?" asked the boy, bewildered.

"It's your birfday, mate, and besides, I've been around long enough to know who to trust, and you smell very trustwurvy, Tommy." It was the closest thing to a compliment he had heard from the vampire.

"Thank you."

"Don't mention it, mate. Seriously doh, don't mention it—to anyone."

"Okay, okay, but can I ask you one more thing?"

"You're pushin' it."

"Last one, I swear."

"Go on den, but give us back duh ring, Tommy. I feel a bit naked wiffout it."

"Where did the Lunalus come from?" asked Thomas as he handed back the ring.

"I'm afraid we'll 'av to wait till next time for dat story, Tommy. It's a bit involved." The vampire slipped the ring back on. "And I've gotta be shootin', mate. Ziza's orders."

"Well whatever it is you're up too, be careful."

"I'm always careful." He winked at Thomas and shook his hand. " 'av a brilliant birfday, and, Tommy . . ." The vampire's tone changed. "Keep an eye on me bruvver for me."

"Sure thing, Malcolm, but why?"

" 'ee doesn't 'av a lot of friends, and 'ee tends to worry a bit when I'm not around. Can't live wiffout me, I suppose." The vampire sped off, and Thomas could hear the echo of his laughter.

Thomas saw Yareli making her way over towards him, followed by LINC. She had what looked like a gift for Thomas. "I was wondering when you were going to show up."

"If I knew everyone was waiting, I would've hurried, but I guess that would've ruined everything."

"Hello, Thomas," chimed his robotic companion. "Standard human protocol suggests that I congratulate you for surviving 148,922 hours, 37 minutes, and 42 seconds."

"Thanks, buddy. I heard you were the one that let the cat out of the bag."

"I assure you, Thomas, that Stella was never once placed into a bag, nor did I release her from this fictional sack."

"It's an expression, LINC. It means—never mind." Thomas figured that this particular battle was not worth fighting. "Hey, can you give me a few minutes alone with Yareli?"

"Certainly, Thomas. There is no identifiable threat in the immediate vicinity, and I require articulation lubricant as well. Should you need any further assistance, I'll be situated at the communal refreshment area conversing with the local Silverback mixologist."

"Thanks, LINC." The artif walked away in the direction of the bar.

"So, I got you something." Yareli said this like she had practiced her delivery. "I hope you like it." She handed him a bag made of animal hide. The hide was decorated with beads in amazing ornamental designs.

"Thanks, Yar. You didn't have to get me anything." He stared at the bag.

"Well open it," commanded Yareli.

"Okay, okay—it's heavy."

"Just open it." Her patience was obviously wearing thin. Thomas could not help but smile. He opened the bag and reached inside. He pulled his hand upward, unveiling a remarkable work of art. He was astonished. It was a masterfully carved pipe. The long pipe stem was decorated with meticulously placed feathers and beads. Thomas was speechless. "Do you like it?"

"It's completely narsh . . . where did you—I mean, where is it from?"

"I made it, Thomas." The words did not seem real to the boy. After all of the animosity she had shown him, she still had found the time to make this beautiful gift. He was humbled.

"Yar, it's amazing. Thank you so much. This is the first peace pipe I've ever owned."

"It's a *chanunpa*."

"A what?"

"A *chanunpa*. Peace pipe is a term your people use. These pipes were used for a lot of different occasions and ceremonies."

"So you're not trying to make peace?"

"No, Thomas. I'm trying to be your friend."

He did not know how to respond to this at first. He opted for a subject change. "Should we smoke out of it?"

"Yes, we can smoke it . . . if you want, but it's mostly just symbolic."

"No, you're not getting away with that. Let me just get around to everyone, and I'll meet you outside on the balcony." He looked around for a second. He thought about his last statement and realized there was no other place he would rather be. "On second thought, let's just go outside now."

They made their way to the balcony that overlooked the jungle. The two of them looked off of the cliff that jutted from the side of the pub at the perfectly round moon. They both leaned over the railing. Yareli had packed the pipe, and she took in a drag. When she exhaled, the smoke seemed to dance in the night sky. It twisted and turned until it disappeared above them. "Your turn," she said. Thomas accepted the pipe. He placed it on his lips and inhaled.

His exhale was not as poetic. He choked when the smoke hit his lungs and it blew out into Yareli's face. "Sorry . . . Yar," said Thomas while still coughing. He bent down to catch his breath.

"No big deal, Thomas. It happens. That stuff's poisonous, you know?" They both laughed a strangely familiar laugh and then looked at each other in silence. Thomas was the first to speak.

"You know, Yar—" began the boy, but his words and their new-found friendship were inconveniently interrupted by the sound of a glass breaking from inside.

Yareli placed the pipe into its holder, and they rushed inside. Anson and Ziza were arguing. The old man stood calm, holding his staff, and Anson looked infuriated. "Where is he, Ziza?" growled Anson.

"I've told you, I will not divulge his whereabouts." Anson's face was flush with anger. "Maybe some fresh air will calm you down."

"I don't *need* to calm down. I need to know where you sent Malcolm." His irritation turned to fury. Thomas noticed Anson's shirt tear down the back. Emfalmay stepped between the two men.

"This is neither the time nor place, Anson," said the Lion.

"Leave us be. This is none of your business. This is between Ziza and me."

"It would appear that I am between Ziza and you," said Emfalmay as his eyes began to glow.

"There is no need for this," said Ziza, trying to calm down both sides. "Your brother volunteered for this mission. I'm sorry, Anson, but I will not compromise him."

"You're impossible," said Anson. He turned and jumped towards Yareli and Thomas. He morphed into a werewolf in front of the two of them. Thomas moved to block him from leaving.

"Anson, we can talk this out." The werewolf did not agree and threw the boy to the side. Thomas was sent flying into a table. Anson growled as he leapt from the balcony.

Ziza appeared next to Thomas. "Happy Birthday, my boy," said the old man as he and Onjamba helped Thomas off of the ground. "I'm sorry about that."

"Are you okay, Thomas," asked the Elephant.

"I'm fine. I'm going to see what's bothering him so much. He doesn't seem himself." He looked over at a stunned Yareli. "Sorry, Yar. Rain check?" She nodded. Before Ziza could protest, he was out over the same balcony wall.

The wind rushed passed his ears as he plummeted to the forest floor. It was still scary when he jumped from high places, but only temporarily. Once he landed, the fear was instantly replaced with adrenaline. He lowered the goggles. If he was going to track a were-wolf in a dark jungle, he was going to need all the help he could get. He looked around for any clue as to what direction the werewolf had taken off in, but it did not take a detective to figure out that he should follow the torn shards of clothing.

He had been tracking Anson for some time now. He thought about the party, and more importantly, about Yareli. She *did* want to be his friend. This comforted him as he looked for the angry werewolf. Thomas looked up. He and Yareli had looked at the same sky from the balcony, but now it had a completely different implication. The moon was full.

Thomas followed the garment trail to a clearing. In the center of the clearing, massive rocks were leaning against each other in a towering configuration. He found his monstrous friend at the base of the rock pile.

Anson stopped and climbed up the tall stone formation. When he reached the top, he arched his back, forcing his snout up into the air, and began to howl. The melancholy song was beautiful. His fur glistened in the full moon's light. Thomas listened to the beast's melodious lament for a few seconds before he approached. "Anson, it's me, Thomas. Can you come down here so we can talk?"

"I know who it is. I smelled you two kilometers back . . . by the way, you shouldn't smoke. It's a filthy habit."

"It was more of a symbolic thing."

"Leave me be, boy."

Thomas searched his thoughts for the right words. "Malcolm will be fine. Could you just come down?"

The werewolf leapt off of the jutting rock and landed directly in front of Thomas, moving menacingly towards him. The boy backed up and lost his footing. He fell to the ground as the beast advanced. Anson was terrifying in his canine form. He was far more intimidating than the first time Thomas had seen him as a werewolf. "You don't know that," he growled. "Why did you follow me? I want to be alone." Thomas was frightened by the lack of control he saw in the werewolf's eyes.

"I'm sorry, Anson."

"Sorry? *Sorry?* What are you sorry for? This has nothing to do with you, boy." His head hung low now. "This is between Ziza and me. Just leave me be." Anson grabbed his head and began to shake. Thomas scurried backward on the jungle floor. "I am not well right now. If you haven't noticed, the moon is at its fullest, which means I'm not altogether in control right now. I do not want to hurt you, Thomas." He showed his teeth. The drool squeezed through his incisors and dripped down to the earth. Thomas's anxiety was masked only by his concern. He of all people could sympathize. He knew how it felt to be helpless while a loved one was possibly in trouble.

"You don't scare me."

"Really . . ." The werewolf bayed at the moon and then advanced towards the unsuspecting boy. "How about now?" The howl had transformed from a beautiful, sad song into a chilling, angry bawl. "How does this feel, Thomas? Do you still think I'm in control? One wrong move, and I could tear you apart." The boy continued to back off as the werewolf advanced. "Come on, Thomas, make your move. Let me show you how out of control I can be." Anson lunged towards the boy. The werewolf stood over his prey. The wolf's teeth were now close to Thomas's forehead. His eyes were wide and focused. He was more animal than man in his current state. "Leave me alone," said the werewolf as saliva sprayed out of the corners of his mouth. Thomas did not know what to do, but one thing was certain.

"I'm not going anywhere, Anson." The boy stood and brushed himself off. "Let's talk about this."

"There is nothing to talk about. If Ziza will not tell me where he sent him, then something's not quite right, is it?" Anson grabbed his head with his claws. "Malcolm could be walking into certain death for all I know." He lifted his head and began to howl upward.

The uncontrollable howling slowly transitioned into heavy sobbing as the large beast slumped down onto his knees and covered his face. "It's just that he's my younger brother, you know?" The large creature sniveled as he fought back the ceaseless track of tears pouring from his swollen eyes. "By four minutes and thirty-seven seconds, but younger nonetheless."

Thomas laughed aloud. "Younger brother, eh?"

"Perhaps I am stretching that part a bit." A smile broke through on Anson's elongated face. "He wouldn't tell me where he sent him."

"He probably didn't want you to go chasing after him."

"Ziza is a smart man—stubborn, old, and insufferable, but wise indeed."

"Your brother can handle himself." The boy moved closer to Anson and sat down.

"I know, Thomas, but I hate not knowing what's going on. He's all I have left, and I just don't know what I would do without him." Thomas put his arm around the werewolf and the two just sat in silence. Thomas thought of his father and how similarly he felt.

"Is there anything I can do?" asked the boy.

"The patient must minister to himself, Thomas."

"Well the least I can do is walk you back to Warwick's." Thomas stood up.

"Is that meant to be a dog joke?"

"No . . . n-n-not at all, Anson."

"A shame really . . . the opportunity did present itself." The two laughed once more. "I would be rude to refuse your offer. It will be a while before I sleep'st so sound, and I could use the company." Anson lifted himself off the cold ground. "I hope you will accept my apologies for throwing you back at the bar."

"I probably deserve some of the blame. I did jump in front of a feral werewolf." The boy smiled at Anson.

"I don't usually lose control like that, but the full moon can still be a bit much for me."

"Is that why you are still . . . you know, furry?"

"Yeah, it kind of has to wear off, more or less, when I get like this."

They had been walking for miles through the jungle back to Warwick's. Thomas told Anson the story of the night he had been whisked away from his home in New Salem. He was trying to get Anson's mind off his brother, and it seemed to work. Anson had calmed down for the most part. They took the elevator in the waterfall up to Warwick's.

They entered the silent bar. Sinclair was finishing up cleaning up with the help of his family. "Hey, boss, you aw'right? I didn't realize it was full tonight. I 'ad a bet on duh late game, I did. Mind, ya know, just bloody preoccupied I guess."

"I'm fine, Sin, don't worry yourself. Thomas here talked some sense into me."

"Just trying to help." He extended his hand for a shake. "So I guess I'll see you tomorrow then?" said Thomas to the werewolf.

"Sit down and have a drink with me."

"I don't know if I should. I have training tomorrow."

"Come on, it's the least I can do after ruining your birthday party." The boy stood there for a second, weighing the pros and cons.

"I guess one can't hurt." Thomas moved to a barstool and sat down. Anson walked behind the bar.

"I was saving this for a special occasion, and it just so happens to be someone's birthday." He shuffled around underneath the bar. The sound of a glass breaking interrupted the sound of the waterfall. "Oops." Sinclair moved and in a second's time had swept the mess up with a tiny broom in his left hand and a dustpan held in his foot. Sinclair disposed of the debris and quickly began to turn off the holovision sets. The Gorilla grabbed his hat and walked towards the exit.

"Good night, gents." Sinclair placed his cap onto his head and loped towards the exit. "See ya tomorrow."

"Good night, Sinclair," the two chimed in unison.

"Ah, here it is." He produced a dust-covered brown bottle with a stopper in it from under the bar. Anson pried the stopper free using his teeth and spit out the cork. The sound of a glass being struck by a cork rang in the background. The werewolf raised the liquor to his lips and swallowed. "I absolutely love this whiskey. It's from a local distillery back home." He put the bottle on the bar after taking a second big swig. "Good whiskey is a good familiar creature, if it be well used." He looked at Thomas. "Well . . . go on . . . it's your turn."

"I was thinking more along the lines of a beer . . . I probably shouldn't . . ."

"That's what makes it so good." Anson slid the bottle closer to the boy. Thomas poured some of the whiskey down his gullet. Within seconds, the boy began choking.

"Smooth," said Thomas as he placed the bottle down on the bar. Anson reached for the bottle as he made his way back around the bar. The whiskey lifted off the bar and flew into Anson's open palm. This feat caught Thomas off guard.

"Can I do that?" asked the boy.

"Eventually," answered Anson.

"Narsh." The werewolf once more partook of the brown liquid as his transformation slowly reversed itself. He sat down next to the boy.

"That's better," Anson said as he passed the bottle back to the boy. Thomas knew that he could not keep up with Anson's pace with the whiskey, so he put the bottle back onto the bar top. Anson now sat half naked with his torn clothing hanging from his body. His bare feet dangled under the barstool. One bead of water slinked down his curved face. "What a hell of witchcraft that lies in the small orb of one particular tear."

"Okay, Anson. If you want me to drink this with you I've gotta know."

"Know what, Thomas?"

"Why Shakespeare?" Thomas passed the bottle back to Anson.

"Well done, Thomas. You've been paying attention." He drew yet again from the bottle. He motioned in the direction of the boy with the bottle. "The better question might be why not?" The boy pondered this hypothetical. "There are few who did more in as little time."

"Your brother had mentioned that you knew him . . . but then he played it off like he was joking."

"Actually, he was my best mate, Thomas—up until the twenty-third of April, 1616, that is."

"What happened then? Did you guys have a falling out or something?"

"No, Thomas. He died. That was the day he was untimely ripped from this world. I changed a little that day . . . and so did my brother."

"Don't take this the wrong way, but it doesn't seem to affect him as much—nothing seems to."

"I find no offense in these words. We all grieve in our own way, Thomas. My brother makes jokes. I quote. Who is to say which one of us is doing it the right way?"

"I suppose you're right."

"I started quoting William to celebrate the beauty of what he was able to do with such little time he had. Up until meeting him, I never realized how much I was squandering this gift called life. I wasted time, Thomas: and now doth time waste me. He helped me change my outlook on life. To see him use his gift of words was mesmerizing. I had never met someone with so much raw talent—well, that was until I met you."

"I don't deserve that comparison. Shakespeare was a great man, and I sincerely doubt I'll ever be half as talented."

"Our doubts are traitors and make us lose the good we oft might win by fearing to attempt," said Anson.

"But . . . I don't even come close."

"It wasn't just the man's talent, Thomas. It was his compassion. He took me into his family. The way he loved Anne and his children . . . and he let me be a part of that. I see this compassion in you too, Thomas.

"I think you've had too much to drink."

"Are you really trying to argue with a man who's centuries older than you?" Thomas shook his head no. "I didn't think so." Anson turned away. "I was a beast—a monster—when I first met William. He found me in an alley behind the Theatre quivering after a particularly horrid evening. I craved the flesh of humans at one point, Thomas, but I always fought those cravings. I'm not proud of those days. It was William who took the time to show me there was another way. We became best friends, William and I. We were inseparable. He let me be part of his family and his professional life. I was a member of the King's Men acting troupe."

"You were an actor?" asked the boy.

"How do you think I know so many Shakespeare quotes?"

"Fair enough."

"William helped me teach myself how to live again."

"Where was Malcolm?" asked Thomas.

"At that point, I hadn't seen my brother in quite some time. Malcolm and I had gone our separate ways some 200 years before. Our kinds have been arch enemies for as long as anyone could remember, and my brother, at the time, was running around with a group of vamps. He was still using at the time."

"Using?" asked Thomas, not familiar with the turn of phrase in this context.

"He was surviving off the blood of humans. His bloodlust was insatiable. Malcolm was still running with his Maker and several other vampires when we accidentally ran into each other one night following an amazingly dreadful performance of *Hamlet* at the Globe."

"Accidentally?" asked Thomas.

"Completely accidental. William and I were to meet each other at The Skulking Loafer, a rather dodgy pub not too far from the theatre. The Skulk was not much to look at, but it was our local. I was going home to change and have a bath beforehand. We were going to drown our sorrows. I arrived first and excused myself to the loo, and unbeknownst to me, my brother and his vampire friends walked in the door. William had also come in while I was washing up. I had not been completely forthright with him about having a twin who too was immortal. So he approached my brother as if it were me. The meeting was not at first cordial. If I hadn't come out of the loo when I did, history might be a bit different."

"Talk about good timing," said Thomas as he drank from the bottle and then handed it to Anson.

"Better three hours too soon than a minute too late." He took another swig of the whiskey. "If William hadn't thought he had just been ignored by his best friend that night at a local watering hole, I might have gone forever without ever reuniting with Malcolm." Anson paused in contemplation. "After some awkward introductions, the three of us had a great time that evening. I found myself indebted to William for bringing us back together."

"I guess he decided to quit hanging with those other vamps then, and you guys have been cool ever since?"

"Not exactly, Thomas. You see, Malcolm was far gone at the time. He was a mere shell of the man I knew and loved. He was almost lost, but I convinced him to trust me. I swore to him that we would find a way together. William helped, like he had done with me, to quench Malcolm's thirst."

Thomas stared at the werewolf intently. "How did he do that?"

"Let's just say the local butcher never looked at William Shakespeare the same. He would bring home every type of blood imaginable, but alas, none worked well enough. Yes, it helped knock down the need to hunt, but it wasn't enough. It still left him feral and did nothing to tame his cravings. Those nights were the kind you wish you could forget. I remember having to physically knock him down. We had to lock him up on some occasions. I am not proud of the way I treated him. He needed tough love, and I provided that."

"It seems like you have so much more control over your affliction." The boy paused for a second, wondering if he had chosen the proper words.

"I crave blood because of hunger, Thomas, just like you may crave a peanut butter and jelly sandwich. If you don't get one, it is no big deal, but what my brother deals with is closer to if I asked you to go without air. He needs human blood to live, and that's when we realized that if we were to be brothers, then we would have to learn how to cope with this fact. The only solution was for us both to learn magic. It was William's idea, actually. The first thing I had to learn was control over my transformations. I needed all of my strength to be able to hold Malcolm down when his episodes became dangerous. I studied every book on the subject I could find. *Taming the Wolf* by

Macallister Greer was particularly enlightening." He drew once more from the bottle. "It took quite some time to perfect the process, and as you can see, it's not always so perfect."

"What did Malcolm study?"

"Malcolm spent his time learning alchemy—more specifically, transmutation."

"Transmutation?"

"It's turning one element into another. Malcolm was always better with metals and such. He displayed such natural talent when it came to alchemy. We needed very little in the way of money after he figured out how to produce gold from almost any metal."

"What about silver?" Anson glared at the boy. "Oh, yeah, sorry." Thomas grinned. "But how did changing metals into gold help you with Malcolm's bloodlust?"

"It didn't, but I started to think that if it can be done with metals, then why not liquids. I must admit it seemed impossible at first. I began with water, it being the purest liquid, therefore the easiest to alter. The practice proved more difficult than I originally anticipated. I wanted to give up. I questioned if all we were doing was right. One night it all came to a head.

"This particular transmutation attempt I had been working on for almost a year, and I was confident it was finally going to work. So confident that I thought it was ready to test on Malcolm. I can still hear his screams from that night. Something had gone terribly wrong with the process, and it reacted badly with his body. He convulsed for hours in my arms as I let him drink of my own blood. Werewolf blood is not a vampire's first choice, Thomas, but when you've been drinking nothing but cattle and swine blood, it might as well be human blood. He made it through the night, and when he healed, I swore I would never try again.

"I had conceded that my brother might have to live with this eternal burden." Anson sniffled, rolled his eyes up and chuckled. "But when I told William of my decision, he said something I will never forget." Anson's face turned happy and sad at the same time. "He said 'How poor are they that have not patience! What wound did ever heal but by degrees? Thou know'st we work by wit, and not by witchcraft; And wit depends on dilatory time.' It dawned on me that it might take some time, but that was the one thing Malcolm and I had in excess. I had promised my brother I would cure him of his bloodlust, and if he was willing to keep trying, who was I to not try too." The werewolf looked at the boy. "You know, William had twins." Anson looked down. "The boy passed away at the age of eleven." He looked back at Thomas. "I sometimes think that's why he understood our pain and suffering and how important helping my brother was to me."

"I guess you finally did figure it out then, right?"

"In the end it came down to science that was unknown at the time of William. We magically altered the molecules and atoms of the water to turn it into human blood. It turned out that William was only half right. It took wit and a bit of witchcraft. Unfortunately, he never got to see the transmutation work. It wasn't until we met up with Newton years later that we solidified the blend."

"Sir Isaac Newton?"

"The same."

"Man, did you guys have a strictly knights-as-friends rule?" Thomas jokingly asked.

Anson laughed out loud and almost spit out his drink. "He wasn't a knight when we knew him, Thomas."

"So, Warwick's Red Ale is actually a magically altered glass of water made to simulate human blood?"

"Yes and no. The chemical makeup of the water has been transformed, thus the new liquid is, in fact, real human blood—with one caveat. There are no white blood cells present in Warwick Red Ale."

"Okay, now I'm confused."

"Malcolm and I were stuck. We did not know what else to do. We had reached an impasse with our experiments, and I decided to start looking elsewhere for assistance. The science was very limited back then. In fact, I would say we were doing things that no one else was even attempting to do. Alchemy and science were one in the same in the 1600s. It was not until Swammerdam had discovered red blood cells that we had our first breakthrough. We were trying to replicate human blood exactly the way it is, but after reading Swammerdam's findings, I started to think that maybe there was only a certain component of blood that vampire's needed for survival."

"Red blood cells," said Thomas.

"Precisely. We started our new experiments immediately, and before long, we had transmuted water into something passable, but it was not enough. It helped Malcolm, but he still needed to supplement his hungers with animal blood. Something was still missing."

"When did gravity boy get involved?"

"Soon after, actually—not long after the Great Plague."

"That's when you guys started to work together?"

"Yes, Thomas. We shared everything we had with him, and Isaac was fascinated with our findings. He wanted to help right away." Anson paused for a second. "He was a nice man—a bit touched, mind you, but nice, nonetheless. We would spend hours locked in his laboratory working on the transmutation. His servants thought him mad—which he was. Some nights Isaac would not go to sleep until 5:00 AM or later. He was simply marvelous at alchemy but like I said, a bit off. But his obsession was the key to discovery. After years of experimentation, we had successfully transmuted water into a red-blood-cell-rich elixir. Malcolm could live a normal life again—well besides the whole undead thing.

"It would be years later that we would discover that the hemoglobin in the red blood cells is the very thing that vampires require for sustenance. Their bodies cannot produce it. We also postulated that the human DNA in the white blood cells is what vampires are addicted to. Without the white blood cells being present in the newly created blood, Malcolm was able to begin quieting his cravings. He is now able to rely solely on this blood for his survival. It astounds me when I think that if it wasn't for a man taking pity on a stranger in an alley, none of this would have happened."

"William was a good friend, huh?"

"The best. William brought Malcolm and me back together all those years ago. They are the only two friends I have ever had."

Anson looked forward and paused. "It's hard having friends when you're immortal. Everyone you love eventually dies. That's why I can be a bit overprotective of Malcolm. We've been together so long, and the thought of losing him again and being alone, well . . ."

"You're not alone, Anson." The Knight Mage pivoted on his stool to look at Thomas. "I would be honored to call you friend." The werewolf looked at Thomas, seemingly surprised by these simple words.

"And I you, Thomas." Anson handed him the bottle, and Thomas drew deeply from it.

"I don't know where Ziza has sent your brother, but I do know one thing. Ziza knows what he's doing, from what I gather, and if Malcolm does get into any trouble, I'm here to help. I promise you that." The boy attempted to hand the bottle one last time to Anson, but it was too late. The werewolf was snoring his tears away, his head cradled by his crossed arms down on the bar. Thomas lifted the bottle and saw there was not much left. He finished off the bottle. "Good night, friend." He placed the empty bottle next to the Anson's head and began to stumble home.

23

desperate

Thomas Scargen had somehow eluded capture by Captain Marcus Slade and his Riders. The Captain had always gotten his man, and now he was in uncharted territory. Scargen was in Sirati, and Marcus and his Riders could not follow. To make matters worse, Arkmalis had killed Franklin Hawthorne—a murder that Marcus knew was unnecessary. *That decision will come back to haunt us, he thought. It is unwise to make enemies of dragons.*

Evangeline had seen inside of Hawthorne's mind. This man struggled and did not give up much, but she had seen the close friendship between Hawthorne and Bartleby Draige, the dragon that had helped Thomas Scargen—a fact that disturbed the Captain. *The only thing dragons hold in higher esteem than credits is loyalty.* This did not change the fact that he was ordered to find the Scargen boy. And if he could not get the boy in Sirati, he would have to wait until Scargen left the safe haven. He needed to know when and where that would be, and the Seer was his only option.

Captain Slade stood next to the imp in silence. Marcus had descended into the bowels of Grimm Tower into the Seer's cell. The only noise to be heard besides the echo of Corbin's trumpeting was the creaking from the metal walkway. Marcus was unsure if it was meant to hold this much weight. Corbin finished playing the summoning horn, and all they could do was wait. Marcus choked a bit.

The smell was almost unbearable for a human, but Marcus insisted on hearing this information firsthand.

"I told you the odor was not fit for 'uman consumption. You could die from some of the stuff I've smelled," said the imp servant. "Still beats the stench from the Depths. That much is certain. Dere's only so much brimstone one should ingest, I'd imagine—no matter what your species."

"I'll be fine, Corbin." The Captain looked around the man-made swamp and saw nothing. "How long does this usually take?"

"Shouldn't be long now . . . dat's if I played the bloody tune right." Marcus did not have time for a mistake of that sort. His anxiety subsided when the surface of the water started to boil. Bubbles formed around the top of the Seer's head as it broke through the surface of the bog. Water ran off his body as he rose from the swamp. The gigantic heap of creature was nestled inside a mound of living fungi and algae.

Marcus looked at the odd creature with complete astonishment. *This is the thing that's supposed to help me find the boy?* thought the Captain. "What is this, Corbin? How am I supposed to take this seriously? You are just wasting my time."

"I assure you, Cap'n, this is no waste of time. The Seer sees everything, well wif duh 'elp of 'is rock anyway." As if on cue, the rock with a jewel embedded into it appeared from the water.

"I have tried everything I know to find this Sirati in the past, but to no avail, and even if I knew its whereabouts, it would matter little," said Marcus.

"The Seer should be able to 'elp you. Like I said before, 'ee's all-knowing." Marcus looked at the big-eyed bulky mass that protruded from the putrid swamp. His oversized eyes were blank as the stone spun in circles.

"Seer, answer one question for me."

"As you wish, Captain of the Bats . . . Slade . . . Marcus Slade . . . Captain Marcus Slade." The Seer's knowledge of his name caught Marcus off guard.

"How do you know my name?"

"It is my curse to know things, to see things, to know and see things others do not. I have seen you before in my visions, Captain, and . . ." His large tongue shot out of his massive head and snagged a frog mid-jump. It was gone with a crunch. "Delicious morsel . . . crunchy delicious morsel. I have seen you before . . . yes, before in my visions. Secrets you have . . . pain." The Seer was silent. "You must tell her—"

"Enough, Seer . . . I'm not here to discuss me. I am here for help finding the Scargen boy. I cannot follow him where he is now."

"I know," answered the Seer. "I know everything . . . everything to know. The innocent Scargen seems to be the only reason I receive guests, in turn guests receive information on futures to come. *Déjà vu*, I think. Orac has *déjà vu* again. I have found the innocent Scargen in London . . . was he not in London? I already know the answer. Visions are never wrong."

"He was in London, but we were too late. He's in Sirati now, but he can't stay there forever." Marcus's stared into the Seer's blank gaze.

"Impossible it is to see into Sirati. Strong magic protects that place, ever-shifting and hiding, hiding and shifting. Wise Captain of the Bats knows this already, I gather. I gather Marcus Slade knows that even Orac cannot see into that place. Impossible, strong magic."

"I am well-versed in the impossibilities of Sirati, Seer. What I need to see is the first thing the boy does after he leaves Sirati. Can you do that for me?"

The floating rock spun faster. The heap grew farther out of the water. The Seer's hands opened outward, and energy circled the creature. The orbs from Corbin's wristcom floated steadily above the Seer. An image glowed from the stone.

A massive man toddled his way through the front door of what looked like a bar. A woman and a tall, thin man accompanied him. It was hard for Marcus to see, but it looked like they were vampires. Thomas Scargen was nowhere to be found.

They entered the establishment filled with more vamps. The vision seemed to center on the oversized vampire. He seemed uncomfortable in his current environment, which was odd considering his size. A vampire of his stature should have little to worry about. The hulking man made his way to the bar. The tall, thin vamp took over from there. The bar was familiar to Marcus.

"This is a blood bar in a remote part of Romania. The town is filled with humans, but run by the vamps. The bar sits on a massive vampire hive controlled by a mad queen. Dark things happen there." The image focused on the vamp bartender. "Jalia Lartor," said the Captain. "I know her." Jalia was someone Marcus had relied on in the past for information—a spy of sorts. The relationship between the vamps and the Tower was tentative at best. Arkmalis had been clear that they must keep an eye on these vampires. If they ever broke the truce, they could be a threat to the integrity of the Grimm Legions. The General was nothing if not practical. "What does this have to do with the boy?"

"Patience, Captain of the Bats, patience."

The group of vamps walked over to a booth. A fat vampire sat there with beautiful human women surrounding him. The bulky vampire spoke. "Are you Fredrick Vilkari?"

"Who wants to know?" asked the fat vampire.

"A friend of a friend."

"I got a lot of friends, big guy. You might want to be a bit more specific."

"Does the name Malcolm Warwick fall into that category?" asked the thinner vamp.

"Don't say dat name too loud, mate. It could be duh last words you utter. Sit down." Vilkari motioned to his seated companions to leave. They scattered on his order.

"What is this?" asked the Captain, interrupting the Seer's vision. "Where is Scargen?" The image faded as the stone fell into the water, and Orac's pupils returned.

"This is what I see. The view is what it is," said the Seer.

"What are you hiding, Orac?"

"Nothing. Orac has nothing to hide. This is what I see. Cannot change it even if Orac wanted to. This has something to do with the innocent Scargen. Always right, my visions. My visions are always right."

Marcus knew that he was telling him the truth, and this worried him. He had hoped the vision would be easier to decipher. "I hope for your sake that this information proves useful."

"My sight is always right, Captain of the Bats." The strange beast began feeding on the toadstools that infested the mound he rested in. "Orac is tired, visions are tiring. I need to rest . . . rest is needed."

"That is all, Seer."

"Thank you, Captain of the Bats. Orac must rest." The clairvoyant heap lowered back into the bubbling swamp. The light orbs raced back into Corbin's wristcom.

The imp rushed up the ladder and opened the hatch. Marcus followed shortly behind him. The Captain turned to the small-statured servant when they had finally shut the hatch door. "Thank you, Corbin. That experience was quite enlightening."

"Enlightening? It was a big waste of time."

"Don't be so sure of that." The two had reached the main floor. Marcus looked down onto his wristcom and hit a few buttons. An image of an attractive pale woman appeared. She was the vampire that Marcus had befriended some time back and the bartender at the bar from Orac's vision—their spy.

"Hello, Captain," the woman whispered. "To what do I owe the pleasure? It has been a while."

"That it has, Jalia. I see you're still bartending."

"Nothing gets passed you." The frustrated captain managed a smile. "Hey, Kreeg. I gotta take this. Cover me?" said Jalia to one of her coworkers. The image bobbed up and down as she walked to what looked like the back alley behind the bar. She pulled out a rolled cigarette and lit it. She took a deep drag.

"I see you still enjoy your dragonweed."

"It gets me by."

"You know that stuff will kill you?"

"Too late," said Jalia as she giggled. "What's going on, Marcus? I don't have a lot of time to chitchat. We're in the middle of happy hour."

"I have some information that may be of use to you."

"I'm listening," responded Jalia.

"You need to be wary of strange visitors."

"What do you mean?"

"There may be someone coming to the hive that does not belong, and he seems to be working with one of your patrons."

"What patron?"

"Are you familiar with a Fredrick Vilkari?"

"Unfortunately, yes." The vampire's expression looked like she just ate something rancid. "He's a lazy, fat, human-lover. Oh, sorry. What I mean is he is always seen with human women in town. He brings them here all the time. It's disgusting really. What about him? I mean he's repulsive to look at, but he seems harmless."

"I think he is helping Malcolm Warwick."

"Malcolm Warwick? The blood traitor? Nobody's seen him in centuries. He's here?"

"Yes. I believe so, but considering the circumstances he will most likely be in disguise. I've been told he's not looked at too kindly around the Hive."

"That's an understatement." She inhaled more smoke. "Where did you get your information from?"

"A reliable source. That is all I can say. I just need you to be on the lookout for any strange man hanging around with Vilkari."

"I can do that."

"There is one other thing." Marcus paused. "There will be other vampires looking for Warwick. They seem to be his friends."

"How should I handle this?"

"Vilkari is the key. Keep an eye on him. He will lead you to Warwick, and make sure you tell Scornd about this."

"She's not going to believe this. She hates him. There's some seriously bad blood between those two." She smiled at her unintentional pun.

"Then Scornd will act swiftly to capture him. Just do not tell her your source, and don't mention the others just yet. If I know her, once she captures Warwick, she will assume others will come looking for him. I need to know if and when they arrive. Can you handle that? They are more important to me than Warwick."

"Of course I can handle it. What kind of question is that? I'll get you all the info I can, as soon as possible. Just know, Marcus: it's going to cost you." She took one more puff from the rolled cigarette and tossed what was left aside. "I gotta go back inside. Gotta get back to the bloodsuckers. Kreeg's probably in the weeds by now. Later." The hologram of the vampire disappeared.

Marcus was certain that Malcolm Warwick and these other vampires held the key to finding the boy. The Seer was never wrong.

24

hangover dreams

"*Aloha kakahiaka*, Thomas," said Lolani, the Hawaiian woman he had met when he first arrived in Sirati. Thomas pulled his eyes open. The sight of light made him retreat back to the safety of his pillow. The sudden movement awakened a pain deep in his skull. His mouth was dry, and he was still wearing the clothes from the night before. Thomas was hungover. He flapped his lips together trying to form words. She handed him a glass of water. He guzzled the water in seconds. He put the glass down and wiped his lips with the back of his hand and tucked his head back under his pillow. After a few seconds of hiding, he realized she was not going anywhere.

"Hello . . . Mancer Lolani." Thomas yawned, still a bit lethargic from the late talk with Anson—not to mention the bottle of whiskey. Lolani sat down next to the bed. "What time is it? It's still dark out." Thomas sat up, jarring Stella from her sleep. The cat had been nestled safely between his legs. The cat voiced her protest and jumped down off of the bed. Stella ran to Mancer Lolani and leapt into her lap. She rubbed the feline's head three times. She then stood and placed the cat on the floor. The cat purred and blinked slowly, then walked away.

"It does not matter what time it is, Thomas. It is now."

"What are we doing up so early?" The boy desperately wanted

just fifteen minutes more of sleep. He turned away from Lolani and yawned.

"The earth awakens with the coming of the sun. We don't want to miss it."

"So what am I gonna be fighting today?" He stretched his arms above his head.

"Your mind, Thomas."

"My mind? What are you talking about?" The boy turned around to see the plump Hawaiian woman had already climbed down from the tree house and was scurrying towards the dense jungle, walking stick in hand.

"I don't have all day, Thomas." She giggled loudly as she continued to walk.

"The smart people are still sleeping!" He raised his voice so she could hear him. "Technically the day hasn't even begun!"

"Meow," said Stella.

"Who asked you, anyway?" said Thomas, slipping on his boots as quickly as possible. He jumped down from the tree's balcony onto the solid dirt.

Thomas struggled to keep up with Lolani. He was tired and the last thing he wanted to do was go on a brisk jaunt through the jungle. "I haven't even eaten breakfast yet." The peculiar fruit almost hit him directly in the nose. He caught it at the last second and bit into it. "Thanks." Thomas had never seen anything like it, but he was hungry.

They walked for what seemed an hour to the boy. His feet were tired and his head still ached. Lolani stopped and turned towards Thomas. "We are about to enter the oldest part of the jungle, Thomas."

"How do you know that?"

"The trees told me."

"You can talk to the trees?"

"No, Thomas, look how big they are." She smiled at the boy and quickly began to laugh out loud as she disappeared into the jungle. "You coming, or you just gonna stand there?" Thomas followed the fading laughter. "Today, you are going to think a little differently than you normally do."

"What's wrong with the way I think? I'm pretty damn smart."

"Being smart is important only if you think it is, Thomas."

"What do you mean?"

"It's obvious that you wish people to think of you as a smart person."

"Yes, what's wrong with that?"

"Nothing, Thomas, but what is right about it?" He stared with a blank, confused look. "You have a preconceived notion that *smart* means *better*, I'd imagine."

"I guess . . . I never looked at it like that before."

"And that's why we are here." They crossed a small stream and climbed up the embankment. "We are going to go on a spirit walk. First, you must work on your mind's perception. Then, you can deal with your fears."

"My fears? What do you mean my fears?"

"These are questions only you can answer, Thomas. You need to start with rethinking everything you've ever learned. Distance, time, gravity—all concepts that limit you."

"Wait, are you trying to tell me the law of gravity is not real?"

"Yes, Thomas, sometimes."

"What do you mean *sometimes*?" Thomas picked up a stone and dropped it.

"What I'm saying is the rock might fall because it wants to, not because someone a long time ago said that it must."

"You've got to be kidding me."

"What would a young bird do if he knew of such human limitations as gravity? Look at your friend Bartleby, or Malcolm for that matter. They determine when and where they will land. Leave this atmosphere and where does the law stray? It is cute to try and package everything in a nice little container, Thomas, but that is not reality. The true reality is that there is no reality, at least past what we have been told to believe. People's beliefs and assumptions make up who they are. If you can't see past this simple truth, you will never be free." The boy pondered this idea as they continued towards their destination.

They passed through a line of trees into a clearing. Thomas heard the distinct sound of moving water as they walked over to the side of a massive river. The wind lightly tickled the surface, rippling the top of the river. Two magnificent trees jutted out over the rushing water. Each tree had a branch that formed a natural platform, twisting above the river. The twin trees dwarfed the two of them. Lolani began to climb the tree on the left. She pointed to the other, indicating Thomas should do the same.

He placed his feet carefully on the knots and in the holes as he balanced himself above the river, trying not to slip on the moss-covered wood. When Thomas reached the hand-like formation, he looked across and saw Lolani already sitting, legs crossed and eyes closed, hands resting on her knees, palms up. "You have great power within you, Thomas, but everybody does. You have been able to tap its source periodically, but your ability to control and consciously use it is at best mediocre. True power comes from accomplishing something, not the potential of one day accomplishing it. Everyone has this potential, Thomas, but it takes hard work. It takes focus and purpose. The control you seek so desperately is an illusion. You need not fear your lack of control, but you must start making decisions and sticking with them. Trust your choices. There are no bad decisions. Every decision leads you down a different path. The path is what matters. Everything around you may change, but you cannot control that. You can only control you." She opened one eye. "Well, go on and sit. We have a lot to do today."

"What do you want me to do?"

"Nothing, Thomas."

"Nothing?"

"Nothing."

"Oo-kay." Thomas sat there for several uncomfortable minutes with his eyes closed. "What should I be thinking of?"

"Whatever you want—or nothing—as long as you understand it's your choice."

"All right . . . think of nothing—or not."

"Now you're getting it."

Thomas opened his eyes. "I can't imagine that's true."

"Imagination is the key, Thomas. If you cannot imagine it, you cannot do it. This is the only thing that can limit you." She began to glow a faint white color. Lolani lifted out of her natural chair and levitated about one foot in the air.

"How are you doing that?"

"No limitations. All your true power flows from within, Thomas. The world outside is only what you think it is. The only truth is inside of you. Do not dwell on what happened before or what might come . . . walk in the now. The present is your moment."

Thomas closed his eyes and let his mind go blank. He could hear the bubbling and churning of the river. He tried but could not concentrate. His eyes popped open. "I don't think I can do this."

"You need to stop thinking. Your mind is clouded like this river. Your preconceived notions are the river's flow. The waves muddy the water and make it hard to see the bottom. But if you eliminate the current, the waters become still, and everything becomes clear."

"Yeah, but you can't stop a flowing river," said Thomas as if he had outwitted her.

She shook her head and raised her left hand towards the river as she closed her eyes. She began to float again. Her body began to shake. White light erupted from her form.

The flash made the boy squint. Lolani was no longer shaking, but still radiated white light. The jungle seemed quieter. The bubbling and churning had ceased. Thomas looked down at the water. He could not believe it. The river had stopped. The waters were still. Lolani looked at the boy. "Preconceived notions, Thomas." She lowered her hand, and the river continued its travels.

"Good visual," said the boy as he stared at the river.

"I want you to sit here until you understand what you have just seen." The boy turned from the river to look at Mancer Lolani, but she had vanished. He adjusted his position and closed his eyes.

Okay Thomas . . . focus. Think of nothing . . . nothing . . . nothing. The boy sat still and did not move. His mind exploded with all sorts of thoughts. He tried as hard as he could to control the rambling nature of his contemplations. *Yareli doesn't hate me.* He shook his head. *Where's my father?* He knew thinking of this was not a good idea right now. He tried to clear his head again. Another thought jumped into the old thought's place. *Where did Ziza send Malcolm? That is Ziza's problem, Thomas, not yours. Great—now I'm arguing with myself. This isn't working.* Thomas opened his eyes and looked at the rushing water. He closed his eyes again. He thought again about the river and its momentary stillness and focused his mind on that moment. He sat there—eyes shut—focusing on the calmness of the water.

Minutes passed. The minutes collected into hours, and hours washed by like the river's current. Thomas had no idea how long he had been sitting there, but the stiffness in his back had finally subsided. He could feel the wind sweeping across his face. He could hear the Earth breathing. The boy concentrated on the river. His breath slowed down and his body relaxed. Thomas began to align his own breath with that of the Earth's. He thought of nothing but the moment. Serenity coursed through him, as if all his fears, failures, and insecurities had lifted. His mind was reborn. Thomas had never felt this happy and calm. Energy circulated in his veins. He could feel his limitless potential, and for the first time in his life, he felt at peace. His body slowly lifted off of the platform.

"Now, I want you to think of your father."

Thomas dropped back down on the branch. The boy had been startled by Lolani's voice. He opened his eyes. She was sitting directly across from him again. The sun was setting. The fall along with the thought of his father awoke the boy from his meditation. "How long was I meditating?"

"Time is another man-made obstacle, Thomas."

"Why do you want me to think about my father? I haven't stopped thinking about him. He's still miss—"

"I know." Her words cut off his. "This is what you need to heal. The question of your father's whereabouts is eating you alive. This makes you vulnerable."

"I just hope he's safe. I don't know what I would do without him." Tears welled up in the corners of his eyes. Water trickled down, slowly carving a twisted path.

"Your reaction is more than understandable, but it leaves you susceptible to attack. This will not do."

"He's my dad, damn it. Am I supposed to just forget about him?"

"No, Thomas. That is not what I am saying. We are going to travel deep into your mind and unlock and explore this pivotal dream of yours. There may be clues that will answer some of these questions you have. All I ask from you is your total focus."

"I will do my best." Thomas settled back into his meditative state.

"I wouldn't expect anything less. Now, Thomas, listen to my voice. Breathe deeply. Relax and let all worries escape your mortal frame." She paused, giving the boy time to realize her instructions. "I want you to think about your father—more specifically, your dream."

Thomas was still. He began to remember the beginning of his dream. The last few weeks had been hectic, but he could not forget the vivid vision.

"Now, Thomas . . . take my hand." Before he could question her instructions, he found himself holding her hand. He opened his eyes, astonished by their proximity. They were both on the platform in Egypt standing behind Dr. Carl Scargen's lifelong colleague Sigmund. He was studying a bizarre artifact.

"Wait, are we—"

"Yes, we are in your dream, Thomas." Lolani cut off the boy again. "We need to be alert and search for clues. This is the one shot we have."

"So they can't see us, right?"

"No, they cannot. We are in your subconscious," said Lolani as she looked around and closed her eyes. "This does not feel like a normal dream. The images are too coherent. Usually when I am inside a dream, the images are all over the place—drastically different from reality." She walked over towards Sigmund to get a better look at what he was examining.

Thomas was preoccupied by the image of his father. The boy stood in front of Dr. Carl Scargen, staring at him as he worked on a diggerbot. "He looks so happy."

"That's because he's talking about you, Thomas."

"That should just about do it, Digger 211. You should be as good as new," said Carl Scargen, turning away from the large artif.

"Nothing looks too out of the ordinary." She was surveying the area when her eyes settled upon the dark artifact in Sigmund's hand. "But something isn't right about the stone."

"How do you know, Mancer?"

"I can sense it, Thomas. It is cursed; very strong, dark magic indeed. This rock might hold the answers we seek." Her eyes narrowed as she studied the stone. "I am not familiar with these symbols. They are similar to the Ancient language, but they are certainly not the same."

"Yeah, but something tells me that if you spent ten minutes looking at this thing you could figure it out your damn self," Sigmund said to the Doc.

"But I think I know who might be able to decipher these markings," said Mancer Lolani.

"Let me guess . . . High Mancer Bebami," answered Thomas.

"Precisely. We need to learn as many of those symbols as we can before we leave this vision. They might hold the key to your father's location." She moved closer to discern the symbols. Thomas also turned his attention towards the stone.

"Like I said, Doc, I'm stumped." Sigmund looked at Thomas's father. "You might be useful after all."

"I guess I'll have to save your ass again. Toss the rock over here, let's see what my keen sense of language can decipher," said the Doc jokingly as he leaned over and extended his hand.

"This is the part where everything goes crazy." Thomas looked dismayed as if he could change the outcome. "I will stick with my father."

"I will stay with Sigmund." Sigmund placed the rock into Dr. Carl Scargen's hand. A blinding flash emanated from the stone, instantly followed by dark smoke. Thomas flinched backward from the light and found himself coughing from the smoke. "I lost him."

"I can't see him anywhere," said Lolani. "I am losing the connection."

"I'm coming over to you." As he exited the smoke, so did the cold, hooded figure. The image stunned Thomas. He almost fell to the ground. The boy froze, and his eyes focused on the man's face. He noticed something new he had not before: bandages, similar to the wrappings of a mummy, covered the man's features. This man petrified Thomas. Lolani was nowhere to be found.

"Mancer Lolani . . . where are y—" The draining of Sigmund's soul from the husk that was his body cut off his words. The body fell to the ground and exploded into dust.

"Sig!" The boy began to sob as the madman laughed out loud. After a huge jolt forward, Thomas found himself in a seated position on the tree. Lolani had already abandoned her perch and was hurrying along the jungle floor, obviously worried. It was deep into the night. *How long were we under?* "Mancer Lolani!" Thomas yelled at the plump woman as she waddled away in the moonlight.

"I have to hurry, Thomas, or I will forget the symbols. I have to report them to the High Mancer. I'll see you at Maktaba tomorrow. I am sure Ziza will want to . . . *accelerate* your training considering the new circumstances. You better get a good rest."

"New circumstances?" questioned the boy. He tried to move, but could not. Thomas was exhausted. His body ached, and his eyes were having a hard time seeing anything in the dark. Thomas had forgotten to grab his goggles and his wristcom. "What time is it?" The boy was disoriented, and Mancer Lolani had vanished into the foliage. He yawned and closed his eyes. Darkness flowed around him, and Thomas was immediately asleep.

25

like a glove

Thomas opened his eyes slowly. A monkey stared at him and twisted its head. The boy sat up, startled as the primate worked its way down the branch that was his impromptu bed. Morning was creeping into the sky as shadows painted stripes over the flowing river. The boy was groggy. He yawned and stretched his arms over his head.

"Damn," said Thomas. "I gotta get home." He jumped down and zoomed through the woods. He arrived at the tree house and walked in to find LINC. The artif was interfacing with Sirati's mainframe. The artif broke off his connection when he saw the boy approach.

"I have spent the last 22 hours, 37 minutes, and 14 seconds attempting to ascertain your whereabouts, Thomas Scargen."

"Sorry, LINC. I fell asleep in the jungle." The words sounded odd even to Thomas.

"That is not a logical place to initiate REM sleep. The beacon in your wristcom directed me to your bedside table, but you were not in the device's vicinity."

"Yeah, I didn't bring it with me. Lolani rushed me out."

"Here is the previously mentioned wristcom." The robot produced the wristcom from a compartment that slid open in the middle of his back. "It has been broadcasting a repeating signal."

"For how long?"

"Approximately 47 minutes, 35 seconds."

"Approximately?" Thomas clicked the wristcom onto his arm. He could faintly hear a noise. Someone had called and left him a message. He cringed at the fact that it could be Veronica again, but the image that now was suspended above his wrist was that of Elgin Neficus. He looked down.

"You are needed at Maktaba in exactly one hour. There is much to discuss about . . . your future. Do not be late." Thomas looked at the time of the message. It had been sent forty-nine minutes prior.

"Great," said the boy. He ran up the stairs and changed out of his forest-worn clothes. He hurried back down the stairs. "Hey LINC, wanna take a walk with me?"

"I simply do not possess the emotional capacity to yearn for or desire things, but the proposal of promenading with you is improbably intriguing. I hypothesize the intrigue stems strictly from my prime directive of protecting Thomas Scargen."

"I'll take that as a yes."

They reached the elevator with a few minutes to spare. Onjamba was waiting for them, holding the door open with his trunk. "Come in. There is plenty of room." Once they funneled into the car, the Elephant let the door close. He had the same silver platter in his hand that he had the first evening of Thomas's training, which now seemed like years ago. "Hello, Thomas. I trust you slept well last evening." The Elephant winked at the boy as he raised the tray top with his trunk. A plate with one huge egg—sunny-side up—stared at Thomas. There was also a piece of rye toast. "You mustn't forget to eat. This is a most important meeting, and breakfast being the most important meal and all."

"That's the biggest egg I've ever seen."

"It is an ostrich egg—my specialty." Thomas used the silver fork that was next to the plate. He scooped up the large egg and slurped it down with one bite. Onjamba looked stunned. The boy grabbed the piece of toast and took a bite out of it. He placed the fork back down on the platter.

"That was delicious, Onjamba . . . I needed that." He continued to chew. "You are in the wrong profession, my friend."

"Unfortunately, I don't know if the world is ready for a talking Elephant chef; besides Thomas, it was just an egg."

"Fair enough." The elevator chimed, signifying that they had reached the uppermost floor.

"Here we are," said the Elephant, straightening his vest as the door slid open. Two Sentry Mages again stood at attention on either side of the open doors. Anson met them as they exited the elevator. The now familiar thumping sound began to beat on his eardrums.

"I trust you slept well, Thomas," said Anson as he smirked at the boy.

"Am I the only person that doesn't think it's funny that I was unconscious in the middle of the predator-filled jungle?"

"You're right . . ." Anson held back the laugh. "It's not funny."

"It's a little funny, huh?" said the boy.

"If it makes you feel any better, I slept for two days after my first spirit walk," said the werewolf.

The faint knocking sound echoed in Thomas's ears. He tried to ignore it and continue his conversation with Anson, but the werewolf had walked ahead. They moved in silence the rest of the way to the circular table. The rhythmic pounding grew louder as they walked closer to the mysterious door. Thomas knew something was beyond the door but had stopped mentioning it. Apparently no one else heard the hammering beat—at least no one would admit that they did.

Ziza stood at the head of the table. Mancer Lolani and Neficus flanked him, seated as usual. Emfalmay was behind Ziza. Anson took his spot to the left of Lolani. "Hello, Thomas. I was afraid after you had not answered Neficus's call that we might not be seeing you this morning," said Ziza.

"I left my wristcom at the tree house. I was in such a hurry I—"

"That is not important, my boy. The important thing is that you are, indeed, here. Now, I will get right to the point." The old man moved slightly closer to the circular door. "So far, you have been performing beyond our expectations. You have learned to use your power, and—more importantly—you have learned how to control these powers. Your exercise with Lolani was most enlightening. It proved that you are ready to take the next step." The old man turned around and was now facing the strange door. "The Council has decided to share with you how these powers work in an effort to expedite your training." The boy's ears perked slightly. Thomas could not believe what the old man had just said.

"How can you possibly explain magic?" asked the boy.

"It is all based on quite a simple concept. Everything around you, Thomas, is made up of subatomic particles. These particles, when formed into different combinations, make different things. My staff, this table, the centerpiece that Onjamba was nice enough to arrange . . ." Thomas looked at the Elephant as he waved back with his trunk. "And all of us here are constructed from the same tiny elements." The boy was intrigued by where Ziza was going with this, but the annoying thumping was distracting him. It was getting noticeably faster and louder. "What we can do, Thomas, is not difficult to explain, but incredibly difficult to do. We manipulate these particles." Ziza waited for the concept to take root before watering it any further.

"And I thought it was magic."

"It *is* magic, Thomas—that's the point. Magic is just a convenient word to describe what we do. It seems mystical and fantastic, but it's quite natural, I assure you. All the *magic* we do is just varying levels of altering these particles. Once you grasp this solitary truth, nothing is the same." He stared right at the boy. "Some are better than others at it, and with practice, still others can become most proficient at the skill. That is why you can move faster and how you can manipulate energy. You are rearranging these particles."

The boy was trying his best to comprehend what Ziza was telling him, but the noise had grown to an almost unbearable level.

"Does it work that way for all magic users?" he said as he grabbed at his head.

"Necromancers work entirely differently, and this fundamental difference is what divides us. The distinction is intention, Thomas. We *ask* these particles to cooperate with us to achieve a goal. A user of dark magic *forces* these particles to do their bidding. Ours is a symbiotic relationship; theirs is slave to master. Our method is the natural way of things; theirs is the equivalent of torture. You see, my boy, everything around you is really just one large, living creature, and when you perform dark magic, you hurt that creature." The man paused and looked at the boy. "Your natural ability to influence these particles is extremely advanced. It also happens to be the reason why you are hearing that noise." Thomas eyes opened wide.

"You can hear it?"

"Not exactly. I can feel it, but I have heard the same noise before. You will have to trust me on this. It is also important that you grasp what I am trying to explain to you."

"I get it, I think. Everything is made from the same stuff."

"I need you to show me you understand this."

"How do I do that?"

"I want you to open that door."

"Finally," said Thomas as he got up from his seat and moved towards the door.

"Stop!" said the High Mancer. "I want you to open it from there." The boy turned to look at Ziza.

"And how am I supposed to do that?"

"Ask the particles to help you, Thomas. Ask them to alter themselves to force the door open."

"Just like that?"

"Just like that," said The High Mancer.

The boy slumped a bit. He closed his eyes and thought about what Ziza had just explained. He began to picture these small particles that make up everything. More specifically, he thought about the particles around the door. His hands rose up and reached out as if he were grabbing the door. *Here goes nothing.* He pictured the particles surrounding the door forming into two hands that gripped the sides of the circular portal. The knocking continued at a fevered pace.

KNOCK, KNOCK, KNOCK, KNOCK, KNOCK . . . *Concentrate.* He tried to imagine the hands pulling against the door. He could see these invisible hands rocking the door back and forth. As he was doing this, it came to him. *I understand. I get it. I can move these particles just the same as I can move my own hands. They are both the same.*

At that moment, Thomas Scargen understood how he had been accomplishing the remarkable things he had done since the night he had met Yareli and Wiyaloo up on the cliff. The hands were no longer imaginary to the boy. They were quite real. "Let's try this again." He reached out with the particled hands and grabbed the door again. The boy vigorously pulled it back and forth. The room shook from the sheer power of the maneuver. The sound of cracking wood filled the floor as the Cheetahs that flanked the door raced out of the way. The alien insignia in the middle of the door began to glow white. Thomas's eyes burned, and his muscles ached—as if he were ripping the door off of its hinges. And then it happened: the door crumbled as the two hands pulled apart. Shards of wood went flying in all directions. Thomas threw what was left of the door aside with the hands he had constructed from the particles around the door. The noise stopped, and Thomas felt instant relief.

An object glowed and hovered in the doorway. It appeared to be a large glove—a gauntlet. It flew towards the boy and stopped in front of him. Thomas's eyes burned as the artifact rotated in front of him. He was speechless.

It was made entirely of a light gray rock—almost white, but not quite that pale. A large groove on the back of the glove resembled a still pool. This opening seemed to be covered by a shield. Thomas could see himself in its refection. He could now see his eyes were glowing indigo. A burning sensation filled his body. The power of this object was overwhelming. He could feel the glove's actual existence. "What is it?" asked the boy. He wanted to know. He needed to know.

"It is the Gauntlet. It is the reason I brought you to my home.

If you choose to do so, you may wield it. The Gauntlet has spoken, and it has chosen you. It is a most formidable weapon when used properly, and it could most certainly help you find your father. We have been waiting for some time now for the one meant to wield the Gauntlet. It has been a long time coming." He walked closer to Thomas. "You are not the first. In fact, someone close to you was one we thought would be the next wielder."

Thomas pondered this for a second. *Anson?* he thought. *It's gotta be Anson.* "So what do I do now?"

"I suggest you think long and hard about this decision. Sometimes things are not as they seem, Thomas. Your power seems to have unlimited potential. This is one of the reasons you were originally sought out, but do not take this responsibility lightly, my boy. The Gauntlet casts an ominous shadow. You need to genuinely ask yourself, 'Do I want this?' Once there is a connection between it and you, it will be impossible to break its hold."

"Its hold?"

"The Gauntlet melds with your body. It needs you—and you begin to need it."

"How do you know all this?"

"I bore the Gauntlet for some time," said Ziza with a grin.

"Can anyone put this thing on?"

"No . . . the Gauntlet chooses whom it wants to join. The wielder must be pure of heart and intention. It is a great honor to be chosen, but it is also a great responsibility." The old man seemed mesmerized by the glove. "Many have tried to wear the Gauntlet, but few have been successful." A hologram appeared above the table. "You can see here a list of the potential bearers." It was a list of different people and cities from all around the globe. Moving holograms of all of them floated next to their names.

LEWIS ASHFIELD—BIRMINGHAM

MORTIMER P. SCREWDLING—EL PASO

VICTORIA DARLINGSWORTH—LONDON

GRAYDEN ARKMALIS—HELSINKI

MUMP—THE SWAMPS OF NEVERLORE

YARELI CHULA—BOWDLE
THOMAS SCARGEN—NEW SALEM

Thomas's eyes flashed to Yareli's name. *That explains the cold shoulder.* The image was of a younger Yareli, but she had the same determined look on her face. Before the boy could dwell on it, Ziza continued.

"Truth be told, Morty from El Paso would have made a fine Gauntlet wielder, but the Gauntlet had other plans, and do not even get me started on Mump. He was powerful enough, but refused to leave his precious swamp," said Ziza.

"What is a *Mump*?" asked Thomas.

"You don't want to know, Thomas," said Anson. "Trust me. I could go another five centuries without running into something like that. It took weeks for that stench to wash out of my clothes." He sniffed himself. "One of the curses of having such a good sense of smell." The boy and the wolf shared a giggle, and then Thomas looked back at Ziza.

"I noticed Arkmalis on the list. Is this the man that's after me?"

"One and the same."

"What happened?" Thomas studied the holographic image of the adolescent Arkmalis. Arkmalis could not have been older than twelve. In the holographic simulation, he was smiling.

"I had sought him out based on his potential. His power was great—there was no denying that. He was a prodigy. The Gauntlet boomed when he was around, but he was far too young for this responsibility. He lacked patience and focus—two evils I have warned you about. He did not want to train, and he did not want to study, but his skill was natural." The old man looked directly at Thomas and raised his left eyebrow. "I could never have predicted his fate."

"What happened to him?"

"A Necromancer saw the boy's weakness and used it to twist and manipulate him. He promised him everything. Grayden left to become a disciple of this man. His spirit was crushed and destroyed." The last statement seemed to hurt the High Mancer. "Grayden was ten years old when he left Sirati. I will always regret that day." He closed his eyes and shook his head. "Tollin Grimm destroyed this boy's life."

"Who's Tollin Grimm?"

"He was a man I called friend a lifetime ago when I bore the Gauntlet."

"What happened?"

"He betrayed me, Thomas, and I guess in a way, I betrayed him."

"What do you mean?"

"Vengeance clouded my judgment." The old man paused. "I fought Tollin."

"Because of Arkmalis?"

"No, Thomas, this was well before that. I was . . . young . . . brash . . . stupid. There was a girl that I loved. Her name was Alana Wrencrawl." He stopped pacing and his face changed ever so slightly as if he had just remembered what love felt like. "She was my everything." The old man paused and looked up at the tree. "We created this place together with the help of the Gauntlet's power. It was our dream to change the world. You see, Thomas, not only is everything made of the same *stuff* as you put it, but we and everything on this planet are all also connected by these particles. The trees, the earth, the sea, the sky are all one. This planet is one big living organism. We do not simply *live* on it; we *are* it. We as a people had forgotten this simple truth." Ziza was now pacing.

"Sirati was to be the prototype for a new world, a shining example of technology and nature coexisting for the betterment of all living things." The old man leaned hard on his staff. "Tollin lived here then. We were close. He had been essential in my success with the Gauntlet and Sirati. He was my best friend. We were not always mortal enemies." Ziza appeared to be reliving some of the pain as he spoke. "The problem with dreaming, Thomas, is, sooner or later, you have to wake up."

"What happened?"

"He killed her." A tear ran smoothly down the old man's face. "Tollin wanted Alana, but she loved me . . . and I her. I admit I did know his feelings for her, but you do not choose who you love, my boy." Ziza bowed his head down. "He thought I had betrayed him. To him, there was no choice. If he could not have her, then no one could." Ziza paused and looked at the boy. Tears swelled and fell. "Love is powerful, Thomas. If it goes unanswered, it can also be quite dangerous."

"What did you do?"

"I found him three months later in a remote mountain village in China. We had studied magic in those mountains together in our youth." He almost smiled as he paused. "He had been hiding there, seeking atonement. He regretted what he had done and searched for peace. As soon as he saw me, he knew there would never be peace for him. I attacked him without pause." Ziza slowly shook his head. "We fought for hours. I sometimes think if I would've let him be . . . " He roused from his thoughts and looked up at the boy. "At the end of the battle, he was severely disfigured—his face unrecognizable. And the Gauntlet left me with a permanent reminder of my vengeance." He lifted the mangled arm. "Power always comes with a price, and there are consequences to your actions, Thomas." He pulled his disfigured arm from his sleeve. The muscles and bone were tangled in a gnarled mess. The exposed appendage was far worse than the boy could have ever imagined. Ziza sheathed the arm once more. "The Gauntlet will take from you over time, and if you misuse it, it is not kind."

"What happened to the Gauntlet?"

"It fell off of me as I was about to destroy Tollin. It lay dormant on the ground as I tended to my injury. It can only be used to serve good, and killing out of vengeance is never good."

"But he killed her."

"That's how I felt at the time. I felt betrayed. I could not fathom how the Gauntlet had failed me at the moment I needed it the most. He killed someone I loved, so he deserved to die." The boy nodded in agreement. "But I was wrong, Thomas. I acted in anger. Tollin deserved justice, not death. Who was I to carry out such a sentence? It would have made me no better than him. I should have shown him mercy. Nothing good is born of hate."

"I didn't think of it like that."

"I grabbed the Gauntlet and left Tollin to die. He was uncon-scious and severely wounded. I thought it only a matter of time. It was not until later that I realized what I had almost done. Killing him would not have made the pain any easier to carry, and nothing I did would have brought Alana back to me." Ziza looked up and then over to Thomas. "I swore afterwards that I would find the next Bearer. Even if it took a lifetime, I owed the Gauntlet at least that much. I owed Alana at least that much. Our dream of a new world was not dead as long as I had hope." Ziza looked around and smiled. "I assembled a new Council of Mages. It had been centuries since the last Council had met, but I needed to ensure that if something were to happen to me, the Gauntlet and its Bearer would be protected; Alana's dream would be protected. The Council was the only way of achieving this goal."

Thomas saw the love in Ziza's eyes. He had never seen him like this before. Thomas thought of Yareli. He desperately wanted to know why she was not standing here in his place. *I wonder what went wrong.* It bothered him that he did not know, but he would not ask. *If she wants to tell me, she can. Otherwise, it's none of my business.* The boy refocused.

"What happened to Grimm?"

"He was destroyed by the Gauntlet."

"You said the Gauntlet fell off of you before you could de-stroy him."

"This is true, but, Thomas, I was not the last Bearer. There was another." The idea had not occurred to Thomas.

"Where's he at now?"

"Assumptions, Thomas," said Lolani. "The last Bearer was a woman."

"Sorry, Mancer Lolani. I didn't mean it like—"

"She is no longer with us," answered Ziza cutting off the boy's apology.

"She's dead?"

"She died destroying Tollin Grimm."

"How did she—"

"Tollin awoke, determined to destroy me for what I had done to him. The remorseful man that I had fought was not so anymore. That man died that day; I killed him. He spent years practicing dark magic and trying to find any artifact or weapon he could get his hands on to try and match the Gauntlet and me. He did not know I was no longer the Bearer. Tollin had searched for decades before finding the Scythe."

"Do I even need to ask?"

"The Scythe is his weapon—well, *was* his weapon. It changed him, Thomas. He had committed murder, but that was a crime of passion. The dark power in the Scythe tainted the man I had once called friend, and it drove him to complete madness. His vengeance turned into obsession. He was obsessed with destroying Sirati and destroying me, and he had the power to do both. If not for her, we would all have been doomed."

"Who was she? Where did she come from?"

"We knew her only as Mary. She showed up at one of the force-fields requesting an audience with me."

"How did she find the place with all of the defensive magic protecting Sirati?" asked Thomas.

"Things were not always the way they are now, my boy. There was a time when no such protections were needed. But where was I . . . oh, yes . . . she showed up out of nowhere. You see, Thomas, usually I see these people and their energies well before I meet them. That is how I originally discovered you." He had not thought about how they knew about him. "But I was caught off guard by Mary. Young Grayden had clouded my judgment. He was still living here at the time, and I truly believed he would be the next Bearer. I did not see her coming.

"She told us that she had nightmares about what Tollin Grimm was hoping to do with his newfound strength. Once we had met, her power was obvious to me, but quite new to her. Mary had explained to me that she was having visions—visions of her fighting Tollin. I convinced her to let us train her—that she would fare better against him if she had more knowledge and control. I also knew she had come for the Gauntlet. I had wanted so desperately to find the next Bearer that I had not noticed her until she showed up at my doorstep. I was obviously overjoyed with these events, but one boy was not."

"Arkmalis?"

"Grayden became increasingly jealous. He was no longer the golden child. He became angry and despondent, and eventually he ran away. Tollin was waiting for him with open arms." Ziza looked down for a few seconds and shook his head back and forth. He then looked up. "I fear my haste to find the next Bearer forever doomed that child." Ziza paused. "Mary was selfless and genuine. The Gauntlet thundered the first time she entered here. In fact the only time it has been louder was today, my boy, and since the Gauntlet will only serve the kind at heart, I knew I did not have to fear her." The boy tried to comprehend the meaning of this last statement.

"She was extraordinary, Thomas, but a loner. When she was not training, she studied. On the rare occasions when she was not doing either of these, she kept her distance. I think she understood there was no returning from this fight, so she tried hard not to befriend anyone. Mary was focused on one task and one task only. She wanted to save the world, Thomas . . . by stopping Tollin Grimm."

"And you were just going to let her try by herself?"

"There was no letting her or not letting her. She would have fought this man with or without my help." He looked over at the Gauntlet. "When the time came, she accepted the Gauntlet. She spent the next six months preparing for her destiny, and then Tollin made the first move."

"What did he do?" asked Thomas.

"Tollin attacked Cairo. This is where I had met Alana, and he knew what that city meant to me. He also knew I would not sit back while he destroyed innocent lives. He was trying to provoke a response from me. Before welcoming Arkmalis into his fold, he had still thought I wielded the Gauntlet, but it had been many years since I had. He did not have the foresight to see that the Gauntlet had chosen a new symbiont. He took his anger out on Egypt."

"Wait, Cairo was attacked by terrorists. They detonated a bomb.

It's what started the Tech War. I might have gotten a C- in World History, but I remember that much."

"It did start the war, Thomas, but there were no terrorists—just a lonely madman. When word got out to the Global Alliance what Tollin was doing, they had no choice but to send in the Hunters. They unleashed a weapon on Tollin they believed would stop him, but it backfired. The loss of life was dramatic, and in the end, Cairo and Ancient Egypt were buried."

"All of this because she had chosen you over him?" asked the boy.

"Unrequited love—it is an old tale, Thomas," said Anson.

Ziza nodded his head in agreement. "When I did not come to Cairo, he began to make his way to Sirati," continued the High Mancer. "There was no way I was going to let him destroy my home and Alana's dream. I began placing protections on this place, and Mary used the Gauntlet to hide Sirati. This place is forever shifting, never in the same place for too long thanks to her."

"This place moves?"

"Yes, Thomas. The only people that can get in must be invited. Mary made this place safe for all of us." Ziza smiled for a brief second. The corners of his mouth moved slowly downward. "I wish I could say the same for Cairo."

"To think all these years I was taught that a bomb had demolished Cairo and buried Egypt."

"A madman's obsession destroyed Cairo, but Grimm did not start the war. Tollin became the catalyst for others to rally around."

"Who?"

"The governments were scared, and they needed a defense against future attacks. With their experience in fighting magic users and their containment methods, the Hunters were the logical choice, and they rapidly began gaining support."

This just keeps getting more confusing, thought the boy. "So that's how they started."

"No, Thomas," interjected Anson. "The Hunters are as old as magic. Our kind has been fighting their kind for millennia. They have been responsible for, or have escalated, almost every war or major military conflict in the last four thousand years. They have had different names over the years, but they have always been dedicated to the task of destroying those who practice magic."

"Really?" asked the boy.

"Iraq, Vietnam, World War II, the Civil War, the Inquisition, and let's not forget the Crusades . . . all the Hunters' doing," said Ziza as he paced back and forth.

Thomas thought of their uniforms and the insignia on the armbands. "I guess they were pretty Nazi-esque now that you mention it."

"They used Tollin's assault as an excuse to eradicate our kind from existence, and if they could not do that, they would hide us all from the world." The old man looked down. His body weighed heavier on his staff. "If only they realized that everyone is capable of these amazing things, and that we are no different than one another . . ." He was somewhere else for a few seconds and then again came back to the present. He looked up and spoke to everyone. "Once Sirati was protected, we left to cut Tollin off."

"We?" asked Thomas.

"Yes, I went with Mary. I was afraid she still was not ready. I knew I could not take him by myself, but together, I thought it was possible."

"The two of you destroyed Tollin Grimm?"

"No. I was incapacitated early in the battle. I was caught off guard by his apprentice."

"Arkmalis?"

"Yes, even at ten years old, his power was astounding. I did not fight back. I had let this happen. I felt like part of me deserved his anger. I tried desperately to get him to come with me back to Sirati, but it was too late. Tollin had shown him dark things—terrible, dark, evil things. Things a ten year old should not see. He was no longer the boy that I had found."

"How did you survive?"

"Grayden would not kill me. He waited for his master to come and do it, but he never came. He could not."

"What happened?" asked the boy.

"A massive explosion had thrown Grayden and I backward. When I turned to see where the power expenditure had originated, I saw Mary incinerating Tollin with a final energy discharge from the Gauntlet. He was instantly reduced to dust. I will never forget that moment. She had completed her mission and saved the world. Tollin Grimm was no more." He looked at Thomas and then again to the Gauntlet. "There is much more to tell you, but it must wait until you accept the Gauntlet's invitation—if you accept it."

Thomas looked down. "The Gauntlet is my best hope for finding and saving my father." His head craned back up, and he looked directly at Ziza. "I don't have a choice."

"There is always a choice." These words resonated with the boy. "The Gauntlet can make you powerful, but it will change you—infect you." The old man stared at the levitating glove. "Think about this long and hard, Thomas. This connection is for life. If you decide to bear it, it will be forever." There was something in the way he had said this that frightened the boy.

"I'm gonna need some time."

"Take all you need, but now you should go home and rest. Tomorrow we will be taking your training to a new level."

"Who am I training with tomorrow?" Neficus stood. He had remained silent for the whole meeting. *Oh no*, thought the boy. A grin stretched across the gaunt man's face.

"Me, Thomas. You are training with me," said Neficus. "And I assure you, we won't be meditating next to a river. It's about time you got your hands dirty."

He walked towards the Grove in silence. LINC walked behind him. Thousands of thoughts were rifling through the boy's head. *That was a lot to take in at once.* He looked up at the trail that ran to his house, and he saw something completely unexpected.

Bartleby was wrapped around the base of the tree, snoring. Fargus was awake on top of him. "Hello, Thomas," said the gremlin in a somber tone.

"Hey, Fargus," said the boy. Bartleby began to stir. His head shot up, and Fargus bounced on his body. The dragon's eyes were blood-shot and swollen. Bartleby sluggishly lifted his head.

"Dere's somefing we gotta tell ya, Thomas." The dragon's demeanor was distressing to the boy. He seemed to be fighting back tears. "Ya see it's . . . it's about 'awforne." He began to sob. "Somefin's gone terribly wrong."

"What is it?" Thomas needed to know what had happened, but he was frightened by the dragon's tone.

" 'awforne's been m-m-m-m—," tried Bartleby.

"Hawthorne's been what? Come on, Bart. You can tell me. It can't be that bad," said the boy.

"Oh, Thomas it *is* dat bad. 'awforne's been m-m-m-m-m—"

"Murdered, Thomas. 'awforne's been bloody murdered," finished Fargus. Bartleby began to cry aloud. The gremlin put his hand on the dragon. "Let it out, Bart. Let it out."

Thomas paused for a second, trying to grasp the statement. "What? No . . . that can't be true. Why would anyone want to kill Franklin? It doesn't make any . . . sense." His eyes began to tear. A new thought crept into his mind. "Who? Who . . . would do some-thing like this?" The boy was confused. "Who did this?" Anger infested his blood. He could not believe what he had just heard, and he wanted answers. "Who did this, Bartleby?"

Steady tears silenced the dragon. He lowered his head in defeat.

The gremlin looked up at the boy. "Grayden Arkmalis, Thomas. It was Grayden Arkmalis," answered Fargus.

26

the tale of delonius draige

"How did it happen?" asked the bewildered boy.

"They ambushed him at the Dodgy Toadstool," said Fargus as he looked at Thomas. " 'ee didn't stand a chance, did 'ee?"

"What's the Dodgy Toadstool, and who's they?" asked Thomas.

"It's a magic-friendly bar in Dover. General Arkmalis and 'is Riders set 'im up. Lenore showed us duh footage from duh recon orb an that. It was 'ard to watch, mate."

"I'm sorry, Bart. This is all my fault."

"No, it isn't, Thomas. You didn't kill 'awforne. Grayden Arkmalis did, and dat man will have to answer for 'is crime." The dragon sniffled. "We came back to tell you the news. Would've been 'ere sooner, but I 'ad to settle some affairs at 'ome. Den we went to bloody London to look for 'osselfot, but 'ee was nowhere to be found." Bartleby looked heartbroken. "Den I slept for two days." The boy looked at the beast, surprised. "It's part of a dragon's mourning process, Thomas, it couldn't be 'elped."

"I appreciate you guys coming and telling me the news in person."

"We aren't just 'ere for dat, Thomas. We came to tell you dat Fargus and I are in."

"What do you mean?"

"Whatever you are planning on doing, we are 'ere to 'elp. 'awforne would've wanted dat, and besides . . . it seems dese people are still looking for ya." His head turned towards Thomas. "I guess I would be lying if I didn't admit dat revenge did factor into our decision. Duh 'awfornes took me in when I 'ad nuffin', Thomas. The least I can do is avenge 'is murder."

"I'm not sure revenge is the answer, Bart. It always seems to lead to more suffering . . . but let's not talk about that right now. You must be a mess." He looked at the dragon. Tears flowed through the cracks in his scales. Thomas thought of how much Franklin had reminded him of his father.

" 'ee was my best mate. Dey don't make dem like dat anymore, do dey?"

"No, Bart, they don't."

Bartleby closed his eyes. The dragon's head quickly shot into the night sky. He let out the deepest of growls. "Arkmalis!" The constant stream fell from his eyes. Fire shot from his nostrils as he breathed in and then out. Thomas moved closer to Bartleby as the dragon lowered his head. The boy patted him on his neck.

"Let it out, big guy."

"I'm sorry, Thomas. It's like it's 'appenin' all over again."

"What's happening all over again?"

"Duh 'ole situation just makes me fink uv my parents. They were also murdered, Thomas."

"I wanted to ask you about them back at Draige Manor, but Franklin had asked me not to."

" 'ee was always trying to protect me," sniffled Bartleby.

"It's just that the holofilms were vague on the details of what happened to them after the War."

"I 'ad dem edited. It's 'ard for me to talk about, but I suppose you deserve to know."

"You don't have to tell me, Bart."

"No, I want to tell you. It 'elps me to talk about it. 'awforne was duh only one who knew some uv duh troof, and now 'ee is gone. It's about time I shared duh 'ole story wif someone."

"If you want some time to talk wif duh boy an that, the artif and I can just pop off," said Fargus.

"No, Fargus. You should 'ear dis too, and LINC has more than proven 'is allegiance."

"Thank you, Bartleby Draige, for your warranted vote of confidence."

Bartleby forced a smile. "I'm done 'iding fings from my friends." He sobbed a bit and turned towards the boy and the gremlin. "If dere's somefin' I've learned from 'awforne's deaf, its dat life is too short for secrets."

"Go on den," said the gremlin.

"Yeah, Bart . . . if you're all right to talk about it," said Thomas.

"I'm fine." The dragon sniffled. "Well, as fine as I'm going to be, anyway." He sat up and looked at the boy. "Duh story starts well before dat holofilm. Duh 'uman's war was escalatin', and some of our kind wanted to 'elp. My dad was da leader of dat movement. Duh Dragon Council convened to decide if dey would 'elp duh 'umans fight dere war. Duh idea of a German victory was unnerving to some of my kind."

"Wait a second. Dragon Council? The holofilm didn't say any of this, and there was definitely no section in Spells about a council of dragons. I totally would've checked that out."

Bartleby looked at the boy with surprise. "You've been readin' up on me, 'av ya?"

"Yeah, I know a little bit now about your . . . kind."

"Well, good. Dat will make tellin' dis tale a bit easier. Duh 'olofilm obviously doesn't tell duh whole story, does it? As far as the Council is concerned, 'umans don't know it exists. It's actually forbidden to tell them. As far as I know, you and 'awforne might be duh only two. I'm pretty sure Ziza doesn't even know it exists."

"It's about time I know something he doesn't." The boy looked intrigued.

"Now, where was I?" asked the dragon rhetorically.

"You are in Sirati, Bartleby Draige. You have not moved a millimeter," said LINC.

"I meant where did I leave off in my story?"

"Then perhaps you should have said so." LINC's optics shuddered for a split second, and he began to talk, but this time he sounded just like Bartleby. "Duh story starts well before dat holofilm. The 'uman's war was escalating, and some of our kind wanted to 'elp. My dad was the leader of dat movement. When the Dragon Council convened to decide if dey would 'elp duh 'umans—"

"Fanks, LINC."

"You are most welcome, Bartleby Draige."

"As I was saying . . . my father spoke on your people's behalf to duh Council. 'ee was one of duh higher-ranking officers, and 'ee wasn't alone in 'is convictions. My muvver for one was on 'is side, and so was my Uncle Pascal. My father and 'is bruvver were Silvas. My muvver was an Incendias." The dragon looked at Thomas to make sure he understood what that meant. Thomas apparently passed the silent test because Bartleby continued. "Others joined dem to make dere position known to duh Council, including my father's best mate Larson Ragnor and his wife Ilyana Ragnor. Larson was a Dracavea. 'is wife was an Aequos."

"Could she shapeshift?" asked Thomas. Bartleby's head tilted towards the boy.

"You 'av been reading, 'avn't you? I'm pretty sure she could. Dere were several pictures uv Larson with a beautiful Chinese woman, and I just assumed it was probably Ilyana."

"Narsh," said Thomas.

"My father was duh strongest—and possibly duh smartest—of all duh dragons, and I'm not just sayin' dat because 'ee was my dad. When 'ee talked, uvver dragons listened. Dis angered and scared duh Council. 'ee also 'ad plenty uv support, and on top uv dat, 'is faction consisted uv at least one uv each uv duh dragon races. My father knew dat if 'ee could get duh support uv all duh races, 'ee could turn duh vote."

"Is that important?"

"Very . . . dey couldn't pretend it was duh ramblings uv one daft dragon. The image uv all uv dose races workin' togevver on somefing was impressive, and it almost didn't 'appen. My father finally convinced a young Glacias to fight wif dem. 'is name was Aldrich Baldemar. It also 'elped dat duh two most respected dragons on duh Council were on 'is side."

"Who were they?"

"Larson Ragnor and my uncle, Pascal Draige. The Council couldn't openly tell 'im no wiffout dealing wif some backlash, but dey would not give duh full support and resources of duh Council to duh 'umans. Dey were scared dat knowledge of dere existence would spread, and soon dey would be 'unted and killed by duh very 'umans dey would 'elp. Duh 'umans weren't keen for duh 'elp right away eiver." Bartleby paused. "Churchill 'ad 'is doubts. Dragons seemed untamed and uncontrollable, and to 'im, dat meant unreliable. Dat was, until 'ee met my father. Dey decided to let a small number of our kind fight wif duh Allies.

"Dere was ten total. Six served in the European campaign, two in duh desert, and two in duh Pacific. Duh deal made it so as few people as possible would know uv duh dragons. Most uv dere attacks would be at night so dey wouldn't give away dere existence. I was seven when dis all 'appened. Mrs. 'awforne would always watch after me— by Mrs. 'awforne, I mean Franklin's great-great-grandmother—or was it 'is great-great-great-grandmother . . ." Bartleby stumbled a bit. Thomas could tell the mention of the Hawthorne name had just hit the dragon. He began to sob. "It's probably best if I let my dad tell dis part uv duh story. I mean 'ee did live it, didn't 'ee?"

"What do you mean?"

"My dad left me videos describing dis part uv 'is life. 'ee wanted me to know what 'appened dat night."

"What night?" asked Thomas.

"I'll let my dad 'andle dat question." The dragon reached over and began pushing buttons on his left wrist. A holofilm began to play in front of them. It was Bartleby's father.

"The War started to turn. We were making a difference, and victory seemed imminent." Delonius Draige's demeanor shifted. "Everything changed after Dresden." Thomas could see by the dragon's expression that the next part was going to be difficult. Bartleby paused the image.

"I don't know how familiar you are wif your people's 'istory," said Bartleby.

"World War II was one of the only things I truly found interesting in History."

"Den you know about Dresden?"

"The firebombing?"

"Dat's what your 'istory books say, but on dat night dere was a lot more goin' on den dat." Delonius began to speak again.

"Larson Ragnor was my second in command. We were close, but very different. I wanted to help the humans and make a difference in the world. The Draige name was synonymous with honor and loyalty. Larson was also there to help. He believed in the cause, but he was arrogant and brash. He enjoyed the recognition far too much. He did not shy away from the spoils of war either, and he had such a temper." The dragon's eyes fell.

"I still don't know exactly what happened that night. There were six of us—two squadrons of three—flying the evening of February 13, 1945. Your mother, my brother, and I made up the first squadron. I was their leader. Larson led the second squadron with his wife and the Glacias, Aldrich Baldemar. Aldrich was the least experienced, but he made up for that with his grit.

"The beginning was a complete blur. My adrenaline was on overload that night." Delonius paused. "War is never pretty, but what happened that night was beyond ugly. We were supposed to fly in fast, hit a few strategic targets, and then teleport the hell out, but war is anything but predictable, my son.

"It was hard to see that night. Larson's team was following us after we made our third run, and smoke was everywhere. It had taken them a while, but the Germans had managed to unleash an anti-aircraft attack. I began to pull up as we completed our run, and I glanced behind to see the run by Larson's squadron. I only caught the very end of it, but Ilyana was plummeting to the earth. She was hit by anti-aircraft guns and crashed to the ground. Larson followed her down into the black clouds. I lost sight of them. I raced to see what was happening. Your mother and your uncle Pascal flanked me.

"Once we cleared the cloud cover, we could see Larson screaming above what appeared to be the corpse of his wife Ilyana. Before I could comprehend what was happening, Larson lost it. He went mad. The crazed dragon began to burn everything—houses, cars, buildings . . . even people—thousands of people. He spared nobody."

Thomas looked over at Bartleby, who had lowered his head. *This must be difficult for him*, thought the boy, looking back up at the holofilm.

"Pascal was the first to realize what was going on, and he was faster than I. He darted down to try and stop Larson, but he was in a rage. Pascal was smaller than Larson . . . and he did not stand a chance. Pascal tried his hardest to restrain him, but he couldn't. Aldrich rushed to help, but when he went to grab the front of Larson, he was engulfed in flames. He quickly used his ice breath to put out the fire. His scaled skin protected him, but he did not close his eyes in time. Aldrich Baldemar was permanently blinded.

"Larson struggled with Pascal. Your uncle tried to detain him, but in the end, he was no match for Ragnor. Larson threw Pascal off of him. Your uncle didn't have time to regain control of himself." Delonius paused. Tears began running down his face. "Pascal landed on a wooden plank that jutted out of a collapsed building. Larson had killed my brother." The image of Delonius Draige was silent for a few seconds. He was visibly shaken.

"I landed and grabbed my brother. I was too late to save him. I'll always remember his last words." The dragon on the holoscreen began to cry. "He said, 'Do not blame him, Brother. He knows not what he does. It has been my absolute honor to serve under you and to have the sincere pleasure to call you brother. I love you. Goodbye, Delonius.' Pascal fell silent in my arms.

"I was speechless. Larson approached me. His eyes were red with anger and betrayal. He offered these parting words: 'I will let you grieve this night, but know this, Delonius. I blame you and only you for her death. We would not be here fighting the human's war if it weren't for you. I did not intend to harm your brother, and for that, I apologize. There will come a day when we will settle this, but this is not that night. When next we meet, we will be enemies.' He disappeared into the flames and smoke. This dragon had killed my brother, but I couldn't say anything—it was my fault his wife was dead." Thomas was crying now. He had never known these dragons, but he could feel their pain . . . Bartleby's pain too.

"Des had taken it upon herself to see after Ilyana. She was our field medic. If anyone could help Ilyana, it would be her. When she got to the fallen dragon, your mother was surprised. In Larson's anger, he had not confirmed the death of his wife."

"She was still alive?" asked Thomas.

"Yes, but barely," said Bartleby.

"She was critically wounded but hanging on by the smallest of threads," said Delonius. "She leaned in and begged your mother to keep her alive long enough so she could deliver."

"What? Ilyana was pregnant?" asked Thomas. Bartleby paused the holofilm.

"Well, yes . . . not in duh way 'umans are pregnant, sort uv more like a bird," said Bartleby. Delonius continued.

"She needed to lay her fertilized eggs before it was too late. I lifted Pascal, and Des did the same with Ilyana. We fashioned a leash of sorts and tethered Aldrich to me. He tried his best to follow with his new handicap. I ripped open a teleportal and the others followed. We landed safely on the top of a large hill just outside of Cornwall in the Bodmin Moor. Ilyana laid the two eggs and passed shortly after. She made Des promise she'd find a home for the eggs and explain to Larson what had happened. Your mother accepted the terms, and Ilyana slowly slipped from our world.

"We buried both of them on that hill. Pascal Draige had died at the age of 172—young for a dragon. Ilyana Ragnor had passed at the age of 247. We officially resigned from active duty the next day. The eggs were given to the Council: a suitable home was to be found.

"I demanded a trial of Larson Ragnor. I wanted to lead a group of us to hunt him down so he could answer for his crimes. The Council refused. They said that the only possible witness to the crime was blind. The truth is they were trying to tell me 'I told you so' for interfering in the War. I quit the Council that night and never went back. I would not be a part of such a cowardly organization." The holofilm ended.

"That still doesn't explain what happened to your parents. Did Ragnor come back?" Thomas had blurted these things out without thinking about what he was asking. He quickly realized that Bartleby was working towards that, but it was not an easy journey for the dragon. "I'm sorry, Bart. I know this must be difficult. If you wanna stop, I underst—"

"No, Thomas. It's important to me dat you know dis . . . even more so dat I get it off my chest." The dragon paused and inhaled slowly. He pushed out the next sentence with his exhale. "It was years later when it 'appened. I was 115 at the time. I 'ad been out drinkin' wif some uv my mates. I 'ad just moved out uv my parent's 'ome, and we were doin' a bit uv celebratin'.

"When I got to my new 'ome, dere was a 'olomessage from my father." Bartleby looked instantly upset. He punched some keys.

A holofilm of Delonius emerged. "I do not have much time, Bartleby. Larson Ragnor has abducted your mother. I know I am walking into a trap, but I have no choice. Larson has no reason to kill your mother. If he has me, he will have no reason to keep her." Delonius Draige began to tear up. "Please, Bartleby, do not try to follow me. I couldn't bear losing you. I am immensely proud of you, Son. You will do great things, my boy, and I will always love you." The holomessage ended, and Bartleby paused for a second.

"I found dis later." Bartleby used his claw to change the holofilm on the holographic display. A black dragon appeared. "Dis is what Ragnor had sent 'im."

Larson was standing in front of an energy cage that held Desdemona Draige. The female dragon cowered in fear at something off-camera. Human guards circled the cage. A Middle Eastern man in a lab coat was looking at a projection from his wristcom behind the dragon. Thomas thought about what this meant. Larson aligned himself with humans to help him with his revenge.

" 'ee didn't look like duh gentle friend uv my father's anymore. 'ee 'ad gone bloody mental, and when 'ee spoke, 'ee seemed distant—not all dere, if ya know what I mean."

Thomas watched as the dragon in the holofilm coldly finished giving his terms. "Come alone, or believe me, Delonius, she will die." The video dissipated.

"Dat was duh last time I saw my parents." Bartleby began to cry again. Thomas patted his side. He had so many questions, but one kept gnawing at him.

"Who were those humans?"

"I never found out. I used to fink dey were 'unters, but it seemed unlikely. Duh 'unters never before 'ad interfered in duh affairs uv dragons. I sought out duh Dragon Council to inform dem uv duh situation and to again ask for dere 'elp.

"A lot 'ad changed since my father 'ad pleaded to dem to 'unt down Larson. Duh Council 'ad a new leader. Aldrich Baldemar was duh new Head Dragon. 'ee was sympathetic wif my cause, but proved just as cautious as duh last. It seemed as if 'istory was repeating itself. The official verdict was dat dere was no proof uv dere deaths, so no formal inquiry could be made wiffout a bit uv evidence.

"I fink I knew I was going to have to do this alone from duh start. I searched for dat damned dragon for years. I almost 'ad given up. I 'ad resigned myself to duh fact dat I would never avenge my parents deaf, but den I received a tip. I never knew who 'ad sent me duh information. I assumed it 'ad come from someone on duh Council who wanted to finally see justice."

"Where was he?" asked Thomas. The boy was intrigued.

" 'ee was in Australia. According to my source, 'ee 'ad apparently acquired a rather massive fortune and spent most uv 'is time 'oarding it. I 'ad finally tracked 'im down." Bartleby stopped. Real regret washed across his features. "I fought I 'ad 'im cornered, but I was no match for 'im. I 'ad still not reached full maturity, and 'ee was duh biggest dragon I 'ad ever seen. I fought as 'ard as I could, but in duh end, all my anger and 'ate was not enough to avenge my parents. I laid dere powerless and defeated." The dragon curled his head towards his body. " 'ee explained to me dat duh 'umans 'ad destroyed bofe uv my parents. 'ee 'ad meant no 'arm to my muvver, but duh 'umans 'ad killed 'er anyway. 'is issue was wif my father, and 'ee 'ad no intention uv killing me. 'ee was actually merciful dat day, believe it or not. I can't quite remember 'is last words, but it was somefing to the extent uv 'ee couldn't 'av me following 'im. Duh last fing I do remember was duh tearing sound right before I passed out." His mechanical wing moved slightly. "Larson Ragnor had ripped off my wing." He made a wincing face as if he could still feel the pain of the incident.

"Oh Bart . . . I'm so sorry . . . I . . . didn't know."

"It's okay, Thomas. I dealt wif it a long time ago. Dat's when I went to live wif 'awforne's parents. Duh gremlins . . ." Fargus looked at him and then looked away. "Duh gremlins made me dis." He fully opened his electronic wing. "I just wish I 'ad 'ad duh strengf to find my father and muvver when I could 'av 'elped." His eyes met Thomas's. "I swear to you dat I will 'elp you find your father, even if it kills me."

"I appreciate that, Bart." He looked at the dragon and patted his head as he leaned over. The dragon yawned and smoke billowed out of his nose. "You look like you could use some rest." Bartleby was one step ahead. He had again wrapped himself around the base of the tree.

"You don't mind if I crash 'ere tonight, Thomas, do ya?" He yawned again and laid his head down on the ground.

"I would be honor—" His words were drowned out by the dragon's snoring. Fargus pulled down his goggles and put his hands behind his head. "Good night, Fargus."

"Good night, Thomas." He rolled over on his side. "And fanks."

"For what?"

"Ya know, for being 'is friend an that. 'ee needed dat, and I'm horrible at dat stuff."

"You're a good friend too, Fargus."

"I would appreciate it if you could keep dat to yourself."

Thomas effortlessly jumped up to his balcony. The snoring grew louder. "Are you gonna be able to sleep through that?" asked the boy.

"I mean, to be 'onest, I don't fink I could sleep wiffout it any-more. It's just dat . . . I kinda find it sooving. Ja know what I mean?"

"Good night, Fargus."

"Good night, Thomas." The boy closed the door behind him as Stella meowed in his direction.

27

inner demons

"Take this," said Mancer Elgin Neficus as he handed the boy a large, black cast iron cauldron. The weight pulled on the boy's taut muscles. "Follow me." Thomas silently followed Neficus. He had not been looking forward to his training with the Necromancer. Neficus made him feel uneasy, and Thomas had not slept well after hearing the news about Hawthorne.

After struggling with the cauldron for what seemed like an hour, they reached their destination. They stood in the middle of a vast gorge. The fog whispered across the ground in roving formations. Thomas could see bones scattered on the ravine's surface. The weight of the iron cauldron was increasingly wearing on Thomas. His eyes focused on a massive skull with tusks curling forward out of it. He turned to either side, and it dawned on him: they were standing in an elephant graveyard. "Put it down here." Neficus pointed to a particular clearing among the scattered remnants of a once great creature.

"What are we doing out here in the middle of nowhere?" Thomas plopped the pot down as dust rose from the disturbance. "This place is kinda creepy, Neficus."

"When one is conjuring evil creatures and such, it helps to be surrounded by death." Neficus said this without so much as a smirk and promptly began his preparations. The Necromancer pulled out two vials from his cloak pockets. He poured the contents of the first one into the cauldron. The second he shook then also emptied into the now glowing pot. Neficus lifted his head, and his eyes had been replaced with darkness. He began chanting, *"Eerah natusum apacarita, Eerah vipannaka uparatta Narg, vigatta, natusum."* The kettle hopped. *"Eerah natusum apacarita, Eerah vipannaka uparatta Narg, vigatta, natusum."*

Thomas could hear a bubbling sound coming from the cauldron. The sound grew louder and more violent until he could see the dark liquid thrashing and churning in the cauldron. The black tar boiled over and sprung to life as it hit the graveyard floor. Thomas was quick to move. He jumped backwards and assumed a defensive posture as one *Eerah* after another slowly flopped out of the cauldron. They systematically flowed towards the boy. *All right now, don't panic. You've done this before . . . you can handle this.*

"Attack," commanded Neficus. The *Eerah* listened. They pounced at the boy, but Thomas dashed out of the way. The *Eerah* blobbed together and changed course. They were moving as a team.

Thomas planted his right foot and pushed both palms forward. "Haaaaaaaaa!" Blue spheres of energy peppered the attacking blob. "Remember me?" Thomas's hands pulsated with every release of an orb. The light, one by one, consumed the dark beings. More *Eerah* advanced and joined together, forming one rolling mass. The enormous black wave spiraled and splashed as it flooded towards the boy.

Thomas pulled back both of his arms on the right side of his body as he dug in his back foot once more. "Maybe this will jog your memory." His hands pushed forward. "Haaaaaaaaa!" A beam of blue energy exploded from his palms. The beam connected with the dark wave. Darkness was replaced by light as the stream of bright blue energy eradicated the *Eerah* instantaneously. Thomas powered down. "That was easy. I thought you said you were good at this." Elgin Neficus just stood there, speechless.

"We've just begun, Scargen."

"And I thought I was going to get to Warwick's early."

"I see you lack the reverence you should have for the Black Arts. Maybe this will earn your respect, boy." Neficus's pupils promptly turned into darkness, and he began to chant incoherently. It was a language Thomas had never heard. Neficus turned his palms up. The sky lit with electricity, dancing around the ominous clouds that had quickly moved in above them. A glowing circle radiated below Neficus. In the center of the ring was a symbol that was unrecognizable to Thomas.

"Neficus? Are you all right?" asked the boy.

The Necromancer resumed speaking English, but not to Thomas. "I summon thee, Demon of the Depths, servant of Narg. Manifest yourself before me in this mortal realm. I summon thee to do my bidding and bind you to me." A single lightning bolt struck the ground between the two men, and a crack formed at their feet. A huge plume of black smoke poured forth from the fissure in the graveyard. The cloud formed into the outline of a massive beast. The smoke solidified.

It was somewhat human in shape but easily fifteen feet tall. From what Thomas could tell, it was male. *If demons even have sexes*, thought the boy. The monster was jet black aside from the pieces of bone that jutted out in various places. A skull plate adorned his face, and huge bony horns protruded out of either side of his head. His stretched arms touched the ground, and his knuckles rubbed against the dirt alongside his goat-like legs. A tail swung back and forth behind the demon. Bony spikes decorated the end of it. Insects of all types crawled around the foul beast.

The demon knelt down before Neficus. It still dwarfed the man even in his new posture. "What is your name, demon?" The creature raised his head to look Neficus in the eyes as acrid, dark smoke encircled the demon's body.

"My name is Mephist, my lord." Mephist's words echoed an unholy octave, but there was no mouth to be found on the demon. "What is it that you summoned me for?"

"Yeah, Neficus, why did you summon him?"

"To destroy you, Thomas."

"Wait, what? This is supposed to be training. Just because I easily handled your test, doesn't mean you should overreact with this . . . *thing*." The monster intimidated Thomas.

"It is a lower-class demon—barely above a lurchon. You should be able to handle it at this stage of your training."

I need to ask someone what a lurchon is, thought the boy. "He doesn't look lower class to me. From here, he looks pretty freakin' upper class."

"If he proves too much for you, Scargen, I can always call him—" The demon now stood and interrupted the argument between the two men.

"I need you to directly order me to do your bidding."

"What was that?" asked Neficus.

"You have alluded to the fact that you want the boy destroyed, but you have yet to order me to do it."

"I order you to destroy Thomas Scargen."

"I accept your orders, master. Destroy the boy." His first movement was so fast, Thomas barely had a chance to dodge the blow. The displaced air knocked back Neficus. Thomas, regaining his composure, fired two blue orbs at Mephist. The black beast deflected the attack. His movements were blurs to Thomas. The demon struck the boy in the back, sending him rocketing forward. Thomas rolled with the assault. He flipped up onto his legs and shot a stream of electric blue current from his hands. Mephist was caught by the blast and reeled back. He quickly turned and sent a torrent of dark energy at Thomas, both hands extended. The first one caught Thomas in his left shoulder. The boy screamed from the burning sensation. "I love the smell of scorched human flesh," Mephist exhaled.

"Well get a whiff of this." Thomas unleashed an onslaught of blue blasts. The demon easily dodged the attempts, and before Thomas could react, the beast's shoulder made contact with the boy's side. He flew across the gorge until a huge boulder stopped his momentum. The boy dropped to the ground face first.

"That is enough, Scargen. I am putting a stop this. This has gone on long enough."

"No, Neficus." The boy lifted himself off the ground and brushed himself off. "I can deal with him." The demon advanced towards the boy. *Let's see if he likes my new trick.* Thomas closed his eyes and lifted the large boulder and an elephant skull using telekinesis. Insects and dirt fell from the objects. He focused his attention and hurled them at the demon. Mephist batted the skull out of the air, shattering it to dust, but the boulder made contact with the demon, knocking him down. "See, no problem." Thomas was looking at Neficus when the darkness overtook him. It wrapped around him and held him down on the ground. Mephist stood over the boy.

"You should know that I am no minor demon. I assure you of this. I am the Extinguisher of the Light, Wielder of the Darkness, Destroyer of Worlds, Tormentor of Souls. I have fought alongside great kings, dictators, and emperors. Death and despair follow in my wake. I am Mephist, High Demon of the Depths, and I do not take orders from insignificant mortals."

"Don't forget the Regurgitator of Too Many Words," said Thomas as he pushed outward, trying to stall the monster.

"You arrogant fool," said Mephist as he moved to finish the boy. Neficus raced over to help Thomas, but the demon brushed him back with one quick arm movement. "I am bound to you, this is true, Necromancer, but I only need do your bidding, and I will be free."

"That is impossible. I specifically summoned a lesser apparition."

"Take it up with the boss if you like, master. When I am done with the young one, I will be free to harvest the souls of any living creature in my path."

"I forbid you to harm the boy, demon."

"I am only required to perform your first request. The only restriction being that I cannot kill my conjurer. It does me no good to destroy anyone who can release me from my torment. It appears you are safe from my wrath, master, but I cannot say the same for the boy. Now if you don't mind . . ." Neficus stared at the demon as Thomas struggled to break free of the black smoky web.

"I will not allow you to harm him, Mephist."

"As if you have a choice." Neficus slapped his palms together and turned them towards Mephist. Black energy flowed from his hands. The beast had to act quickly to avoid the stream. The two fought as Thomas struggled. Neficus was holding his own, but the demon was strong and fast. Mephist avoided the last attack from Neficus and appeared behind the Necromancer. The demon telekinetically lifted the bones of a long-dead Elephant and hurled them at Neficus. The Necromancer was hit by a flying rib cage and dropped to the ground. He did not get up. The demon turned his attention to the boy. Suddenly, Thomas heard a roar.

Thomas turned to see the origin. Emfalmay landed in the clearing, eyes glowing. He pulled his sword off his back, and it ignited. The energy blade glowed the same light green color as his eyes. The Lion arched his head upward and roared again.

"Here, kitty kitty," said Mephist as he signaled to come closer.

Emfalmay ran at the demon as three more Lions dropped in, surrounding the beast. There were two Lionesses that Thomas had never met and one younger male Lion, Emfalmay's son Emkoo. The Lions all held two-handed energy axes like the Sentry Mages.

Emfalmay leapt and swung at the demon. Mephist dodged effortlessly. The other Lions engaged. The four of them moved as a unit, but the demon was fast and wasted no time unleashing his counter attack. He shot his arm out and the black webbing engulfed one of the Lionesses. She was lifted off of her paws and thrown backwards. Her fate now mirrored Thomas's. Emfalmay roared louder and directed the sound at the demon. Mephist was caught off guard and reeled from the sonic attack. The remaining two Lions pushed the advantage. Mephist recovered and rolled to his right. Emfalmay slashed the air with his sword, and an energy wave was sent towards the demon.

Mephist knocked the wave in the direction of the young male Lion. The impact knocked him out instantly. "Emkoo, nooooooo!" roared Emfalmay. Thomas tried again to escape, but the dark webs only tightened the more he struggled. He wanted to help, but he could not do anything.

Emfalmay stood and stared at the lifeless body of his son. Mephist turned and hit the last Lioness with another dark web. She fell to the ground, imprisoned. It was down to Emfalmay and Mephist.

The Lion awoke from his trance and approached the demon,

twirling the sword in his hand. "It is time to send you back to your anguish, foul beast."

"Are you sure you're capable without your friends?"

"I need no help to defeat you," said Emfalmay as he again rushed in towards the demon. The two began their dance. Their movements were so fast they appeared as blurs to Thomas. The motion began to slow as Emfalmay slashed the demon across the back. Black liquid poured from the cut. Mephist laughed as the wound mended itself. The Lion jumped back.

"You are a formidable opponent," said the demon as he turned to face Emfalmay. "But you have an obvious weakness." Mephist raised his hand and the unconscious Lion lifted off of the graveyard floor. Emkoo was motionless. "Is this your son?" The demon motioned with his hand, and Emkoo was drawn close to Mephist. "He reeks like you." Emfalmay roared and charged. The demon's words countered this attack before it could begin. "Continue and he dies." The Lion stopped. He extinguished and dropped his weapon.

"You win, demon," said Emfalmay as he fell to his knees. Mephist released his hold on the young male Lion and moved towards Emfalmay.

Thomas still writhed in his dark prison. He could not help Emfalmay or Emkoo in his current state. He began to worry. *This thing is pure evil, and if I am to realize my potential, then it is my responsibility to do whatever is necessary to eradicate this evil from the world. If I can't defeat this demon, then how do I stand any chance against Arkmalis? If I don't act soon, this demon will destroy Sirati. If Dad is still alive, I will need help to save him. The real question is what would Dad do?*

The epiphany awoke the boy's energy level. He pushed his arms apart, and energy pulsated from his body, melting the dark rope that contained him. He stood on his feet, peeling off the remnants of the demon's prison. He looked over at Mephist as he lifted Emfalmay in one hand and raised his other to strike down the Lion. Thomas said the first thing that came to mind.

"Hey, Mephist." The demon's head twisted in the boy's direction—the Elite Guard at his feet. "I wasn't done with you."

Mephist let go of Emfalmay, and the Lion dropped. The demon seemed drawn to accomplishing the task he had been summoned to do: destroy the boy. He moved purposefully towards Thomas.

Thomas looked up into the sky. "I have made my decision." The boy tensed up. "I accept your partnership. I will bear the Gauntlet." He had but a second as the creature lurched forward once more, just missing the boy's midsection with his black claws. Thomas landed on one knee after dodging the thrust of the demon.

Thomas looked up and could see something streaking across the forest's canopy. The boy raised his right arm to meet the stone glove. The force of the meeting nearly knocked Thomas off his feet. The surge of energy was incredible. Elephant bones instantly turned into dust as electrical current sparked from the Gauntlet and began to encircle Thomas. Neficus sat up and shook his head. He looked dumbfounded. Thomas's eyes fumed as power rippled through him. He was lifted off his feet, empowered by the glove. The energy was invigorating. The boy gritted his teeth and closed his eyes as the sensation climaxed and then stopped.

Thomas landed in the crater his energy output had created. He felt incredible, indestructible. A sense of calm permeated his essence. He looked down at his new right hand and turned it over. A circle with the symbol that adorned the door that had housed the Gauntlet appeared on his palm. The icon glowed orange but quickly changed to the calm blue color that was encircling his form. Thomas clenched his hand in a fist. The stone hand felt like his own. The two were one.

Mephist regained his focus and continued his assault. He hurled a black smoke ball at the boy. Thomas batted the blast skyward like he was returning a serve. The demon ran head first, barreling towards the boy. Thomas extended his gauntleted arm and stopped the beast midcharge. He grabbed Mephist's left arm. "You should have left when you had the chance."

"You don't frighten me, boy." The demon smiled.

"Trust me, I will," Thomas said with little emotion. The demon jumped backward and seemed startled to see Thomas grasping what remained of his left appendage. The boy tossed the withering arm as it contorted and vanished into black smoke. He calmly walked towards the demon. "You won't be harvesting anyone's soul today, Mephist."

"Do you know to whom you speak? I can grow that back in two days, silly mortal."

"The only one who's gonna realize his mortality today is you, demon." The boy's eyes were still glowing. The beast started to laugh out loud. His cackle became so loud that Neficus clasped his cupped hands to his ears. "Have it your way, but don't say I didn't warn you." He planted his right foot back for support and moved the Gauntlet backward then quickly forward. "Haaaaaaaaaaaaaaa!"

When the beam hit the demon, his laughter was replaced by screams of torment and rage. The whimpering beast seizured as the energy blasted straight through his back. Thomas was steady as he controlled the beam. "Now to make sure you won't be growing back anytime soon. Haaaaa!" he yelled louder this time, and the beam grew. The energy engulfed Mephist where he stood. The demon disappeared into ash. Thomas stopped the expenditure, realizing the task was complete. He powered down and so did the Gauntlet. He turned over his rock hand. The symbol on his palm had vanished. "Now that's training." The boy remembered the Lion. "Emfalmay!"

Thomas raced over to the Lion, but he had already moved to check on his son. Thomas moved to free the two Lionesses and made his way to where Emfalmay was standing.

"You performed adequately, Scargen," said Neficus. That was the closest thing to a compliment he expected, but Thomas was more concerned with the fate of Emkoo.

Emfalmay held his son in his arms. "Emkoo!" he shouted as he shook him. The young Lion choked to the relief of Thomas. Emkoo blinked a few times. His eyes shot open. He pushed his father's arms off of him as he stood.

"I am fine. I'm sorry, Father. I was careless. It won't happen again," said Emkoo as he walked away. Thomas moved to follow, but Emfalmay's paw stopped him.

"Leave him be. He needs time to deal with his failure." Emfalmay looked at Thomas. "I owe you an apology. I am sorry I doubted your loyalty at first." He looked back at Emkoo as the young Lion walked away. "Thank you for saving my son's life. I will never forget what you did today. My pride is forever in your debt." Emfalmay looked back up at the boy, but his stare moved past him. "Looks like someone else wants to talk to you."

Thomas turned his head around to see Ziza standing there with his walking stick in his mangled hand. His glance lingered on the Gauntlet. "It suits you, Thomas Scargen of New Salem. It truly suits you." Thomas slowly turned his body.

"That thing gave me no choice. He was gonna hurt the others, and he wouldn't shut up. Do they all go on like that? I am a High Demon . . . blah, blah, blah, blah."

"Yes, they do," said Ziza as he giggled. "Demons like to hear themselves almost as much as humans do." He smiled at the boy.

"At some point during the battle, I knew I was meant to wield this, and now with it on, I feel . . . incredible."

"I remember the feeling all too well, Thomas. The way you handled Neficus's test was admirable, but make no mistake, Mephist will be back. A demon of that level cannot simply be killed. Technically it's not alive to begin with. At least in the way we are."

"So that thing's coming back?"

"Yes, not anytime soon—not after what you did to him, but his embarrassment will only last as long as it takes for him to rematerialize."

"How long will that take?"

"Hard to say . . . months, maybe years." Ziza began to walk in the direction of Maktaba. Thomas sighed and lifted his newly ornamented arm.

"It's lighter than it looks."

"Heavier too, my boy." Thomas's eyes looked deep into Ziza's. "Come, there is something you need to see. You too, Emfalmay, and Neficus." Ziza leaned in towards Neficus. "There is no need to dwell on this longer. Mistakes happen."

"I have conjured many a demon in my time, High Mancer, and I have never made a mistake. There must be another explanation."

"The Black Arts are unpredictable. Sometimes what has to happen happens, no matter what your intention," said Ziza. Thomas looked back to see the High Mancer wink before turning to catch up to him.

28

a friend in need

When they reached the meeting floor in Maktaba, the others were waiting. Everyone took his or her place at the table. LINC stood off to the side. Ziza limped to the head of the table. Everyone's eyes shot in Thomas's direction when he sat down. They all stared at the Gauntlet. He noticed that Yareli was the only one not looking. This was the first time he had seen her since finding out that he had essentially stolen her destiny. The guilt was too much for him to handle, so he had avoided her. There was no avoiding her now. She finally turned and looked at him. He waved with the gauntleted hand. *You moron. What are you thinking? Are you trying to rub it in?* He stood there confused for a second. His eyes looked back and forth, but then he just decided to sit down.

"Hello, everyone. Thank you for coming here." Ziza paced back and forth. "I wish it were under better circumstances. I can see that every one of you has noticed Thomas's new *accoutrement*. There will be plenty of time for questions later. I told Thomas if he joined with the Gauntlet, I would further explain its power, and I am a man of my word."

"Narsh," said Thomas under his breath.

"I will begin by telling you that the Gauntlet is an old weapon. How old and who created it is a mythology all its own—a tale for another time perhaps. The simplest answer is no one is sure of its origins. If you so desire, you can peruse the countless volumes of speculative theories that I have collected over the years. We might not know exactly how it came into existence, but we do know quite a bit about its use—firsthand in my case." He lifted the deformed arm. Everyone paused and looked at the man's crippled appendage. "The Gauntlet is powered by stones. Each stone has its own unique attributes. As most of you know, when Mary wielded the Gauntlet, it contained all of the stones, but now it is empty."

"I don't understand. What happened to them?" asked Anson.

"Mary had defeated Tollin Grimm, but in doing so, she had used all of her own power. I arrived just as the Aringi Captain swooped down and grabbed the Scythe and Grayden Arkmalis. I moved over to the girl as she lay there on the jungle floor. She was still alive but just barely. I'll remember that smile on her face as long as I live. I tried what I could to revive her, but it was futile."

"I'm sorry, Ziza," said Thomas.

"Thank you, my boy."

"What does this have to do with the stones?" asked Yareli. "What happened to them?"

"Patience, my dear," said Ziza. "Mary died in my arms. Her body lifted out of my hold and into the churning sky. The wind and dirt swirled around her as her eyes hollowed and her lifeless body glowed. The Gauntlet released itself from Mary and levitated high above her. The Gauntlet flashed all of the individual colors of the stones. The jewels rocketed out of the artifact they had lived in for centuries and flew off in separate directions. They raced across the gray sky farther away than one could see. I caught Mary's body, and the Gauntlet dropped at my feet. The stones had gone. She had given her life to save us all, and the Gauntlet was reset." Ziza faintly smiled. "I will never forget her sacrifice." The old man closed his eyes and sunk down on his staff. "I brought her and the Gauntlet home to Sirati."

"Why didn't the stones do that when you lost the Gauntlet?" asked Anson.

"I pondered that question myself for years. The only explanation

is that it only happens when there is a death while wearing the artifact—a defense mechanism of sorts." Everyone seemed to be taken
aback at this last revelation, except Thomas. He was thinking about
his dream.

"Could the black stone in my dream be one of these jewels?"
asked Thomas.

"I had that very thought, my boy, but none of the stones is black,
and from what Lolani had said, dark energy emanated from that
stone. The stones in the Gauntlet do not give off such energy—quite
the opposite actually. I'm sorry, Thomas, but I am unfamiliar with
this artifact."

"The symbols didn't help?"

"I have not deciphered the glyphs as of yet, but I will, Thomas. I
promise you this. It is a variation of an extremely old language, and
it is proving most difficult. What I do know is if your premonition
has come to pass, your father is in danger, and to defeat Arkmalis and
his new partner may require more energy than the empty Gauntlet
can provide." He moved closer to the boy. "Finding the stones has
become a priority."

"You said if I accepted the Gauntlet I would have enough power
to save my father."

"Yes, and I also told you there was more to know about the
Gauntlet. I'm sorry if you misunderstood. I did not intend confusion, and I did not mean it to sound like simply putting the Gauntlet
on would facilitate your father's rescue, but it is the first step."

"I'm listening." Thomas had hoped it would be that easy, but
deep down he had known better. "What's the next step?"

"We got a lead on one of the lost stones. Malcolm has talked with
some of his old vampire friends at my request."

"Why would you do that? You know that's just asking for trouble," said Anson.

"Maybe so, but it was our only lead, and it bore fruit. It had been
brought to my attention that one particular vampire has become
increasingly powerful, performing magical feats that she had not
done in the past. I met with Malcolm privately to see if he would do

some reconnaissance for me. The only issue was he had a history with the vampire in question."

"Who is this vampire?" asked Anson impatiently as he stood.

"Her name is Amara Scornd. She is one of the Exemplar."

"What's an Examplar?" asked Thomas.

"She is one of the six original vampires, my boy," answered Ziza "And a commanding Necromancer. We believe she is currently in possession of one of the stones."

"He never mentioned her to me," growled Anson.

"Your brother has a lot of secrets, my son, and this particular one he is not very proud of. It was during his . . . early years." Thomas knew what this meant.

"Where is my brother now?"

"That is why I have called you all here. He has gone missing." Anson slammed his fist down on the table. Thomas put his hand on the werewolf's back.

"How can you be sure?" asked Anson.

"He was scheduled to make a report two days ago, and he never did. We waited to see if he had just been preoccupied, but by now his disguise has to have worn off. We fear his identity has been compromised, and he may have been captured." He raised his staff and the center of the table illuminated into a hologram of an unfamiliar vampire. "This was his last communication."

" 'ello Ziza, just checkin' in." The voice was definitely Malcolm's. "I 'av almost infiltrated the 'ive. I've been 'anging out at the local pub. I use that term loosely, mind you. Vilkari says 'ee's gonna get me in tonight, so I should find out what you wanted to know by tomorrow. I gotta go. 'ere 'ee comes . . ." The transmission ended.

"Frederick Vilkari is one of Malcolm's oldest friends."

"Not Vilkari . . ." said Anson as he stood up. "That vampire is more than just a friend. He is my brother's Maker, and he is driven only by greed and opportunity. I have never trusted that man."

"We have no proof that this man is connected to your brother's disappearance. Malcolm trusted this vampire, and he is our best lead to Malcolm's, and possibly the stone's, location."

"I'm in," said Anson.

Yareli stood immediately after Anson's words. "Wiyaloo and I are in." Thomas stood.

"Thomas, I do not think it would be wise for you to go," said the High Mancer.

"I have to help."

"You have free will to do what you want, I assure you. I would not keep you here against your will, but know that your training is far from complete."

"He got captured trying to get a rock for this Gauntlet, which just permanently became my responsibility. And from what you say, if my father is not alive—if my dream was real, then I'm gonna need all of these rocks I can get my hand on." He raised the Gauntlet. "If I don't go, why should anyone else?"

"I will make sure he will come back to finish his training," said Anson. Ziza lowered his stare and turned away.

"I can tell that there is no talking you out of this, but I want you all to know what you are getting into. Bartleby and Fargus have already agreed to be your transportation."

"I bet that cost us," said Neficus. "We paid him far too many credits for the collection of the Scargen boy."

"He is asking for nothing in return, Elgin. The dragon wants to help our cause," answered Ziza. The High Mancer turned back to the rest of the Council. "From our estimates, there are over ten thousand vampires in this hive. Amara Scornd presumably has the stone, but there is no indication that she knows what she has. It seems to have amplified her power, and she is using her power to control the humans of this town. The town is called Sangeros. It is located in an isolated part of Romania. We believe it is the yellow stone—the Taitokura—the Stone of Experience.

"What does that mean?" asked the boy.

"The stones are not that exact in nature, Thomas. The Gauntlet sometimes has a mind of its own, and one can never be sure how the stones will react." Thomas looked down at his rock hand and the still pool that once held that very stone. "You will leave in the morning."

"Why don't we go now?" wondered Thomas.

"They are vampires, boy," said Neficus, annoyed by the question. "They are powerful, deadly creatures, and you will be extremely out-numbered. If you just run into that hive without a plan, you'll all be dead. We need time to prepare."

"Which leads us to what we are dealing with," interrupted Ziza. "Neficus, can you enlighten us with some of the ways to destroy the undead?"

"Yes, High Mancer." The man stood as the middle of the table opened up again and a three-dimensional representation of a vampire emanated from the holographic projector. "There are only two known ways to forcefully kill a vampire." A holographic man ran up to the vamp in the representation and stabbed at him with a simple wood stake. The animated vamp shrieked and burst into dust. "Wood stake directly through the heart," said Neficus as he pointed at the holo-gram. "This is a guaranteed kill and your best chance."

"It is said that when staked, right before they die, they feel human once again," said Anson under his breath to Thomas. The image reset itself. The same holographic man whirled an axe, severing off the head of the animated vampire, and again, the undead burst into dust.

"Decapitation is another way," said the Necromancer. "Crucifixes, garlic, holy water—all rubbish." Pictures of these flashed as holograms as he said them. The image reset to the static vampire. "Another indi-rect way to kill the undead is sunlight." The vamp was showered with sunlight and immediately erupted into dust. "These are natural kill-ers, and they will show no mercy to a human." He stared downward at the boy. "To them, you are merely food." He looked back up and continued to pace. "Amara Scornd is someone not to be taken lightly, especially if she indeed has the stone. This particular vampire is an Exemplar, as Ziza stated earlier. This means she is very, very, very old."

"How old?" asked the boy.

"Let's just say she is older than most countries and leave it at that," said Neficus. "And there is little information on which, if any, of these methods will actually kill an Exemplar."

"Thank you, Elgin," said Ziza. He motioned for Mancer Neficus to sit. "I'm afraid Malcolm's intel was not very detailed and leaves us with some decisions to make. I will need to think on these aspects while the three of you get some much-needed rest. We also need time for preparation. Elgin, I believe I will need your expertise and help this evening, my friend. Something you said has given me an idea."

"I serve the Council, High Mancer," said Neficus.

"Then with that, this meeting is adjourned. We will meet here in the morning to discuss the plan and enact it." Ziza walked off with Neficus towards his study.

"It is settled then. We leave in the morning," Anson said as he looked at Thomas.

"I don't know what to say, Anson. This is all my fault." Thomas looked away and then turned back towards the werewolf. "It doesn't seem right not doing anything. We are wasting time."

"Wisely and slow, Thomas; they stumble that run fast. We need time to do this right. I appreciate the concern, and I echo your sense of urgency, but patience will win out. Trust Ziza. He needs time to think, and we need time to rest."

"Thomas, I was wonderin' if I could run some diagnostics on your artif an that. 'ee looks like 'ee's due for a check up, doesn't 'ee?" said Fargus. "I mean if dat's aw'right wif you. I don't want to step on your toes or nuffing."

"Yeah, I have been neglecting his maintenance."

"I'll 'av 'im looking like new in duh morning," he whistled as he walked over to LINC. The robot turned towards Thomas as if to ask permission.

"I am not certain that this is the most productive use of my complex functionality."

"It's all right, LINC, you need it. Everybody needs some fine-tuning now and again."

"I am not *everybody*."

"Regardless, you could use it. And thanks, Fargus." Yareli walked hurriedly by. "Hey, Yar . . . can I talk to ya for a second?"

"S-sure . . . walk with me. I'll catch up with you later, Wiyaloo."

"Yes, my lady."

They reached the path that lead to Yareli's apartment. She had avoided looking at him the whole way down the elevator. "I feel like such an ass." Thomas scratched his head with his rocky hand.

"You mean more than usual?"

"I'm trying to be serious here. I didn't know what you were talking about before."

"You rarely do. You have to work on your listening skills." She finally looked at him. Her eyes looked like they were on the verge of tears. She stopped in front of a large patch of grass. In the center stood a monument. He had run by here countless times, but never stopped to look at what it was. Something in the Gauntlet twinged. She walked off the path and stopped to sit on the stone bench that was in front of the ornate dome. He sat next to her and stared at the structure. It was magnificent. Thomas could not believe he had never stopped to look at this beautiful work of art. The Gauntlet again shocked him.

Growing pains I suppose, he thought.

"I come here sometimes when I want to think. It reminds me that anything is possible," said the girl.

"What is this place?"

"It's where she was buried, Thomas."

"Who?"

"The last wielder of the Gauntlet—Mary." His face dropped with this disclosure. "She's my hero."

How did I not know this? It makes complete sense that this is her hero, he thought. "I didn't know you were supposed to be . . . I mean that this could have been . . . I didn't know that you were in line for this." He lifted his gauntleted hand.

"I wanted it so badly. I wanted to save my mother. I thought with that power I could easily handle the Hunters. I figured I'd walk right into their headquarters and take her back. The Gauntlet saw that I couldn't be trusted with such power. It knew I'd use it for vengeance, and it refused me. I was heartbroken. When they found you, I wanted to hate you, but things have changed. Since meeting you . . . things don't seem so bad, and I don't feel angry all the time." She smiled at him for a second before her mouth curved back down. "I'm sorry for how I've treated you."

"It makes more sense now." Thomas looked at her. "I didn't want this." He lifted up the Gauntlet.

"I know, Thomas." She leaned on his shoulder. "I know." She began to cry. He hugged her tightly as she wept. After a few minutes of sobbing, she finally emerged and looked at the boy. "Thank you, Thomas, but I'm convinced the Gauntlet knew what it was doing. This is your destiny, and I will do anything I can to help you find your father."

"I appreciate that, Yar. I really do, and I promise you I will help you find your mother when this is all done." She slinked down into his arms and hugged him tightly.

After a long while, she let go of him and stood up. She leaned down and kissed him on the cheek, and then she walked off in the direction of her place. "Good night, Thomas." The boy sat there and could feel that his mouth was gaping, but he could not move.

Thomas walked back to his treehouse, half guilt-ridden and half mesmerized by what had just happened. Despite the kiss, he could not help but feel responsible for destroying Yareli's dreams, and he might have even gotten Malcolm killed. *If I didn't need that damn stone, he would've never gone.* There would be no telling what happened to the vampire until they got there.

When he reached the treehouse, Onjamba was still awake. He was watering his plants as usual. The water can was in his trunk, and he continued to attend to the plants as he turned to greet Thomas.

"Hello, Thomas. I fixed you a sandwich. I left it up in your room. I figured you'd be hungry."

"Thanks, Onjamba. I think I might forget to eat without you." Thomas began to walk in the direction of the staircase. Onjamba put down the watering can and moved to cut off the boy.

"There's one other thing." The Elephant walked in front of him up the stairs, being careful to duck his head when needed. The two walked into Thomas's dark room. A beam of moonlight shined down on Spells, who was laying on his desk. "Ziza wanted me to bring this to you," said Onjamba. "He said there is some information that might prove useful for your trip."

"Why didn't he just pull me aside after the meeting?"

"I believe it might have something to do with your night stroll with Ms. Chula." The Elephant winked at Thomas and pointed to the sandwich on the desk next to the growing volume. Onjamba ducked back out of the room as the floorboards creaked in agony. "The chapters on vampires might be most useful." The Pachyderm's words trailed off as he descended the staircase.

Thomas looked down at Spells. It had been a while since he had read him. The book had come a long way since his first study days with Ziza. He punched a few keys on his wristcom, and three light orbs shot out from the device. They hovered above the spellbook. He placed his hand on the book and it sprung to life. The binding expanded again as the book grew in size. *The Gauntlet must come with a lot of instructions*, he thought.

"No instructions per se," said Spells as his pages flapped up and down. "Vampires are the current topic, however."

"Show me what ya got," said the boy as he bit into his dinner. He had forgotten to ask what he was eating, but after the day's events, he did not care. It was delicious.

The book rose up off of the table and fanned through its own pages before coming to a stop. The book lowered itself in front of the boy. Thomas looked at the chapter heading, and sure enough it read: VAMPIRES: FACTS ABOUT THE UNDEAD.

"Bring on the bloodsuckers." The subject of vampires, although not as appealing to Thomas as dragons, was still much more intriguing than his old school books. The boy began reading the tome. It felt like one of the few times he had studied in high school, except now he was actually enjoying it. He thumbed through the chapter, quickly getting a general overview of topics covered in the text. He then turned back to the front of the section and began to read.

WHAT IS A VAMPIRE?

A vampire, or Homo Sanguinus, is a parasitic creature that was formerly human. More specifically, a vampire requires blood for sustenance. Human blood is preferred, but a vampire can live off of any type of hemoglobin.

"I already know this crap," said Thomas.

Vampires are natural hunters that live for the thrill of the chase. They have what's known as a bloodlust.

"Let's skip the beginner stuff." He began turning the pages of the book, trying to find something new for him to learn when he came upon this heading.

SUPERNATURAL ABILITIES

"That's what I'm talking about," said the boy. The section glowed a faint yellow color as if it were highlighted.

"I guess the old man wanted you to know what you were dealing with," said Spells.

"I guess so." The boy continued reading.

These are the five main abilities that one will face when dealing with the living dead. Often age is directly correlated with the potency of such abilities—the older the vampire, the more powerful the vampire.

REGENERATION: Regeneration is the ability to quickly heal and/

or replace damaged tissue. Like a human body, the vampire's body possesses the ability to regenerate damaged tissue, but at an exponential rate. A wound that might take a human months to heal from, could regenerate in a matter of seconds for a vampire. The two exceptions to this rule are beheading and staking in the heart—both lethal to a vampire.

PERSUASION: A vampire is said to be able to twist and turn the insides of a mortal with a mere suggestion. Often confused with charm, the propositions of these undead creatures can be difficult to ignore. The only known defense to this ability is awareness.

STRENGTH: All vampires have magnified strength. Mature vampires can lift four times their own weight. As a general rule, the older the vampire, the more amplified their strength becomes. The strongest of all vampires are the Exemplar—the original vampires.

SPEED: Vampires can reach speeds ranging from 160-275 kilometers per hour. Some reports suggest the fastest of their kind can reach speeds as high as 325 kilometers per hour. A vampire can also complete physical tasks faster using the same ability.

Malcolm must be in this group, he thought to himself as he took another bite of his sandwich.

FLIGHT: Vampires undergo a second transformation as they mature. Retractable wings develop out of a vampire's upper back once they reach full maturity—between 500 and 600 years of age. At this age, a vampire can have a wingspan of over ten feet when fully extended. These wings are strong, flexible, and highly articulated for superior maneuverability.

"I never realized how advanced Malcolm is," said Thomas. "I just assumed all of them . . ."—he yawned—"were that strong and fast." He read the topic of the next heading.

HOW TO KILL A VAMPIRE

"Neficus already covered that topic." He yawned once more. "I guess that's enough for tonight."

"Sorry I'm not more of a page-turner this evening," said Spells. "It was *bound* to happen."

"I see what you did there," said the boy. Thomas raised his arms above his head in a stretch. "It's not . . . you. I'm just tired," said the boy through another yawn.

"You need to sleep, Thomas," said Spells.

"When you're right, you're right. It was a long day." He lifted the Gauntlet. "Good night, Spells."

"Good night, Thomas." Booker Spells landed open on the desk. The light orbs returned to Thomas's wristcom as he took it off and placed it on the desk. The boy walked over and sat on his bed.

He finished most of his sandwich and threw the remains at the Saber-toothed Lily on his nightstand. It caught the sandwich with ease. "Nice catch, Lily," said the boy. The plant smiled, exposing its sharp teeth. Lily then chomped on the crust of bread as Thomas crawled under the sheets. Stella jumped onto the bed. The feline circled in front of him and then fell down, lying next to the boy. The cat purred with content as Thomas's thoughts dwelled on what was to come. His new partnership would be put to its first real test, and Malcolm's life was at stake. But then he thought about the kiss, and he managed a smile. He placed his hand on the rock that covered his other hand. "Tomorrow's gonna be a long day," said Thomas. "Good night, Stella." The cat blinked at the boy. His eyes shut, and he fell asleep grasping the Gauntlet.

29

not as they seem

Thomas awoke to find Stella staring at him. She meowed at him to get up. "You hungry, little monster?"

"Meow."

"You can say that again," said Thomas as he yawned and stretched his arms. "I am so . . . achy." He looked up and saw the rock hand. "So . . . that *actually* happened." He grabbed the goggles off the dresser and placed his wristcom on as it automatically adjusted to his left arm. He hastily took care of his morning routine and made his way over to his closet.

Thomas walked into the closet over to his dresser. He opened the second drawer. He grabbed one of his Philadelphia Wires T-shirts. They were his favorite team in the National Robotic Hockey League. He had grown up in Massachusetts, and by all rights he should have been a Boston Bolts fan, but his father was originally from Philadelphia. He had taken Thomas to his first game when he was six, and ever since that day he had been a fan. The shirt made him think about his father's predicament. *I'll find you, Dad. I swear I will—if it's the last thing I do. But I gotta help a friend out first. He's in trouble, and it's kinda my fault.*

He looked at the shirt and something occurred to him. *How am I gonna take off my shirt, let alone put a new one on?* He looked at the size of the T-shirt and then at the Gauntlet. *This should be interesting.*

Thomas reached down and pulled his T-shirt up, and to his surprise it peeled off as if nothing had changed. That's weird. With his new-found confidence, he began to put on the new shirt. He watched as the glove conformed to the size of his normal arm for the time it took him to put the shirt on. Somehow the Gauntlet knew what he was doing and adjusted itself accordingly. "Narsh," said the boy as he pulled up his pants. "Problem solved, huh, Stella?"

"Meow," replied the cat as she stretched and fell back on her spot on the bed.

He walked out of his room and down the spiral staircase, Spells in hand. Onjamba was downstairs watching robotic rugby on the holovision. LINC was sitting next to him. *I guess Fargus finished early*, thought the boy.

"Good morning, Thomas Scargen." LINC's head rotated without his body moving. "The Pachyderm was just explaining the conventions of this athletic competition." His head rotated to look at Onjamba. "I find sports artifs tremendously intriguing. They actively engage in a demeanor that will cause physical damage to their frames as well as compromise systems integrity. This leads me to extrapolate that they have not been programmed as well as I have."

"You have to be joking on that call!" interrupted Onjamba, yelling at the holovision.

LINC's head rotated back towards Thomas. "The Pachyderm believes that the striped artifs have some sort of damage to their optical arrays. He has verbally suggested this 23 times during the course of the match. I am inclined to agree with his hypothesis based on the overwhelming data that suggests these artifs are ignoring flagrant disregard for the rules and regulations of the sport."

Thomas looked over at the Elephant, placing Spells down on the counter. "I guess you two have been busy?" The Elephant bobbed his head in recognition. "Any word on what's going on?" asked Thomas as he fed Stella some food.

"You are to meet everyone at Maktaba." The Elephant stood up. He grabbed Thomas's spellbook and handed it to LINC. "I was told to tell you to hurry up, and that you need not worry about packing:

everything you're going to need has been or will be packed for you." This last statement confused the boy, and he began to speak but thought better of it. "Your guess is as good as mine, Thomas—just a messenger."

Thomas was the last one to enter the large meeting room. To his surprise, the circular door with the odd symbol had been repaired. LINC followed behind him with Booker Spells in his left hand. Flora shot down and grabbed the book, but the vine was not strong enough to pry the text from the artif's clasp. Flora went taut as she struggled to release the book. LINC finally registered what was happening and opened his hand. The vine and Spells were sent flying into the upper part of the tree.

Thomas took his seat, giggling. He looked at his comrades and noticed that Anson and Yareli were oddly dressed. Anson was wearing more leather than he had ever seen on the man before, and Yareli was dressed completely in black. "I'm glad you could join us," quipped Neficus as he walked to his chair. At his seat was a stack of similar clothes, but they seemed about two times his size. His eyes moved back to Yareli. He could not help but stare. She wore a short, skintight dress, and her hair was down. She normally had braids, but this was different. Thomas had never seen her like this—he was mesmerized. She looked amazing. Yareli's facial expression woke Thomas from his thoughts. He quickly turned towards Neficus.

Neficus had been speaking before he was interrupted by the boy's arrival. "As I was saying, you three are going to have to be undercover if you stand any chance in the Hive." Thomas looked around like he was late for class. His eyes met Yareli's, and she nodded and smiled. The white apparition stood guard behind her. "The clothes I have given you will help mask the fact that you are human. I spent most of the night coming up with these." There were three ornate vials in his bony hand. "Each one of these was engineered for your specific genetic makeup. These will alter your appearance."

"Alter our appearance?" the young woman questioned the Necromancer. Neficus handed the first container to Yareli.

"Make you look like vampires. Yours was the easiest to concoct, seeing as your actual appearance did not have to be altered." He stopped beside Anson and handed him his concoction. "Yours was most difficult, considering the magic needed to hide your true forms. We can't have you walking around looking like your brother, nor can we have you reeking like a werewolf."

"I smell fine."

"That may be, Mage Knight, but a vampire could smell your kind from two kilometers out—if not farther. And need I remind you of the state of werewolf-vampire relations? This disguise is your best chance for survival."

"Away, and mock the time with fairest show. False face must hide what the false heart doth know." The Necromancer ignored Anson and continued.

"And last, but not least." Neficus paused behind the boy's chair. "It took me some time to work out how I was going to cover up your new . . . toy." The Necromancer gazed at the Gauntlet. Thomas reached out his stone hand and took the potion. "You will look like a hulking beast of a vampire. It was the only way I could mask the size of the Gauntlet, and it will make more sense if you have to use your power." Thomas was elated but confused.

"But the glove can shrink when needed. There's no reason for me to be a big vampire."

"Your naivete is unnerving, to say the least," said Neficus.

"Patience, Neficus. Yes it is true, Thomas, the Gauntlet can momentarily adjust its size, but only momentarily. The glove is also powerless if not at full size."

"Oooooh," said the boy, a little embarrassed.

"Now that the lesson is over, may I continue?" asked Neficus looking directly at Thomas. The boy nodded his head yes. The Necromancer returned to his pacing. "Where was I before the second interruption . . . ahh yes. There is one small caveat with your disguises."

The boy leaned over to whisper to Anson. "How did I know that was coming?"

"These mixtures will do what I have said, but the effects are temporary."

"How long?" asked Anson.

"Approximately?"

"I'd actually prefer specifically," replied the wolf.

"Approximately . . . seventy-two hours. Which should be plenty of time."

"Let's hope so. The last thing I'd want to be is a werewolf trapped in a vampire hive," said Anson.

"So we don't open these babies till we get there?" Thomas asked.

"Precisely, my boy," interrupted Ziza. "You will be meeting Malcolm's contact when you get to the Tapped Vein. It is where Vilkari frequents."

"What's the Tapped Vein?" Thomas inquired.

"It's a vampire bar, for lack of a better word, in Sangeros—the one Malcolm spoke of in his last communication."

"I'm guessing beer is not on draft," added Yareli.

"This is where you will find Fredrick Vilkari. Whatever you do, do not reveal your true identities to this man. We do not know what has happened to Malcolm. Trust is not an option." The High Mancer paused for a second to make sure everyone understood. "There is one other thing. Use your powers only as a last resort. There are few vampires who possess such skills, but feel free to use powers obviously associated with their kind." He grinned. "Here are your new wristcoms." Three dark communication devices floated in front of the three of them. One was noticeably bigger.

"Why?" asked Thomas.

"In case we get caught," answered Yareli. "The information contained on any one of our wrists could be dangerous in the wrong hands."

"Oh," sighed the boy. *Plan for the worst.* The reality of what they were about to undertake finally hit Thomas.

Ziza followed them outside. LINC was loading Bartleby's storage containers while Fargus sat on the artif's shoulder, looking at his handheld. The artif was carrying two cases of Gloop, and the gremlin was prepping the dragon for the mission. He was whistling, and in between tunes, he was taking swigs from a bottle of Gloop. "You guys almost ready?" asked the gremlin. "Do you 'av any idea 'ow 'ard it was to wake 'im up? I nearly went up like a match, wif all 'is snoring an that. At the end of duh day, I 'ad to wave a bit of meat in front of his nose, didn't I? Almost lost me 'and."

"You make it sound as if I was trying to kill you. I was simply takin' a nap, wasn't I?"

"A nap? It's just, I've never met anyone else who takes two-day naps. No matter 'ow many times I see it, I still don't get it. Sounds a bit more like hibernation, doesn't it?" Bartleby snorted a flame at Fargus. "See what I mean? Dis is what I'm talkin' about. It just isn't right, is it? I'm fed up."

Yareli, Anson, and Thomas got on the back of the dragon. Fargus situated himself on top of Bartleby's head. Ziza walked closer and pet the dragon's head. "You take care of them, Bartleby."

"I won't let anyfing 'appen to dem, High Mancer."

"Good luck, everyone. This will be dangerous. There is no denying that, but I could not think of a more capable group to pull this off." He backed away and bowed his head. "Goodbye, my children." Bartleby flapped his wings as they lifted off of the ground. LINC's turbines kicked in, and Wiyaloo floated upward. They shot out through the shield opening, and Bartleby formed a teleportal. The dragon, robot, and spirit ghost passed through the tear and disappeared over Sirati.

30

a fat vampire

The sky ripped apart. LINC crossed through, quickly followed by Wiyaloo and Bartleby. The dragon carried the girl, the werewolf, and the boy. Bartleby slowed as he approached the desolate hillside. The beast landed two and a half kilometers from the town of Sangeros, as planned. "Stupid question," said Thomas. "Why is it dark out?" The boy knew the local time was around eleven o'clock in the morning.

"There's nothing stupid about that, Thomas," added Anson. "That's most peculiar."

"It's pretty convenient for a bunch of bloodsucking night owls." Thomas looked at Anson. "Well, not Malcolm."

"I feel a strange magic," said Yareli. "Very strong."

"I too sense it," said Wiyaloo.

"Duh only fing I can feel is duh free uv you still on my back," said Bartleby.

"Sorry, Bart," said Thomas as he dismounted the dragon. He helped Yareli down as Anson leapt off.

"Whatever is keeping Sangeros in the dark is incredibly strong, ancient magic." Yareli was on her knees, feeling the earth. "The ground is cold, and the trees are almost dead. There hasn't been light here for some time."

"According to my reconnaissance scans, there appear to be no living creatures present in the immediate vicinity. The only life form readings I am detecting are emanating from the town of Sangeros," said LINC.

"This place gives me the creeps," said Thomas as he cringed.

"There are a lot of questions that need answering." Anson looked towards a line of decaying trunks that flanked the town. "Let's find some cover. We don't need to be seen just yet."

They moved at a brisk pace, following Anson. Thomas looked around as they ran. There was something unnatural about the whole scene. Thomas found it unsettling. The tree's bark was a cold, stark white, and pieces were peeling from the trunks. Large, jagged boulders marred the landscape. Death was at home here.

Sangeros was situated in the valley below the tree line. Thomas pulled down his goggles. The specs began to scan the area. "The town is full of warm-blooded humans." The humans registered in a red hue on Thomas's overlay. He looked from side to side. "But there are a bunch of cold-blooded vamps walking amongst them."

"Can you see the Tapped Vein?" asked Yareli.

"Yes. It's filled with vampires." Thomas lifted the goggles.

"I can smell them," said Anson. "I better take my medicine before one of them gets a whiff of me, and Thomas make sure you switch your wristcoms."

"I almost forgot: we get to play dress up." Thomas grabbed his costume out of one of Bartleby's storage compartments and threw his wristcom in with the others. He lifted up the oversized outfit.

The other two were already dressed in their disguises so they drank their concoctions. Yareli grabbed at her stomach and dropped the vial. She then rubbed her hands in her eyes. She looked at Thomas. He could see her pupils had turned red and she was far paler, but for the most part, she was unchanged.

Anson, on the other hand, was going through a transformation—but different from the changes he had grown accustomed to. His face bubbled and churned. The man who looked back at Thomas did not look like his friend. He gritted his teeth as the final stage passed. He now looked older and thinner.

"How do I look?" He smiled, exposing his fangs.

"I'd say closer to your age," said the boy. "Definitely creepy."

"Well, go on, Thomas. Drink up." Yareli tapped her foot, arms crossed.

"Oh right. If you will excuse me." Thomas walked behind the nearest boulder and began to disrobe. The boy stood there, naked in the cold air. He raised the container to his mouth and drank. "This stuff tastes like crap." He finished the vial. Thomas looked down in time to see his left hand inflate. He then turned to look at his right hand. Flesh wrapped around the Gauntlet, hiding the rock hand. Thomas was looking at the hands of a giant. He wiggled his fingers. His torso stretched and his feet grew. He had the weirdest sensation of his head growing. He felt so much larger. The boy could now look over the boulder at his other friends. He began dressing. He bent over to put his pants on, and he staggered backward, falling with a thump. Thomas sprang to his feet and grinned with embarrassment. He hopped on one foot while pulling on his boots.

A sharp pain interrupted his dressing. It started in his stomach and spread throughout his body. His eyes were on fire. Tears ran down his oversized cheeks. Thomas could feel his teeth tearing downward. And as quickly as it came, the sickly feeling subsided. He looked down again and could see that his skin looked much paler. Thomas came out from behind his makeshift dressing room. He lifted his leather jacket onto his shoulders as both of his arms slid through the sleeves.

"You look scary," said Yareli.

"Thanks . . . I guess," said Thomas, fumbling his words as he attached the bulky new wristcom. The bass in his voice caught him off guard. "I sound scary too." He turned to Fargus, who was whistling along, fixing something on Bartleby's armor. The gremlin was lost in his work and not paying attention to the commotion. "Boo!"

The gremlin jumped off the dragon, frightened. It took him a second to regain his composure. "That was well out of order. Do you always knock about, scarin' the smallest guy you can find? You shouldn't pick on people dat are smaller than you, is all I'm saying.

Would you like it if say a giant snuck up on you while you were minding your own business and yelled at you? Ja know what I mean? We'll see 'ow funny dat is next time ya need ol' Fargus to do somef-ing." Bartleby was doing all he could to hold back from laughing out loud.

" 'ee was just 'avin a laugh Fargus, dat's all. Weren't ya, Thomas?" explained the dragon.

"Yeah, sorry, Fargus." The boy giggled. "I was just trying out the new pipes."

"Come on, LINC. I know when I'm not wanted an that. I've got a few more fings to adjust on you," said Fargus. "I've got an idea."

"Adjustments?" squeaked LINC. "Are you sure you know what you are doing? I am a highly sophisticated piece of machinery."

"Don't worry a bit, mate. I fought about it last night after you left, and now it seems I 'av some down time." The gremlin patted on the artif's leg.

"I must stay and protect Thomas Scargen. That is my prime directive."

"It's fine, LINC. You can't come with us anyway. Vampires don't usually associate themselves with artifs, and besides, from the looks of this town, these people have probably never seen anything like you."

"These vampires seem completely unsophisticated." The artif's head spun towards Fargus. "It appears as though my original assessment of not having any time to dedicate to your previously discussed endeavor was premature and grossly inaccurate."

"What did 'ee say?"

"He's all yours," said Thomas.

"Thomas, please remember to remove yourself from any situation that involves dangerous activities or individuals," said the artif.

"I will, LINC." The artif and the gremlin walked away from the group. Fargus was whistling as usual as he performed calculations on the hologram above his handheld device.

"Well, I'm knackered. I fink I'm gonna sleep for a bit. If you need us, just ring me." The dragon toddled off to find a suitable bed for a nap.

"Wiyaloo will follow us invisibly," said Yareli.

"For as long as I can manage," added Wiyaloo.

"What does that mean?" asked Thomas as he turned to look at the Spirit Warrior with a confused look on his face.

"It means there are some places I cannot follow, and I sense such a place nearby."

"It's the source of all the bad mojo that everyone can feel?" asked Thomas.

"Correct," said Wiyaloo.

"What are the odds we will go into that place?" The Spirit Warrior raised his eyebrow. "Don't answer that."

They walked down the main street of Sangeros. Thomas tried as hard as he could to maintain an air of confidence, but the place was truly creepy. There were no signs of modern conveniences anywhere, and the townspeople looked like they were a century behind. The three of them looked out of place in the dark town. "I'm gonna kill Neficus," said Thomas. "We stick out like a sore thumb."

"That's where we are supposed to meet Vilkari," said Anson, pointing to a pub sign that read: THE TAPPED VEIN. Anson walked through the door with little hesitation. Yareli followed and, reluctantly, so did Thomas. He had to turn sideways to enter the bar.

The lights were dimmed low in the bar. Inside, they were no longer conspicuous. Neficus's choice of disguises could not have been better. "Remind me to apologize to Neficus," added the boy. "This place is vamp heaven." Vampires of all shapes, sizes, and colors filled every shadow of the murky bar. The bar looked like it was made from slate. The décor was predominately black with touches of red.

The three of them walked up to the bar. The Tapped Vein seemed to have several different drafts. *I wonder how many types of blood they serve?* thought the boy. There was a stunning female vampire working behind the bar.

She turned around and jumped backward when she saw Thomas, spilling some of the drink she was pouring. "Whoa! You are gigantic," said the female bartender as she delivered the drink to a vampire one seat over. His appearance had startled the woman. His new form was massive and intimidating, even to other vampires. "What you drinking, Goliath?" asked the bartender as she collected herself.

"Do you know where I can find Fredrick Vilkari?" Thomas got right to the point. "We share a common friend."

"He's over there at that table." Thomas looked over to see a fat man drinking a blood-red cocktail, flanked by two girls.

"That's him?" asked Thomas, staring at the man in the red booth.

"I guess you were expecting someone more . . . vampiric," joked the bartender.

"Thank you for your time," said Anson as he placed some credits on the bar top. The three of them made their way over to the booth.

"Are you Fredrick Vilkari?" asked Thomas.

"Who wants to know?" asked the pudgy vampire, sandwiched between what appeared to be two human women.

"A friend of a friend," clarified the boy.

"I got a lot of friends, big guy. You might want to be a bit more specific."

"Does the name Malcolm Warwick fall into that category?" asked Anson, trying to get to the point.

"Don't say dat name too loud mate," said Vilkari, lowering his voice. He looked side to side. "It could be duh last words you utter. Sit down." The man motioned at his seated companions. "Get duh 'ell out of 'ere, girls." They shuffled out of the booth. The last one turned back and blew him a kiss. "Sit down, please." He motioned for them to enter the booth. Yareli and Anson sat, but Thomas had to remain standing. He was too big to sit. The boy stared at Vilkari as the fat vampire leaned in. "I was wondering when someone was going to show up looking for 'im. We go—" Vilkari cut himself short and looked at the boy. "What are you staring at?" asked Vilkari, noticing Thomas's fixation.

"Nothing . . ." said Thomas, as if he had just been caught doing something wrong. The boy could not wrap his head around the fact that he was talking to an obese vampire.

"Don't mind Grok here. He's only the muscle," voiced Anson. "Not much upstairs, I'm afraid." Thomas was offended and impressed at the same time with Anson's cunning. "I'm Hobart, and this here is Vixen." Yareli nodded. "We've been running with Malcolm for the last two hundred years or so." Vilkari brushed off Thomas's stare and continued.

"We go back centuries, me and Malcolm," said Vilkari. " 'ee was my best friend for years actually. Well, up until 'ee disappeared in London all dose years ago." Anson looked over at Thomas. "I must admit, I fought 'ee was dead, but den 'ee turns up 'ere askin' all sorts uv questions. It took some convincing for me to believe it were 'im in duh first place. Bloody good disguise, that. 'ee was obsessed wif Amara Scornd in particular. 'ee kept askin' about dat necklace of 'ers. It was odd to say duh least, but like I said, we were best mates back in duh day, so I did what I could."

"So you know where he's at?" asked Anson.

"Dat's not exactly a secret around dese parts. 'ee's been found out. The Mistress herself figured it out, but I still don't know bloody how. Like I said, I didn't even recognize the geezer."

"What's Scornd's beef with Malcolm?" asked Anson, trying to get a little more information about the situation.

"She claims that 'ee's a blood traitor, and if dere's one fing that vampire's can't stand, it's a blood traitor. As you know, it's the worst crime possible to kill our own kind. Don't get me wrong. I love duh guy and all. Like I said, we go back a piece, but if I 'ad to venture a guess, I would say 'ee's probably rachnid food by now."

"What's a rachnid?" blurted out Thomas.

"Trust me, you're going to find out. 'ee's most likely being kept in the center of duh 'ive. It is 'ome to fousands of vampires, myself included."

"Where is this Hive?" asked Yareli.

"You're sittin' on it, aren't you, my pet? This whole damn town is sitting above duh largest vamp 'ive you've evva feasted your pretty lit'l eyes upon." He reached across to grab Yareli's hand.

"I would not do that if I were you," said Yareli.

Vilkari leaned back in his booth and took a swig of his blood. He wiped his mouth with his sleeve. "If I know Scornd—and I do—she's torturing poor Malcolm as we speak. She's been waiting quite a while for 'er revenge, and she's going to enjoy every bloody second uv it."

"How do we get in?" asked Anson.

"Wait, you fink you're gonna just waltz in duh bloody 'ive, grab 'im, and then pop off like nuffin' happened, don't you? Amara Scornd is not a vampire to be trifled wif, my friend. She'll have you all destroyed—even Muscles over dere." He pointed at Thomas.

"What do you propose we do then?" asked Anson.

"I'd propose you should get duh 'ell out uv 'ere while you still 'av legs to walk wif. You're as good as mortal if you get caught."

"That's not an option, Vilkari. We are here to rescue Malcolm, and that's what we are going to do."

"Well, don't says I didn't warn ya." He took another swig of the blood. "You guys are crazy. I like dat. So, what do you need from me?" asked Vilkari.

"Take us to the entrance to the Hive, for starters," said Anson.

"I can do dat, mate: I owe Malcolm at least dat, but I can't guarantee your safety."

"Will you help us find him?" asked Anson.

"I will do whatever I can to 'elp. If 'ee's alive, 'ee's gonna need all duh 'elp 'ee can get." The fat vampire struggled to free himself from the plastic booth. "I just 'av to make a few quick 'olocalls to clear my schedule. If you'll excuse me." He got up, looked back at them, and leaned on the table. "I'll meet you guys outside in five minutes." He grabbed what was left of his blood and made his way to the door.

"I do not trust that man," said Wiyaloo.

"Me neither, but he's all we got," remarked Yareli. "We need him to find the Hive and Malcolm."

"We must stay vigilant, but we do not have a choice. We follow Vilkari," said Anson.

"Agreed, but keep a watchful eye on this man," said the spirit ghost.

"As always, I trust in your counsel," said Yareli.

"I'm not gonna lie: I'm freaking out a bit," said Thomas. "I mean . . . we have no idea what we're walking into."

"Present fears are less than horrible imaginings," responded Anson.

"Is that supposed to help?" asked Thomas.

31

seduced

They had not gone far from the town of Sangeros when the fat vampire came to an abrupt halt in a minefield of large jagged rocks. "So where is it?" asked Thomas. "I don't see anything around here. Just a bunch of stupid rocks."

"It's right 'ere. We're standing on it, aren't we? It's all underground. There are bleedin' caves after bleedin' caves after—guess what? More bleedin' caves. Now all we need to do is find duh bloody door, don't we? I know it's around 'ere somewhere." The vampire played with his chin as he pondered over several massive stones that rose out of the ground, walking from one to another.

Vilkari finally chose the rock slab to the far left. He took one last sip out of his goblet and threw the glass, half full of the Tapped Vein's special brew, at the ragged stone. It erupted on impact, and the contents began to trickle down. The maroon liquid defied gravity and stopped moving. A symbol began to carve itself into the rock. The blood swirled and bubbled and started to fill the grooves of the insignia. Smoke poured from the smoldering rock. The smell from the vapor was harsh and biting. When the smoke cleared, a dark mark was etched into the entire face of the boulder. "I fink I found duh door." The pudgy vampire grinned and proceeded to lean over and grab a part of the marking that looked like a handle. He twisted it as the door smoked and pulled free of its surroundings. "Ladies first." The fat man looked at Yareli and winked.

"Thank you," replied the girl as she entered the dark tunnel. Wiyaloo pulled on Thomas's arm and began to whisper.

"This is as far as I can go." The spirit ghost's words reverberated in his head. "I will inform the others of this location." The beast paused. The silence was long enough for Thomas to think Wiyaloo had already vanished. "Please look after Yareli."

He could feel the breeze from the spirit ghost's departure. *A place Wiyaloo can't enter, this is going to be loads of fun.*

"So are we doin' dis?" asked Vilkari, looking directly at Thomas, his left arm invitingly extended. Anson had followed Yareli, and now it was the boy's turn. He walked through the opening, and his feet found no ground. He began to fall.

Thomas righted himself and braced himself for the landing. He crashed onto several bodies, all in different stages of decay. His new weight shook the ground. He stood up and saw a landing area covered in human bones. Vilkari landed next to him, wings extended.

"Thanks for the heads up," said Thomas.

"Oh yeah, duh drop. I forgot. It's a precaution. Don't want any 'umans lurkin' about all by demselves, do we?" He walked to another door and slid a huge stone slab to the side like it was a screen door. "You guys comin'?" Yareli and Anson passed the fat vampire.

Vilkari entered the long chamber, and Thomas followed. The rock door slammed behind him, startling the boy. He turned around to see the origin of the noise. *Why do I have the feeling we just entered a crypt?* When he turned back, the others had gone on ahead of him.

Thomas hurried to catch up to rest of the group, and he walked directly into a spiderweb. His new height had betrayed him. The boy squeamishly brushed the webs off of his head. "I guess they don't have a maid." Torches burst to life down the length of the tunnel. Thomas could now see that webs adorned most of the walls and ceiling.

"It's not pretty, but it's 'ome," said Vilkari as he laughed nervously.

"Where does this lead?" asked Anson.

"To a main hall that all of the tunnels extend from. Once we get dere I can lead you to where Malcolm is most likely being 'eld. If I didn't know any better, 'ee's probably in duh rachnid nest."

"How will we know when we're close?" asked Thomas.

"Trust me, mate. You'll know," said Vilkari.

The farther they traveled into the Hive, the more outwardly unsettled Vilkari became. The tunnels were anything but straight—twisting and curving this way and that. The boy was uneasy himself, but he should be. He was a human in a vampire hive. This was Vilkari's home. The obese man should have nothing to fear. "Are we lost?" asked Thomas.

"Lost? No, why do you ask?"

"Well, we seem to be lost. I'm pretty sure we've past here before, but I can't be positive because everything down here looks the same—dirt, stone, spiderwebs. Are you sure you know where you're going?"

"Yes, we're almost dere." The fat vampire picked up his pace. The three of them followed, but for some reason, Thomas had a distinct feeling that something was wrong. They reached a large opening that seemed to connect all of the catacomb tunnels. The walls were covered in markings, which in turn, were covered by an uncanny amount of spiderwebs. "We're here," said Vilkari.

"Where is *here*?" The torches flickered and then extinguished. Thomas could not see anything, and he did not have his goggles with him. He had left them with Bartleby. When the torchlights reignited, they were surrounded by vampires. "Oh, so when you said 'we're here,' you weren't telling us—you were telling them."

"Who are your new friends, Fredrick?" The voice was cold yet warm, evil but soothing. She moved from the shadows slowly, seductively. Her black hair ran down her long neck. She wore a red leather jacket that stretched down to the floor.

"They are the associates of Malcolm's that I had told you about," said Vilkari.

"Friends of Malcolm the blood traitor?" Here eyes scanned the three of them. "Malcolm Warwick betrayed his own kind. You associating yourself with such filth does not speak very highly of your taste in company." She smiled a fake smile. "How rude of me. My name is Amara Scornd. I am the Mistress of this Hive."

"I can't believe this," said Thomas.

"Believe it," said Anson. "Malcolm has never been the best judge of character."

"Silence!" exclaimed the Mistress. "Take them down to the rachnid cells." The guards advanced. Thomas grabbed the first vampire and threw him into four others who were approaching. He moved to stop the next assault when he heard her clear her throat. The boy turned around to see Amara holding Yareli by her neck. "I don't think you want to do that." Thomas relaxed and extended his huge hands above his head.

"Web them up with Warwick. Make sure you take their wrist-coms. There could be something worth looking at on them."

"But you said you would free Malcolm if I—"

"Warwick will be punished accordingly, Vilkari. You would do yourself well to drop the subject, unless you want to end up in the Pit as well."

"No . . . Mistress."

"Good to see you come around." She turned towards her guards. "Just because he is your progeny doesn't mean you can protect him forever." She turned towards Thomas. "Bring the big one to my chambers. He looks like he might be of some use to me." She winked at the boy and stormed out of the catacomb.

Anson leaned over to the boy and whispered. "Be careful with that one, Thomas. Look like the innocent flower, but be the serpent under 't."

The guards took Anson and Yareli away. Two guards grabbed Thomas and forced him down a different catacomb. The farther he went downward, the more the tunnel reeked of mold. He passed what he thought had to be the rachnid cells. He glanced to the left and saw a room full of human cocoons with tubes running from them. Red liquid traveled through the tubes. Thomas could make out several different faces embedded in the cocoons. The people all seemed to be asleep. Large spiderlike creatures meticulously tended to the webbed victims. One of the creatures moved closer. Its head and torso were humanoid, but they were attached to the body of a horse-sized spider. *I guess that's a rachnid.* Thomas was pulled into a room and forced to kneel. A third vamp guard grabbed the boy by his face.

"We're going to give you a little something to drink—just to take the edge off," said the guard as he waved a capsule full of green liquid.

The elixir's color reminded him of the gremlin Gloop, but he had a suspicion that it would not taste as pleasant. "Thanks, but I'm not thirsty," said Thomas.

The guard punched the boy across the face. Thomas lifted his head, and the guard grabbed his face again. "I don't remember asking." The guard squeezed the boy's cheeks in an effort to make him open his mouth. Thomas began to squirm. The two vampires fought hard to stay in control. *What am I trying to do? Even if I try to escape they would kill my friends.* Thomas succumbed.

A vampire wearing a black lab coat approached. The guard handed the vamp the capsule. The capsule was attached to a mechanism the doctor held. The doctor leaned over and squeezed the trigger of the device. A tube shot out the front of it and into the boy's mouth. A large mouthpiece covered his lips. The apparatus forced the green liquid down his throat. He choked. The fluid gurgled as one of the guards forced his mouth shut, and the doctor released the feeding tube. "I guess you didn't like it." Thomas had never tasted anything so disturbing. It burned the inside of his throat. "I guess I should have warned you of the taste, but where's the fun in that?" He felt the change almost immediately. All the strength and power that Thomas had started to grow accustomed to was gone. The boy was powerless. He sank down. "Take him to her now," commanded the doctor. "You mustn't keep the Mistress waiting."

"Yes, Doctor."

The guards pulled the boy down a flight of stairs that had been dug out of the cave. *There's no moldy smell down here.* They came upon a small room. It resembled a waiting room. The two guards lifted Thomas onto his feet.

"Go on through that doorway," the guard on the left told him. Thomas did not see any other option so he followed the order. "The Mistress is waiting."

Thomas entered Amara Scornd's lair gingerly. Now powerless, the extra bulk that Thomas was carrying made maneuvering much more difficult than he had anticipated. He felt helpless. His movements were also slight because the room was laid out like a museum. Trinkets adorned every corner of the expansive room—priceless artifacts from different places and time periods. He was fairly certain he saw a Van Gogh painting on the far wall.

From the looks of this stuff, she must be ancient, the boy pondered. *Although you can't tell by looking at her.* He gazed at her. *Sure she's got red pupils, but she's so hot.* Thomas started to feel a sturdy attraction to Mistress Scornd. He could not quite understand it, but he was mesmerized by her, and he could not help but stare.

"Grok, was it? You like what you see?" she asked as a smaller version of the rachnid he had seen on the way over jumped up and crawled on her shoulder.

"What? Yes . . . I mean . . . yes, my name is Grok." A peculiar giggle followed his rushed words.

"I want you to make yourself comfortable."

"What the hell is that thing?"

"My pet here? She is a rachnid—a human-spider hybrid, if you will. She'll be about six and a half feet tall when she's fully grown."

"What are they doing here?"

"We share a common love with the rachnid." Scornd giggled. "Both our kinds need blood. They help by keeping the humans alive so we can bleed them."

"How do they do that?"

"Well, with the same venom I'm sure you just enjoyed. It keeps the humans in a stasis of sorts. All the humans you saw this evening are all ours. We produce a significant amount of the bottled blood used by vampires all over the globe."

"You farm them?"

"It's more like milk them," corrected Scornd. Thomas shuddered at the thought and then realized that was what he had seen.

"And they just line up for that?"

"They have been programmed over the years to do just that. They have no idea that anything exists outside this small town. We like to keep them in the dark."

"I noticed that as well."

"You mean the perpetual darkness?"

"That's what I was getting at."

"It's a little enchantment I came up with. It's actually quite brilliant."

"Beautiful and humble," interrupted Thomas. He did not know where his courage was coming from, but he felt drawn to her.

"It has made our way of life easier, to say the least."

"I can see that." Thomas tried to remain calm. "I am . . . impressed."

"Big, brawny, and smart. It is I who am impressed." Scornd simpered and turned.

"So what's with how antiquated everything is in Sangeros? There wasn't even a holovision in the bar."

"You sure are curious. I like that." She smiled at him. "The humans in the town are all under my . . . influence. It is similar to the influence all of us vampires share, but mine is a bit stronger."

"Really? I hadn't noticed." They exchanged flirtatious smiles.

"It is just far easier to deal with controlling them when they don't have access to the outside world. Their ignorance ensures that our business thrives and, more importantly, that we do not starve."

She had made her way over to a bar that was located under what Thomas was sure was an original Dali. Mistress Scornd bent down to pick up a bottle. "Would you like some?" The red liquid that sloshed up and down the side of the glass container drew Thomas's attention. "It's a 2036 AB negative—quite expensive. It's the rarest blood there is, which in my opinion makes it the best." She had already begun to pour him a glass. She handed him his goblet and raised her glass. "To new . . . friends."

"New friends." Thomas clinked his glass against hers. He did not know what to do. He could not drink the blood, but he really did not have a choice. The last thing he wanted was to have these vampires know that he was not actually their kind, especially in his weakened state. Thomas raised the glass to his lips and pretended to drink. A globule of the scarlet elixir stroked his lower lip. It took all he could muster not to spit. He smiled as he withdrew the goblet from his mouth.

"You missed a drop." She wiped her finger across his bottom lip. She then placed her finger in her mouth. "Like I said, it's expensive— mustn't waste a single drop." Mistress Scornd turned and walked towards the center of the room. She took off her jacket and threw it to the side. Thomas let out a breath he had been holding for about a minute's time.

"It's very good," said Thomas, doing his best impersonation of how Grok would say this. He followed the Mistress. She turned to meet him, and the two almost ran into each other. She pulled him in tight, stood on her toes, and kissed him. Thomas was taken aback by the gesture, and even further so by the tart, metallic taste in the Mistress's mouth. He did not let that stop him from embracing her closer. Her body was frigid and warm at the same time. As he kissed the vampire, he quickly opened his eyes and noticed a nearby vessel. He quietly poured the glass into what he could now see was a mid-to-late-fifteenth century Ming vase. *My father would kill me for that*, he thought.

Thomas felt a sudden twinge somewhere near his chest—more specifically, her chest. Thomas backed away. He felt a surge of energy in the glove for a split second, and then it ceased. He grabbed his right arm tightly and stumbled back. He then saw the cause of his disorientation. Dangling from her neck over her well-placed cleavage was the yellow stone. The jewel was embedded into a necklace that hung around Scornd's neck. The ornament was in the shape of a spider. At the center of the spider's body was the Taitokura, the Stone of Experience. The charge he felt guaranteed its authenticity.

Almost immediately, the power overload snapped him out of her influence. He shook his head trying to reset himself. *Spells said they have the ability to seduce. I'll have to be more careful.*

"That's a beautiful necklace," said Thomas as he tried to gather himself. "It must've cost a small fortune."

"I fashioned the amulet myself."

"What kind of rock is that?"

"I'm not certain." She slinked closer to the boy. "I . . . *borrowed* it from a man I met some fifteen years back, and it's been my good luck charm ever since." She placed her finger on his bottom lip and tugged. "I'm a bit of a collector of beautiful things, if you haven't noticed, and I usually get what I want." The outside parts of her lips arched upward. The innuendo hung like one of the many tapestries in the room. "But why are we talking about this silly bauble? I liked our last topic so much better." Mistress Scornd leaned in to kiss him once more. He turned his head. "What's wrong, Grok? Why do you fight yourself?" She turned his head to look into his eyes. Thomas could sense the power of the stone. "There's something so . . . different about you. I can't quite put my finger on it." She pulled closer and stroked her finger, complete with red nail polish, down his cheek.

"You don't know the half of it." *If you knew the truth, I'd be in one of your blood bottles.* The boy grinned at her. He kept staring at the necklace, which was inconveniently hanging in front of Amara Scornd's bosom. This did nothing to dissuade the Mistress.

"Why don't we try that again?" She bent forward and tilted her head to the right.

"Sorry, not interested." He looked away and promptly looked back into her red eyes. Thomas pulled her close and started kissing her again. He felt her frozen lips once more and a similar shock from the stone, and again the boy withdrew. *Stop letting her do that to you.* "Nope, no interest whatsoever." *It's definitely the right rock.* "Just isn't doing it for me, sorry." Her mouth gaped open. Her eyes thinned. She was infuriated.

"I am Amara Scornd, Mistress of the Hive, and one of the Exemplar. No is not an answer I hear often." She looked away from Thomas. "Guards!" Three vampires rushed in. "Dorin and Griscom, take him to his friends." She pointed to the two vampires holding the electric staffs. The two guards grabbed the boy under both of his arms. "Fisbol, stay here with me. I need . . . satisfaction." The third vampire moved over to Amara Scornd. "Maybe some time with your blood traitor friends will help you to . . . reconsider." She giggled as she pulled Fisbol closer to her. Thomas was taken out of the chambers.

The vampire guards—Dorin and Griscom—drug Thomas down one of the many dim catacombs. *I wonder what they have done with Yareli and Anson*, he thought. He again tried to use his powers, but nothing. *This isn't getting any easier.* They stopped in front of a door that was covered by a red glowing force field. The field dissipated as they passed through the entryway. The guards drug him into the cell.

The detention center resembled a spider's nest. *I guess this is the rachnid's lair that Vilkari was babbling about.* The ceilings seemed to go endlessly upward, covered by layer after layer of what looked like silver and white ropes. Ten or so rachnid climbed across them, spinning new strings. The chamber was littered with their webs.

Thomas looked around and could see his friends. At the moment, they were faring far worse than he was. Yareli and Anson were webbed up, dangling from the ceiling like stored food. Several rachnid attended to the chore of containing them. The rachnid here were older than the one in Amara's room, and much bigger. They were getting ready for another visitor. *I guess they're waiting for me*, thought the boy.

Dorin and Griscom held him against the wall. Three rachnid dropped down and began the task of entombing the oversized boy.

He tried to struggle, but his efforts proved futile. He was a fly in a web. They circled his large body and spun their webs. In seconds Thomas's fate now mirrored his friends', and without the use of his magic, he felt defeated.

From what Thomas could tell, Yareli and Anson had also been given the drug. Anson and Yareli seemed distant and drained of energy. Their cocoons slightly rocked back and forth, dangling from the webbed ceiling.

While he was busy contemplating his friends' statuses, the rachnid had finished their task. The guards vacated the webbed prison. The force field filled the hole once more.

"Yar . . . Anson . . . are you awake?" asked the boy. The werewolf lifted his head. It was the only part of his body that was not covered.

"Thomas, is that you?" Anson's eyes squinted as he looked in his direction. "I can't smell you. I never realized how much I rely on my other senses." He shook his head back and forth. "I haven't felt so . . . human in centuries." His head shot up, and he looked from side to side. "Where's Yareli?"

"I'm here," answered the girl. "What did they feed us? I feel sick."

"It's rachnid venom," said Thomas. "It seems to suppress our powers. I'm just glad the two of you are alive." He turned his head as far as he could to the left to see his comrades. "She has the stone. Malcolm was right. I felt its power, and if she knows what she has, she's keeping that to herself."

"That doesn't help us now," interjected Yareli.

"The venom was unforeseen, even by Ziza," said Anson. "We have seventy-two hours—well I guess more like sixty-eight hours— before these disguises wear off."

"So all we have to do is free ourselves from these webs, get the stone, and escape the hive—all without the use of any of our powers." said Yareli.

"Don't forget find my brother," added Anson.

"It's impossible," said Thomas.

"This is a sorry sight," said Anson, "but not an impossible one, my dear boy—"

Their dialogue was interrupted by the whoosh sound of the force field relenting. Two guards carried in a new prisoner. Malcolm hung between Dorin and Griscom, and he did not look good. He was paler than usual, and he looked emaciated. His skeletal frame was balanced perfectly between the two guards.

They propped Malcolm up, and down came the spiders. Malcolm hung in his webs, unconscious. The werewolf was furious. The venom was the only thing keeping these vampire guards alive. "What have you done to him?" asked Anson.

"Shut up, blood traitor," said the guard on the left as he smacked Anson across the face.

"A hit, a very palpable hit." Anson smiled at the guard. The two vampires left the cell laughing. The werewolf stared at his brother's motionless body. "Malcolm." No response. "Malcolm!" yelled Anson once more.

The vampire lifted his head and mumbled to himself and immediately fell back to sleep. Malcolm had obviously been given too much of the elixir, and it had left him incoherent.

"Well, we found Maaaalcolm," slurred Thomas as he yawned. "I feel . . . drained. Oops . . . poooor choice of wooords." He looked over and he was the only one still awake. "I guess I-I'mmmm not the ooonly one . . ." Darkness fluttered into his eyes as reality dropped away. Thomas's head dropped as he slipped into the venom-induced coma.

32

time flies

Thomas woke to the sound of two rachnid working on his webbed prison. His eyes slowly opened. He had not felt this helpless before in his life. "I think you two missed a spot here under my arm." The multi-legged monsters continued their jobs as if nothing was said. "Looks and personality. You guys must be great at parties." Thomas felt cold, anxious, but most of all lonely, even though his comrades were only feet away. He stared across the room. Anson and Yareli were still fast asleep. Anson was making noises like he was having a nightmare, while Yareli sounded like a hibernating bear with asthma. This made Thomas smile. Even in these horrible circumstances, he saw the positive.

He felt like he had been out for some time, but he was exhausted. Dorin abruptly entered the room. "All right, blood traitors, wake up." Yareli sat up mid-snore, but Anson did not wake. Dorin walked over to the webbed werewolf and slapped him. "Wake up, vermin." Anson shot up. "It's time for your medicine." He moved towards Yareli first. "Hello, gorgeous," said the guard. He placed the same contraption on her that they had used on him earlier. Her face twitched and contorted with disgust as she swallowed the emerald poison. Dorin then administered the venom to Anson and then Thomas.

It tastes worse this time, the boy thought. He did not even bother with Malcolm, who still had not had one moment of lucidity since their arrival.

"If I was you guys, I'd get some more rest. You have a date with several hungry rachnid tomorrow. I got 300 credits on you guys lasting at least five minutes. I would hate to be disappointed. Nighty night." With that, Dorin laughed his way back through the portal.

Thomas was scared, tired, and hungry. *There's no hope.*

Thomas then heard a familiar sound. He heard the lowest whistling sound start to become stronger. He could not see the origin of it.

"I fought 'ee'd nevva leave," said Fargus as he appeared in front of Thomas. "I 'av been waiting out dere for like six hours for someone to walk fru dat bloody door." He looked around the holding cell. "Dis place is a bit creepy isn't it—wif all duh bones and webs an that— and what's wit all dem fanged fellows knockin' about?"

"Fargus, you are a sight for sore, drugged-out eyes," said Thomas with a smile on his face.

"When you guys didn't return for almost two days an that, we started to try and find a way in 'ere, didn't we?"

"Wait. We've been in here two days?" asked Anson.

"Yes it's been two days, 'asn't it? You guys look like 'ell too, if you don't mind me saying. Maybe you guys should try a bit of exercise an that. Could do ya a bit uv good is all I'm saying."

"How did you find us?" asked Yareli. The gremlin turned to her.

"It weren't easy, was it? You guys are almost a mile under ground at dis part uv duh 'ive. Dey weren't exactly giving tours of dis place, were dey? I snuck into the joint fru a tiny crack in duh surface. I told dem I would find you guys if I could and try to 'elp an that."

"Why didn't you just come through the door?"

"We didn't 'av any 'uman blood now did we? Besides we couldn't just walk fru duh front door and demand dey return you guys. Dat would 'av been a bit presumptuous on our part, wouldn't it? I over'eard a few of them fanged fellows babbling on about a big show in duh arena tomorrow night, and I just figured it 'ad to involve you guys. So I followed duh one bloke when 'ee said it was time for your medication and dat 'ee was going to give it to ya."

"It must have been my favorite guard, Dorin," said the boy.

"Yeah, I believe dat was his name, duh bloke dat just left, right?"

"That's him."

"Well, 'ee was saying dat you guys are meant to fight some of dem large rachnoids—"

"Rachnid," corrected Thomas.

"Well whatever dey are called, you are meant ta fight dem in some sort of vamp arena. 'ee was goin' on about 'ow 'ee needed to make sure you were well drugged up before den. 'ee said it's meant to be a trial an that, but I wouldn't put much faif in such a judicial system. On a side note dough, I did get to see one of dose venom contraptions close up. Marvelous piece of machinery, isn't it?"

"Not when it's shoved down your throat it's not," answered Thomas.

"Where are LINC, Bartleby, and Wiyaloo now?" asked Anson.

"Well, Wiyaloo disappeared sometime early on duh first day. I guess his connection had severed wif Yareli. Bartleby is still fast asleep, isn't 'ee? Just lazy . . . dragons I mean, and LINC is . . . recovering from some of the upgrades I added. 'ee's waitin' for me to return wif word of what 'appened to you guys an that."

"So you should do just thaaaat . . ." said Anson as he passed back out. Thomas looked over and saw that Yareli had followed the werewolf's example. The loud snoring began again.

"She sounds like a bloody broken vacuum, doesn't she?" Thomas giggled at Fargus's assessment.

"Anson is right: you should get word back to LINC and Bartleby, and you need to hurry because we don't have much time before these disguises wear off."

"What's the difference? Ja know what I mean? Either you're a bunch of vampires captured, or you're a werewolf and two 'umans captured. I don't see duh big deal is all I'm saying."

"They have this rule about killing their own. That's why the rachnid are involved. They will be all over us if we are discovered to be human. We would end up in one of those bleeding rooms to rot for decades, and I can't even imagine what they'd do to Anson if they discover what he is."

"When you put it dat way, I guess it sounds a bit worse, doesn't it? I'll move as fast as I can, Thomas."

"Tell them that the stone is definitely the one. I felt its power. Tell them they must be ready to move. Then I need you to get back here. I have a plan, and there's something important I need you to do, but first I need to know . . ." He motioned for the gremlin to lean in. Thomas whispered, "How much Gloop do you have left?"

33

spy games

Marcus lifted one of the straps across his aringi. The beast screeched as the Captain tightened the leather belts. Its head pivoted violently from side to side. Evangeline looked on as she saddled her own bat. The two were in the aringi stables. The Newts went about their business, feeding the large bats and cleaning the stables. The lizard-like creatures were more than capable of harnessing the aringi, but it was something Marcus preferred to do himself. Evangeline always took care of her own aringi as well. She shared a certain unexplainable attachment to her beast.

Marcus had had no luck finding Thomas Scargen. They had no choice but to go to the vampire hive and follow up on the Seer's premonition. Farod, Jurdik, and Taunt had been out flying earlier and were now in the mess hall. Evangeline and the Captain were to meet up with them and leave to visit the vampire bar where Jalia worked. "In all my years of tracking, this is truly a first. This Thomas Scargen is either really slippery or really lucky." The Captain looked over at Evangeline. Her eyes met his, and he could not help but smile.

"I wasn't sure your face still did that," said Evangeline as she stroked the back of her aringi's ear. The bat straightened its neck, and its eyes rolled upward. The aringi's purr reverberated through the stables.

"There's not a lot to smile about these days," said the Captain.

He looked away. He did not know what to say next. He decided to change the subject. "That beast would do anything for you." Marcus looked back towards Evangeline. "It's amazing how close she is to you. These bats usually seem distant."

"I've seen your mount show affection to you before, Captain, and if you have no connection with the aringi, then why do you always choose the same one?" She looked at him for an answer. "And you're telling me you haven't named him?"

"No, I have not. My aringi is my transport, and that's all. I am the Captain of the Riders. I have no time to be emotionally attached to anything." He regretted the lie as soon as it left his mouth. She turned her head away from him. "What I mean is . . . once you name them, they become more than just transportation." His aringi seemed to look at him and tilt his head. Evangeline looked back at him.

"And what's wrong with that? I believe my connection with Pria helps us when we are in flight and in battle. Isn't that right, Pria?" She scratched the top of the aringi's head.

"Pria can't understand a word you're saying," joked Marcus.

"I don't believe that. I believe my affection for Pria makes our psychic bond stronger."

He smiled again and looked at his bat. "Well, maybe you have a point. The way you fly is amazing, and you can't argue with results." She grinned and lowered her eyes then went back to the task at hand. He cleared his throat. He felt awkward and again decided to change the subject. "So, are you about ready? It's a long shot, but we aren't finding anything out just sitting around the Tower. The Seer has never been wrong before. Something must be going on in Sangeros."

"Almost there," she said as she continued strapping the under-belly saddle to Pria, occasionally throwing her bat a dead rat. The beast snapped the treat out of the air and purred.

"I should try to contact Jalia one more time before we leave." He looked down at his wristcom and hit a few buttons. The sound of the wristcom trying to connect echoed in the stable. A holographic representation of Jalia sprang out of the display.

"Hello, Captain Slade. I was wondering when you were gonna call me. Do I have news for you." She appeared to be walking somewhere crowded.

"You were supposed to call me when you found out anything."

"Oops, you know how my memory is."

"It has nothing to do with the excessive amounts of dragonweed you smoke, does it?"

"Don't judge me. Immortality can be boring."

"What's the news, Jalia?"

"Oh, right—anyway the craziest thing happened a few days after our last conversation. I was working another double shift—one of the drawbacks of being immortal in a town with no sunlight. It's about 5:00 AM, and in walks Vilkari, but he's not with those human skanks he's normally here with. He walks in and sits at his usual booth. About ten minutes later, in walks this other vamp, but this guy I've never seen before. I might forget a lot of things, but I don't forget a face. So this other vamp goes over and sits down in Vilkari's booth. I don't think anything of it, and then all of a sudden, you popped into my head. I remember what you said about the fat vampire and anyone strange hanging around. So I start thinking that this bizarre vamp must be Malcolm Warwick, like you had said." She stopped and took a swig from a bottle.

"And?" wondered Marcus. "Was it Malcolm?"

"Well, yes, but I found that out later. I did what you said to do and alerted the Mistress of this new vampire and the possibility of who he could be. She immediately arrested him, but, from what I heard that night, he never said who he was. They tortured him and tortured him, but he still said nothing. It wasn't until his disguise wore off that Scornd believed it was Warwick. She was excited, to say the least. She rewarded me with a nice 1788 B negative. She was not happy with Vilkari, but he ended up making some deal with her."

"What kind of deal?"

"Mistress Scornd assumed someone would come looking for Warwick, and that they would probably come looking for Vilkari—

seeing that he was Warwick's contact. He was to lead them right to her in exchange for his freedom, and that's exactly what he did when the three came around. What a piece of work. The joke's on him, though. He's been confined to his quarters. Last I heard, he was pretty pissed off."

Marcus felt a rush go through him. *Could one of these be Scargen?* "Can you describe the other three to me?" asked the Captain.

"Sure . . . umm—well, one was an older man, pretty tall and thin. He looked funny next to the other one who was frankly the biggest vampire I'd ever seen. He had to be like seven foot tall and just as wide."

"They were definitely vampires?"

"Yep, all three. I do know my own kind." This disheartened the Captain. That put a damper on his hypothesis. "The girl was the most peculiar to me, though. I mean, I guess it's just that I've never seen an American Indian vamp before." The words took a while to register as she kept talking. "I'm not being racist or anything; it's just one of those things, you know."

"Did you say American Indian?"

"Yes. Why, is that not cool to say? Is Native American better?" Marcus hit a few more buttons on his wristcom and a touch screen display emerged next to the hologram of Jalia. He used his hands to navigate through profiles, and he stopped on one.

"Is this her?" he asked. The image had stopped on a three dimensional representation of Yareli Chula. Her vital information was listed next to her.

"That's the one. She looks a bit paler now, but like I said, I never forget a face."

Marcus grinned and looked over at Evangeline. She looked confused. "If that's her, and she is disguised as a vampire, then who's to say the other two are not disguised as well." The Second smiled.

"I'll call Farod, Jurdik, and Taunt and tell them to get down here," said Evangeline as she walked out of the hangar stable.

"Wait . . . you mean she's not a vampire?" asked Jalia. "She sure smells like one."

"You cannot say a word of this to anyone—but no, she's not a vamp, and I believe the other two aren't either."

"I don't know about that. The big one was plenty powerful when he was captured. He threw a couple of the guards around like ragdolls."

Scargen—it has to be—there's no other explanation. "I trust they are being held somewhere in the Hive." His confidence had returned to him. Soon he would tell the General that he had found the boy, and he could get things back to the way they were. "What are the odds of a prisoner exchange?"

"I don't think that's gonna happen."

"Why not?"

"Well, I'm actually on my way to the Pit as we speak. Their trial begins in like half an hour."

"Trial?" asked the Captain.

"The trial is just a formality, really. Malcolm and his fellow blood traitors are gonna be fed to the taranchers." The Captain knew of these hefty, feral rachnid, but they stood no chance against Scargen and his friends.

"They will destroy the taranchers, Jalia. These are powerful Mages you are dealing with."

"I doubt that. They are so filled with rachnid venom, they won't be doing much of anything."

"Rachnid venom?"

"Yeah, they are probably close to paralyzed at this point." Marcus was stunned. He had heard stories about the effect of this venom, but he had thought it was just a myth. This changed everything. He had to think fast.

"Listen to me, Jalia. Do you know where Vilkari is right now?"

"Yes, he's in his quarters."

"Do you think he'd help Malcolm and his friends escape?"

"I think he'd do just about anything to embarrass the Mistress after what she's done to him, and besides, he's Malcolm's Maker, which means they share a progeny-maker connection. He has to help Malcolm. It's in his blood."

"Then I need you to free Vilkari."

"Why would I do that?"

"I need these prisoners alive. The General will be most displeased if anything bad happens to them. It will negate our treaty, and I don't think either side wants that." The hologram was silent for a few seconds.

"What's in it for me?" asked Jalia.

"I guess I was waiting for that question. You will have my respect, and the General and I will be indebted to you."

"And . . ."

"100,000 credits."

"Don't get cheap on me now, Captain."

"Okay, 200,000; but how can you be sure you can free him?"

"A woman has her ways, Captain. Don't worry about a thing."

"I'm transferring the credits now. Tell that fat vampire that if he doesn't save Malcolm and his friends, he will have a new enemy who is far more powerful and less forgiving than Amara Scornd, and Jalia . . ."

"Yes, Captain?"

"Please don't forget."

"It's odd how much more I remember when 200,000 credits are involved. Bye, Captain." She smiled as her image disappeared. The display screen dissipated as well. Evangeline walked back into the stable. Farod, Jurdik, and Taunt followed.

"Get ready to move," commanded the Captain.

"Why, what's up?" asked Taunt as he chewed on what looked like some sort of animal's leg.

"Amara Scornd is holding Yareli Chula and Malcolm Warwick captive."

"What does that have to do with the Scargen boy?" asked Farod.

"The girl is pretending to be a vampire and I think her companions are also in disguise."

"Meaning?" asked Taunt.

"Meaning that the boy is with them, and he is currently a prisoner in the middle of a vampire hive, which doesn't bode well for us recovering him."

"Oh," said Taunt. "We better get going." He threw what was left of his dinner onto the ground. Several Newts sprang for the boned meat, fighting each other over the scraps. "Pathetic Newts. They act like they don't get fed or something."

"Two meals a week is scarcely enough for these creatures to function, Taunt," said Farod. "It's a wonder they live as long as they do. Their physiology is remarkable."

"Forget the stupid lizards. We got some vampire ass to kick," said Jurdik as he looked over at the rest of the Riders.

"Hopefully, it will not come to that," interrupted the Second.

"But if it does, we are equipped for it." Taunt raised his forearm. The T27 opened up to reveal a crossbow attachment loaded with wooden stakes.

"You really do think of everything," said Jurdik.

"I just did some calculations, and there was a 77.6 percent chance that we'd eventually face vampires when you factor in what we do and who we do it for."

"And they are amphibians, Jurdik," said Farod as he looked over at the squat man. "Not lizards."

"Riders, mount up," commanded Marcus, trying to stop an argument before it could start. The five of them walked outside of the stable and lined up straight across. Marcus called telepathically to his bat. The five aringi rushed out of the stable and straight into the sky. They all came shooting downward and simultaneously snatched their Riders off of the ground.

Marcus instructed his aringi to form a teleportal and typed all the pertinent information into his wristcom. The sky ripped open. Taunt went first, followed by Jurdik and Farod and then the Second. Marcus leaned up to his bat. "Let's get going . . . Teros." The aringi screeched approvingly at Marcus. The name seemed to fit the bat. The two sped through the opening in the sky.

34
the pit

Thomas jolted out of his slumber. His eyes sat heavily in his skull. The rachnid venom was taking its toll on the boy. The last thing he remembered was Fargus begrudgingly leaving through one of the rachnid tunnels. The feeling of loneliness crept back into his head, an apparent side effect of the venom. He blinked and shook his head back and forth. "Anson . . . Yareli . . . wake up," he said under his breath. The two slowly roused. "We don't have much time. I need you to listen." The werewolf and girl turned to Thomas. They, too, looked weary. "Now, when Dorin goes to feed you the venom, do not struggle. I want you to drink it. Drink as much as you possibly can."

"Are you mad?" exclaimed Anson. He had become increasingly agitated over the last few days. If he had had the ability, he probably would have transformed by this point, and this inability seemed to have shaken him. He had not quoted the Bard since the first day in the Hive. Thomas took this as a bad sign.

"I don't have time to explain. The guard's coming. Just, please, do it." Thomas had a plan, but if one thing went wrong, they would all be dead. Dread gripped his cold, wrapped body. The reality of their predicament was daunting, but he had to remain strong. "You'll have to trust me, Anson."

"That I can do, friend," replied the werewolf. His brother was still motionless next to him. Malcolm was alive but just barely.

"Be ready on my signal." The force field that covered the doorway lowered. Two vampires entered the room. Griscom and Dorin now stood in front of the webbed group. Dorin walked first to Anson and inserted the tube into his mouth. The werewolf pretended to struggle for a second, but then he accepted the liquid. He consumed a great deal of the venom. Anson smiled when the tube was removed. This did not go unnoticed.

"He's so far gone, he's enjoying this rachnid slop," muttered Griscom. Dorin turned to see the werewolf's grinning face.

"O true apothecary! Thy drugs are quick," said Anson, feigning madness. Thomas knew this was a good sign. The guard smacked the werewolf across the face. Anson growled.

"Silence, blood traitor," hissed Griscom as he made his way over to Anson's wilted brother. The guard raised Malcolm's head, and Dorin shoved the device into his gullet. The fluid poured into his mouth. Nearly half of it fell to the ground, but enough was consumed to placate the guards. They continued on to Yareli. She looked at Griscom with disgust as Dorin delivered the drug. She, too, drank the poison as fast as she physically could. Thomas was the last to get administered his daily dose of venom.

"He's a big one. We need to make sure he gets plenty of this crap." The guard clutched the boy's jaw, and the process was started anew. Thomas did not fight the invasion. He opened wide and surrendered to the delightful taste of Gloop.

Remind me to thank that little bastard, thought Thomas as energy slowly began to flow through his massive form. Fargus had done it.

"I'll be right back with your escorts for this evening. There's a big show in the Pit tonight, and you guys are invited."

"I suppose we're Mistress Scornd's honored guests?" asked Thomas.

"You could say that," said Dorin as he began to laugh. The two vampires left the cell and the force field reestablished itself.

Everyone stared at the door, waiting for the bloodsuckers to back away. The hum from the force field was the only thing to be heard. A ragged cough broke the silence. It was Malcolm. Heads turned. "What are all you staring at? 'avn't you ever seen a vampire before?" asked

Malcolm. "And dose disguises of yours are bleedin' hysterical. I know my bruvvers foul stench anywhere—even when you don't smell like a wolf. And as for da Goliath outfit, Tommy, it's bloody marvelous. In fact, Yareli seems to be duh only one who's being 'erself dese days—well, and Fargus." The gremlin appeared on the web bump above Thomas.

"Dat's one 'ell uv a nose," said Fargus. "I fought you couldn't smell me?"

"I can't, but I can 'ear ya whistle." Malcolm smirked.

"It's good to have you back, Malcolm," said Thomas.

"I can't believe you'd be so irresponsible as to even attempt to undertake such a task without me. The sheer audacity."

"It's nice to see you too, Anson—and yes, I feel better. Fank you for asking, my bruvver." He looked at Anson. "I 'ad to try to get the bleedin' stone. Tommy needs it, don't ya, Tommy?"

"Yes, but—"

"But nothing. I found duh stone. I just got a bit sidetracked, dat's all."

"We don't have time for this," said Thomas. "They will be back soon. I guess you've probably figured out that Fargus replaced the venom with Gloop."

"It wasn't even dat 'ard to do, to be honest wif ya. I mean dese fang blokes aren't too bright, are dey?" said Fargus. "I mean besides Malcolm an that."

"The Gloop should give you enough energy to start fighting off the venom," said the boy. "They want a fight in the Pit, then we'll give them one they'll never forget. Just so everyone is on the same page—be ready to move on my signal, and remember, until then, keep acting like you're still all venomed up."

Dorin and Griscom reappeared with two other vamp guards. Fargus quickly disappeared. They were systematically torn from their web cocoons. Malcolm collapsed when he was freed.

"I got you," said Anson as he helped his brother to stand.

"All right, let's get these on." The guard heaved glowing shackles at his prisoners. And as for you, big man, try this on for size." He swung an oversized shackle at Thomas.

"You guys think of everything," joked the boy. The guard closest to him twirled the staff in his hand and pushed on the back of the boy's knees, forcing him to kneel.

"You will not be laughing when we get to the Pit, blood traitor. That much I can promise you." He and another guard picked up Thomas and locked him together with the other three. Anson lifted Malcolm, still weary from the ordeal.

"Put him down," commanded Griscom.

"Not so fast, Grisc. If we let him carry him, it will save one of us the trouble," said Dorin.

"I like the way you think," said Griscom.

The four convicts were chained together as they marched to the Pit. Anson carried Malcolm in his arms. The added weight did not seem to hinder the werewolf.

They passed bleeding room after bleeding room as they walked the hallway towards their judgment. The thought of the fates of all of those humans was painful for Thomas now that he knew what was going on in these rooms. *This has to stop*, he thought. Thomas could feel his power returning. He just hoped his companions were feeling the same. He would soon find out.

They entered into a circular room with two sets of doors. The guards began to unlock their shackles.

"This is exciting, Dorin. Better than the usual human games that go on in the Pit."

"I know. That never ends well for the little blood bags, does it?" said Dorin. "I'm pretty sure we're still undefeated." The vamp guards laughed out loud as Griscom unlocked Malcolm's shackles.

"Looks like someone has decided to wake up. It just might be a bit too late, blood traitor," said Griscom as he removed the cuffs.

"You know what dey say—better late den never, right, Griscy?"

said Malcolm to the vamp guard. He turned and looked at his brother. "I fink I can walk on my own now. Fanks, Bruvver." Anson placed him down. Yareli wrung her wrists.

"Go through there," ordered Dorin. They were pushed forward through the double doors with the energy staffs. The other side of the door was too quiet. The doors rocked open with the force of their collective weight.

The crowd erupted into a deafening cheer. Thousands of vampires surrounded the Pit in stone booths that had been carved from the walls of the cave. The booths were stacked one on top of another and climbed far up above them. The floor of the Pit was covered in maroon stains. *Human games*, thought the boy.

Thomas remained calm, even in the midst of this spectacle. He was scared, but he needed to focus if his plan was going to work. "Looks like a sellout," said Thomas to his stunned comrades. "I guess they're expecting a good game." The doors behind them slowly shut, cutting off their last means of escape. Then as fast as the crowd began to cheer, they stopped. Mistress Amara Scornd had entered the Pit. She made her way to the platform that overlooked the arena. The doctor Thomas had met on his first day in the Hive walked out with the Mistress, stationed to her immediate left. She walked out to the precipice to engage her fans and began to speak.

"Welcome to the Pit!" said Amara Scornd. Her words loudly echoed through the arena. "Tonight we have some special guests." Cheers interrupted her. "I bring before you four vampires who have committed the heinous act of treason." The crowd remained silent. "The severity of which is evident by the deeds of their leader, Malcolm Warwick." The crowd hissed in unison. "I know, I know. This man refuses to do the very basic of vampiric deeds. He refuses the blood of the humans." Gasps of horror filled the spacious arena. "And I do not know if all of his followers do the same, but I am prepared to pass judgment solely based on the company they keep." The crowd roared at these words. "Malcolm has knowingly and purposefully killed one of his own kind." The crowd began to stir at this assertion.

"That was centuries ago," Malcolm admitted to his companions.

"It was a bleedin' accident. I 'ad told that wanker that we shouldn't be messin' about wif a loaded crossbow. 'ee told me ta bugger off, and then proceeded to keep playin' wif duh damn fing. 'ee shot 'imself, if ya must know. Not duh smartest vampire I've evva met. Poof . . . he disintegrated right in front of me. Amara walked in, and I took off. I can't believe dat dat's what all dis is about, a stupid four-'undred-year-old grudge. Women."

"Excuse me?" asked Yareli. "Women?"

"Man, you just keep making friends, don't you?" asked Thomas.

"It's a talent, I suppose." Malcolm made a cigarette appear from his hands and lit it. He took a long drag and exhaled. A look of sheer ecstasy appeared on his face. "I 'av missed dat. I must admit."

"That makes all who associate with this blood traitor"— Amara looked over at Thomas and winked—"accessories to murder, the most unthinkable of murders. He killed an immortal."

"Did she just wink at you?" asked Yareli.

"Wink?" Thomas tried to play off the gesture. "She must have . . . umm . . . stalactite dust in her eye or something."

"I can't believe you," said Yareli, shaking her head. The Mistress continued.

"Malcolm Warwick and his cohorts stand accused of the murder of Metrius Scornd, my beloved son."

"You didn't say it was her son," said Anson, looking at his brother.

"Details . . . look, it's not as doh it was 'er real son, is it? She gives dat name to just about everyone she turns. She was 'is Maker. I really don't see what all duh fuss is about."

"What say you, my friends?" asked Mistress Scornd. "What is your verdict? Are these blood traitors innocent?" There was an eerie silence that filled the Pit. "Or are they guilty?"

"Guilty, guilty, guilty," the vampiric mob chanted. "Guilty, guilty, guilty."

"She knows how to get the crowd going. I gotta give her that," said Thomas, trying to play off his feeling of terror.

"The people have spoken." Amara turned towards Malcolm and the rest of them. "For the crime of treason and the murder of an immortal, the court finds you . . . guilty as charged." The crowd roared once more. "You are hereby sentenced to death by tarancher." Amara Scornd pointed her hand at five massive doors across from Thomas and his companions.

The doors in front of them opened, revealing the giant beasts. Vampires with electric prods maneuvered the five rachnid from their stalls. These creatures looked wild, untamed, and desperately hungry. They were easily twice the size of the rachnid in the cell.

I guess they're taranchers, thought Thomas. The monsters began to scream at one another. "Okay, guys, get ready . . ." said the boy, but something sounded off. His normal voice was back. "That can't be possible. It's only been—"

"Sixty-five hours, twenty-two minutes, and thirty-five seconds," informed Anson. "I've been trying to keep track." Thomas turned to see his friend morphing back to his original shape. The two twins, now identical again, stood side by side, although Malcolm still was hunched.

"Almost seventy-two hours—that's great, Neficus. That's just freakin' great." The boy could barely turn round before one of the beasts charged him. Thomas sped out towards the tarancher and delivered a blow with the still-disguised, gauntleted hand. The tarancher soared backward into two of the others. The guts of the beast covered Thomas's disguised hand. The tarancher was dead. The remaining taranchers gathered themselves around the carcass of the one Thomas had killed and shrieked. It was not long before the remaining four split up into two groups. Two remained on the ground, while the other two took to the ceiling.

"Good job, Tommy. Now you've made dem angry," said Malcolm as he grinned, bearing his fangs. "I don't like killing fings unless dey're angry. It also 'elps dat I 'ate bleedin' spiders."

Thomas could feel himself begin to shrink. A quick downward glance confirmed the transformation. The flesh was swirling off of the Gauntlet. Dark green slime covered the top of the stone glove. The glowing emblem had returned to the palm. Thomas stood exposed before the vampire hive in his true form. He rolled his sleeves up and cuffed his pants. He grabbed his belt and ripped it across to the last hole so his pants would not drop. The last thing Thomas needed was to be falling all over the large clothes as he fought.

The remaining taranchers began their assault as the vampiric crowd stood silent. It would only be a matter of time before they would smell their blood. "I smell a werewolf!" somebody yelled.

"Me too!" said another vampire from the crowd.

"I smell humans!" cried yet another crowd member.

"I guess dere's no use in 'idin' anymore, Anson," said Malcolm as he looked his brother in the eyes.

"I suppose not," replied the werewolf as he barreled towards the first attacking rachnid. Anson leapt and transformed in midair. By the time he landed on the monster, his shirt had already been shredded. He howled as he arched his head upward. The large rachnid began to thrash in an attempt to knock off his predator, but it was useless. Anson's right paw came down across the tarancher's abdomen. Blood spurted out of the wound as the beast fell and skidded along the ground. Anson landed on his hindquarters and moved to the next tarancher. The crowd voiced their disapproval as the tarancher shot a web at the charging werewolf. The web snared Anson. He fell to the ground, and the beast began to draw Anson towards it as it advanced.

Malcolm landed in front of his brother, his fangs exposed. The vampire raised his hand and telekinetically halted the creature in mid-run. Anson broke from his cocoon, and the momentum forced him upright. He broke his gallop and slid in next to his brother. "Hold him," Anson commanded.

"What do you fink I'm doin, trying to take 'is bloody picture?" The werewolf pushed his two paws forward. Orange energy poured out of his paws and straight at the frozen beast, reducing the monster to ash in seconds. "It's like you're a bloody exterminator, Anson," said Malcolm.

"I will praise any man that will praise me," replied the werewolf.

"That's as close to a thank you as I'm gonna get, isn't it?"

"I would say so . . . considering all the trouble you have gotten us into."

Yareli stood next to Thomas, unsure of what to do. "I'm not much help without my quiver and bow," she said as she looked at the boy.

"Well, where is it?"

"I left it with Bartleby."

"Why'd you do that?"

"Well I didn't think vamps would take too kindly to someone carrying around a weapon that shoots sharpened wooden projectiles. That's why."

"I see your point." Thomas chuckled to himself. "Stay close to me, then. I promised Wiyaloo I'd keep you safe."

"I said I wouldn't be much help. I didn't say I was helpless. I don't need you to keep me saf—" A rachnid's web shot and lassoed the girl. The sticky white line retracted upward.

"Yareli!" the boy shouted. He brandished his gauntleted hand and sent a light blue pulse in the direction of the offending tarancher. The oversized bug moved out of the way at the last second, and the ceiling evaporated, exposing the night sky above. Large chunks of limestone and what used to be stalactites fell towards Thomas. The boy jumped to his right, but as he did, tripped over some of the rubble. As the dust cleared, the boy flipped over to see a new tarancher racing towards him. There was no time for Thomas to recover. He closed his eyes and prepared for the worst.

He was roused by a resounding squish sound accompanied by the feeling of warm liquid squirting onto his face. His eyes popped open to see Bartleby Draige standing atop a pile of smooshed tarancher.

"Nasty lit'l buggers, aren't dey?" said Bartleby as he raised his back left foot and made a foul face. Bartleby had dropped in through the hole Thomas had made in the ceiling.

"It's good to see you, Bart!" exclaimed the boy as he wiped the rachnid goo out of his eyes. "What took you so long?"

"I was finishing my nap. I do need my beauty sleep every now and again." He winked at the boy and took off back into the sky.

The vampires systematically began to enter the battle from the crowd. They began to surround Thomas, Malcolm, and Anson. Yareli was still dangling from what was left of the Pit's ceiling. They had taken care of three of the taranchers, but this was something entirely different. Beside the fact that their new foes were immortal, they were severely outnumbered.

Thomas moved quickly. He jumped in front of the first wave of attackers and pushed the Gauntlet forward. The mob of vamps was engulfed by the blue energy. Limbs were torn away, and vamps were cut into pieces. The force dissipated, and the vamps, though injured and maimed, still advanced. Some grew back legs and arms, while others literally pulled themselves back together. Their bodies were mending and splicing as they continued towards the group. "What the hell do I do now? They're not playing fair."

"We don't have the proper weaponry," said Anson as he fired a purple sphere into the charging vamps. The explosion left a hole in the Pit's floor. Vampire bodies were strewn everywhere, but again they regenerated themselves and progressed forward.

"I think I liked the taranchers better. At least they had the decency to stay squished," said Thomas as he looked over at Malcolm.

"And it's not as doh dere's a pile of wooden stakes just lying about, now is dere?" asked Malcolm. "We can only 'old dem off for so long. Dere's at least 10,000 bleedin' vampires in dis bloody 'ive—not includin' yours truly, of course."

"Then this is where we'll stand," said the boy as they faced outward, back to back. The vampires would move in for the kill sooner or later. It was only a matter of time, even with Bartleby firing down into the vampire crowd—but one thing was certain: Thomas and his companions would not make it easy for the vampires. Thomas heard a familiar hum and looked up. The sound of turbines firing echoed above as the artif made his entrance.

"I will facilitate the extension of your life processes, Thomas Scargen," said LINC as he rushed into the cavern through the newly made skylight. He hovered above the companions as the tops of his robotic forearms opened up and what looked like Gatling guns sprung out. LINC stopped above them and began to rotate at the hip. As he started to fire, instead of bullets shooting from the barrels, wooden darts were projected at the advancing vampires. Leaving his weapons at incredible speeds, the wooden darts methodically found their targets. Vampires were exploding into dust all around them.

LINC's a vampire-killing machine, thought the boy. "I guess those are the upgrades Fargus was talking about."

"Remind me not to piss Tin Man off anytime soon," quipped Malcolm.

"I'm just hoping he's not hiding silver shards in there somewhere," said Anson with a smile.

"Well, now that we got most of these bloodsuckers occupied . . ." Thomas craned his neck to where Amara Scornd's throne was. "Fargus, do it now!" he screamed. The gremlin appeared on the throne behind Amara Scornd. He reached down and snatched the amulet containing the yellow stone off her neck.

"Fanks, luv," said Fargus as he sped off towards Thomas. Before Mistress Scornd could comprehend what had happened, the gremlin disappeared. Her scream filled the cavern. Energy began to pour from her.

"Bartleby, let's get out of here," said Thomas. "She looks pissed." The beast landed as he sprayed the surrounding vampires with fire. The vamps scattered like startled rats. Thomas jumped onto the dragon. "Go!"

"Ya don't 'av to tell me twice."

"Come on, Yareli," said Thomas. He looked up to see the tarancher that had webbed her up was moving in to strike her down. "Stop playing around."

"*Ta'tai,*" said Yareli as the webs exploded outwards. She began to fall. The tarancher tried to catch her with a new web, but the gust had knocked it backward. Thomas raised his arm.

"Haaaaaaa!" he yelled, and an energy beam shot from the top of the glove to the tarancher's body. The power stream incinerated the rachnid, leaving a stain on the ceiling.

Yareli landed on her feet, forming a crater on impact. Dark green liquid rained down on her as she ran towards the dragon. "Like I said, I'm not a lot of help without my quiver and bow," said Yareli as she wiped the venom off of her face.

"Get on," said the boy.

"Look," said Yareli. The boy looked skyward, and a stream of sunlight poured into the dark cavern. Hundreds of vampires exploded into ash in the solar bath as the remaining undead scurried to avoid the solitary shaft of light.

"Look what I found." Fargus appeared on the dragon's head, twirling the necklace around his finger then back the other way.

" 'old on to somefing," said Bartleby as began to take off straight up. Malcolm soon followed, holding his brother under his furry arms. LINC was the last to go. He continued annihilating vampire after vampire as he flew upward.

Red flashed in front of the dragon, forcing him to halt the escape. Amara Scornd now blocked the only path to the exit, staying just inside the protection of the darkness that remained. She flapped her wings to stay in place, as energy circled both of her hands. Her power was impressive even without the stone. "Give me back my amulet, or I will destroy you all," said Scornd. Bartleby tried to alter course, but Scornd mirrored his movements. The power that emanated from her was intense. She moved her hands back, preparing to incinerate the dragon and his crew. "Very well. I will just *take* it back." There was no time for Thomas to react. She began to move her hands forward. The boy braced for the impact.

"I'm the one you want, you daft vamp," said Malcolm. Anson was still in his arms. Scornd's eyes darted to Malcolm.

"Blood traitor!" screamed the Mistress as she moved upward towards Malcolm.

"And just so you know, your stupid son, as you call 'im, shot 'is bloody self wif duh crossbow. Not too bright, was 'ee?" said Malcolm. She shot an energy attack at him. He rolled to the right, dodging the blast. "I blame parenting." Anson shot his hands forward as the two brothers barreled in the direction of the Mistress. Orange energy poured from his palms at Scornd as she advanced, but it was blocked by the Mistress's shield defense. She altered course and shot into Malcolm, hurling him backward. The blow forced Malcolm to lose his grip on Anson. The werewolf plunged back down into the swarming vampires.

"We have to help," said Thomas.

"We've got our own problems," said Yareli as the boy turned to see what she was talking about. Two winged vamps hovered in front of them. Thomas recognized Dorin and Griscom immediately.

"LINC!" shouted the boy. "Help Anson."

"Protect the werewolf. Ensure Anson Warwick's safety." The artif rocketed back down into the sea of vamps, unloading his darts on the advancing horde. Anson moved with precise grace, tearing into vampire after vampire.

"Look out!" cried Yareli as one of the guards fired a blast toward them from his energy staff. The boy ducked as the beam of energy just missed his head.

"That was close," said Thomas as Bartleby turned in the direction of the two guards. The dragon advanced on the undead creatures. Fire streamed from Bartleby's mouth. The two guards split off in two directions just out of the way of the fiery assault. Bartleby made a hard left turn and adjusted his route. He was now behind Griscom.

Thomas sat up on the dragon and focused his power. He moved the Gauntlet forward. "Haaaaaaaa!" A light blue orb flew in the direction of Griscom, hitting him in the wing as he retreated. The injured guard plummeted towards the ground.

A flash of motion streaked above them. Thomas looked skyward to see that Dorin had moved in fast and now hovered above the dragon, matching Bartleby's course. "I've got you now, you filthy human," said Dorin as he moved to seize the boy. He lunged at Thomas and grabbed at his arm. "This is where you die, boy."

The stake ripped through Dorin's back and straight out of his chest. Black blood squirted from the fresh wound. A look of calm settled on the vampire's face just before he exploded into ash. Bartleby pulled up and turned.

The female bartender from the Tapped Vein hovered in front of them with a large wooden stake in her hand. The weapon was covered in Dorin's black blood. "Shitty tipper," said the vamp as she winked at the boy and flew away.

"Is it me, or did dat seem a bit off?" asked Fargus. "Bloody amazing, but a bit off."

"What was that all about?" asked Thomas.

"There's no time for speculation," said Yareli. "We have to help Malcolm."

"I'm on it," said the dragon as he shot off towards the dueling vampires.

Thomas could see Malcolm Warwick and Amara Scornd moving at incredible speeds. Malcolm kicked the Mistress in her chin, and she flipped backward. He moved in quickly to follow up on the blow, but she had already countered. Amara landed a devastating punch, and Malcolm reeled backward. Malcolm steadied himself and regained his composure, but it was too late. Amara was powering up for another attack.

"You will die, Warwick," said Scornd as energy coursed around her body. Her pupils were on fire. She was forming a sizable energy sphere above her head. They would not get there in time. The Mistress moved her hands forward. Malcolm was doomed.

A blur sped past them and hit Scornd as she released the sphere. She was sent flying sideways. The blast, intended for Malcolm, shot upward into the grotto's ceiling. Vilkari now hovered where the Mistress had just been. Bartleby flew up alongside Malcolm. "Get out of 'ere now!" insisted the obese vampire as he hovered next to the group. Bigger pieces of earth and limestone began to crumble down from above. What was left of the roof began to collapse.

"But what about you?" asked Malcolm. The ceiling now resembled a half-completed puzzle from underneath.

"I'm gonna do what I should've done a long time ago." Vilkari pulled a stake from his jacket and held it in his hand. "You are my progeny, and one of my best mates. Dat means I am responsible for you." He lifted the stake. "It probably won't kill duh old bitch, but it will sure slow 'er down." The two smiled and locked arms. "Now get going. You don't 'av much time before dis 'ole place collapses." Vilkari released Malcolm.

"Fank you, Vilkari."

"No, Malcolm. It is I 'oo should fank you. You made me see what I 'ad become." The fat vampire flew off in the direction of Amara Scornd.

"Goodbye, old friend," muttered Malcolm. "Where's my bruvver?"

"I have secured your sibling, vampire," said LINC as he floated next to Malcolm. The werewolf dangled from the artif's hands.

"What took ya so bloody long, Tin Man?"

"I was eradicating the existence of 283 of your species while facilitating the protection of Anson Warwick."

"I got twenty-four of them," said Anson as he looked at his brother and smiled.

"You'll 'av to try a bit harder next time, won't ya?" said Malcolm. "I must admit, I was worried dere for a second—but only a second. It's good to see you, Bruvver."

"My recommendation is that we suspend this dialogue pending our escape into the protection of the sun's radiation," said LINC.

"The artif does make a fine point," said Anson.

"Sounds like a bloody good plan to me," said Bartleby as he flew towards the expanding opening in the ceiling. Thomas held on as the scaled beast soared upward out of the darkness. Malcolm and LINC followed the dragon through the new hole in the earth.

An explosion from within the cavern ended any attempts of following them. The sun's rays would be enough to dissuade any vampire retaliation, at least in the immediate future. The Hive had now vanished into a pile of rubble. The same cold energy that surrounded Amara seconds before now encircled the rubble. The glow began to fade and then slowly dissipated.

The dragon continued to gain speed as he glided through the morning air. It was the first afternoon sunrise Thomas had ever seen, and it could not have been more beautiful. The townspeople were stirring. They flowed out onto the streets and stared up at the sun, awestruck. The white trees surrounding the village reached for the heavens.

Wiyaloo appeared next to the dragon. "It is good to see you again, Thomas Scargen, and thank you once more," said the spirit ghost.

"It's good to be back." The boy smiled.

Bartleby landed at the site where they arrived. The boy was relieved to see daylight once more. *But not as relieved as the towns-people*, he thought. He grabbed some water from Bartleby's storage unit and splashed it on his face. He then grabbed a bottle of Gloop and chugged it. "This stuff is addictive." He laughed as he threw Yareli a water container. "And by the way, Yar, green is definitely not your color."

"Thanks," she replied sarcastically as she washed off her face and hair. Malcolm grabbed a bottle of Warwick Red Ale his brother had brought with him.

"Fank 'eavens. I fought I was gonna 'av to drain poor Tommy over 'ere," said Malcolm as he raised the beverage to his lips. "And by the way, Tommy, nice glove, mate." The vampire slightly lifted his head in a nod.

"This old thing?" joked the boy. He reached into the storage container and grabbed the three wristcoms. "Here ya go." He tossed them to their rightful owners. LINC landed with a thunderous thump next to the boy. "That was totally narsh, LINC."

"Fargus Hexelby deserves accolades for the upgrades to my weapons systems. He is skilled in the field of robotic anatomy and program implementation. He is not as versed as my creator is in these particular areas of expertise, but no one on this planet is." Thomas thought of his father and his unknown fate.

"The stone!" exclaimed Thomas. The thought of helping his father had reminded him of the very thing they had sought after in the first place.

"You mean dis beautiful fing?" Fargus was roosted on Bartleby's head. He was still twirling the amulet as he whistled. Fargus's eyes were fixed on the necklace. It looked like he was hypnotizing himself. "Duh way I see it, it must 'av been dis trinket 'ere dat kept dose nice folks in duh dark for so long. I bet dose fellows are well 'appy to see a bit of sun, an that."

The boy snapped on his own wristcom. "It all makes sense now. She said she had used dark magic of some sort, and I bet the amulet

enhanced her powers at least tenfold. I can feel its energy from here."
His eyes locked onto the prize. *I wonder what it will do to me. Ziza
said the rocks can be unpredictable, and how in the hell does it get into
the Gauntlet?* "Do you mind if I take a closer look at it, Fargus?"

"Now why would I mind? It's meant to be yours anyway, isn't
it? 'ere, catch," said Fargus as he tossed the amulet to Thomas. The
boy lifted the Gauntlet to catch the necklace. The instant the yellow
stone touched the boy's rock palm he vanished.

35

blossoming

Thomas materialized and almost fell over. The sudden teleportation was jarring, and the change in time of day was disorienting. He was standing at the base of a pagoda temple as the sun dissolved into the horizon. Cherry blossom trees surrounded Thomas. Each tree had a plaque with engraved Japanese characters. He knew they were Japanese because his father's colleague had once shown him similar markings from a dig he and his father had done in Nara. The pink blossoms had sprouted, and the abandoned petals littered the path. The blossoms danced in sporadic gusts that swayed the paper lanterns adorning the sides of the pathway. Thomas felt at peace. It was the first time since leaving Sirati that he had a chance to catch his breath. He had no idea where he was, but he did not care. He looked down at the Gauntlet. The yellow jewel rested in his palm, still set in the necklace. *It had to be the stone touching the Gauntlet that teleported me here,* he thought, *and from what I've seen, here must be Japan.* "Computer, where am I?" the boy asked his wristcom.

"Cannot per-r-r-r-form this function cur-r-r-r-entlly," stuttered the wristcom. The holographic display shook as if something was interfering with the signal.

"So much for calling for help," said Thomas to himself as he surveyed his surroundings. *By the looks of the place, I'd say no one has visited here for some time.* The path before him led directly to a steep set of stone stairs that led to the entrance to the pagoda. The temple, while striking, looked like it had seen grander days. Thomas walked towards the stairs. When he reached the base of the staircase, he paused for a moment. A monolith leaned crookedly on the side of the pathway. Foreign markings covered the rock slab. The symbols were not Japanese, but they did look similar to the markings on the yellow stone. Then Thomas saw it. The same symbol that was on the palm of the Gauntlet was at the top of the monolith. "I must be in the right place," said Thomas as he looked around. "The right place for what is the question." The temple was eerily quiet. "Something tells me I'm not alone." The boy looked up the stairs. *I guess I climb.* He tucked the jewel into his oversized coat pocket and began to ascend the stone staircase, trying carefully not to trip over his elongated costume.

When he reached the top of the stairs, he looked down on the temple's grounds. The temple was atop a massive hill. Cherry trees guarded the perimeter. He turned around and made his way to a large, elaborately carved door. He knocked twice on the door. No answer. The only sound he could hear was the echoing of his knocks. "I guess I should just let myself in." He slid open the door and entered.

He stood at one end of a long hallway. Marble posts held up the high ceilings. The interior was breathtaking. The archaic structure was covered in battle scenes. Thomas stared at the artwork. There was painting after painting of great warriors. They were samurai— Thomas was certain. *You don't grow up in an archeologically friendly household and not know what samurai look like.* As he progressed down the path, the paintings changed. They began to depict warriors from different eras. The boy's attention was directed to a painting of an adolescent boy squaring off against a demon. *Arkmalis.* The boy recognized him from the hologram. His eyes were quickly drawn to another painting farther down the hall.

It was a rendering of a female from behind. She was perched atop a large baobab, similar to the ones in Sirati. The Gauntlet was attached to her right arm. *That must be Mary.* The stone glove in the picture glowed an odd hue of purple. Thomas looked down at his rock hand and turned it over. "You've never done that for me." He looked around to see hundreds of paintings of Gauntlet wearers. His mouth hung open. "Narsh." But it was not until his eyes rested on the canvas farthest down the corridor that Thomas began to comprehend the true wonder of the Temple.

This particular work of art was of Thomas facing down several advancing vampires in the Pit. He was taken aback. He had never seen himself painted before. This, coupled with the fact that the painting was of an event that had only just transpired, confused the boy. "What is this place?" asked Thomas. He now stood in front of the open paper door. He cautiously moved towards the entrance, but somehow the boy knew there was nothing to fear. His footsteps echoed down the empty hall. He could smell smoke as he walked through the archway. At the far end of the room, Thomas saw a boy who could not have been older than ten years of age. He floated above a pillow meditating—his eyes closed. The young Japanese boy wore a dark gray robe with blossom-colored accents. His head was shaven, and his hands were hidden in his sleeves. Melted mounds of wax surrounded him. The wicks of the candles drowned inside the hot liquid wax. Thomas pondered if he should interrupt the meditation, but before he could decide, the young boy spoke.

"Hello, Thomas Scargen. I have been waiting for your arrival."

"Really?" Thomas did not know what to say. "You knew I was coming?"

"Precisely. The appearance of the next Gauntlet Bearer has been foretold for decades."

Thomas looked down at the gauntleted hand. "Sorry I kept you waiting. I didn't know I had an appointment." He smiled.

"I knew you'd come, eventually. My name is Itsuki Katsuo, and welcome to my home. This is the Temple of Yokan." The young boy still levitated with his eyes shut.

"How did you know I was coming?"

"I am the only person that can help you. Logic dictated that ultimately you had no choice but to find me."

"Help me with what?"

Itsuki's eyelids raised, and his stare met Thomas's. "Attach the stone in your pocket to the Gauntlet on your arm."

"It seems that the Gauntlet knew exactly where you would be. Once I came into contact with the yellow rock, I—"

"So you have found the Taitokura, very exciting . . . very, very exciting. The stone will take some time to connect."

"I was wondering how that was gonna do down, but aren't you a little . . . I don't know . . . don't take this the wrong way, a little young?"

"Do not be fooled by my age. I have been preparing for this my entire life. It is my family's legacy since the early wielders of the Gauntlet. We have been Augmentors for centuries."

"Where is your father? Maybe he should help. I would think he would have more experience at—"

"My father is dead." Itsuki's legs extended as he began to walk towards Thomas. "I wish more than anything that he could be here for this moment, but he died shortly after my birth." The young Augmentor took Thomas's arm and began to examine the Gauntlet. "My father, my father's father, his father's father, his father's father's father, along with the rest of my ancestors are buried here at this shrine. Their collected experience is now my own. Such is the power of the Temple."

"I didn't see a cemetery."

"There is not one. They are buried under the *sakura*."

"The what?"

"That is what we call the cherry blossom trees."

"That's what those Japanese characters were?"

"Precisely. My family has always buried its own with the seed of a *sakura* in their mouths. It is said that when the tree grows, so grows the spirit. In this way, their spirits are eternal." Thomas stared in confusion. "Now we have no time to lose, Thomas. Where is the Taitokura?" Itsuki waved his arm, and an ornate box floated into his hand.

Thomas reached into his coat pocket and pulled out the golden jewel. "Here."

Itsuki Katsuo was awestruck. "I have never seen one of these with my own eyes. We have much to do, but first things first." He lifted his empty hand and Thomas's loose clothing instantly conformed to his body. "Follow me."

"Thanks, Itsuki." As he followed the Augmentor, Thomas looked himself up and down, amazed by the fit. "But my friends are—"

"Your friends are fine, Thomas." The Augmentor walked to a large reclining chair. There were no lights in the Temple, though plenty of candlelight danced around the room. "Please, have a seat."

"Okay," said Thomas as he examined what looked like a dentist's chair before plopping himself into it. "But you better not have a drill in that box."

"Not quite . . ." The box opened up to expose several different compartments. Each compartment contained a unique tool. All were foreign to Thomas. Itsuki pried off what was left of Amara's necklace without touching the amulet. The first instrument flew out of the toolbox and levitated in front of the Augmentor. He placed the stone into it. "The hardest part is getting the stone and me prepared." His eyes focused on the now-untarnished Taitokura. It began to glow and rotate in the tool's central clamp.

"Do I really need to be here for this part?" Thomas began to think about his friends and where they were. "My friends don't know where I am, and—"

"I told you your friends are fine. They will be here shortly. You need to rest, Thomas."

"For what?" Itsuki calmly pointed back into the hall he had arrived from. Thomas jumped out of the chair and walked back into the hallway. He turned to the right and reexamined the wall. A new painting was forming. It was going to be one of the larger pieces. The canvas was a depiction of Thomas standing on top of the Temple stairs as he looked down on a battlefield. He slowly walked back into the room where the Augmentor was preparing the jewel and sat again in the chair. "I'm just gonna go ahead and get some rest, like you suggested." Thomas stretched his arms out and yawned. "Wake me when my friends arrive." His head fell back as he sighed. His eyes drifted close. He was asleep instantly.

36

surveillance

The sun had already set, a first in Sangeros for some fifteen years. Marcus peered downward through the visor in his helmet, engaging the night vision. The Captain kept his distance atop a nearby cliff. He had to remain far enough back so they could not detect him or his aringi. Teros awkwardly plodded around behind the crouched Captain. The chase was finally over. They had been tracking the group since the Riders' arrival in Sangeros, and they had finally caught up to them. Marcus's persistence had paid off, but something was amiss. *The dragon is here, the twins, the girl, her spirit. The artif is even here, but where is the boy?* The Scargen boy had somehow gotten away.

Evangeline emerged from the clouds and landed with the slightest noise next to the Captain. The remaining Riders followed suit. Marcus turned to the Second. "We stick with them. My instincts tell me that they will lead us back to Scargen." He turned to the other Riders. "Taunt, see what you can gather with the recon orb."

"Right away, Captain." The Rider lifted his wristcom and pushed a series of buttons. A holo-interface appeared in front of Taunt as a small orb shot out of his device. The miniature surveillance orb flew through the evening sky, barreling towards the motley band. It came to a halt above the dragon's head and began relaying video and audio back to the Riders, who were watching from a safe distance. The Native American girl began to speak.

"We've searched everywhere, Fargus, is all I'm saying!" shouted Yareli Chula at the gremlin.

"Well all I did was frow duh frickin' necklace to 'im. 'ow was I suppose ta know dat would 'appen? I don't know 'ow these sorts uv fings work, do I?" Fargus looked away and began to whistle nervously.

"Small to greater matters must give way," Anson said as he walked between the bickering friends. "It matters not who is at fault. Finding where he is is all that matters now."

"Agreed," said the spirit.

They don't know where he is, thought Marcus. A warning signal rang from the artif as the Captain once again focused on the holodisplay.

The artif whirled and buzzed. A beam shot out of his arm piece and opened up to reveal a holographic display. The artif was intently staring at what appeared to be a map, and on the map was a blinking orange dot. "I have approximated Thomas Scargen's location. The signal is intermittent and indistinct, therefore, an exact position is not possible at this time, but I can triangulate his location within viable search parameters."

" 'ow exactly did you pull dat one off?" asked Malcolm Warwick.

"Dr. Carl Scargen equipped my programming with the capacity to track Thomas Scargen via a minute tracking device inserted into the base of his wristcom."

"Why didn't you mention this before?" asked Yareli.

"No one had asked," said LINC.

"Well 'ee is good for somethin' ain't 'ee?" Malcolm said with a smile. "I guess between you 'elpin back at duh 'ive and figurin' dis out, I might owe you an apology, but don't 'old your bref waitin', Tin Man."

"I assure you I do not require oxygen or any of the other elements contained in the atmosphere for survival, nor do I possess lungs. Therefore, holding my bref, as you so quaintly described, would be highly improbable, mostly due to the fact that I do not participate in respiration or any other pulmonary activities." The artif paused, and his head turned towards Malcolm. His optics blinked and then focused. "But I do suppose I was incorrect in my first evaluation of your usefulness to the group dynamic as well, Malcolm Warwick."

"I'm glad you two have kissed and made up, but where is Thomas, LINC?" asked Yareli in a frustrated tone.

"According to my calculations, he is in Japan," whistled LINC. The collective heads of the companions spun around after this revelation. "Shikoku, to be exact. From the limited information currently available, I have ascertained his present location somewhere near a secluded mountainous terrain. The signal seems to be weakening. From this data I can extrapolate that something near his current location is causing interference."

"How did he get there?" Yareli wondered out loud.

"I would venture a guess that the Gauntlet has something to do with it," interjected Anson.

"Well we best get goin'. Who knows 'ow long it will take dose vamps to catch up, and Thomas could very well be in trouble," snorted Bartleby. "Fargus, download duh destination into my navcom."

"Zoom in on those coordinates, Taunt," ordered Marcus. The virtual screen in front of Taunt zoomed to see the navigation coordinates. His computer highlighted the relevant information. "The intel has been secured, Captain, but it seems vague at best. According to the readout, he is in Shikoku, Japan, but that is all the specifics the artif was displaying."

"Well done, Taunt." Marcus turned and walked away from the cliff. "We need to report this development to the General."

"But aren't we going to follow them, Captain?" asked Evangeline.

Marcus turned back. "Patience, Second. There is no reason to alert them to our presence as of yet." He leaned over and began typing on his wristcom. A holographic picture of Corbin appeared.

"Hello, Captain Slade. I imagine you have news for the General."

"Yes, Corbin. We have found the boy. We are going to follow him from afar and await further orders from General Arkmalis."

"I will alert my master. Good hunting, Captain." The hologram disappeared.

Marcus's attention turned towards Taunt's virtual monitor. The image now depicted the dragon and the others taking off through a freshly opened teleportal. "Send the recon orb through with them. Make it follow the artif they call LINC. He seems to be programmed to protect the boy, and make sure we get a trace on that teleportal."

"Already on it, Captain," shouted Taunt. He deftly maneuvered the tiny surveillance camera using his wristcom. The sphere zipped through the tear in the sky undetected, following the automaton. A second orb shot from his wristcom and traveled to where the teleportal was closing. The second orb scanned the teleportal and its destination.

"We will wait here until Taunt gives the signal," commanded Marcus. He glanced over at Evangeline and caught her eyes and immediately looked away. "This could be our most dangerous mission to date, and I need everyone here at their absolute best." *I'd worry if I thought for one second you'd be in any trouble, but I learned a long time ago you can more than handle yourself.*

"They have moved on from the teleportal's destination," said Taunt. "We're clear."

"Riders, mount up." With that command, the aringi shot down from the sky and landed on top of their respective Riders. Marcus was the last to take flight. "Open the teleportal, Taunt," commanded the Captain. A beam shot from the aringi's headpiece and ripped the teleportal back open. The Riders crossed the open void. Marcus watched as Evangeline passed through the hole. Certain uneasiness filled the Captain. *I wish circumstances were different. We could have been happy together, my love.* He passed through the opening. The sky repaired itself behind him, and all was still.

37

a ghost in the woods

Thomas woke to Itsuki tinkering with a new instrument that he had now placed the gem into. "Your friends have arrived." The Augmentor did not waste time looking at Thomas. "I felt the portal opening. They are somewhere southwest of here. It is probably best that you find them as quickly as possible, considering what is to come."

"I agree," said Thomas.

"And be watchful. I sensed they might not be alone. That could be trouble."

"I think I want to keep you around. You are full of all sorts of safety tips." Thomas smiled, but Itsuki could not be bothered to manage more than a smirk. He remained focused on the task at hand. "Okay."

Thomas left through the sliding rice paper door and sprinted down the Hall of Yokan. He stopped when he got outside the Temple entrance. Fog had settled on the Temple grounds. Thomas looked down at his wristcom. "Computer, what direction is southwest?" After some interference, the computer directed him. He moved with unnatural speed through the *sakura* as the paper lanterns circled in the wind, pushing the grounded clouds aside. He ran down several series of stairs to the bottom of the Temple and passed through a stone gate. It was now considerably darker than when he had entered the Temple.

He barreled through the white-blossomed woods in the direction of his comrades. "Computer, activate LINC's beacon and begin tracking." He had no idea where he was, but that did not stop him.

Thomas came to an abrupt halt when he saw the shrine. He was instantly gripped with a feeling of regret and guilt. Something about the shrine was speaking to him, but he did not know who or what it was.

Various flowers and plants were strewn throughout the gardens that surrounded a statue of a female. The beauty of the shrine was only tarnished by the feeling of complete dread that resonated in Thomas. The feminine sculpture was situated in front of a large open pagoda. Inside, there were several scrolls with Japanese characters on them. "Computer, translate," Thomas pointed the wristcom's display at the parchment. A scanning light ran up the scroll.

The translation floated above his wristcom. "Would you like me to read the translation aloud?" asked the wristcom.

"Sure, let's hear it."

"My dearest love, my heart remains forever yours—in this lifetime and the next. If there is a way, I will find you in the afterworld. There we shall be together for eternity. My heart plays games with my eyes. I see you in my dreams, in the Temple, and in the forests. I know my vision betrays me, and that death is the only manner for us to be entwined once more. Daiki Katsuo." The final few symbols looked familiar to Thomas.

"How about this one?" The computer completed a similar scan.

"My heart grows lonely without you, and I fear I may join you soon. I am not afraid to die, but I am afraid for our son's survival. He is learning at an exponentially fast rate, and he is going to be the greatest of all the Augmentors. I only worry that he will not be able to survive without someone to look after him. I yearn for your companionship. I swear sometimes in the evenings, I can hear your delicate voice singing to the child. The notion is driving me slowly mad with loneliness. Daiki Katsuo." Thomas instantly recognized the name after seeing it the second time. The characters on one of the trees matched these final characters on the scroll. Thomas turned his attention to the third and final scroll. The light scanned up and down the writing.

"Time will not divide us much longer, my love. I see you in everything now. The boy is showing an understanding of our ancient tools that I never had, nor my father or his before him. Itsuki has embraced the finality of my situation, and he meditates more and more for me. I hope he will be able to take care of himself. He is still so young, but so wise. I am proud to call him my son. My time in this realm is short. I will soon be in your arms once more. Daiki Katsuo." Thomas stood there, wondering.

"He was an idiot sometimes." The female voice echoed from behind Thomas. The boy jumped with surprise. He swirled around to see what best could be described as a ghost—the likeness of which resembled the statue of the young lady. "I was there the whole time. He was not seeing things." She was glowing white. She wore a plain, unlined, white kimono. "I did not mean to startle you. Where are my manners? I have been dead for some years now, and I forget the simplest of etiquette. My name is Moriko Katsuo. You must be a friend of my son." She moved closer to Thomas. The spectral figure had no legs or feet dangling from under her clothing as she floated over to the boy. "I still sing to Itsuki every night. I will never forgive myself for leaving him." Her face saddened as she spoke, and Thomas's feeling of unease increased.

"I am Thomas Scargen." She bowed to him, and he reciprocated.

"My son has spoken your name recently."

"That's odd, because tonight is the first time I have met him."

"Details . . ." Two blue flames appeared between Moriko and Thomas, hovering in the air. "I was wondering where you two had gone." The spectral flares zipped at Thomas and danced around him. They quickly focused their attention on the Gauntlet as Thomas opened his rock hand and raised it. He stared at the flames as they explored the exterior of the rock glove. The boy was hypnotized by their movements and their ghostly song. He did not know whether to be frightened or to laugh. "Do not worry, Thomas. They are harmless . . . well, mostly. But you need not worry: they like you."

"I think they like the Gauntlet more."

"The Gauntlet is you, Thomas." She placed her hands into the opposite sleeves and began to float away. "I must admit: they are good judges of character."

"Where are you going?" asked the boy as he unsuccessfully tried to touch one of the flames.

"You want to find your friends, right?"

"That's why I'm here."

"Well, follow me, but be warned. Do not stray far from me. I am by no means the only spirit that walks these woods, and between you and the *sakura*, I am one of the nicer ones." The apparition winked at Thomas as she turned and proceeded down the rock path that exited the garden shrine.

"You'd be surprised how well I can handle myself." The apparition continued without response to Thomas. He picked up his pace to a jog. "Wait up." The two blue wisps followed in his wake.

They walked on quietly for some time, not saying anything to one another. The sounds of various nocturnal creatures and the song of the wisps filled the void. Thomas began to grow impatient. "According to my beacon, we have already moved past their position."

"It would be wise not to rely on such trinkets in this forest. They can be deceiving. Your friends will be meeting us shortly."

"All right, I'll trust you." Thomas started to look around. "But I can't be following you around all night."

"That will not be necessary, young man." Moriko's glowing finger pointed to a path that diverged from their current passageway. The two blue flames highlighted the way. "Your friends are right down there in a small clearing."

"Thank—" The boy turned as the woman vanished into a white

mist. The two wisps followed suit. "It was nice meeting you!" yelled Thomas to the empty woods.

Thomas collected himself and then ran down the new path. The smell of a campfire filled his nostrils. "Bartleby."

The dragon was sitting down, smoking a fresh pipe of dragon-weed. " 'ee can't be dat far away, can 'ee? I mean right, LINC. What are your bleedin' sensors saying?"

"My sensors are not fully functional at this time." The artif tilted his head like a confused puppy.

"Yeah, for some reason, electronics don't work well around here." Thomas stood there smiling as the realization came to his companions at their own speeds. Yareli ran to him and embraced the boy tightly. She slowly let go and backed off awkwardly.

"I was just . . . worried," said Yareli as she looked down and then back up.

"It is good to see you, Thomas Scargen," said Wiyaloo. The fox sniffed the boy. "You smell like a spirit."

"Yeah, it's a long story," said Thomas nonchalantly.

"That's probably why I did not smell you coming. I thought it might be the dragon's pungent aroma." Anson walked towards the boy and hugged him. What was left of his shirt hung from him like cobwebs. His pants had also seen better days. "Hello, Thomas."

"I would 'av smelled you myself, Tommy, if I was a 'undred per-cent." Malcolm half saluted as he lit a new cigarette. "Filfy 'abbit I know."

Fargus appeared on LINC's shoulder. "We should grab dat stone and get the 'ell out of 'ere before there's more trouble. Ja know what I mean? Who knows what kind of nonsense could be knockin' about in dese woods. Better to be safe than sorry an that."

"Can't do that, Fargus. I've met my Augmentor." Thomas looked back at the collective blank stares. "I'll try to explain on the way." Bartleby extinguished his pipe and lowered his back so Thomas could mount him. He pulled Yareli up onto the dragon as Fargus rested on Bartleby's head. Malcolm drew his wings and grabbed Anson under his armpits. LINC's turbines fired, and Wiyaloo also took flight.

"Hey, Bart, we will be able to see the Temple as soon as we get above the trees."

The dragon broke through the tree canopy. "Now, correct me if I'm wrong, but I am goin' to assume dat's duh Temple you were referring to," said Bartleby.

"That's the one."

"It's beautiful," said Yareli.

"Everyone, 'old on to somefing," said Bartleby. The dragon hung in the air for a second then dashed towards the Temple of Yokan.

38

revelations and reinforcements

The smoke from the dragon's pipe had not cleared yet as General Slade and the others uncloaked. They had been following the group since they had crossed the teleportal. "Augmentor? What does he need one of those for?" asked Marcus as he spun to look at his Riders.

"It might have something to do with the amulet he stole from Amara Scornd." The Second's mind began to churn. Her face changed as if she had realized something. "The stone in the necklace must be one of the Gauntlet's," said Evangeline as she figured it out in her head. "Scornd had no idea what she had."

"That's probably for the best. That kind of power in a vampire's hand is dangerous, to say the least," said Marcus.

"You are saying you trust Arkmalis with such a stone?" Evangeline's question was direct and caught Marcus a bit off guard.

"I am a soldier. I do not have the luxury of asking such questions or questioning orders." He turned away from the other Riders. "Besides, he wants the boy—not the stone."

"Yeah but soon as he catches wind of what that stone is capable of, you can bet that will change. He will probably try to augment that Scythe of his. That would be a sight to see. That thing already scares the piss out of me," added Taunt as he shivered jokingly and hooted in the direction of Jurdik. Farod did not laugh.

"Enough," said Marcus. The tone of his voice ended the giggling. The Captain pivoted and looked Jurdik in the eyes. "This is no laughing matter, and the weapon you speak of is not the General's."

"What do you mean?" inquired the Second. "He has wielded it as long as I've been around." Marcus quieted his tone to respond to Evangeline.

"He inherited the weapon, so to speak."

"From whom?" asked the Second, outwardly surprised by this fact.

"A far more powerful Necromancer than Grayden Arkmalis," said Farod. "I was young, but I will never forget his power."

"Most of the men from those times are dead or have had their memories erased. The General didn't want anyone questioning his place as leader, but he needed someone to lead that had experience in such matters and someone to maintain the aringi—so he spared Farod and me. I spent the next several years recruiting new Riders for the General."

"Wow," gasped Jurdik. "So there's some guy out there whose powers trump the General's?"

"No," said Marcus definitively. "That man is dead. The last wielder of the Gauntlet defeated him. Grayden Arkmalis is by far the strongest of our kind." These words woke Marcus from the tale. "We must inform the General that the boy wears the Gauntlet." Marcus grabbed his wristcom. "You have never seen its power, but I have. We are going to need reinforcements. The General himself may be needed to end this." He pressed a few buttons, and the holographic version of Corbin stood atop his wrist, but the image was fading in and out.

"Hello, Capt'n." The words also were scratchy. "Any word on the whereabouts of duh Scargen boy?"

"We have located the boy, but there are new concerns."

"Such as?" The words were followed by white noise.

"The boy has already acquired the Gauntlet."

"What was dat, Captain? I am afraid somefing seems to be interfering wif duh transmission."

"Yes, this place is tampering with all of our tech. The boy has the Gauntlet."

" 'ee 'as? Duh master will need to know of dis right away."

"Wait . . . there is more, Corbin. We think that the boy has found one of the stones."

"Dis will not make the General 'appy. Is duh boy alone?"

"No, he has reunited with his friends. They are on the move, but we are tracking them with a recon orb."

"I need to relay dis information to duh General. Is dat all, Capt'n?"

"We are going to need reserves."

"You need a few more Riders? Dat should be no problem. I'll alert—"

"No, Corbin. We need a battalion of Lava Trolls, two squadrons of Riders, and as many *Eerah* as the General can summon."

"Dat's a bit extreme for one boy, Capt'n, isn't it?"

"He's eluded Hunters and escaped a Vamp Hive—not to mention evading us. I don't think I am being excessive. We cannot take any chances. This boy's energy is off the scale, and the Gauntlet, let alone the augment, is just going to make that signature rise exponentially. We have no idea which stone the boy has, but we both know that it only takes one to tilt the scale."

"Duh boy must need someone to 'elp him wif dis process. Dat should buy us some t—"

"He has found his Augmentor. That much is certain."

"We *don't* 'av much time den, do we? Where are you and your men currently?"

"The closest I can tell you is somewhere in the mountains of Shikoko, Japan. Our nav tech also seems to be malfunctioning. Whatever is affecting our communication is also interfering with our positional locators."

"Malfunctioning? How am I supposed to get you your reserves if I don't know where to send dem? Obviously I need to get approval from the General, and you know how 'ee is when it comes to details."

"Not knowing where we are makes it virtually impossible to create stable teleportals, Corbin. Taunt will try to form a stable connection before our next communication to make sure."

"Very well, Capt'n. I will 'av a response for you as soon as I can locate the General." Corbin's shaky hologram dissipated.

Locate the General? That imp is never more than three steps behind Arkmalis. The thought disturbed Marcus. *What is the General up to? No matter.* "Taunt."

"Yes, Captain."

"I want you to try to establish a stable teleportal. Jurdik, Farod, the Second, and I are going to fly ahead and figure out exactly what we are dealing with."

"Yes, Captain," said Taunt as he stood at attention. Marcus turned towards Evangeline.

"We will be receiving reinforcements shortly, provided we can make a secure connection."

"It's not that simple. There are countless variables . . . if the teleportal collapses mid transfer, there could be some serious ramifications. You can't just open a teleportal that size without doing some heavy calculations first. I also have to run a litany of stability tests and survey the area for optimal connection scenarios. It's going to take some time, Captain," said Taunt. "Easily three to four hours to establish a solid teleportal the size we need."

"You've got an hour." He turned to the other men. "For now, I do not want to give away our location. Our mission is to continue to follow the boy. Jurdik, take point." Marcus leaned down. "I am not going to lose him now because that recon orb starts to malfunction like the rest of our tech." He closed his eyes as he telepathically called his aringi. "Riders, mount up." The Captain was picked from the clearing like a mouse by a ravenous owl. Evangeline, Farod, and Jurdik followed Marcus's lead. Jurdik and his aringi flew to the front of the squadron. The winged creatures vanished into the fog.

39

preparations

Corbin scuttled across the skull-lined floor of the main chamber. The imp had particularly bad news to deliver to a particularly ill-tempered man. Needless to say, there was urgency in the imp's waddle. He had lost his master—not an everyday occurrence. He was determined to find the General as quickly as possible. *Time is of the essence. The boy is in our grasp, all we need is to close our fist.* He could already hear his master's words.

Corbin winded his way up the Tower's exterior staircase. *Down to the Seer and now up to duh Tower, my lit'l 'ooves can't take much more of dis.* The lofty tower that reached for the night sky was the last place the imp had not yet looked for the General. *The master must be up 'ere,* thought the perspiring imp. His small legs began to cramp from all the steps.

When he reached the top, he snuck along the stone wall that encircled the highest point of the Tower. He could hear General Arkmalis talking to someone. Corbin peered over the rock wall. Grayden Arkmalis was talking with a hooded man formed from the lava well that resided in the center of the Tower. He had seen his master communicate through the well in the past, but he did not recognize this man—it was difficult to see anything significant from where he was skulking.

The hooded man mumbled something to the General. Corbin

was usually a master dropper of eaves, but he could not make out a word of what this mysterious figure was saying.

"We agree then," said the General as he bowed his head. The hooded figure melted down into the well. The molten magma splashed up and back down. The imp waited for the lava to settle and then moved gingerly over to Arkmalis.

"M-m-m-master," stumbled Corbin.

"Not now, imp," said Arkmalis as he looked out over Grimm Tower. "How long have you been listening?"

"M-m-master . . . I just reached the top of the Tower."

"There is much to do. I need some time to think."

"M-m-m-master . . ."

"Damn it, Corbin."

"B-b-but—"

"If you interrupt me once more, I swear I will send you back to the Depths."

"They have found the boy," blurted Corbin. The General's tongue struggled to form words.

"Why didn't you say that?"

"A thousand apologies, my master, but there's more."

"Out with it already."

"The Scargen boy now wears the Gauntlet." The fire in the well bubbled.

"That was inevitable after losing him."

"There's . . . more," said Corbin. Arkmalis's eyebrow arched as if to insist the imp continue. "Marcus believes he may have one of the stones and has already found its Augmentor. The Captain is asking for reinforcements, master."

"He may be powerful, but he is still just a boy," said Arkmalis.

"The Aringi Captain has requested a battalion of lava trolls, two squadrons of Riders, and as many *Eerah* as you can summon."

"That seems excessive. Marcus better not be wasting my time and resources." The imp and the General stood in silence. "We will give Marcus what he thinks he needs."

"There is one other problem, my master."

"Go on. Out with it."

"There is no location to send them to."

"What? How is that possible?"

"There seems to be interference with their tech. I could barely understand his message. Marcus is quickly evaluating the situation, master, and then will report back."

"Then we better be ready. Time is of the essence. The boy is in our grasp, all we need is to close our fist." The imp smiled upon hearing these words. The lightning flash woke the servant from his self-congratulation. The General again moved towards the well.

Arkmalis's eyes fired red. He began chanting, *"Eerah natusum apacarita, Eerah vipannaka uparatta, vigatta, natusum, Narg."* The lava turned dark and began to fold onto itself. *"Eerah natusum apacarita, Eerah vipannaka uparatta, vigatta, natusum, Narg."* The churning black tar slowly crept upward. *"Eerah natusum apacarita, Eerah vipannaka, uparatta, vigatta, natusum, Narg."* Clumps began to break off and slide out onto the floor. *Eerah* were being born.

No matter how many times he had seen his master summon them, it always was astonishing. "Come, Corbin. There is much to be done before the ensuing battle." The imp struggled to keep up with Arkmalis, who moved with renewed vigor. They had passed the main chamber and were continuing downward as the *Eerah* seeped out of the Tower.

Corbin lost sight of Arkmalis as he entered the interior at the base of the Tower. The imp hurried so he would not lose the General. When he entered the hall, he could see his master making his way to his chamber and the two large doors. The General swung them open and walked inside. The doors slammed back shut. Corbin opened the imp-sized door set in the chamber door and scuttled through the chamber to where he assumed his master was going.

General Arkmalis stood in the center of his immense armory. A multitude of varied weapons adorned every inch of the curved rock surface. Intermingled with the weaponry were display cases filled with dark artifacts and jars full of odd ingredients needed for necromancy.

In the middle of the cavernous room stood an enormous statue made of black stone. The chiseled form was of a massive saddled gorgol perched atop a rock that jutted diagonally out of the floor. Carved chains drooped from the saddle into its mouth. Corbin had seen these beasts before in the Depths. The gorgol were fierce monsters that roamed the Wastelands in packs. These creatures were not to be trifled with.

This particular work of art always impressed Corbin for its facsimile to the real thing, but it scared him more. The fact that the statue was life-size was what he found so unsettling. The gorgol's muscular neck curved in the direction of the imp. The creature's head was the size of Corbin's entire body. He looked up into the hollow eyes of the statue. "Stupid gorgols," muttered the imp.

The General moved towards the wall of axes. Corbin lurked around the base of the sculpture to see what his master was staring at. The imp's eyes followed his master's to the oversized battle-axe. He grabbed the handle of the weapon. The General rotated the axe. The wall began to slide over. The reverberation of stone grinding on stone echoed throughout the armory. Arkmalis waited patiently for the wall to move.

Behind the wall was a chamber. General Arkmalis walked carefully towards the exposed compartment. One weapon hung on the interior wall.

The Scythe was nestled in what looked like two skeletal bird's claws. Its handle was made of bone that the imp could not place. Arkmalis reached up his hand and the Scythe flew into it. He swung the weapon from side to side. The red energy flowed from his hands and began to encircle the weapon. The imp stepped back. "Don't be afraid, Corbin. This old thing doesn't bite." The General walked over to the statue that Corbin still clung to. "I can't promise the same of the gorgol."

Grayden leaned over and touched the statue. Energy emanated from his palm and surrounded the chiseled steed. The rock pedestal shook, and the imp fell backwards. The sculpture shuddered as the stone gorgol's feet exploded into flames. The statue reared up and erupted to life. Lava flowed in the beast's eye sockets as it jumped down from its perch. The dark creature shook its head back and forth, stamping his front claws. Gaseous fumes surrounded the gorgol's red glowing eyes. The mount was long and muscular. "Meet Egnatius," said Arkmalis as he stroked the leathery skin on the gorgol's head. "He is my battle mount."

I didn't know 'ee 'ad a bloody battle mount, thought the imp. Corbin had been in battle with the General before, but nothing of this magnitude. The gorgol roared, exposing his jagged teeth as his head arched upward. The imp scurried across the stone floor and hid behind a display case.

Arkmalis leapt and mounted the dark steed. "Do try and keep up, Corbin. We have an army to prepare." The General rode out of the armory and through the chamber into the grand hall.

The imp caught up with Arkmalis outside of the aringi stables. He had almost run into a Newt while trying to keep up. Corbin walked out in the middle of the General assembling the troops. Arkmalis loomed over the scene atop his battle mount.

Lava trolls emerged from the molten pits, solidifying as they cooled. Still others dropped from under the stone bridge that connected the Tower to the mainland. This is where the trolls lived when not in service. A deep horn sounded, and the bulky lava rocks lumbered up the spiraling walkway. After the trolls were collected together, a second horn sounded, and the monstrous creatures halted. Smoke lifted from the still rock formations.

The Riders had already paired up with their respective aringi. The imp glanced upward as he made his way to the stable entrance. By Corbin's count, twenty or so circled above him. He looked below the flying aringi to Grimm Tower. *Eerah* oozed outward and enveloped the entire fortification. There they awaited the command of their dark master.

Corbin entered the stable. Five Newts were situated just inside the doorway. They were shoveling the aringis' droppings. The stench of guano tickled the hairs in the imp's big nose. The stink was pungent. He pinched his nose as he traversed the mounds of bat feces. He had smelled his share of foul odors before being conjured, but this he would never get used to.

An aringi moved in his stable. The sudden flapping noise startled the imp. He stumbled backward, and his left foot found one of the piles he was trying desperately to avoid. "Stupid bats." The aringi left in the hangar all screeched. He raised his soiled hoof upward and looked at it in disgust. Two of the Newts giggled. "Get back to work," said the imp. Corbin wiped the hoof on some hay. "I 'ope you get shot out of duh bloody sky." The bat made a noise back at the imp.

He reached the last stable where his steed waited for him. He peered into the stall, and looking back at him was his boar. Corbin placed his saddle onto the wild pig and petted the crown of his head. The pig snorted in delight. "I've missed you too, Scroffy."

The imp straddled the razorback as they both left the guano pit behind. His wristcom rang. He looked down at the device to see it was Captain Marcus. The imp promptly answered. The hologram sprung up in front of Corbin. "Hello, Captain. What news have you? I pray it's good."

"Taunt assures me that the teleportal will be up and running within the hour. We can begin moving the army as soon as the link is established."

"Well dat's good news. Duh General will be pleased."

40

hanami

Bartleby landed clumsily on the base below the main Temple. The lanterns blew back from the impact. LINC lowered along with Wiyaloo, Malcolm, and Anson.

"What is this place?" asked Yareli as she and Thomas dismounted.

"This is where I get my upgrade," the boy said with a grin. "This is the Temple of Yokan." The boy motioned with his arm. "There's someone you need to meet." The boy raced up the stairs. His comrades followed.

"Dis place is old, Tommy," said Malcolm as he looked around. "And I should know."

"Ziza spoke of this Temple long ago. He had mentioned a man's name. Daiki Katsuo I believe. I have read countless volumes on the validity of such a place existing. I was not convinced until now that it did." Anson sniffed the cool night air. "The magic here is strong."

"As well as the spiritual energy," said Yareli.

"Agreed," rumbled Wiyaloo.

"Yeah, I believe Itsuki had mentioned that, and Daiki Katsuo is his father. I also had a lovely conversation with his dead mother."

"What?" asked Yareli. Confusion swept through his comrades. Thomas liked finally being the one who knew what was going on.

"I'm sure you'll meet her sooner or later. Nice lady." Again awkward stares followed his words.

"From the sound of it, this Itsuki must be ancient," said Anson.

"I'd say he's definitely mature for his age." Thomas smiled. The group ascended the stairs to the top of the Temple. They settled on the lawn outside of the main hall. Itsuki walked out of the doors and looked out at the unlikely friends.

"Hello, everyone," said the young boy. "Welcome."

Yareli leaned over to Thomas. "You didn't say Itsuki had a kid," she said.

"He doesn't."

"Then who is that?" asked Yareli. Thomas moved over to the young boy.

"This is Itsuki. Itsuki, these are my friends." He introduced the stunned companions. Every one of their faces—except LINC's—had a surprised look on it. The artif spoke first.

"This diminutive human seems rather juvenile for such a prestigious undertaking."

"My foughts exactly," added Bartleby.

"Well 'ee's just a boy, isn't 'ee? I was expecting someone, well, a bit larger to be honest," said Fargus.

"You, of all people, should know that size does not matter," said Anson.

"I suppose you 'av a point an that. 'ee's just so young, isn't 'ee?"

"Stop being so rude, Fargus," commanded Yareli.

"It's okay, Yareli. It is hard for some people to look past appearances." Itsuki came down to the rest of them. His hands were behind him. "I may look young, but sometimes looks are just that."

"How did you know my name?" asked the girl.

"I have wisdom beyond my years," said Itsuki as he smiled. "And Thomas talks in his sleep." Thomas blushed at this revelation. Anson approached the young Augmentor with a quizzical look on his face.

"I have noticed the *sakura* still have their blossoms. They should not be flowering this time of year. How is this possible?"

"Well-spotted, wolfman," said Itsuki. Anson now seemed puzzled by the young boy's knowledge of his alter ego. "This is not a normal place."

"How did you know I'm a werewolf?"

"Like I said before, I have wisdom beyond my years."

"You are far older than you appear. That is, in a way, reassuring," said Anson. "What is this place?"

"This is the Temple of Yokan. This is my home and where I train."

"What are you doing here all by yourself?"

"I have been waiting for your friend Thomas, and I assure you: I am not by myself."

"When you say train, what exactly does dat entail?" asked Malcolm, drawing from his cigarette.

"I am an Augmentor. I have trained both physically and mentally my whole life preparing for this day. This Temple is my ancestral home. My ancestors were samurai, as am I. I have mastered the Bugei Juhappan, trained in the arts of ninjutsu, and studied the disciplines of the Shaolin monastery—to name a few."

"I guess that explains the shaved head," said Thomas. Itsuki grinned and continued.

"The spirits of Augmentors past are all around us. They have taught me the Ancient Language, and I have read and memorized countless volumes on the secrets of augmentation. I alone can attach the Taitokura to the Gauntlet." He looked directly at Thomas and then the glove. "I have been waiting for Thomas Scargen to arrive for quite some time."

"Well 'ee's got 'is bleedin' resume in order, doesn't 'ee?" said Malcolm as he inhaled on his cigarette. He exhaled. "So you're a bleedin' ninja?"

"No, vampire. I have trained in the methods and practices of the Shinobi, or *ninja* as you call them, but I live the way of the samurai."

"How have you been waiting for decades?" interrupted Yareli.

"Time travels differently in this place, hence the blossoms. Excuse me." Itsuki walked past them all and began to walk down the Temple stairs.

"Where are you going?" asked Thomas. Itsuki stopped and looked back.

"I need to tell my mother that we will need more food for *hanami*."

"Hanuumee?" questioned the boy.

"The traditional Japanese custom of observing and reveling around cherry blossoms, or as the Japanese call them, *sakura*," started LINC. "Large groups of humans congregate underneath said trees to consume sustenance and alcoholic refreshments, most notably *sake*. The custom dates back to the Nara period when they would examine *ume* blossoms, but by the Heian period, the practice had shifted to *sakura*. The custom was only initially intended for the elite of the Imperial Court, but soon was adopted by the samurai warriors."

"Most impressive. I couldn't have said it better," said Itsuki. "The samurai saw themselves as *sakura*. Their lives beautiful in a flash and then gone as quickly."

"A metaphor for how fleeting and ephemeral life is," said Anson. "Out, out, brief candle."

"For some of us, anyway. My people believe the trees contain *kami*. *Spirits* is the easiest translation of the word. We give praise to these spirits in hopes of them looking after us in life or in battle."

"That's beautiful," muttered Yareli. The young boy bowed, and the companions did so in return.

"We will need all the help we can get when their army arrives." said Itsuki as he continued down the stairs. Before he could be questioned, he had disappeared into the fog.

"What army is he talking about, Thomas?" asked Yareli.

"I would assume he means Arkmalis's," said the boy.

The dragon growled, and fire shot from his nostrils. " 'ee's 'ere?" asked Bartleby.

"If he's not here now, he will be soon enough."

"Good," said Bartleby as his eyes filled with rage.

"Then what are we doing just sitting here? Let's get the hell out of here while we still can." Yareli looked at the boy.

"I won't stop any of you if you want to, but I'm staying."

"We stand no chance against Arkmalis's army. We should retreat, Thomas."

"The Gauntlet wouldn't have sent me here if I wasn't meant to be here."

"We don't know this boy. How do we know he's telling the truth?"

"I just do."

"What does that even mean?"

"I didn't know you when you showed up in my backyard begging me to leave, but I followed you. Something told me to trust you, so I did. I have the same feeling now. Besides, I have seen things here. Strange things that all point to the fact that I have to stay."

"What sort of things?" asked Yareli.

"There is a hallway inside with a painting of me fighting Arkmalis's army at this Temple. Not to mention the hundreds of paintings of every Bearer of the Gauntlet there ever was, including Mary. That is all the proof I need. Itsuki is my Augmentor—I don't care how old he is. I trust him like I trust the rest of you."

"Thank you, Thomas Scargen. It will be my honor to be your Augmentor." Itsuki had returned as fast as he had left. Yareli tucked her head down in embarrassment.

"How do you know there is an army out there?" asked the suspicious girl.

"I have scouts that are among them as we speak. Their numbers continue to grow, but they will not attack until the morning."

"Scouts? We are just supposed to take your word on that?" asked Yareli as she waved her hand at what looked like a fly of some sort that buzzed around her face. The bug then flew at Itsuki's direction. He quickly brandished a set of chopsticks from behind his back and caught the insect between the utensils.

"Whoa," said Thomas. "You just snatched that bug out of midair. It's pretty narsh having a samurai-ninja-Shaolin monk on our team." Thomas grinned at his Augmentor as he looked at the insect trapped between the chopsticks.

"A bug, yes, Thomas, but not the kind you think," said Itsuki.

"What do you mean?" asked the boy.

"Look for yourself." He moved the chopsticks closer to Thomas. On second inspection, he could now see a tiny orb, not a bug, was clenched between the two pieces of wood.

"What is that?" asked Thomas. "Fargus, come here." The gremlin walked over and examined the item wedged between the chopsticks.

"Dat's a bleedin' recon orb . . . it's used for spying on unsuspecting people an that."

"You wanted real proof about this army, well here ya go." Thomas took the orb with his rock hand and squished it. "Are you in, or are you out?" Everyone was quiet. "I won't hold it against you if you leave. I understand." They had been through hell the last few days, and he could not deny them their chance to leave. "You have to make up your mind right now," commanded Thomas. "I need to know who's on board." He looked out at his friends.

"I intend to ensure your safety from a close proximity, Thomas Scargen," said LINC.

"I expected as much," chuckled the boy.

"You just saved my ass, Tommy. I can't leave ya now." Malcolm lit another cigarette and slugged down a gulp from his bottle of Warwick Red Ale. "Besides I'd like to see 'ow dis all plays out." He blew out a smoke ring.

"Thank you, Malcolm."

"Cowards die many times before their deaths; the valiant never taste of death but once." Anson smiled at Thomas. "I'm in too, friend."

"Well I'll open a teleportal if any uv you decide you be wantin' to leave, but I made a promise I would 'elp you find your dad, Thomas, and dat's exactly what I intend to do."

"Aw'right," added Fargus, nonchalantly agreeing before he began to whistle once more. All eyes moved to Yareli.

"Wiyaloo and I are staying too," said the girl.

"Agreed," said Wiyaloo. Yareli's arms were folded across her chest. She did not look happy.

"What are you all staring at?" asked Yareli. No one dared answer her, and they all averted their gaze.

"So we stand and fight," said Thomas.

"But first, we eat," interrupted Itsuki. "And ask the Spirits for their blessing." The dragon's stomach howled with excitement.

"Sorry," said Bartleby.

They had settled in under the large cherry blossom trees in a clearing next to the Temple. Blankets had been laid down on the ground. Some were covered with food and the others were occupied by the group. There was even a blanket big enough for Bartleby, who was still cramming his dragon-sized mouth with sushi made especially for him. The dragon had fashioned large chopsticks out of two *bō* that Itsuki had in his armory. Thomas was amazed at how easily everyone but he could use the simple utensils. He gave up after a while and used the simplest of utensil, his hands.

The paper lanterns glowed around them as the translucent mother of Itsuki attended to them. She had not said much this evening. She barely seemed like the same woman Thomas had come across earlier.

"Can you talk to your scouts?" asked Anson.

"Yes." The young Augmentor answered like he was waiting for the question.

"We need to know their numbers." Anson looked over to Itsuki. The Augmentor closed his eyes. His pupils seemed to shift around under his eyelids. His eyes squinted hard and then abruptly popped open.

"There are almost two full squadrons of bat-like creatures."

"Aringi Riders," corrected Thomas. Itsuki smiled at the boy and then closed his eyes again.

"There is a large amount of *Eerah*, I believe they are called." His eyes opened. "My scouts estimate about four thousand of them."

"What?" asked Yareli, surprised by the size of the *Eerah* army.

"Leave them to me," said Thomas confidently. Itsuki squinted even harder this time.

"Oh no." When his eyes released their grip this time, he looked directly into Thomas's eyes. "They also have a force of about fifty or so rock creatures with glowing red eyes. More of these beasts are still emerging from a gigantic teleportal. These creatures seem to be making my scouts apprehensive."

"Lava trolls," said the twins simultaneously.

"What is a lava troll?" asked Thomas. He was a little upset he was back to his normal position of not knowing anything.

"I will field the inquiry," said LINC, to Thomas's surprise. "Lava trolls, or *Trollus scorias*, are massive creatures whose exoskeletons are made completely of lava rock, and their blood is made up entirely of magma. They are traditionally dim-witted beings that rely almost strictly on brute force." Thomas stared at LINC, waiting for an explanation. "I perused your textbook while you underwent your nocturnal recharge. I returned to our domicile early the night before we departed, and I fortuitously found your book open on the desk. I decided to read the volume in its entirety in case there arose a necessity for such pertinent information." Thomas lifted one of his eyebrows.

"So . . . those odds aren't so good. We are going to need a plan," said the boy.

"And some help," said Itsuki. The Augmentor's mother approached the companions. The two wisps accompanied her, weaving in and out of the companions. She carried a tray with a bottle of *sake* and several small bowls. "Now we make an offering to the Spirits." Itsuki lifted a bowl off the tray as his mother passed out the bowls and quietly filled them. "Spirits, we make to you this offering," said the Augmentor as he raised his bowl. "May the spirits be with us . . . *kanpai*." They all raised their bowls and drank. The conversation continued, but something grabbed the boy's attention.

Thomas saw Moriko Katsuo put the tray down and walk off towards the trees—the two flames followed. She stopped and appeared to be staring at one tree in particular. It seemed odd to the boy until he realized that it must be the tree her husband had been buried under. He slipped away from the group towards the floating apparition. The two wisps met him and began to twirl around him. When he reached Moriko, her shoulders were shaking as if she was crying. He stopped next to her.

"He was the best husband a woman could ever want—and a better father," said the Augmentor's mother. "I miss him so much.

There is not a minute that goes by that I do not think about the two of us and what we had together. He was my world." She smiled. "Love is the most powerful magic there is. You would be wise never to forget that, Thomas Scargen."

"I won't, Mrs. Katsuo, and I'm sure one day you'll be reunited with him."

"Perhaps one day, but for now, my boy needs me. He can barely get a thing done without my help." Thomas grinned. Itsuki seemed capable of taking care of himself, but it was not an argument worth having with a ghost at this hour. "Thank you, Thomas."

"For what?"

"For coming here. My son can realize his dreams because of you. Not every mother gets to see that you know." She sniffled, and for the first time during their interaction, she looked away from her tree and directly at Thomas. "And for listening to the sentimental ramblings of a dead woman." She bowed, and Thomas did the same. He straightened back up to discover she had vanished.

"Disappeared on me again." He made his way back to the festivities. Itsuki noticed Thomas and nodded his head in his direction.

"It has been my pleasure to meet you all, but I must return to my work, or all of this will be for naught. Our main objective is to gain enough time for me to attach the stone. I trust you will form some sort of plan before morning." He looked at Anson.

"It will not be easy, but I think we can hold them off for a bit. I will catch everyone up to speed in the morning. Malcolm, LINC, and I will keep watch and discuss our plans. Everyone else needs to get some rest. What we face tomorrow is daunting, to say the least." Thomas could not argue with this logic. The artif and the two immortals did not need as much rest as the others, and he wanted his battery to be full come morning.

"There are plenty of rooms and beds inside the smaller temple. I will see you all in the morning. *Oyasuminasai.*" Itsuki bowed, and the companions reciprocated. He then walked towards the larger Temple's doors.

"I still can't get used to the whole bowing thing. I mean I never know when to do it, or how long to remain down . . ." Thomas looked at Yareli. "I'm gonna go grab my stuff from Bartleby and then crash myself." He yawned and walked in the direction of the already sleeping dragon. "Good night."

"I'll go with you," said Yareli to Thomas's surprise. "I have to grab my clothes and my bow anyway." The two said good night to everyone and walked over to Bartleby.

"Thanks . . . for staying I mean," whispered Thomas as he reached into the dragon's side compartment.

"You didn't think I was really going to leave? I said I'd help you find your father." Thomas handed her the bow and quiver. "Besides . . . I want to make sure that nothing happens to you. I can't have you going and getting yourself killed."

"Oh," said Thomas as he quietly closed the storage container. It was the only thing he could think of to say. "Well I'm glad you stayed." She smiled as they walked towards the smaller temple. He thought of his conversation with Moriko, but he wasn't sure why.

They entered the temple. Doors lined the corridor on both sides. "I guess I'll be sleeping here." She pointed at the first room. "Good night, Thomas." She entered the room, but then poked her head out. "I'm glad I stayed too." She grinned once more and disappeared into her room.

Thomas entered the room across the hall and plopped down in the first bed he saw. Thoughts rushed through his brain. He was excited about the coming battle. This would be a real test of his powers, and though excited, the notion scared him too. He thought of Yareli and his friends and the fate he had decided for them. *I hope I made the right choice.*

41

an army

The last of the lava trolls were crossing over the teleportal's threshold. Several aringi were needed to hold open the portal, and they were growing tired as a result. This bothered the Captain: he needed his Riders and their beasts to be ready for battle in only a matter of hours.

They had sent out scouts, but they had proven unreliable. Their tech malfunctioned more frequently the closer they got to the Temple. Taunt had been the first to see the correlation and had moved his teleportal experiments farther into the forest. He was able to establish a stable connection and open a constant teleportal. Outgoing holes were the only kind that worked, and even these could only be maintained for five minutes at a time, which made moving personnel tedious.

They had established the link with Grimm Tower for three hours. It had taken that long for the *Eerah* and the two squadrons to get through. The *Eerah* had collected into one enormous shape, churning and folding over itself while they waited restlessly for their summoner. Lava trolls continued to clomp through the teleportal.

Two squadrons of aringi were on site, including twenty-seven pilots and ten Newt handlers. The Captain's squadron was running one short due to the untimely death of Dalco Jakobsen. Twelve Riders flew with him. Evangeline, his Second, had thirteen in her squadron, and each squadron had Newts at their disposal.

The commander of the lava trolls would soon be making contact with Marcus. Together they would await the coming of General Arkmalis. The plan was simple. They were going to overwhelm the enemy with sheer numbers. It seemed too easy, and this unsettled Marcus. He worried about Evangeline. He knew his worries were unwarranted—she had proven time and time again that she could handle just about anything—but he still was apprehensive. He could not shake the image of the dragon. It was all he could think of as he stood there patiently awaiting the arrival of the Commander.

Evangeline walked over to the Captain. "I don't know how much more of this Pria can take," said the Second.

"I was thinking the same of Teros." Marcus had said the words before he realized what he had done.

"Teros?" Evangeline was smiling. How could he have blurted out the name? He waited for her to say *I told you so* or *what happened to them being just transportation*, but it never came. "The name suits him, Captain. Teros . . . a remarkable name for a remarkable creature." She patted him on the back. He felt her compassion surge through him. "Don't look now, but here comes Old Smokey."

"I wish you wouldn't call him that," giggled Marcus. "He has a name." The massive gray monster lumbered over to them. Smoke lifted off of his bulky frame, and where his feet fell, he left burnt footprints in the earth. His eyes glowed orange, and he carried a large stone axe over his right shoulder. The ground shook as he approached.

"Is something funny, Captain?" echoed the Commander as smoke poured out of his mouth.

"Why do you ask?"

"I could hear you laughing at the nickname your Second has given me." The two stopped smiling.

"I'm sorry, Commander . . . I-I didn't mean—" The troll commander cut her off.

"There is no need for an apology. I may be made of stone, but I have a sense of humor." He swung his axe off of his shoulder and onto the ground. The earth shook as he leaned on it like a cane.

"You should hear what some of my men call your Riders." All three laughed out loud.

"It is good to see you again, Commander Suvios."

"Likewise, Captain."

"We have a lot to discuss," said Marcus. "Once the General arrives, of course. How many more of your trolls are there?"

"By my count, there are only ten or so remaining that haven't crossed. That puts our total at just above three hundred."

"Good. What we are dealing with should not be taken lightly." The flow of lava trolls through the teleportal ceased.

"And just what are we dealing with?" asked Commander Suvios.

"A boy and his friends," said General Arkmalis from atop the gorgol. He carried Grimm's scythe on his back. A trail of flames unfolded from the gate behind him. His abrupt appearance had startled Marcus and caught all three of them off guard. "Simply a boy and his friends, Commander."

"Yes, General," said Suvios as he and the rest of the army kneeled down. Corbin came bouncing through the portal on his boar. The imp and his pig rushed back and forth, trying to avoid the small fires Egnatius had left in his wake. The sight would have been comical if not for the General's demeanor.

"Captain Slade, instruct your men to shut down the teleportal," commanded the General. The Captain turned and raised his fist. The opening collapsed into itself with a resounding whoosh. "You didn't start the party without me, did you Marcus?" The General leapt from his mount.

"No, General. We were awaiting your arrival to begin discussing tactics."

"Very good. I didn't want to have to play catch-up." He smirked. "Now get up and let's begin." The army stood as one. Arkmalis motioned for them to follow him.

Marcus, Evangeline, Suvios, and Corbin walked with the General. The gorgol followed behind. They made their way to a clearing in a copse of cherry blossom trees. Commander Suvios had to duck to clear the branches. "First things first," said the General. "What intel do we have on the boy and his friends?" Marcus punched a few keys on his wristcom. A holographic screen appeared in the center of them. A three-dimensional representation of Anson and Malcolm Warwick emerged.

"These are the Warwicks—powerful Mages in their own right, but there is more." The image of the two changed. A werewolf and a winged vampire appeared. "They are both immortals—difficult to kill, to say the least." He hit another key. An image of a Native American floated above the ground. "This is Yareli Chula. She is also a powerful and skilled Mage, and a Summoner." The image of her Spirit Warrior popped up next to her. Footage of the two in action began to play. "He is a formidable opponent. From what we know from our intel, he cannot be killed unless she is." The hologram altered into a dragon. "Bartleby Draige, he is a fearsome beast. We all know what dragons are capable of." The Captain's eyes met with Farod's.

The image shifted once more. "That brings me, last but not least, to our target and the most powerful of all of them, Thomas Scargen. He now wears the Gauntlet. This is a tremendous weapon, as we all know. The boy is naturally skilled, and there is no telling how far his powers have increased. Do not be fooled by his inexperience: he is extremely dangerous. We also have reason to believe that the Gauntlet may have been augmented. If you couple this with a rather troublesome artif protector"—footage of the android now played—"we are looking at one hell of a fight." The holoscreen went blank. It rotated and transformed into a three-dimensional map of the Temple and surrounding areas. "Commander Suvios, you have the floor."

"Thank you, Captain Slade. As you can see from this representation, there is an open field that runs for one mile from the base of the main temple to this tree line here. This is where we plan to start the engagement. We have them severely outnumbered, and if we can keep them out in the open, we have the advantage. The *Eerah* will go in first, followed by the first wave of my trolls." Holographic *Eerah* oozed out from the tree line. Behind them trudged a line of lava trolls. "The *Eerah* proved ineffective in their first encounter with the boy, but we hope this will keep them occupied long enough for my trolls to advance and the aerial assault to begin. We will coordinate with Captain Slade and his attack." Marcus moved over to the map and began to speak.

"The first squadron, led by the Second, will fly out in coordination with the first line of trolls, followed by the second squadron, led by me, shortly thereafter. They have four combatants capable of flight. Of those four, the dragon is the most dangerous."

"Well planned, Marcus—a bit theatric, but well-planned nonetheless," said the General. "How long until your men are ready? I wish to get this over with as quickly as possible. Our army should be able to destroy a mere boy and his band of freaks in no time. Wouldn't you say so, Marcus?"

"Permission to speak frankly, General?"

"Granted."

"I strongly advise we hold off our attack until morning for two reasons. The first being that our aringi are undoubtedly drained from maintaining the teleportal for so long, and they will be less effective if we attack now."

"And the second?"

"If we wait until morning, the vampire will be eliminated from the equation."

That would convince Arkmalis. He was a General first. He understood that fresh troops and better odds were always advantageous. "New plan," said the General. "We attack at sunrise. Suvios, inform your trolls of our change in plans. Evangeline, you tell the Riders the same, and Corbin . . ."

"Yes, General?"

"Make my bed."

"Yes, your most powerfulness," said the imp as he bounded away on his boar.

"And Marcus, this plan of yours better work."

"I am confident, General."

"And if that doesn't work, there is always plan B."

"What is that, General?" Arkmalis reached over and put his hand on the Scythe.

"Well . . . *me*, of course."

42

the battle beckons

Thomas walked out of the smaller temple. He had not slept well, but he was appreciative of what little rest he did get, and it felt nice to be back in his own clothes. He was wearing his blue Scargen Robotics shirt. The shirt reminded him of his father. Thomas thought it was appropriate, considering the circumstances.

The sun barely had emerged, and morning fog still infested the temples. A light wind stirred across his face. Yareli was already awake and had also opted for some of her own clothes. She stood near Anson, who was explaining what was expected of her. Bartleby was stretching his legs, and Fargus seemed to be doing some final diagnostics on the dragon. Thomas made his way over to where LINC, Anson, and Malcolm were discussing battle tactics.

"Good morning, Tommy," said Malcolm as he came closer. Thomas smiled at the vampire. LINC was emanating a holographic representation of the battlefield.

"As I was saying, if we become overwhelmed, we will fall back to the main temple. We can use the higher ground to our advantage." Anson froze where he stood. The howl of the wind had ceased. "Something's wrong," said Anson as his head pivoted anxiously.

"What is it?" wondered Thomas.

"We're not alone, are we?" said Malcolm.

"By the pricking of my thumbs . . . " Anson sniffed the warm air. "Something wicked this way comes." The companions turned to the opposite side of the large field that was surrounded by cherry blossom trees.

Eerah began to seep out of the tree line. The dark creatures sped their way towards the Temple. Anson was quick to take the lead. "Wiyaloo, I need you to cut them off."

"As you wish, Anson Warwick." The foxlike beast barreled towards the *Eerah*'s line.

"Malcolm, help him," commanded Anson. The vampire followed behind the spirit ghost. Yareli drew an arrow out of her empty quiver. "Yareli, save your arrows. There are far worse things in the woods this morning." Thomas sped past the others.

"I got this," said the boy as he passed Anson.

"Thomas, no!" yelled Yareli. "You need to be here for the augmentation."

"I'll be fine," said Thomas as he charged in behind Malcolm and Wiyaloo, who had already engaged the *Eerah*. The vampire fired energy blasts as Wiyaloo threw pulses from his staff. The dark wave shifted and folded. It now moved with new resolve at the two combatants. For every ten they managed to destroy, another twenty would take their place. "Hey, guys, do you need some help?" asked the boy when he reached the ghost and the vampire.

"I suppose we could, Tommy," said Malcolm.

"Agreed." As the words left his mouth, Wiyaloo turned and, with a twirl of his staff, unleashed an energy attack on an oncoming mass of *Eerah*.

Thomas crouched, pulled back the Gauntlet, and moved it forward quickly. A stream of power exploded from the stone glove. "Haaaaaaaaaaaaaaaaaaaaaa!" A hole formed down the middle of the dark ocean. The response from the *Eerah* was swift. The tar-like creatures began retreating back into the forest.

"I fink dey recognize you, Tommy," said Malcolm as he stopped his assault, watching the *Eerah* retreat.

"They are not getting away that easily." Thomas sprinted forward and rushed into the black mass. The tar creatures formed over top of him. He began destroying the *Eerah* from the inside. Their fear was heard through an echoing shrill. They recoiled and drew back to the tree line. The boy gave chase. A wall of porous dark rock abruptly stopped him. He looked up to see two massive stone creatures, both cradling bulky rock weapons. Their eyes and the inside of their mouths glowed orange as smoke lifted from the openings. The first beast swung his rock sword down at Thomas, and the boy rolled left to avoid the attack. The second monster stomped above him, but Thomas sped forward out of the way, narrowly avoiding being crushed by the large foot. He turned to retreat, but he was now surrounded by these giants. They scorched the earth where they trod, leaving smoking footprints in their wake. Hundreds of these monsters stomped rhythmically out of the forest. *This can't be good*, thought Thomas as he jumped back and threw a pulse at the stone goliath in front of him. The energy flowed from the Gauntlet. The blast disintegrated its right leg. Lava spilled from the wound as the rock creature crumbled to the ground, shaking the earth.

Thomas raced towards the fallen beast, the only way back to his friends. He was severely outnumbered and needed help. The rock soldiers followed, wildly swinging their colossal weapons. LINC rocketed out to meet Thomas. The artif stopped, hovering twenty feet above the battlefield. The artif's assault crumbled three of the stone monsters, but still more advanced. Anson ran at Thomas also. When he reached the boy, he sprinted past him and leapt towards one of the rock beings.

He was in his werewolf form before he landed on his first victim. He began tearing into the troll's rock flesh before what remained of his shirt hit the ground. Magma oozed from the incisions Anson inflicted on the monster. His moves were primal. The stone guard fell to the ground as the werewolf landed on his next enemy. Malcolm and Wiyaloo turned their attention away from the *Eerah* and towards the new threat. The three of them stood back-to-back-to-back, fending off the menace.

"I'm guessing *they* are the lava trolls?" asked Thomas

"Well spotted, Tommy. What gave it away?" said Malcolm.

"Okay, okay, stupid question." Thomas ducked under the swing of a stone sword. "Any tips?"

"Well dey are mean sons of bitches, but dumb as rocks." The vampire winked at Thomas as he avoided the downward smash of a large rock hammer. "See what I mean?" Malcolm laughed aloud as Thomas turned and blasted a hole through the assailing troll. The troll bled out molten rock as he collapsed to the ground. His fiery eyes extinguished as smoke rose from the rock carcass.

A foreboding darkness blotted out the morning sun. The shadow grew large as Thomas looked up to find the origin of the shade. Aringi blanketed the sky. Bartleby, who was already circling above, darted towards the squadron. Anson bounded off his current stone victim and galloped in the direction of the group. "LINC, Malcolm, Wiyaloo, assist Bartleby," commanded the Mage Knight.

"Already on it, Bruvver." Malcolm's wings unfurled from his jacket as he leapt into flight.

"I am afraid I cannot comply with that order, Anson Warwick. Dr. Scargen's programming is extremely specific on matters involving his son in direct mortal danger. My prime directive is to protect Thomas Scargen."

"We discussed this last night. You will be doing just that. If we can't stop this aerial assault, Thomas is at risk."

"It's all right, LINC. Yareli, Anson, and I can handle things down here. Bartleby and Malcolm need your help." Thomas spun to see three charging lava trolls. "Haaaaaa!" yelled the boy, blowing the beasts backward into more approaching trolls.

"Understood, Thomas. You have override authorization." LINC fired off in the direction of the ominous swarm.

"Be careful, you crazy bucket of bolts," said Thomas under his breath. Yareli ran up next to him. She planted her feet, reached into the empty quiver, and grabbed a white translucent arrow. She nocked the glowing arrow into the bow, pulled the string tight, and let loose. The shaft cut through the smoke-filled air. Its destination was a group of lava trolls that were forming to their left. The arrow transformed into a stampeding herd of buffalo. The force of the animals rumbled through the group of trolls.

"I've been working on that one," said Yareli as she winked at Thomas. The trolls still advanced. Anson approached and reared up on his hind legs. He began to form an energy sphere between his two paws. The orange glow glistened across his fur.

"You two get back to the Temple. There are far too many of them. We need to gain the higher ground." Anson let the orb loose. It traveled into the middle of the lava trolls that were loping towards them. The explosion tore through the surrounding giants, flinging rock pieces in all directions. Yareli and Thomas stood there, staring at the aftermath. "Now!" yelled Anson.

The three darted back to the Temple of Yokan. The slow, heavy steps of the trolls ensured them ample time to regroup once they reached their destination. "I'm going to see how far along Itsuki is with the stone," said Thomas as he doubled his speed and zoomed up the Temple stairs. He moved through the Hall of Yokan and skidded to a halt in front of the floating boy. The jewel levitated in front of him. Its power was never more evident to Thomas. Itsuki's eyes popped open.

"It is time." Itsuki grabbed the stone and slammed it into the opening at the top of the Gauntlet. His arm blazed a golden hue. The Gauntlet pulsed with power. "So . . . that's it?"

"Yes, that's it."

"I just thought there'd be some sort of ceremony or something." Thomas raised his hand and slowly moved each one of his stone fingers individually. He stared at the Gauntlet as his forearm tensed. "I gotta tell you. I don't feel any different."

"Give it time. There is a small adjustment period," said Itsuki. Thomas's eyes began to burn. "You can also expect to"—Thomas's body dropped to the ground—"lose consciousness." Itsuki's last words trailed off to deaf ears as Thomas lay there still.

43

air supremacy

arcus's Riders moved in rigid formation. What was left of the two squadrons filled the gray sky. Marcus had thought their presence was going to be a surprise. They were not prepared for such a quick response. The dragon had not been alone. The robot, a Spirit Warrior, and a vampire that was apparently immune to the sun had joined the dragon. Marcus was not familiar with such magic, and anything he was not familiar with worried him.

Their numbers had been reduced by ten already. Bartleby Draige alone had killed four of his men. Marcus could sense that the dragon's anger was fueling the beast. The artif was also quite distracting and had taken out three aringi. Two of the men had survived the fall, but just barely. The spirit ghost had killed one of Evangeline's men, and the vampire had ended the life of two of Marcus's Riders.

His main concern right now were several spirit animals that were terrorizing his Riders. A large bald eagle chased two of his men. A pack of wolves had just dissipated, but not before taking out an aringi. It was a constant barrage of animal attacks.

The source of the attacks was the one they called Yareli Chula. She had established a spot on the top of the Temple and was hindering the effectiveness of Marcus's Riders. He had to do something. "I'm going to see if I can take care of our surface-to-air problem," said Marcus into his headset.

"That would be a big help, Captain," responded the Second.

Marcus flew straight at the Temple. He cut through the air, gliding downward on his aringi, and began firing on the girl. She moved like a blur, but the longer he occupied her, the less damage she could do to his Riders. He bore down on her and was about to begin firing again when a white flash halted him.

His beast pulled up. He turned to see what the disturbance was. It was the girl's Spirit Warrior. The ghost fox spun his staff and fired a spread of energy blasts at the Captain. Marcus peeled left and avoided the attack. The ghost followed. "It looks like I'm not going to be able to take care of the surface-to-air problem."

"What happened?" asked Evangeline.

"Let's just say I'm . . . preoccupied." He cut right and spun back towards the fox. He fired at the apparition who moved quickly to avoid the laser attack. "I'm going to need you to take care of it. Take three of your men."

"Yes, Captain, as soon as I can shake the vampire." He turned to see that she was being chased by the winged man. He acted instantly.

"Taunt," he yelled into his headset.

"Yes, Captain," answered his Rider.

"I need you to focus on the vampire."

"Roger that, Captain." Taunt broke off and moved towards Malcolm Warwick. The vampire did not see him coming. He was preoccupied with catching Evangeline. Taunt swooped in behind the vampire and opened fire with his crossbow attachment. Malcolm was vulnerable. The stakes sailed straight at the vampire, center-mass.

Right before the first piece of wood entered the undead man, the robot flew in the way of the stake and caught it with his right hand, followed by the second stake in his left. Taunt's plan had not worked, but at least Evangeline was now free to attack Yareli Chula.

Marcus still could not shake the Spirit Warrior. He spoke into his headset. "Farod, break off the dragon and turn your attack to the artif and vampire."

"As you wish, Captain. Do you need any help with the fox?"

"No, I can handle him. Just occupy those two while Evangeline takes out the archer."

"Yes, Captain."

"Evangeline, you are free to take out the surface-to-air problem."

"Affirmative, Captain." Evangeline dropped down and began her run at Yareli Chula.

Marcus rolled again, narrowly avoiding a white energy blast. Farod and his men joined Taunt in the fight against the artif and the vampire. One of the men got close enough to shoot a red energy rope from his T27 at the vampire. The glowing cord missed the leg of Malcolm Warwick. He turned and ripped through the wing of the oncoming aringi. The bat and its Rider plummeted to the battlefield.

The Second made her first run on the archer. Yareli Chula moved with dexterity to avoid the blasts from the aringi. Evangeline pulled up and turned to begin her second run. "I was unable to eliminate the target on the first run. Attempting a second run." She flew in faster this time.

Malcolm Warwick had begun to systematically attack Farod's men. The robot had moved on, but Marcus did not know where he had gone. The crowded sky had become confusing. Aringi, dragons, vampires, spirit ghosts, artifs . . . it was getting harder to keep track. Marcus looked downward to gather his bearings when he noticed something peculiar. The trees on the south side of the Temple had seemingly relocated. *Trees just don't up and move*, he thought. A white energy pulse rocketed past him, barely missing the aringi's right wing. This woke Marcus from his ponderings.

The spirit ghost had chased him to the clouds. They were at a great distance from the rest of the battle. The Captain crossed through a cloud, and the fox was waiting for him. He went into a defensive spiral to avoid the burst of energy. Marcus looked down to see that the robot was surrounded. Two of the Riders were successful in attaching energy ropes around the artif. The robot struggled to free himself, but more energy lassoes looped around the android. Marcus was pleased with this turn of events, but his pleasure was quickly interrupted.

He glanced around to find the Second. He finally could see her. He spotted her looping around the far side of the Temple to make what he assumed was her third run. He looked behind Evangeline and saw the great beast closing in. It was the dragon—*Bartleby Draige.* She didn't know he was there. "Evangeline—" But he was too late.

The dragon's fiery assault had enveloped Pria and Evangeline. The bat had closed her wings to protect her Rider, but at the cost of flight. The aringi slowed and pulled up. Her right wing was on fire. Draige swooped down and grabbed the beast with his talon. The dragon ripped Evangeline from Pria. He dropped the aringi to the battlefield floor, Her wing was still on fire, the other torn.

The Captain was horrified, but he was helpless. Marcus was in a dogfight of his own, and the fox was not letting up. Out of the corner of his eye, he saw his Riders pull the artif apart using the electric lassos. The two halves had been thrown in two different directions. He refocused on the dragon—who must have seen the artif because he threw Evangeline aside and bolted towards the falling halves of the artif. He saw Draige catch the top half of the artif and then dash in the direction of the robot's other half.

Marcus was no longer concerned with his dogfight. He zoomed straight downward as tears streamed out of his eyes and white blasts whizzed by his head.

"Evangeline, can you hear me?"

No response.

The white blasts stopped abruptly. The spirit ghost must have sensed no more danger to his master and broke off the chase. Marcus pushed Teros to his limit.

"Evangeline, please respond."

No response.

He dove to catch his falling Evangeline, but he knew it would be too late.

"Damn it, Eva, answer me!" His anger had gotten the best of him.

No response.

Captain Marcus Slade feared the worst.

She's . . . gone.

44

branching out

"It begins." Itsuki looked up onto the wall. His eyes found their target. The sword shined brilliantly. The hilt of this *katana* was a carving of demons circling the blade, but it was not always this way. He reached up, and the sword flew into his hand. He had only used the weapon once in combat. A forest demon had threatened the Temple. The young boy had inadvertently summoned the monster while trying to pay homage to his ancestors. Itsuki met the beast and defeated it, and in doing so, found a name for his blade: *Onikira*—the Demon Killer.

The craftsmanship was striking. Itsuki was a true artisan, and although he had only used *Onikira* in battle once, he was proficient with the sword. He sliced through the air with a couple practice swings. The blade felt like a natural extension of his arm. He walked out of the room. A new painting was forming. He paused to see what it was. *This could be important.* He stared intently as the invisible brush created yet another masterpiece. This picture was one of the biggest in the hall. He stepped back to see the whole scene. The image of Itsuki standing across from a massive man holding a glowing scythe filled the frame. Cherry blossoms and lava trolls speckled the background. This unsettled Itsuki. *This does not bode well.* He rushed down the hall and out to meet Yareli and Anson. He knew his part had just begun.

"Where's Thomas?" asked Anson with a puzzled look on his face. He had turned back into his human form.

"He's currently . . . unavailable."

"What's that supposed to mean?" questioned Yareli.

"His body and the Gauntlet are preparing themselves."

"So, where is he?" asked Yareli.

"He's sleeping."

"We need him, Itsuki," growled Anson.

"Perhaps I can be of assistance."

"I'm sure you are very adept in the martial arts, Itsuki, but that won't do us much good against this enemy," warned Anson.

"I assure you, my skills reach far beyond the martial arts." The young boy walked to the edge of the steps and looked down on the impending ground assault. *It is time*, he thought. He placed his sword in front of him and began levitating as his eyes went blank. His eyes burned the exact color of the cherry blossoms. His body was enveloped by the same warm light, and he began chanting, "*Senzo . . . Kami . . . Noboru, Senzo . . . Kami . . . Noboru.*"

The Temple shook. The cherry blossom trees swayed back and forth. The first row of *sakura* below them now glowed. Their swaying became more violent as Itsuki continued his chant. Branches formed into long arms, and faces grew out of the gnarled trunks. The eyes of the trees opened. The newly formed arms slammed to the ground and pried themselves from the earth, pulling free. Their roots weaved together to form legs and feet. The placards with the characters now adorned their wooden chests. Enormous samurai swords appeared in their bark-covered hands. Itsuki's chanting ceased.

The wooden troops were quick to enter the fray. They moved with speed and purpose and descended upon the rock beasts. Blossoms floated to the ground behind the charging foliage. Each progressive row began to spring to life and join in the fight. They moved with grace, wasting no movement. Spirit swords clashed with stone ones. The smell of sulfur crowded the field and now wafted up into Itsuki's nostrils.

Anson looked over at Yareli and then back at the Augmentor. "I didn't see that coming," said Yareli as she stared at the wooded army.

"Once more unto the breach, dear friends, once more," said the werewolf as he rushed in behind the attacking forest. He transformed his two-legged sprint into a four-legged gallop. The wolf sped towards his prey. Yareli drew a spirit arrow and placed it into her bow, following Anson's lead.

Itsuki's eyes opened, and he dashed down the ancient stairs, sword drawn. *Onikira* blazed the color of the blossoms. He moved through the advancing forest, trying to get to the front of the line. Itsuki paused once he saw them standing on the blossom-covered battlefield. Three of the trees were waiting for him. The smallest of the three turned. Itsuki immediately recognized his father. He stood towering over the boy. His familiar face was alive in the bark of the tree. His elongated branch arms appeared to be strong, and the right one carried a blazing oversized samurai sword—a *katana*. A second, smaller sword—his *wakizashi*—was tucked into his midsection in a belt-like root, which also held the sheath for the *katana*. His legs were made of his twisted roots. The character on his chest confirmed the young Augmentor's suspicions. He was Daiki Katsuo, father of Itsuki, husband to Moriko Katsuo. The other two trees were much taller. *They must be older ancestors.*

"Hello, Father," said Itsuki as if he had talked to him yesterday. He bowed.

"Hello, Itsuki." The three trees bowed in unison. "I am proud of you, Son."

"Thank you, Father."

"What are your orders?" asked Daiki of his son.

"We need to destroy as many rock creatures as possible. Thomas Scargen is in the middle of his augmentation, and we must buy him some time."

"Understood," said his father as he and the other two trees bowed. Itsuki reciprocated the gesture. The four ran in different directions. The trees were going to lead their respective armies. Itsuki was running to the head of the trees. He moved quickly through his flowery kin. *Onikira* stretched behind him, extending from his straightened arm. He could see the opening amidst the stampeding trees. The young Augmentor burst through the moving tree line.

He was met with the thunderous clap of a downward-striking hammer. The impact shook the earth around the small boy. He swiftly ran through the bulky legs of the lava troll. He stopped and jumped upward, slicing the beast up the middle. The two parts of the creature fell, leaving a pool of magma. The tree army yelled in triumph. Itsuki, now in front of the trees, turned towards the army of cherry blossom trees and raised *Onikira*. "We have all waited for this day for quite some time. Today, my ancestors and I fight for Thomas Scargen and the future of this world. We will not all survive this day, but we will fight with honor, until the last *sakura* stands. The Katsuo name shall burn in our enemies' souls. We are now one." The trees cheered with him. He lowered his sword and turned it in the direction of the oncoming lava trolls. "*Kougeki!*"

Itsuki charged at the first troll in his way. With two slices, the lava troll was armless and defenseless. One of the taller trees ended his pain abruptly with a quick slice. The head of the troll rolled in front of the young Augmentor. Itsuki jumped the disembodied head as he eyed up his next two victims. He moved at the first troll and struck. The top part of the beast slid diagonally off of his lower body. Itsuki ran up the falling beast and leapt at his next prey. With a flash, *Onikira* found its target. Itsuki slid down the creature, bisecting it. He turned, and with a flick of his wrist, he removed the foot of a third oncoming lava troll. The moan from the creature echoed as it slammed into the pool of magma flooding from the other trolls. Itsuki could not hear anything. He was now one with his sword. The gentle uprising of his chest was steady.

He paused and took in the scene. It was breathtaking. The horrible acts of war were disguised beneath fluttering blossoms. The *sakura* moved with poetic grace. They were systematically destroying every lava troll in sight—still more advanced. Out of the corner of his eye, he saw the wolfman leaping across a series of lava trolls, viciously destroying each one he landed on. He moved with purpose and strength. *And I thought I was doing well.*

He was awoken from his musings when an aringi crash-landed at his feet. His wooden slippers shook. The beast must not have seen the young Augmentor yet as it writhed in pain, screaming. One of its wings was ripped and broken—the other burnt. The Rider fell shortly after with a breaking sound. It was a girl, which caught Itsuki off-guard. Her helmet resembled a cracked egg. She looked lifeless. The beast still stirred. It had now seen the young Augmentor and began acting like a protective dog, putting itself between him and the girl Rider. It circled left, and the young boy slowly countered. Itsuki tightened his grip on *Onikira* and looked down at the blade. "You ready, my friend?" he whispered to the sword. He moved quickly at the injured creature. The beast's scream was deafening, but ended shortly after it had started. With one stab, he had quieted the aringi. He moved towards the fallen Rider with caution.

His victory was short-lived. Laser blasts were unleashed from the sky at the feet of the young Augmentor to keep him away from the girl. Itsuki flipped backwards to avoid them. He landed and parried the last few shots with *Onikira*. A massive bat glided past the boy. Its hindquarters extended, plucking the female Rider from the earth.

Bartleby rushed over Itsuki's head shortly thereafter in the opposite direction. Suddenly, the bat's burnt wing now made more sense. *The dragon must have been the reason for the aringi's untimely fall. But something's wrong.* The dragon was not in control as he moved closer to the Temple. He appeared to be holding two shiny objects in his talons. Itsuki sprinted, matching the dragon's speed and trajectory.

Bartleby came crashing down towards him in the direction of the Temple. The dragon crashed into the top of the Temple, barely avoiding the room that Thomas slept in and just missing Yareli, who had gone up to the high ground.

Itsuki stopped where Bartleby had crashed. Fargus jumped off the dragon. He grabbed his head and shook it. "That fall has me a bit beside meself." He whipped out his multifunctional device and ran towards the remnants of LINC's body that Bartleby had clutched in his talons. The artif's torso was in one claw and his legs in the other. "Ya need ta let go, Bart. I need to make sure 'ee's still functioning. 'ee 'as been knocked about a bit, 'asn't 'ee?"

"Yeah, I'm fine. Fanks for askin'." Bartleby opened his claws and the top and bottom parts of LINC spilled onto the ground. The gremlin began his work immediately.

"What happened?" asked Itsuki.

" 'ee got ripped apart. Dat's what 'appened. If ya 'avn't noticed dere's a bunch uv aringi up dere."

Malcolm landed next to him. His wings retracted into his coat as he lit a cigarette. "We are completely outnumbered," said the vampire.

"Agreed," said Wiyaloo, appearing next to Malcolm.

"The trees are holding their own, but they cannot keep up this pace," said Anson as he landed next to his brother.

"The trees will fight until they are piles of wood," said Itsuki. "But the wolfman is right. They cannot do this alone."

A large, deep horn interrupted the conversation. Itsuki turned and could see its source. It was being played by one of the lava trolls. The aringi instantly broke off their attack. He looked down on the battlefield, and the trolls began to retreat as well. He moved to the edge of the Temple stairs. Itsuki gave the order for the trees to cease their attack, and the wooded army backed down and stood at attention. The lava trolls stood guard directly across from the trees. The Temple was silent. Another horn blast resounded through the Augmentor. He began to see movement.

Two trolls came forward and began walking towards the Temple. Between them rode a small imp on a boar, carrying a flag of some sort. Itsuki directed his attention to the imp and his flag, and then he recognized it. *It can't be.* It was a flag of truce. The companions exchanged confused looks.

"We need to stall so Thomas's augmentation can be completed. Is that correct, Itsuki?" asked Anson.

"That is correct."

"Then we need to hear what they have to say, and take as long as possible doing it. Everything hinges on this."

45
ultimatum

Corbin's boar waddled much like the imp. He was sandwiched between two of the lava troll guards. The imp bounced on the small beast as he held up a white flag. He was about to deliver a message to the other army and looked terrified. Marcus was gliding down to meet them. He was the Captain and needed to be there for such things, but his thoughts dwelled on Evangeline. He had left her in good hands—Farod was a capable healer—but she was severely injured. She had broken her left leg on impact, and the dragon had crushed several of her ribs. She was also severely burned. Teros touched down on the ground, and Marcus disembarked. "Hello, Corbin," said the Captain.

" 'ello, Cap'n," said the imp, who had settled into the middle of the still battlefield beside the two trolls. Marcus recognized them immediately as the two that normally guarded the main hall of Grimm Tower. "I guess we wait."

"Yes, Corbin, that's precisely what we do." The two trolls began talking to each other like no one else was there.

"So, what are we doin' again?" asked Gibgot.

"I swear you never listen, do you?" said Fronik. "You 'av to be duh dumbest lava troll I 'av ever 'ad duh displeasure to serve wif."

"Well I was right busy, wasn't I? I 'ad like five uv dose bleedin' tree folk trying to tear me apart." Gibgot looked over at Marcus and smiled confidently.

"Dat's not what I saw. You were fighting what looked like a stationary sapling." Fronik cocked his stone brow.

"You know I 'av a slight astigmatism in my left eye, and 'ow dare you question my warrior-like instinct in front of 'im." He pointed his thumb at Marcus. The Captain might have grinned on a different day, but not now—not while he did not know her fate.

"It's 'ard to question something dat doesn't exist, now isn't it?"

"Well, Mr. Know-it-all, 'ow do you suppose I got chosen for such an important and prestigious mission as dis one?"

"You mean duh mission you 'av no clue about? The one you can't even remember?"

"Dat's duh one."

"We were duh two lava trolls standing duh closest to duh Commander." Gibgot looked stunned for a second but recovered quickly.

"You sayin' proximity is duh only basis for our inclusion in dis mission?"

"Dat's exactly what I'm sayin', ya half-witted poor excuse for a boulder."

"Well you say proximity, and I say fate," remarked Gibgot. Marcus looked across the battlefield trying to drown out the ramblings of the two trolls. All his thoughts were on Evangeline. "Fate has frusted us into duh spotlight to carry out dis important and monumental mission for General Arkmalis." He paused. "I intend to do whatever I can to make sure it goes off wiffout so much as a 'itch."

"Dat's brilliant, Gibgot. The only fing standing between the General and total annihilation is you." He scratched his chin as pebbles fell to the ground. "If only you knew what dis mission entailed. I guess fate 'as yet to 'elp you wif dat one. I swear you are barkin', mate."

"If I'm so crazy . . . den why was I chosen for dis mission?"

"Oh, 'ere we go again."

"Enough, you two!" commanded the Captain. "I can't hear

myself think. Gibgot, we are here to negotiate the surrender of Thomas Scargen."

" 'ee knows my name," the troll said partially under his breath. "Oh . . . so I was chosen to deliver the terms of surrender?" asked Gibgot. Fronik slammed his palm onto his face.

"That is actually my job as official speaker for duh General," said Corbin. "You two are 'ere to look scary."

"Dat doesn't seem to be a good utilization of my particular skill set," said Gibgot. "Lookin' scary doesn't take much skill, does it?"

"Not for you, it doesn't," laughed Fronik.

"Hey . . ." said Gibgot.

"Corbin will give the terms. I will assess the situation, and yes, you two are here for . . . intimidation." Marcus turned away and once again looked across the battlefield. This time he saw three people walking towards them through the fog. Two of them looked identical—save for a few articles of clothing and complexion. He knew right away who they were. *The immortals.* Anson and Malcolm Warwick were approaching. Between them walked an Asian boy. He had seen the boy when he rescued Evangeline. His skills were impressive. He could not sense much from the immortals, but he could sense wisdom in the boy. He was older than he looked.

A new shape lumbered through the fog. It was the dragon. Anger boiled inside Marcus. Bartleby had been Evangeline's attacker. *I need to control myself.*

They reached the midpoint of the field and stood twenty feet across from Marcus and the rest. He could now see more differences between the twins and how young the boy really was, but where was Scargen? Malcolm Warwick spoke first. "You guys surrenderin' so soon?"

"What are your terms?" asked Anson.

"I guess there is no need for introductions, Anson Warwick. Let us get to the point."

"Where words are scarce, they are seldom spent in vain," responded Anson.

"Shakespeare—I do not make enough time to read his words." Marcus looked over at Anson. "We will give the terms, but first one question. Where is the boy?"

"I am afraid that is one question you will never know the answer to, Captain Slade," said the young boy. "What are your terms?"

"Who is this boy?" asked Marcus.

"That, too, is none of your concern. Let's hear what you have to offer." Anson stepped closer. Bartleby paced behind his comrades.

"Corbin, come forward and read the terms." The imp marched forward and stuck the flag into the ground. Hitting a few buttons on his wristcom, a holographic screen appeared in front of him. The screen was covered with words. The imp began to read aloud.

"The great General Arkmalis—"

"Dat son uvva bitch is 'ere?" snarled the dragon.

"You must control yourself, Bartleby." Anson turned to look at the dragon. "This is neither the time nor the place."

"The great General Arkmalis deems your chances of survival minimal, but being the merciful man that he is, he is willing to give you a chance to end this now," said Corbin.

"Am I supposed to take dat fing seriously?" asked Malcolm. The imp scowled at the vampire.

"Continue, Corbin," commanded Marcus.

"Yes, Captain. Where was I? Oh yes . . . the terms of surrender are as follows. Firstly, the great General demands that you hand over the Scargen boy, or the General himself will destroy everyone here. If you comply, your lives will be spared."

"Well dat's not gonna 'appen—not while I still draw bref," quipped Bartleby. Marcus thought for a second of slaying the dragon, but decided that this was not the time.

"Bartleby, if you cannot control yourself, then you need to go back to the Temple," said Anson. The dragon lowered his head. "Is there anything else?"

"Secondly, if you do not intend to surrender the boy, there is one alternative. You are to choose a combatant to face the General man-to-man."

"And what are the rules for this duel?" asked Anson.

Corbin continued reading without acknowledging the question. "The rules for combat are as follows. There can be no interference by others during the battle. General Grayden Arkmalis will battle your chosen warrior." Marcus watched the twins exchange glances. "The two combatants will face each other"—Corbin looked up from the text to gauge his audience's response as he continued—"to the death."

Marcus did not know of this stipulation, and he felt confounded by Arkmalis's arrogance. *Why not just take the boy by force?* thought Marcus. *The General's confidence will be his undoing.*

"If a combatant is defeated, and no one will face the remaining combatant, that side is deemed the loser. These are the terms." The hologram disappeared into the imp's wristcom.

"How long do we have to decide? We need some time to discuss."

"Well, by saying that, it is obvious that you intend to fight," noted Marcus. "Then we will give you five minutes to deliberate and pick your combatant." Signaling for his aringi, he vanished in a mass of wings and flew off toward the General. He soared to the ridge where Arkmalis was waiting for him. Marcus dismounted and made his way to the General.

"General," said the Captain as he kneeled down.

"Get up, Marcus. What news do you bring me?"

"They do not intend to surrender Scargen."

"Then I guess they will challenge me. When does the duel begin?"

"Well, they need some time, General. I gave them five minutes."

"They're stalling, Marcus. Where is the boy? We are getting nowhere with these tactics. I will enter the fray and speed up their decision."

"They will choose the most experienced, the most powerful."

"Do we have any idea which one that is?"

"Anson Warwick will come," said Marcus with certainty.

"The werewolf? An immortal."

"Yes, General, but everyone has a weakness, even immortals." Marcus's look was reassuring. "I have such a weapon." Marcus reached behind his back and produced a blade. "Primitive, but lethal when used correctly." The Captain held in his hand a small dagger. "It is pure silver. It is the only thing that will kill such a monster." The hilt was carved from bone. The polished silver of the blade threw light across the General's face as Marcus turned the weapon.

The General snatched the dagger out of Marcus's hands and placed it in his belt. "Of course I know silver kills werewolves."

"Your attack must be precise. It must pierce the heart if you mean to slay him. Draw the beast close and then strike."

"Come now, Marcus. How hard can it be to kill a wolf?" Arkmalis mounted the gorgol. "Start sending your Riders back through the teleportal. Their services are no longer required. I will take care of these pests. It ends now," said the General as he kicked the sides of the gorgol. The monstrous creature ran like a blur into battle.

Captain Slade wasted no time. He flew to where they had taken Evangeline. He ran over to Farod. The healer was attending to the Second. She was completely unconscious, but at least she was breathing. Jurdik and Taunt had made their way over to check on Evangeline as well. Marcus relayed the General's order. "Tell the Newts to get the aringi ready for departure," said the Captain to one of the younger Riders. The young man turned and ran off in the direction of where the Newts where attending to the aringi.

"That dragon must be stopped. Why are we just sitting back and watching this?" asked Farod as he attended to Evangeline.

"They are our orders," answered Marcus. "I don't like this any more than you do."

"I almost had that vamp. One more minute and I would've had him," said Jurdik as he nursed a slight flesh wound. "Stupid blood-suckin' freak's lucky I ran out of darts."

"Don't blame the tech," said Taunt. "There's only so much you can fit into the T27s." A noise came from the direction of the fallen Rider. Everyone turned to witness Evangeline beginning to wake.

"Is-is . . . Pria . . . all right?" asked the Second as she looked up at Marcus. He did not know what to say. She was barely coherent, but the last thing he wanted to do was upset her.

"She is . . . fine, Eva. Get some rest." She smiled and slipped back into unconsciousness.

"Why did you lie to her?" asked Jurdik.

"She doesn't need to deal with that right now." Marcus felt a twinge of guilt but focused on what needed to be done. "I want you to begin the retreat, Taunt, and, Farod, make sure she is safe." Farod nodded.

"What if he loses?" asked Taunt.

"I will stay here and make sure the trolls and the imp get out of here if Arkmalis is to fail," said the Captain.

"Why are you staying?" asked Farod. "You owe him nothing."

"I have a score to settle for Evangeline. My orders were to get my Riders out of here, and I'm doing that." Anger replaced the sadness within him. "Now get going, Farod. That is an order."

"Yes, Captain." The bats descended on their Riders, and they began to fly away. Farod's aringi grabbed Evangeline. Marcus was pleased. His general was being hasty, but it meant that Evangeline had a chance. Marcus and his aringi flew over the battlefield, but this time as observers.

The General entered the battlefield on the back of his fiery mount. He trotted out to the center of the clearing and rallied the lava trolls. He stormed into the forest of warriors. The Scythe hacked and cleaved limb after limb, pruning the tree spirits. The two sides were once again engaged in combat, but this time the General's army had a distinct advantage—Arkmalis had entered the battle. Marcus's thoughts still belonged to Evangeline. *I need you to get through this, my love, and I will destroy the monster that did this to you.*

46

face-off

"'e's ridin' on duh back uv a bloody gorgol," said Malcolm as they looked down at the General.

"What is a gorgol?" asked Itsuki. He had never heard of such a creature.

"Gorgol are foul beasts of the Depths," answered Anson. "They, like my kind, are pack hunters—extremely proficient pack hunters."

" 'oo's ridin' on duh back uvva gorgol?" asked Bartleby as he glanced down at the battlefield. The dragon's face changed when his eyes answered his own question. "Arkmalis!" Bartleby darted off the Temple without any discussion.

"Bartleby, no!" cried Yareli, but it was too late. The dragon was powered by vengeance and dashed straight at the man atop the shadowy creature. Bartleby extended his talons and collided with the gorgol. Arkmalis was sent soaring. The General dug the Scythe into the ground to slow himself. Bartleby sped towards Arkmalis and landed in front of the General. The dragon unleashed a focused inferno. Arkmalis raised the Scythe and formed a shield. The fire burned around the energy shield as Bartleby moved forward, intensifying the flames. The General was forced back under the strain of the blaze. The dragon pushed harder, and Arkmalis dropped to his knee.

A single Rider approached Bartleby from above. The dragon was too fixated on the General to notice. An array of laser blasts rained down on the fire-breathing dragon. His shield deflected the first few attacks, but it failed before the third shot hit his artificial wing. Bartleby looked away from his intended target to see where this ambush had come from. Itsuki recognized the Rider immediately. It was Captain Slade. The Rider flew down close to Bartleby, who now directed his fire at the Captain. Slade dodged the flames as he glided upward.

Bartleby regained his focus and continued his fiery attack on the General, but he could not see the gorgol pounce from behind. The beast latched onto the back of the dragon and bit down. The gorgol found an unprotected spot through the dragon's armor. Bartleby roared fire and reached up to grab the gorgol. The dark beast's teeth let go of their grip and began to gnaw on the dragon's talon. Green blood spurted out of the wound. Bartleby pulled his claw free of the beast's mouth and grabbed his attacker. He lowered his head and threw the gorgol. The dark beast cried out when it hit the ground. The gorgol got to its feet and growled at Bartleby. The dark steed slinked behind its master. The dragon turned his attention to the General, but it was too late.

Arkmalis stood holding the Scythe, laughing. Bartleby leapt at the General. Arkmalis turned and slashed his weapon through the air. A wave of energy was released by the Scythe and hit the dragon before he could reach the General. Bartleby shot backwards from the explosion. The unconscious dragon flew towards the Temple's base. Captain Slade gave chase to finish what his master had started.

Itsuki motioned with *Onikira* from the top of the Temple's stairs, and the trees moved at his command. Two of the larger trees extended their branches like a net and caught the flailing dragon. Yareli jumped in front of Itsuki. "So much for saving my last arrow," she said as she let the projectile loose. A herd of wildebeests galloped at the single Rider. The Captain banked left and took off in the opposite direction.

The large trees began to walk the dragon up to the Temple. Itsuki could see that Bartleby did not look good. Green blood stained his claw, and sparks flew from his artificial wing.

"Someone has to stop that man," said Yareli.

"I will go and face him," said Anson with calm certainty.

"Werewolf, allow me. I have trained for this day for decades," pleaded Itsuki.

"I am the ranking Mage, and this is my duel."

"Augmentor rule number twenty-three clearly states—"

"With all due respect, Itsuki, your rules do not apply here. I know you are a capable warrior, but this is my responsibility. You may still yet need to draw your sword, but it is my duty to defend Thomas. I accept the duel."

"I will go wif you," said Malcolm.

"No," said Anson. His voice was firm. "You need to stay here in case I am not successful. Promise me you will do this. Without him . . . all will be lost. I need the one person I trust the most to ensure that everything will be fine. Besides, according to the terms, only one man is supposed to face the General."

"O-okay, Bruvver . . ."

"Yareli," Anson commanded. "I need you to establish a shield around the whole Temple when Bartleby arrives. Can you do that? I do not trust the General to keep to his word, and we need to protect Thomas."

"Y-y-yes, Anson." She looked at him. Her expression revealed her uncertainty. "Please be careful."

"Fargus, work on LINC. We may need his firepower, and see what you can do with that hotheaded dragon. We might need to make a hasty exit."

"Bruvver." Anson turned and was met by his paler counterpart. Malcolm hugged his brother tightly. "Fank you for everyfing." Anson looked at his brother with pride. He stepped to the precipice of the Temple, looking down at the destruction.

"There is a tide in the affairs of men, which, taken at the flood, leads on to fortune; omitted, all the voyage of their life is bound in shallows and in miseries. Farewell, my friends." Anson began to walk down the Temple stairs.

Malcolm turned to Fargus. "I will need to see what is happening down there."

"No worries, mate. I 'av just duh fing." Fargus lifted up his hand-held device, and three recon orbs appeared from the top of the contraption. They floated down behind Anson as the werewolf began to quicken his gait. A holographic image of the action appeared in front of Malcolm. Every so often, the camera angle would change. Anson had already reached the base of the Temple.

"Now dat's well done, gremlin," said the vampire.

"It's about time someone recognized my talents."

Anson charged the battlefield. He leapt and transformed into his wolf state before landing on one of the lava trolls. He blasted a hole through the unsuspecting monster's back, making quick work of the beast. The lifeless rock crashed to the ground. The wolf raced across the field dismembering or incinerating any troll that stood between him and Arkmalis. He reached the General and slowed his pace to a walk.

"Call off your troops." Anson's eyes squinted, and his teeth clenched. "I will fight you." A slight growling sound reverberated after the words.

"Stand down," commanded the General as he held his fist up. The lava trolls began backing off and settled to a position behind their General. The stone goliaths all kneeled down with their weapons holding them up. A row of smoldering sculptures backed the Necromancer. The General jumped off of his mount, and the gorgol ran off as instructed. The tree samurai ceased their attack and withdrew back to the base of the Temple. They stood just outside the shield that Yareli had established. Their blossoms floated down to the battlefield.

The two men stared intently at one another. Arkmalis was still. Anson was crouched as his body slowly moved up and down with each breath.

"Anson Warwick, I presume? I don't believe we've ever had the pleasure." The snarling werewolf changed back into a man. He straightened himself up and cleared his throat. His pants were the only part of his clothing that held on to his athletic body.

"I don't believe we have."

"I am Grayden Arkmalis, First Necromancer and General of the Grimm Legions."

"I am Anson Warwick, as you know, Mage Knight of the Council of Mages." An awkward silence lingered.

"I shall enjoy killing you, wolf."

"I did not know so full a voice issue from so empty a heart. But the saying is true: 'the empty vessel makes the greatest sound.'"

"You *dare* mock me?"

"I do not mock you, General. I pity you." The General's face twisted in disgust.

"Pity this," said Arkmalis as he spun and swirled the Scythe towards the direction of Anson. The werewolf backflipped over the weapon's attack. He landed already transformed, and growled at the General. "Down, boy," teased Arkmalis.

Anson was crouched in an offensive stance. His claws were extended. He pulled back his right paw and quickly pushed forward. An orange sphere flew from his extended hand.

The energy blast was easily batted away by the General's bony weapon. He spun and countered with a whirl of the Scythe. A shockwave shot from the weapon. The werewolf leapt over the blast and barreled at Arkmalis. He snarled as his right paw struck out at the General's face. Arkmalis moved his head to avoid the beast's strike. Before the General could collect himself, Anson slashed upward with his left paw. This blow caught Arkmalis across his face. The General yelled with anger. The mask had blocked most of the blow, but his claw had met skin near the General's chin. He reeled backward as blood spurted from the three streaks embedded in the General's face. He covered the wound with his hand. The werewolf slowly paced back and forth in front of the General. He growled. "That's better. Your face could use some character. That mask is rather boring."

"You will die, wolf." Arkmalis cut through the air with the Scythe. The blast caught Anson in his left arm, and he spun round. A second blast hit him square in the hunched back. The werewolf rolled forward, avoiding the third attack. Anson quickly lunged to his left and twisted back in the direction of the General. The werewolf zigzagged back at the source of the blasts, dodging the General's furious assault. He charged Arkmalis again. The back of the General's hand connected with Anson's elongated jaw. The wolf yelped as he flew to the side.

Anson planted his paws and skidded to a halt. Blood trickled from his lips. The fur stood up on his back as he rapidly breathed in and out. His body bounced rhythmically. His voice rumbled as he showed his teeth and threw his palms outward. Streams of orange flames shot out at the General. Arkmalis had little time to react, but that was all he needed. He sped directly at the wolf and sliced at Anson with the Scythe. Anson dodged and ripped at the General. The two began to exchange blows at a confusing pace. The holographic images of them began to blur. Itsuki could not follow their actions. The blurring moved back and forth as flashes of energy sporadically escaped from the indistinct mass of man and wolf, but neither opponent seemed to be getting the upper hand. The distorted image separated back into two forms. Arkmalis stood fifteen feet away from Anson. He was bloodied, and his neat and tidy uniform was torn in several places. He breathed heavily as he leaned on the Scythe.

The werewolf, unlike Arkmalis, was not exhausted. He had clearly pressed his advantage. He moved his paws back, and magic poured forth in the direction of the slumping General. The blast connected with his target and pulled Arkmalis away from his weapon. He soared across the field and landed in a sitting position. His head dropped. Itsuki felt relief. The battle was over. Anson had bested their general. *The painting was wrong*, thought Itsuki. Thomas would be safe. The werewolf had the General down. He moved swiftly and advanced to finish Arkmalis. He lunged at the General.

The massive man caught the werewolf in midair. Arkmalis had somehow managed to stand. Anson's furry chest was met with an upward stabbing motion. Anson gurgled. The wolf collapsed to his knees.

"Anson!" screamed Malcolm. The end of the blade was sticking from his chest. Itsuki stared in disbelief.

"What have you done?" asked Anson.

"I believe I have killed you, Warwick." The victorious general smirked. "The blade is made of pure silver. That is your weakness, is it not?" asked Arkmalis as he reached down and grabbed the werewolf's fur. "Thanks for playing, wolf." Arkmalis picked up the bleeding beast and threw him. The Scythe flew back into his hand as Arkmalis laughed aloud.

47

something found

Thomas opened his eyes and stared straight up to an unfamiliar ceiling. He immediately sat up and looked around his new environment. The walls and ceiling were made of rock. The color of the rock seemed familiar to Thomas. Markings similar to the one on the Taitokura adorned their surfaces. *It looks just like the Gauntlet.* He looked down to compare the two, but something was wrong. He was looking at his naked arm. The Gauntlet was missing.

The boy stood and began to inspect the room he was in. His eyes darted all around the sparsely decorated space. He saw nothing except the bench he had just awoke on and an arched doorway at the far end of the room. Thomas's mind flooded with questions. *What happened? Where is the Gauntlet? Where am I? Where is everyone? Are they all right?*

Two figures appeared in the doorway, postponing Thomas's panic attack. Thomas could tell that they were both male, and they were whispering. The man on the right was dressed in all white, and an aura of the same color surrounded him. He was obviously the elder of the two, and his power was great. He finished what he had to say, and the other man bowed to him. The mysterious stranger in white continued walking. The other man turned to Thomas.

He was a young black man wrapped in robes similar to those common in Sirati. This seemed odd to the boy. The man had an athletic build and could not have been over the age of twenty-five. He confidently moved towards the boy. When he saw the dark man's face, it looked strangely recognizable. "Hello, Thomas."

"Do I . . . know you? You seem . . . kinda familiar."

The man extended his hand. "My friends call me Ziza."

"What?" Thomas was confused. This man had no signs of the deformity that the man he knew was currently saddled with. He had no walking staff, and his hair was black and full, but he recognized the man he knew in this man's eyes. *Have I traveled back in time?* he thought, but before he could fully consider the possibility, the man spoke once more.

"You have not traveled through time." The boy looked at the young Ziza.

"Then why do you look so young?"

"This is how I looked when I carried the Burden."

"The Burden?" asked the boy.

"The Gauntlet, Thomas. This is how old I was when I last wielded the Burden."

"How is that possible?"

"You are inside the Gauntlet." The words took a few seconds to register in Thomas's brain. It seemed like an impossibility, but what did he know about augmentation?

"What am I doing inside the damn thing?" asked the boy. "I was sort of in the middle of something."

"The stone has begun to awaken. It takes time for the stone to reestablish its connection with the Gauntlet, during which time the Gauntlet is powerless—hence the unplanned nap. I believe the Gauntlet also wants to introduce us to you."

"Define *us.*"

"All the Gauntlet Bearers," said the robed figure.

"That's who that other guy was? One of the other Bearers?"

"Yes, you could say that." Ziza turned in the direction the man in white had traveled. "We are all here to help you." He turned back.

"How can you help me?"

"We have the collective knowledge of generations of Bearers. Any questions you have we can answer. Our experiences are now yours. Everyone who has ever wielded the Gauntlet, alive or dead, is in here. They are the way they were when they wore the Gauntlet as well. There is a wealth of untapped knowledge at your fingertips, and all you need to do is ask." Thomas thought about the possibilities.

"This sounds amazing and all, but I don't really have time for this right now, Ziza. My friends are fighting for their lives, and they need my help." He was growing impatient and felt odd without the massive rock dangling from his right arm. It had been only minutes, but he missed the weight of the glove.

"Your friends, for the time being, will have to make due without you. The Gauntlet will not reactivate until it is ready. At that time you will awaken and the augmentation will be complete." Ziza turned to walk out of the room and waved for Thomas to follow. The boy ran to catch up with the young Ziza. He crossed the threshold of the room he had appeared in and entered the massive hall.

He looked up at the high, arched ceilings with his mouth open. The sight was stunning and otherworldly. The hall was also made of the same material as the Gauntlet. When he finally looked down to see where they were walking, he noticed there were hundreds of people moving this way and that, in and out of other halls and doorways. They were all dressed from different time periods and places which at first seemed odd, but the more he thought about it, the more it made sense to him. The anachronistic group stopped what they were doing when Thomas approached. They all stared at him.

"What are they looking at?" asked the boy as the two men walked down the center of the vast angelic hall.

"You are the new guy, Thomas. They are naturally curious."

"Well tell them to back off. They're bugging me out," whispered Thomas as they walked passed. "Are you sure there's no way to speed up this process?"

"I'm afraid not, Thomas. It would be like trying to speed up a sunrise or the rotation of the Earth. It happens at its own speed."

"Approximately how long we talking about?"

"It's not an exact science."

"Well, I'm no good to my friends if they are dead when I get back." They reached the other end of the hall. On the ground were several dark circles surrounded by more of the symbols that were on the stone. Ziza stepped on one of them, and it glowed. Thomas was hesitant, but he too stepped on one of the circles. The two men shot straight up into darkness. Thomas was now looking down on the onlookers.

"You remind me of myself." The man sniggered. "All adrenalin, no brain cells."

"What's that supposed to mean?"

"You rush into things without any preparation. Sometimes it's better to wait, examine, and then act, Thomas. I am pretty sure my older self has stressed this to you. Besides, there's someone you need to meet." Something about the way he said this last line made the boy believe him.

"Is that where you're taking me?"

"Precisely."

The glowing circle stopped, and Ziza and Thomas exited. They were in a narrower hallway now, but just as tall. At the end of the hallway was a giant set of doors. The same emblem from the palm of the Gauntlet was embedded on these doors as well. Thomas looked at his hand, forgetting again that he was not wearing the Gauntlet. The boy's curiosity got the best of him. "What's up with that symbol?" Thomas pointed at the door.

"That is the *Glophitis*," answered Ziza. This confused Thomas even more.

"What's a glow-fight-us?"

"It's one of the power runes from the Ancient language."

"What's it mean?"

"That's a good question, Thomas. There are a few ways to decipher it, but the simplest translation would be *gauntlet*."

"I probably should have guessed that, all things considered." The two exchanged a laugh as they walked towards the mysterious entry. The doors swung open. The boy's excitement was coupled with fear of what lay beyond. They entered the room.

Books were in shelves that stretched to the ceiling. It reminded Thomas of Maktaba, but this place was more ethereal. There was no Flora here, but her expertise was not needed. The books were floating back and forth, sorting themselves. There was a desk at the other side of the room, and behind it stood a hooded figure. The muted lighting made it hard for Thomas to see this person.

"Ziza, who's tha—" His words were cut short as the hooded figure moved from behind the desk.

Thomas could discern that the person was a female almost immediately, but little else of the woman's identity was obvious. She carried herself with elegance and grace—a large book resting in her hands. "Hello, Thomas Scargen." Her voice was quiet but strong and somehow familiar.

"Who are you?" asked the boy. He could not place the voice, but something told him he had definitely heard it before. He needed to know who this woman was.

"I am the last Bearer of the Gauntlet." Her form was silhouetted from the intense light that bled around her. He could see that she had let go of the book she had been reading. It floated out of her opened fingers and slowly levitated to its home in the shelves.

"Mary?"

"Yes, Thomas."

"I can't believe it's you. I've heard all about you. What you did was . . . amazing . . . so incredibly . . . narsh." He stared in awe and said the first thing that popped in his head. "You must be ridiculously powerful."

"I suppose I was when I carried the Burden." Something about this woman's voice was assuring to Thomas. He found safety in her tone. She moved closer to the boy. "There's something you need to see."

"What is it, Mary? I can call you Mary, right?"

She moved even closer. "Yes, Thomas, you can call me Mary . . . but . . ." She reached over and pulled down her hood.

Thomas looked at her uncovered face and looked away, but then quickly back again. He could now see her face, and he was entirely bewildered. *It's impossible . . .*

"I was hoping . . . you might call me something else," finished Mary.

He could not be absolutely sure, but he was fairly certain of the woman's identity. *It can't be . . . She can't be . . .*

"Mom?" asked the boy.

"Yes, Thomas," answered the young woman. Tears welled up in Merelda Scargen's eyes as she looked at her son for the first time in fifteen years. "We have a lot to discuss in a short amount of time."

48

the blood of a silva

Malcolm sprinted past Itsuki, slicing through the silent air. He met his brother's floundering body with open arms. The impact stopped the wolfman abruptly. Malcolm had caught Anson. He turned to fly back to the Temple, back to the security of the shield that Yareli still maintained.

The vampire's feet touched ground and promptly started to run. He lowered the unmoving, bleeding body of his twin. "You're gonna be fine, Anson. Your body will 'eal dis wound as soon as I pull out duh blade." Malcolm went to grab the shaft, but Anson's shaking hand stopped him.

"Mustn't remove . . . it's made of—" The werewolf coughed up blood. "It's made of pure . . . s-s-s-silver." Sorrow filled Malcolm's eyes. Anson looked into the sorrow. "Death . . . is a fearful thing." The vampire let go of the knife.

"We don't 'av a lot of time den, do we? Wiyaloo, see if you can't 'elp stop some of dis bleeding." Malcolm waved at the fox. Itsuki could not help but think how difficult this had to be for the vampire—not only because his brother was dying before his eyes, but he was covered in his blood as well.

Wiyaloo swept over behind the werewolf. He cupped his paws around his head. The spirit ghost began to glow white. "The injury is severe," said Wiyaloo. "I am not sure I can be of assistance."

"It's worse den I fought. I 'av to change it before it spreads."

"Change it?" questioned Yareli.

"I 'av to change the silver into somefing else, don't I? Quite frankly, anyfing else before too much of it gets in 'is bloodstream."

"Is that even possible?" questioned Yareli.

"I've turned plenty of uvver metals into silver and gold, but reversin' dat process, well I'm not sure it's ever been done before."

"If anyone can . . . you . . . can . . . Malcolm." With those words, Anson fell unconscious. His furry body slowly morphed into a human again. His human form was a sickly blue color.

A look of horror washed across the vampire as the reality of the situation settled on his face. Malcolm shot up and began looking around. "I need candles."

"I'll be right back," said Itsuki as he ran into the hall and into his inner chamber. He grabbed as many of the candles as he could. The young boy rushed back outside. He returned in time to see Malcolm drawing a circle on the ground using the blood that was pouring from his brother's wound. The vampire continued to draw a second circle inside the first. He then sketched a series of lines running to several crudely drawn symbols.

"Dat should do it," said Malcolm. The markings were foreign to Itsuki, but several of them reminded him of the symbols on the stone. " 'ere." Malcolm took the candles out of Itsuki's arms. He placed several candles on the ends of the lines he had just created. Candles of varying heights now encircled the blood ring. Malcolm grabbed his brother and brought him into the center of the circle. He put his body on the ground and stood in front of Anson. He widened his stance and then closed his eyes. The candles ignited, their flames wriggling and dancing in the wind. The vampire drew his hands together. The sound of the clap ignited the blood circle, and the force extinguished the candles. Smoke slithered up into the sky. The crimson lines now glowed white. The stench of burning metal filled Itsuki's nostrils. "I 'ope dis works," said Malcolm as he placed both of his hands on the hilt of the dagger. The weapon began glowing the same white that the circle was burning. Anson's body shook as Malcolm firmly held the knife. The glow intensified as Anson's body convulsed. The werewolf's entire body was enveloped by the iridescent illumination. The radiant light imploded into the short sword. The vampire looked down at the blade and yelled, "*Argentum mutatio plumbum!*" These words echoed in Itsuki's ears. The white light escaped in a huge, blinding flash.

When Itsuki's eyes refocused, he could see Malcolm readjusting his fingers. After a quick inspection he yanked the blade from Anson's rib cage. Anson sucked in life. Malcolm stared down at the blade that was now dull gray. From what Itsuki could tell, the vampire had done it. The dagger appeared to be made entirely of lead.

Blood still exited the wound, and it was not sealing. The werewolf lay down into his brother's arms. Malcolm lifted him up and moved him out of the circle. He placed him down, leaning up against the Temple. "Wiyaloo, 'elp me." The spirit appeared next to the two brothers.

"Is this a dagger I see before me?" asked Anson with a smirk.

"Please, Bruvver, conserve your energy." The concerned eyes of a sibling stared back at the werewolf. "Da wound isn't 'ealing."

"You did it, Malcolm . . ." Anson remarked as he coughed up blood. "You did what you could." The wolfman again choked. "I just want you to know that I'm so very proud of you." The vampire had begun to cry. Black tears streamed down Malcolm's face.

"Please, Anson." Malcolm held his hands over the wound trying to hinder the persistent flow.

"It's okay, Malcolm. I've had more time than most. I'm ready to move on," said Anson, accepting his fate. His eyes fluttered and nearly closed as he coughed blood once more. "This fell sergeant, death, is strict in his arrest." The wolfman's eyes slowly shut and did not open back up. They all looked down in silence. Malcolm interrupted the quiet.

"Damn it, Anson! I 'avn't given up on you yet, so don't give up on us. We have to get this wound closed. Is it possible, Wiyaloo?"

"I do not know," said Wiyaloo. His paw glowed white as it

surveyed the body. "His spirit is holding on, but just barely." The wolf remained still as the fox began to chant.

"Fargus, do you 'av any uv dat magic drink left?" asked Malcolm desperately.

"Sorry, mate . . . I used all uv it back at that bleeedin' 'ive," said Fargus. Malcolm turned back to his dying brother. Bartleby sat with his head lowered, nursing his mangled claw.

LINC was in two parts under the gremlin, malfunctioning. "D-d-d-dr—zzz—n-en-en." The artif was trying to speak, but what came out was a jumble of zaps and stutters. "D-d-dr-ah-ah-g-n-n." Malcolm spun to hear what the artif was trying to say. Bartleby even lifted his head.

"What's duh Tin Man whingin' on about?" asked the vampire.

"I don't know what 'ee's sayin'. 'is bloody circuits are completely fried." Fargus punched at the holographic keyboard.

"D-d-draaaaag-g-g-gon b-b-blood is—zzz—b-beeeelieved to have cer-r-rtain magical qualities. It is s-s-s-said . . . that theeee—zzz—q-q-qualities can range from medicinal propert-t-ties to super huuuman abilities—zzz—most-t-t d-dd-dragon scholars b-b-believe this to be solely a myth—zz." LINC's head dropped again. Sparks flew from his midsection.

"What did 'ee say?"

"Well I fink 'ee was goin on about dragon's blood 'avin magical properties an that," answered Fargus.

"Bartleby, is dat true?" asked Malcolm.

"I 'av 'erd as much, but don't know from experience. What are you finkin'?"

"I'm finkin' your magical blood might 'elp Anson." Bartleby shrugged his shoulders.

"I'll see what I can do." The beleaguered dragon stood up on his three good talons. He held the wounded claw off the ground and hobbled over to Anson. The werewolf was covered in blood as Wiyaloo tried to heal the gash in his chest. Bartleby stopped beside Malcolm. "'ere goes nuffin'." He raised his talon above Anson. A bead of emerald dragon blood rolled down his pointing finger. It followed his curved claw and leapt from it. The single drop fell right into the gaping hole located on Anson's chest. Silent anticipation filled the air.

Nothing happened.

Itsuki began to get nervous. He knew he would have to act soon or the augment would be jeopardized.

"Sorry, Malcolm. For a second there I fought you were on ta somefin', " said Bartleby. He lowered his arm and walked back to where he had been sulking and plopped down. Malcolm watched the dejected creature begin to wallow in his inability to help. The vampire then looked down to Anson's wound. Itsuki's eyes followed.

The blood had suddenly ceased and was replaced with a bubbling green liquid that poured out of the dagger's gash. Anson convulsed. Malcolm grabbed his brother's shoulders and looked down at the cut. Itsuki held his legs. Anson's skin reached across from both sides of the gash and began knitting itself together. He stopped shaking, and the Augmentor let go and stood up. He looked down at the werewolf. Anson's wound was healed. A white scar was the only proof that the werewolf had been mortally wounded.

"If dat 'ad been free inches to duh left, I'd be very un'appy right now," joked Malcolm.

Anson began to laugh, but quickly winced in pain. "Ow, ow, ow," said the werewolf.

Malcolm hugged his brother. "It worked. I can't believe it. It worked. I owe duh Tin Man big for dis one."

Bartleby's head lifted again. "You're welcome."

"Fank you too, my dragon friend." Anson tried to get up and then fell back down. "Rest, Bruvver."

"But someone needs to fight Arkmalis, or Thomas is doomed," said Anson. "All of us are doomed."

Itsuki knew what had to be done. He had always known it would come to this. He grabbed the hilt of his sword. "My time is now," said Itsuki as he purposefully walked past the group.

49
mother

Thomas stared at the woman who had left him and his father fifteen years ago. He had stopped believing that this moment would ever happen. *She has no right.* The boy clenched his fists. His anger was scarcely tempered by curiosity. There were so many questions, but one in particular had haunted him his entire life. He blurted it out without thinking. "Why did you leave?" This woman had abandoned him when he was only two years of age. He had no time for niceties.

"I see you have your father's bluntness."

"I'll give you two some time." Ziza began to walk out of the room.

"You don't have to leave, Ziza." His head turned towards the young Ziza, but his eyes remained on his mother. "I have nothing more to say to this woman."

"I will dismiss myself nonetheless." He walked out of the room. Mother and son stared at each other like strangers. Silent anger filled Thomas. He was attacked by emotions and could not say a word. Silence.

"The first thing you need to understand is that it was the hardest thing I've ever done, but I had to do it."

"You *had* to do it? You didn't *have* to do anything."

"I did what I did to protect you."

"And what exactly did you do?"

"I had to deal with a madman. I loved you and your father. You have to believe that, but I had to face Tollin Grimm."

"Why you? For all these years I thought you had just left us. I . . . hated you." He regretted the admission as soon as he said it.

"You have every right to feel that way. Just, please, let me try to explain."

"I'm listening."

"I started having these dreams."

"I guess that runs in the family."

"At first they were innocent enough. I would do something that seemed impossible, move things with a thought, create balls of energy from my hands. It felt so real. You could imagine I was a little scared. I'd wake up covered in sweat, trying to catch my breath, screaming. It worried your father. There had been unexplained things in the past, but this was different. I dismissed it, because I didn't know what it was, and it frightened me. I wanted to tell your father, but I was terrified he'd think I was insane. How could he possibly understand?"

"You could've tried. He loved you so much."

"I suppose, but everything changed the night I had my first specific vision. I saw a man driving an aerobus full of children. The aerobus was sideswiped by a cargo transport that had run a red light. I could see the children screaming. A feeling of complete helplessness came over me. I shot up in bed. I was disoriented, and I had awakened your father—but he was getting used to it. The dream felt so real. The next day, when I was out running errands, I found myself in my dream. My nightmare was unfolding. I saw the aerobus and then shortly after the transport. They were on a collision course with each other. I moved on pure instinct. I threw my hand up and yelled and somehow stopped the oncoming cargo transport with my mind. At first I had thought the transport must have just stopped, but it soon was obvious that I still held the transport. I put it down as gently as I could and ran away. I had done something extraordinary, yet no one had seen it. I altered the lives of those children, and it was exhilarating. That moment changed everything." Thomas's anger had subsided. He was still upset with his mother, but he could not have imagined their similarities.

"I was at first ashamed of having these powers, but that soon faded. I began to do some research, and I learned there were others like me . . . like us." The boy was caught off guard by this statement. "I was overwhelmed by this need to act, and then it happened. I started to see what I had to do. I saw my future and knew I needed to take action. I snuck into your room and read you one last story. *The Lost Dragon* was your favorite."

"I'm still a sucker for a good dragon story," said Thomas as he smiled. "It's just . . . now I'm *in* one." She returned his smile. It faded quickly from her face.

"I left when you fell asleep. My search for the man called Ziza Bebami started the next day. I had seen him in several of my dreams, and I knew he was the only one that could help me."

"But how could you leave us?"

"The Gauntlet called to me. It needed me . . . I needed it. There was no one else to fight him. I had a responsibility to the world. I couldn't just go back to being a housewife."

"But I was two years old. *I* needed you. *I* needed a mother, and Dad needed a wife. You had a responsibility to *us*."

"I'm sorry, Thomas, but the world needed me more. I loved you with all my heart, but I couldn't sit back and watch Grimm destroy this beautiful world—not before my son had a chance to see it." Thomas thought about how greedy he had sounded. She had left to save the world. "I left everything behind and told no one my real name. I wanted to make sure you were protected. If I had stayed, they would have eventually come for us. I did what I did for you, my son." This reality washed over Thomas. She did not leave because she hated his father and him. She left because she loved them. He began to understand what she had done. He was now doing the same thing she had. He had begun this journey to save his dad, but he now began to realize the responsibility that came with his powers reached far beyond his father. "I loved you and your father, and that's why I trained. The things Grimm did were unspeakable, and the things I could see him doing in the future were far worse. I had to stop him. I was not going to let my son grow up in a wasteland controlled by a madman." Thomas's anger had been extinguished. He was proud of his mother. She did what no one else could and sacrificed herself for them. There was another awkward silence, and then Thomas spoke, choosing his words carefully.

"I'm sorry about saying I hated you earlier." His eyes met his mothers. "You just have to understand, this is all new to me. I thought you had run out on us. I thought it was my fault, and Dad never talks about it because it makes him sad." She looked at him with sadness. "You can't expect me to just be all right with this right away. I do appreciate what you've done, and I—I love you . . . Mom. I'm just going to need some time." That was one of the hardest things he had ever said. She smiled and moved in to hug her son for the first time in fifteen years.

"I knew that one day I would see you again, and I had a pretty good idea that you would be special. I just never realized how special." She smiled at her son, and he felt her warmth. The two embraced. The hug had said more than the entirety of their conversation.

She let go and backed away from the boy. Tears met the curve in her smile. "We need to get you back." She wiped away the dampness with her finger. "Your friends need you. You should know that the power of this stone can take some time to kick in, and it will activate when you least expect it. Just don't give up, and the Gauntlet will not fail you. If you need anything, remember, the door is always open. Good luck, Thomas. He began to feel his body being torn away.

"Who needs luck? Kickin' butt apparently runs in the family. If you haven't been keeping score, I'm the son of the woman who destroyed Tollin Grimm."

"Destroyed Grimm?" Merelda Scargen looked at him as if he were telling a lie. "I did—" Her words were abruptly cut off, and Thomas was pulled backward and upward away from his mother.

Back to the Temple . . .

Back to his friends . . .

Back to the battle.

50
destiny

He strode past all of them and walked through the shield that Yareli was maintaining. She was the only one to notice. Malcolm and Wiyaloo were attending to Anson, and Fargus was attempting to repair LINC. "You shouldn't do this," said Yareli. "There has to be another way."

"This is my destiny." The young Augmentor focused on her eyes. "I need you to stay here in case I fail. Nothing can interfere with Thomas while he's in augmentation—nothing."

"I understand." She held the shield despite the volley of energy attacks from an impatient Arkmalis. "I'm sorry for ever doubting you. You have fought well and honor the Spirit." She bowed as much as she could while upholding the defenses. He returned the gesture and turned towards Arkmalis.

"You were just concerned for him. I understood." He looked at Yareli and drew his sword. "I know you will protect him if I cannot. This shield will not falter. The spirits are behind you." He knew she would do everything in her power to keep Thomas safe. He turned to leave, but his departure was interrupted.

"Wait, Itsuki . . ." said his mother as she floated towards her son—blue wisps behind her. "You do not have to do this. You are too young to just throw your life away." The ghost cried and grabbed at the Augmentor's robes. The flames hung in the air next to her. "I need you to stay here where it is safe."

"I love you, *Okaasan*, but this is something I must do. Rule number four. You know my job is more than just preparing the stone." She looked up at him, and he felt guilty. He had to say something to make her feel better. "I promise you that I will be all right." He gently lifted his mother's hand from his robe and bowed. "I must go now."

Itsuki charged down the Temple stairs, his sword extended straight behind him as he ran with great speed. The wisps raced behind him, trying desperately to catch up with him as Itsuki moved closer to his destiny. They shortly gave up their chase and vanished.

Itsuki leapt into the air forty feet away from the General. He cut through the air like the sword he wielded. *Onikira* crunched down on the bone of the Scythe, but it did not break. The General could not have seen him coming, but somehow he had managed to lift his weapon to deflect the blow. Arkmalis pushed with his free hand and an invisible force threw the young boy backward. He landed on his feet, sword out to his right. Itsuki looked up at the masked man.

"Well, well, well. What do we have here?" asked the General. "The wolfman is dead, so they send a child to fight me."

"I am no ordinary child, Arkmalis." The boy's nose clenched, and he turned his head. "You reek of demon."

"You smell my mask, little one. I killed a High Demon and took his mask for a trophy, but that was a long time ago."

"You are the boy from the painting."

"What painting?" asked the confused General.

"So it appears we have something in common," said Itsuki. "I too have defeated a High Demon, but I kept no such trophy. Its foul energy still infests you."

"That's impossible. There was nothing left of that monster."

"It is not left up for debate. You have become that which you killed."

"Who are you?"

"I am Itsuki Katsuo. I am Shogun, and First Augmentor of the Temple of Yokan, wielder of *Onikira*, the Demon Killer. I have been preparing my entire life for this moment. Defend yourself, demon spawn."

The General was silent for a few seconds. Wind whistled across the battlefield. Arkmalis laughed aloud. "From the looks of you, child, you haven't been preparing long enough." He grinned at the boy like he was nothing.

Onikira sliced through the air, and an energy blast shot in the direction of Arkmalis. The young boy raced behind it, sword extended. The General hacked at the energy strand with his blade, and it dissolved. The boy ran up the extended Scythe, and Itsuki's foot connected with the General's mouth. His head snapped to the right as he stumbled backward. Itsuki followed up with a second energy wave from *Onikira*'s blade before he reached the ground.

This time the blast connected with its target. Arkmalis shot back into the line of kneeling lava trolls. One of the trolls extended his hand to catch the General. The hand broke from the troll's body as Arkmalis landed behind the large beast. The surprised creature looked down in horror as lava drained from his handless arm.

Arkmalis wasted no time with his retaliation. He leapt over the flailing lava troll and sent a bolt from the Scythe. Itsuki jumped to his right. The attack missed, but as Itsuki rolled up from his maneuver, he was met by Arkmalis's palm on his chest. "Say hello to the wolfman for me," said the General.

Itsuki saw a flash of light before being lifted off of his feet. The origin was Arkmalis's hand. The blast knocked Itsuki backward. His feet dug into the ground to slow himself. He dug the tip of *Onikira* into the ground to stop himself. His clothing smoked. *He's quick*, thought Itsuki. He charged the General with his sword.

His blow was again blocked. The two weapons bounced off one another, both glowing. The two combatants began to exchange blow after blow. Itsuki would strike. Arkmalis would counter. Their weapons danced as the sound of metal hitting bone reverberated across the battlefield.

Arkmalis spun his weapon at Itsuki's head. The young boy leaned backward as the blade of the Scythe just missed his nose. Itsuki flipped *Onikira* in his hand as he established his position. *"Keeya,"* he yelled as a light red energy sphere shot out of his palm. Arkmalis nonchalantly pushed it aside with his hand. His Scythe cut through the air and sent an energy blade in the direction of the boy. Itsuki was stunned and did not see the last movement of Arkmalis. The blast connected, sending the boy backwards through the air. He landed with a thud. He gradually got to his feet and propped himself up. His robes were now singed and covered in dirt. Blood trickled from the corner of his mouth.

"Is that blood I see?" said the General. "You are clearly no match for me, child."

"We'll just see about that." The boy wiped the blood from his lower lip. "And I told you: I am no child." He began slicing the air with *Onikira*. His hands moved in a blur of speed. With every cut sprang an energy discharge. Dozens of glowing fireballs shot out of his sword, all bearing down on the General.

Arkmalis moved like a machine, systematically blocking the attacks with his weapon—except the last one. Itsuki had charged this one longer and it was at least ten times the size of the others. It knocked the Necromancer off of his feet, and then it exploded. Dust rose from the ground following the detonation.

Itsuki began to breathe heavily. That last attack had worn him out. *It's over*, he thought. The Augmentor slumped down and relaxed. A smile extended its way across his dirtied face. Thomas would be safe. The augmentation would go through as planned. His job was complete. Itsuki stood and dusted himself off.

It started as a soft chuckle but then grew to resounding laughter. He knew the source immediately. The Augmentor was defenseless as General Arkmalis walked out of the dust cloud. His hand erupted into an electric current that shot straight through Itsuki. There was no time to move, and even if he could, his power had been spent. The young boy had given everything, and it was not enough. The surge of electricity shook the boy. He was now being electrocuted by Arkmalis, but he still smiled.

The General replaced his weapon onto his back and now

intensified the attack by adding his other hand. He walked closer as he snickered with satisfaction—until he saw the boy's defiant smirk. Arkmalis pushed harder until the boy dropped to the ground. He ceased the assault. Itsuki's body twitched.

The boy used the sword to sit up. He sheathed *Onikira* and sat down on the dirt cross-legged. He closed his eyes and began to chant.

The General moved to the meditating boy and pulled the Scythe out of its holder. "It is a shame, boy. You are skilled for your age. You remind me of myself in a way." He raised the weapon above his head. "It will be a pity to kill you."

"Itsuki," a familiar voice rang out.

Otōsan? His eyes opened. His father charged the man that would kill his son. The General waved the Scythe and hacked off the branch that Daiki held his sword in. Arkmalis raised his hand, and Itsuki's father was sent flying. The General turned to finish off Itsuki but was met instead by Moriko Katsuo.

"You will not harm my son." Moriko's eyes glowed white as she levitated in the air. The two blue wisps appeared between Arkmalis and Itsuki's mother. "*Kaaaaa!*" yelled Moriko, breathing new vigor into the flames. She pushed her hands forward as the fire encircled the General. Moriko again moved her hands. The flames intensified and swirled around Arkmalis, completely imprisoning him within a blue inferno.

Itsuki was stunned. He had never seen his mother do anything like this before, but he knew her illusion would not fool the General.

"Enough!" yelled Arkmalis. "You insult me with these cheap tricks." The General whirled the Scythe, abruptly extinguishing the firestorm—and Moriko Katsuo. Arkmalis turned and looked at the Augmentor. "You cannot defeat me, child."

"That was never my intention," said Itsuki. He closed his eyes and resumed his meditation. Itsuki could hear Arkmalis's footfalls crunch the earth as he slowly moved closer.

"This is just pathetic. Give me Scargen or I shall destroy all of you. Is there no one here that will oppose me now?" Itsuki opened his eyes again as Arkmalis raised the Scythe to deliver the killing blow. Itsuki was ready to assume his fate.

A blue streak flashed by the wounded Augmentor as the blade sliced towards him. The Gauntlet blocked the Scythe before it could reach Itsuki's neck. "Hey, sorry I'm late. I was doing this whole augment thing . . . kinda lost track of time," said Thomas, kneeling in front of the Augmentor. Itsuki's eyes met his savior's. Thomas's eyes glowed light blue. "Let's get you out of here."

51

a duel

Thomas turned to Itsuki. The Augmentor's eyes flashed a faint pink color and then closed. "Don't worry, my friend. You are safe now." Thomas picked up his fallen companion and sped back to the Temple. The Cadet Mage raced up the stairs. He slowed to a stop in the middle of his friends. Thomas handed the broken boy to his mother as she floated over. "You know what they say—any fight you can walk away from . . ."

Itsuki choked and strained to speak as his mother now held him. The blue wisps circled the young boy.

"We have a proverb that is similar." He looked right at Thomas. "Fall seven times, stand up eight." The Augmentor forced himself to his feet. He wavered but remained upright.

"Thank you, Itsuki."

Itsuki dropped to one knee. "If the Bearer cannot fight, the Augmentor must. Rule number four."

Thomas walked over to the now-grounded dragon. Bartleby's bionic wing sparked, and his armor was scorched with burn marks. He was bickering with Fargus while the gremlin was working hard trying to piece together LINC. "I told you dat dis would 'appen if we didn't put more power in duh shields."

"Well 'ow was I supposed to know we would be facing twenty aringi at once, let alone dat Grayden Arkmalis would be knockin' about wif a bloody *gorgol*. I can't tell duh bleedin' future, now can I? It's not like I'm a soothsayer with a bloody crystal ball, am I?" Fargus feverishly worked on the artif. The robot was split at the waist. The tiny mechanic was working to seal what looked like a fluid leak. Lubricant stained the gremlin's yellow hands as he worked feverishly. The robot's legs twitched ten feet away as if still attached.

"LINC," said Thomas, taken aback by the situation as he stooped beside his damaged friend.

"I assure you T-t-t-om-m-mas . . . It l-l-loooooks cons-s-s-sit-erab-b-b-bly w-w-w-worssssss—zzz—thaaaan it . . . feeelz-z-z." His one working optic rotated to look at Thomas. The other had been fried and dangled out of its socket.

"You look great, LINC." Thomas's tear duct began to overflow. "I'm sure Fargus will have you lookin' good as new. I'll be back in a little bit to check in on you." The robot's arm awkwardly transformed into a cannon.

"I m-m-muuust . . . deeefend T-t-t-thomas Scargen—zzz." The cannon clumsily reverted back into a hand that now reached towards Thomas. His hand dropped, and the light in his only working optic sensor dimmed and then extinguished. His head tilted to the side, lifeless.

"LINC."

"It's aw'right. 'ee's just . . . resetting, isn't 'ee?" said Fargus as he continued to work on the motionless artif. The boy knew Fargus was trying to make it sound better than it was, and he appreciated the effort. He could not remember a world without LINC, and if anyone could repair him, it was the gremlin. "I will fix 'im for you, Thomas. I promise. At duh end uv duh day 'ee'll be as good as new. Don't you worry about it one bit." Fargus looked at the holoscreen hovering in front of him.

"Thanks, Farg."

Malcolm and Wiyaloo tended to Anson as Thomas moved closer. He was now sitting up, but still did not look good. Crimson stains covered his chest. The white scar almost glowed. The boy knelt beside his friend and grabbed his hand. Thomas looked down at the were-wolf. "I'm sorry, Anson. This is all my fault."

Anson's gaunt face turned towards the boy. The werewolf stared into Thomas's eyes. "Men at some time are masters of their fates: The fault, dear Thomas, is not in our stars, but in ourselves, that we are underlings."

"Rest, my friend." The boy put Anson's hand down to his side and stood. Wiyaloo continued chanting. Thomas looked at the vampire. "I need Wiyaloo and you to guarantee me that no one here will interfere. This is my fight. I could not live with myself if anyone else gets hurt." He looked around at his beleaguered friends. "There's been enough bloodshed today. I need you to promise me, Malcolm, that you will get everyone out of here if I fail."

"I promise I will, but you're not gonna fail, are ya?"

"I appreciate the confidence."

"Just kick 'is ass, Tommy," hissed the vampire. Wiyaloo nodded his head and grunted in agreement.

"I will, Malcolm." Thomas could see that Malcolm wished he were the one about to face the man who did this to his brother.

Yareli almost knocked him over with her embrace. He forgot where he was for one second. Her arms warmed him. He felt safe. The shield dissolved around the Temple.

"I don't mean to interrupt this beautiful moment, but I believe we have some business to attend to," said Arkmalis, standing directly in front of the two, his oversized weapon strapped to his back. "Shall we," said the General as he lifted Yareli without touching her and tossed her aside.

Thomas focused on the flailing girl and slowed her fall with his mind. The quickness of the first blow caught Thomas square in the jaw. The blow lifted him into the air and backwards down the stepped temple. Before Thomas could catch himself, Arkmalis met the boy's momentum with another strike.

Thomas flew back uncontrollably. He reached down and dug the Gauntlet into the soil, plowing the ground until he slowed to a halt. The boy looked at his attacker as he drew the Scythe off of his back.

"Is that all you got?" yelled the boy as he brushed himself off and spit out dirt. Arkmalis swung the Scythe and a wave flowed outward towards Thomas.

He jumped over the pulse and ran at the General, firing blasts from the stone glove. Arkmalis parried the attacks with his weapon. Each blast was volleyed back at the boy. Thomas knocked aside each return with the Gauntlet. He still advanced. Gaining speed as he moved, the boy leapt, landing in front of the hulking General. Thomas raised the Gauntlet and opened his hand, placing it on the chest of Arkmalis. The General was caught off guard and had no time to react. "Haaaaaaaaaaaa!" yelled the boy. The energy discharged out of the *Glophitis* on his palm. The General shot backwards through the kneeling line of lava trolls. This time they moved out of the way.

Thomas knew it was only a matter of time before Arkmalis would be upon him again and assumed a defensive posture. The attack came from above, and the force of the hit blew back Thomas and created an impact crater. It was followed by another energy pulse that emanated from the Scythe. This one hit the boy straight on. He lurched back, but did not fall. The boy lifted the Gauntlet and showered the General in energy. Arkmalis flew backward as what was left of his shirt was destroyed, exposing his tattooed torso. The General disappeared into the dust cloud.

Thomas could not see where Arkmalis had gone. He heard the Scythe tear through the air and had little time to raise the Gauntlet to deflect the massive blade. Arkmalis swung the weapon again, and Thomas sidestepped the strike. The General spun around to swing the Scythe at his target once more.

Thomas blocked the blow, but Arkmalis unleashed an energy attack with his empty hand. The sheer power of the assault hammered Thomas backward. The base of the Temple abruptly stopped his momentum. The crash almost knocked the boy out. Any thoughts on resting were instantly set aside by Arkmalis's hand, grabbing the boy by his shirt and raising him out of the rubble. His body was limp in the large man's hand. "This is the great warrior? This is the boy that the Gauntlet chose? The next Bearer?"

"Sounds like someone's a little jealous." The boy smiled. "Just a thought." Arkmalis threw him with angry might. Thomas's lifeless mass hurled through the sky. The boy's body landed with a thud.

The sky began to churn with red electricity. The conduit of the charge was Arkmalis's weapon. Lightning shot down from the heavens and surged with contempt around the man's body as he strode towards Thomas. The General laughed as he moved closer. His tattoos began to change color. The pulsing current powering the man's form intensified the markings on his body. The tattoos now glowed red, matching his eyes and the Scythe.

"That's new," said Thomas to himself. The fight was starting to take its toll, and he still did not feel any different. *The augmentation isn't working*, he thought, *and he seems to be getting stronger*. But there was no time to debate this. The boy sprung to his feet and rushed at the General. He swung the Gauntlet with all the power he could muster.

The speed of his uppercut rocketed the man off of his feet. Arkmalis flipped backward and landed on one knee. He raised himself out of the dirt. A drop of blood leaked from the corner of his mouth. The General laughed as he moved his hand across his face, wiping off the red globule.

"So you are human." Thomas inhaled. "That's reassuring." The General lifted himself up and leered at his opponent.

"Enough, boy," said Arkmalis, electricity still circling the Scythe and his arm. "No more games. Playtime is over. Admit defeat, and surrender yourself."

"I'm sorry. What was that? Your mouth was moving, but I really couldn't keep up. Is it me, or do you just like to hear yourself talk sometimes?" said Thomas as he once again darted in the direction of Arkmalis.

The General swung the Scythe, and a bolt of energy released from the weapon. The scarlet expenditure hit Thomas straight in his chest, impeding his progress. The boy shook and convulsed from the current that surged through his body. The electric onslaught ceased, and the boy collapsed. Sparks still jumped off of him, and his clothing was singed and tattered. He slowly looked up to see Arkmalis staring back at him. "Maybe next time you'll pay attention when I am speaking." The General's kick was swift. It caught the boy straight in the jaw, and he was sent flying towards the kneeling line of lava trolls. He skipped across the scorched landscape. Each hit on the ground slowed Thomas. His wilted body burrowed into the ground as he came to a halt. The boy lay motionless.

He was dazed and on the verge of unconsciousness. Thomas Scargen was half-buried in the plowed earth. His bones ached. He tried to move but faltered. He tried once more, but his will and his body were in total disagreement. *I don't think I can do this.* Doubt raced through his mind, infesting his thoughts. *I have let everyone down.* The pauses between blinks became steadily slower. *I can't beat him. There's no way to win.* Thomas choked. *I'm just a boy . . . just a stupid, weak boy.* He looked down as the *Glophitis* disappeared from the palm of the Gauntlet. His head rolled to one side, and he lay silent for what felt like years. He began to mumble. "I've failed everyone . . . I'm sorry . . . what am I supposed to do now?"

"Get up," said a female's voice. "Get up, Thomas."

"I can't," pleaded the boy.

"Yes, you can. You are stronger than that," said Yareli. The voice was coming from his wristcom. Thomas struggled to open his eyes and look over at the hologram floating above his wrist.

"I should've known you'd be calling me at a time like this. The augmentation didn't work," said Thomas, trying to lift himself out of the rubble. He did not want to let down his friends, especially Yareli, but he was exhausted. "The stone must be damaged." The boy fell back down and coughed again. Blood poured from his mouth. "I have no energy left."

"This isn't about a stupid rock, Thomas. I can't believe what I'm hearing. Thomas Scargen doubts himself?"

"I can barely move, Yar, and it actually hurts to talk." He laughed a little after he said this. Blood still escaped down the side of his lips. "It hurts to laugh too." Thomas felt a twinge in the Gauntlet.

"That's good. If you can make a joke, you can't be that tired."

"Or I'm just delirious."

"You have to believe in yourself. You're the only one of us who can defeat Arkmalis."

"Have you been watching the same fight?" Another twinge came from the Gauntlet.

"Trust in your strength. Trust the connection with the Gauntlet. It will not fail you. Believe in yourself. Everyone here believes in you. I believe in you, Thomas, and I'm sure, wherever he is, your dad believes in you too."

Another surge coursed through the Gauntlet. Thomas's eyes popped open. He had lost sight of the reason he was doing all of this. *If I don't save Dad, who will?* His body was battered and in severe pain, but something deep inside was driving him now.

"Thanks for the pep talk, Yar, but if you haven't noticed, I'm a little too busy to chat right now."

"That's more like it," said Yareli as her hologram dissolved.

"All right. I can do this." He braced his arm against the ground and pushed. "I have to do this." The boy drew from a new well of purpose. He pushed with his other arm and sat himself up. Thomas stood on his shaky legs. "Okay. Let's see what this thing can do." He concentrated on the Gauntlet and its power. He thought of everything he had been through—his friends, his artif, and his father. He thought about his mother and the yellow stone, and something shifted inside the Gauntlet. He looked down at the stone glove and moved his fingers. The *Glophitis* flickered orange once more, but then maintained a yellow glow. The golden energy enveloped the Gauntlet. The glow encompassed his whole body then faded. "That's new."

The familiar blue energy began to circulate from the Gauntlet, lifting his body out of the crater. The power coursed through his exhausted form at an exponential rate. It warmed him. The stone was recharging him, and it felt magnificent. Thomas Scargen overflowed with the warm energy. He was reborn. The augmentation was complete.

Thomas studied the advancing General as he landed back on his feet. His eyes burned hot. He could feel the stone's influence, and the power was startling. The energy was refreshing and new. The boy jumped up and threw the Gauntlet outward. "Haaaaaaaaaaa!"

Arkmalis was caught off guard, and the beam hit him in the left shoulder and sent him spinning. He fell to the ground. "Seize him," he ordered. Two of the lava trolls grabbed Thomas. His reaction was quick. He spun and, with one punch, shattered the first beast. Bits of black rock speckled the air. The troll's left arm pounded to the earth. Its large stone sword flew into Thomas's gauntleted hand, and, with a fluent slice, he divided the second troll diagonally. Its torso slipped off and lava oozed out of the fallen monster.

The General charged, the Scythe gripped in two hands. His eyes glowed with rage as he zeroed in on the boy and swung.

Thomas blocked the blow with the borrowed weapon. The oversized sword was gripped in his hand. The two combatants moved with swift purpose. The boy matched every attack by Arkmalis. The speed of their movements became blurs. Their pace lifted the dust and earth around them. Soon they were surrounded in a cloud. Thomas lost sight of his opponent. The boy stepped back and stood still. The General followed Thomas's lead as the dust cloud lowered and dispersed.

The two stared at each other. But something was different. For the first time in the battle, General Arkmalis was noticeably fatigued. Thomas was not. In fact, he was smiling. "What's wrong, General? You want to take a break?"

"I will enjoy wiping that grin off of your smug face." He charged. The upswing of the Scythe splintered the stone sword. Thomas tossed what remained of the sword aside. "Not smiling now, are you, Scargen?" The General spun and, with two hands on his weapon, slashed at the boy.

Thomas did not move. Time seemed to slow down as the blade of Arkmalis's weapon cut towards the boy. Thomas put his hand out and grabbed the Scythe with the Gauntlet. "This ends now." The boy's words echoed. He tightened his fist. The Scythe broke in two. Black energy dissipated from the weapon as bone shards splintered. A look of sheer surprise arose on the face of Arkmalis.

"You can't—there's no way. I-I . . . c-c-can't believe . . ." stuttered the General.

"Well maybe you should start." The movement was almost undetectable. The punch was met by breaking bone. Arkmalis spit scarlet as he wavered backward. Shock infested the man and overflowed onto his face.

"But . . . you-you're . . . you're just . . . a boy."

"Not anymore." He moved his two hands back simultaneously. They flowed forward together, the Gauntlet in front of the other. His palms were pushed forward. "Haaaaaa!" said Thomas as light blue energy sprang from his hands. Cool, focused power emanated from his rocky palm. The General met this beam with one of his own. The cobalt energy rushed into the red. The General was trying desperately to hold his ground. "Haaaaaaaa!" the young man yelled louder. His energy flow increased exponentially. The General was pushed backward, frantically adjusting his feet to balance himself. The blue ocean of energy overtook the crimson output from General Arkmalis, enveloping the large man in a wave of power.

Arkmalis was sent soaring. Thomas sped by and caught him before he could land. "This is for Itsuki." The young man's fist landed in the General's midsection, breaking ribs with the well-placed strike. His anger began to simmer. "This is for Anson." The blow snapped Arkmalis's head back. Thomas could feel the fury begin to bubble. "And this one's for LINC." The uppercut caught the General under his chin. Rage now boiled in the young man's veins. His power was astonishing. "And for what you did to Hawthorne." He lifted the General off of his feet without touching him. The glow from Arkmalis's tattoos diminished back to their original black state as Thomas looked into the General's empty eyes. The man was held frozen and vulnerable. He was powerless.

"Finish me, boy," commanded the General.

Energy rippled across Thomas's form and the extended Gauntlet. Part of him wanted to do as this man asked, but he would not. He could not. *Anger does not control me*, thought the young man. *I control my anger.* Soothing, calm energy began to circulate through Thomas.

The rage that had fueled him was gone and was replaced with a new strength that coursed through his body. He let go of his telekinetic hold on Arkmalis and powered down.

The General hit the earth flat on his face, dropping the other half of the Scythe. The man struggled to get back on his feet. The remnants of a broken man quivered in the still air. "What's wrong with you, Scargen?" Veins bulged from Arkmalis's neck as he spit out the words. "Finish me!"

"No," said Thomas, ignoring the General's rage-fueled plea. "That would make me no better than you." He lowered the Gauntlet and leaned in towards Arkmalis. "And you're not getting off that easy. You will stand trial for your crimes." Thomas paused. "You lost to a boy, General, and now you'll have to live with that failure for the rest of your pathetic life." He moved closer to Arkmalis. "Now, where is my father?"

The conquered general began to giggle. Soon the giggle grew into a full-bellied laugh. Thomas grabbed him and pulled him upward. "Where is my father, you son of a bitch?" Thomas shook the man, but he just continued to laugh.

"Perhaps I have lost . . . but you've won nothing." Arkmalis's body slumped forward, unconscious. The General was still.

52

the man of my dreams

General Arkmalis lay at Thomas's feet, defeated. The young man dropped down to his knees. He felt a wave of relief wash over his body. He could not believe the battle was over. Thomas had won but was no closer to finding his father. He looked at the enemy line. What remained of the General's troops had begun to retreat at the sight of their fallen leader. "That . . . wasn't . . . so bad," said Thomas as he tried to slow his breathing. He tried to ease himself forward and fell backward into a seated position. "Maybe . . . just . . . a short . . . rest." He closed his eyes.

The rattling noise woke Thomas. He opened his eyes, looking for its source, and quickly found it. The handle of the Scythe was twitching against the ground. Thomas stared at the broken weapon as it continued to vibrate, and it slowly began to smolder a sickly black hue. The blade spun through the air in the direction of the handle. The parts levitated towards each other. The blade joined its counterpart, and the weapon began mending itself. Black smoke circled the fresh wounds on the Scythe, pulling and healing the shattered bone. When the smoke cleared, the weapon was reborn.

The Scythe rose up over the young man's head. It spun once and, with a full hacking motion, ripped open the sky. The weapon collapsed to the ground. Thomas tried to collect himself, but he was completely fatigued. The exhaustion from the battle left his muscles throbbing, and he could barely move.

Two large robots floated in through the rip and moved towards the General. Thomas identified them as his father's craftsmanship. The Scargen Robotics logo confirmed his suspicions. They were two of the diggerbots his father had been using for his excavation in Egypt. He tried to move to stop them, but he could not. Thomas was dumbfounded.

A hunched, hooded man crossed the tear's horizon. Thomas peered under the hood and could see the man's face was wrapped in old bandages. It was the Necromancer from his dream. Thomas remembered the man's soulless eyes. He moved on instinct. With what little power he had left, he threw himself at the hooded man. "Where is my father, you piece of—"

The man raised his palm nonchalantly and caught Thomas with an invisible hand. "We mustn't swear at our elders, my boy," interrupted the man. He threw the young man back down to the ground. Thomas was drained and helpless. He felt as if he were being pulled down to the ground. He tried to writhe his way upward, but he could not move.

The bandaged man pointed at Arkmalis's smoking body. The Diggers moved to Grayden Arkmalis and picked up the fallen general. The hooded man placed his hand above the newly repaired Scythe. "Now, Grayden, what have I told you about playing with other people's toys?" His deep voice was soothing. He moved his fingers slightly, and the weapon shot upward. The Scythe slapped into his hand as he closed his fingers around the familiar handle. "If you want something done right . . ." said the man as he turned to look at Thomas. Power coursed from the weapon into his body. Black energy whipped around the hooded man's form. "I have missed you, my dear," said the man looking at the Scythe.

He motioned to the robots, and the artifs disappeared through the tear with Arkmalis's still body. The man pulled the hood back. "You must be Thomas Scargen." He smiled from covered ear to covered ear. The man's whole head was sheltered in bandages, and his eyes were completely black.

Thomas nodded. "So you know who I am, but who the hell are you?"

"You still have not pieced it together, have you?" The man moved closer to Thomas.

"What are you talking about?"

"I must admit. I did not think this is how we would meet. If only your darling mother were around to see her failure come to life."

"What do you know about my mother? Tell me who you are."

"My name, Tom, is Tollin Grimm." He heard the name, but it could not be. This man had fought his mother, killed Ziza's love, and now was the only man that knew of his father's fate.

"I thought you were dead. She destroyed you."

"Obviously we have a very different definition of destroyed."

"She killed you with the Gauntlet . . . Ziza said so. My mom said s—" He remembered his mother trying to say something right before he left. Was she trying to tell him about this man? Could it be true? Was this Tollin Grimm?

"Merelda Scargen could never have destroyed me. No one is as powerful as I."

"How do you know her name?" asked Thomas as he pushed himself up to one knee using the Gauntlet.

"I probed her mind shortly before she banished me into this stone." He lifted his palm to show the black rock embedded into his hand. "She knew she was no match for me, and that she would never destroy me, so she did the next best thing. She locked me away using the brown stone."

"Brown? The stone is black."

"Its color altered once I was imprisoned in it. She then buried me in the sands of Egypt."

"I thought you and the Hunters destroyed Egypt."

"Well . . . I did have a part in it. That much is true, but she was responsible for burying Egypt. I barely had time to access her thoughts. The name Thomas Scargen was all I could distinguish at first. She tried ever so hard to hide the fact that she had a son, but she was far too busy focusing her power on my exile to control her thoughts as well. For fifteen years I pondered on this name . . . Thomas Scargen, Tommy Scargen, Tom Scargen. The syllables bounced around in my head, reverberating for years. I became obsessed with you in my cramped chamber." Grimm began to pace. "I dreamt of one day being freed and finding you. At first the thought of killing you crossed my mind." The man was gesticulating ferociously but then stopped and looked right at Thomas. "But that thought gave way to asking you to join me, the son of my jailer by my side. What better revenge could I wish for? And who could ever imagine that the man who discovered my stone prison shared the same name. What are the chances?" Thomas could not believe what he was hearing. "I listened intently while the good doctor and Sigmund all but told me where I could find you. After I was so graciously freed by your father, I alerted my men to your whereabouts. Hadn't you wondered how they had found you?" Thomas had never thought about it. He had just assumed it was his power levels that had alerted the General.

"How did you get out?" asked the young man.

"I had countered your mother's magic at the last possible second." His tone changed ever so slightly. "There was no way she could have known, and it was the only thing I could do. I simply added a little caveat to my stone prison. If the right person found the stone, I would be released."

"What do you mean *right person*? How was my father the right person?"

"You see, Tom, my escape required a great amount of energy and the touch of an adept Mage."

"My father has no such powers."

"On the contrary, Tom. Your father was an advanced technic. He was extremely talented at manipulating tech. You can attest to that. He had just used his powers to fix one of his beloved artifs before he touched the stone. His energy was the key to my locked prison. His power flowed into the stone, and Dr. Carl Scargen's talents were transferred to me. That is why I can control his toys so easily." Grimm coughed and caught his breath. He turned away from Thomas. "I must confess, Tom, your father was a most unfortunate casualty of my resurrection, and for that I owe you an apology, but rest assured his sacrifice will not be in vain."

"No." Thomas's face changed. He felt an emptiness deep inside. A sensation of pain, loss, and regret eclipsed rational thought. Tears fell from his eyes. He had thought it, but now the murderer himself confirmed it. No matter what he did, he could not change that simple, excruciating fact. His father was dead. *Grimm.* Thomas's eyes went blank as electricity surged through him. "Haaaaaaaa!" yelled Thomas as he flashed the Gauntlet and unleashed a barrage of energy at the man with the bandaged face.

Though the man looked sickly, he moved with astonishing speed and precision. He parried the assault back at Thomas using the Scythe. The young man was knocked backward by his own attack. He heard a stuttering wind pass his ears as he flew back. His lifeless body crashed into the ground and churned the soil into a mound that formed behind Thomas. He slowed and now rested on the raised earth. He tried to stand, but he could not. Tollin Grimm raised his left hand and again held back Thomas with an invisible grip.

"Really, Tom, that was rude—impressive, mind you, in your current state, but rude nonetheless. I was not finished talking. You really must learn some self-control." Thomas struggled to move and speak, but no words could pass his lips. "Let's get a good look at you," said Grimm as he lifted Thomas and began to slowly rotate him. He tried to break free, but he was frozen in the air—on display for his rival to examine. "It appears that the Gauntlet has chosen you. For what reason, I do not know. I must admit I've never understood its choices. Its insistence on its Bearers adhering to good saved my life, but I still think it a flaw. Regardless, it is a very powerful weapon, and you should be proud of yourself." His words seemed genuine. "If only your parents were here to see your great accomplishment." The man laughed aloud. "Oh but I guess that's impossible—both being dead and all—and oddly enough, both by my hand." The words awakened Thomas's last reserve of power. He hit Grimm in his right shoulder with the energy sphere. The mouse had bitten the snake. Tollin dropped the Scythe and twitched in pain, but Thomas was still caught in midair. He had hurt Grimm, but the attack had barely fazed the studied Necromancer. "Are you sure you're ready for such a commitment?" He continued his speech as if nothing had happened. He opened his palm, and his weapon flung back into his hand. "I prefer a more detached weapon, as you can see. Just a personal preference I assure you. I used to think differently, but I was a stupid, naive pawn in those days. Ask your new teacher Ziza Bebami about becoming too attached to such things. I'm sure he can show you what that Gauntlet can do to you."

"I can see what it did to you," said Thomas, using all the energy left in him. Tollin Grimm wielded the Scythe and ripped into the air. A shockwave was sent slicing towards Thomas. It caught him square in the chest, tearing what was left of his shirt apart. The young man screamed inside his head. The pain was almost unbearable, but he was not going to give Grimm the satisfaction. A gash formed across his chest.

"I thought we could be friends, Tom, but I see now that that is not possible. You have proved troublesome, to say the least, and I should have known that that fool Ziza would eventually interfere." Grimm turned away from the young man, and then instantly was inches away from him. He reached up with his rag-covered left hand and grabbed Thomas's face by the cheeks in a forceful grip. "It would be a shame to waste such talents." Thomas could smell the years of decay on the man's bandages. "You have an anger inside you that could be useful. With your power and my wisdom, we could rule the world. Your potential is astounding—even without the Gauntlet. But I fear there may be no swaying you." Grimm released the young man's face. "Something tells me I may have use for you yet." He paused for a second. "Or maybe I should just kill you now. Then the circle will be complete."

He backed away and began to raise the Scythe, but before he could deliver the blow, the sky above the two combatants scratched open and a black dragon poured out of the break. Grimm jumped back into a defensive position. Thomas looked up and saw why. Ziza and Emfalmay were atop Talya Grenfald.

Ziza leapt from the beast, flipping forward, and landed in front of the young man, his staff in his good hand. The stone that rested on the top of his staff burned green as did his eyes. Thomas had never seen this before. "Enough," said the High Mancer as Emfalmay landed next to the old man, sword drawn.

"Hello, old friend," said Grimm as he remained grinning, his weapon at the ready.

"You lost the right to call me that a long time ago," said Ziza as he rolled his staff. The jeweled side now pointed at Grimm.

"Who's your pet?" asked Grimm, pointing the Scythe at the Lion.

Emfalmay roared in response as his eyes blazed.

"Charming," said Grimm.

"Leave this place, Tollin," said Ziza. "We all know you do not have the strength to deal with both of us."

"That remains to be seen, but the odds have perhaps tilted. Another time then, Tom." Grimm took a step backward and passed through the tear behind him. The teleportal whooshed shut. The young man dropped from the unseen hand and crumbled. Thomas raised himself up to his knees and began to cry. Ziza placed his hand on the young man's back while Emfalmay stood guard.

"It's all right, my boy. Let it out."

"Did you know my father was dead? Did you know Mary was my mother?" asked Thomas, confused at his teacher's previous level of involvement. "Did you know Grimm was still alive?" Thomas could barely take in oxygen, his face wet with regret and loss.

"I was not certain of your father's fate or that the woman of my earlier tale was definitely your mother. I had my suspicions, but that was all, and I believed as you did that this man was destroyed." He rubbed the top of the young man's head. "I am sorry, Thomas. I see now that you should have known all that I did. Tollin's interference was unforeseen." A long silence was shared between the two Mages.

"I just wish I could have said goodbye to him." Thomas's tears bled from his eyes, and Ziza hugged his head. Feelings broke through the young man.

"You just did, Thomas. You just did." The two embraced in silence. Thomas passed out in Ziza's arms.

53
funeral for the fallen

Bartleby was giving his best friend Hawthorne's eulogy. The dragon had been crying for some time, but he had managed to deliver a fairly eloquent speech. Anson, Malcolm, Fargus, Ziza, and Emfalmay all sat in front of him. Itsuki and his wooded family stood behind them. Yareli was next to Thomas, holding his non-gauntleted hand. Her touch was all that was keeping him from losing it. He had just found out not long ago that the same man that had been the cause of his mother's death, Tollin Grimm, had murdered his father. He could not shake the image of this man standing over him, and he had been completely helpless.

Meeting his mother had been comforting, but it was not the same as her being alive, and Thomas had yet to discuss the reunion with anyone. He was going to tell Yareli before the funeral, but she had grabbed his hand and had not let go. This helped him to deal with the pain for the moment. *Why bring it up now?* he thought. *I'll talk to her about it when we get home.* It just felt good to be close with someone right now. She leaned onto his shoulder. *I have to tell her a lot of things.*

He had feelings for the girl. Thomas was certain of that, and he was pretty sure she had feelings for him too, but he would not tell her. He could not tell her. Everyone he loved died. He would not curse her with this fate. He would have no time for a relationship anyway.

Thomas would dedicate all of his time to training. He would not feel helpless ever again. If he was to defeat Tollin Grimm, Thomas would have to be as dedicated as him. Still, it was nice to feel close to someone, even if it was temporary.

Bartleby finished the eulogy and moved towards the female dragon. He cried in Talya's arms as she patted his head. Thomas looked at Yareli. She softly let go of his hand. It was the first time in hours he had not been holding her hand, and he felt lost, but it was his turn to talk. He kissed Yareli on the forehead as she hugged him.

The young man made his way in front of the mourners and walked towards the rock that served as a makeshift podium. He looked out at the gathering of people, and he realized his friends and comrades surrounded him. Three white crosses pierced the soil. The cherry-blossomed warriors formed a semicircle around the proceedings. It would have been beautiful if not for the occasion.

Thomas spoke. "Sig, you deserved better. Thank you for being a friend to my father. You were there through some pretty rough times, and I know you stood up for me more than once. You were my father's best friend, and you will be truly missed." The young man looked up. "Franklin Hawthorne, what can I say that hasn't been said by my dear dragon friend? I didn't know the man as well as it felt I did. I instantly connected with him. He reminded me so much of . . . my dad. I know you are in a better place now." He looked over at Bartleby who was fighting back tears. Their eyes met in understanding.

"Many of you never knew my father—I guess actually none of you did. He was a great man, and I'm not just saying that because we're related." Thomas let out a small laugh. "He taught me to be the man that I have become, and if he were here today, he would be proud of the people that I now call friends. He'd be proud of me I think too." The young man's voice cracked. "I miss you, Dad." Tears ran down his cheekbones. He made no gesture to wipe them. Thomas was proud of these tears and would not hide them. "My father would always tell me what he considered the secret to life. He would say, 'Tom, it's pretty simple. Be happy for no good reason.' He said, 'All you have to do is smile, Tom, even when there's nothing to smile about. If you smile enough, you forget what you were so mad about, and everything just seems a little bit easier to deal with.' He lived his life this way, and he might have been the happiest person I've ever met." He lowered his head and took a second to collect his thoughts. "I'll never forget all the sacrifices you made for me, or all the times you put your life on hold to raise me. I regret not being with you when you needed me the most." The young man looked down. "I have this feeling that I could've done something. I could have somehow prevented your death." The young man paused a second to collect himself. "But that feeling fades, and it's replaced with the knowledge that you will always be with me. I have almost seventeen years of memories with you. You taught me to do the right thing and to stick up for those who cannot stick up for themselves, and that's what I intend to do. I'm going to make you proud, Dad." Thomas lifted his gauntleted arm. He looked at the glove, and then out to the onlooking crowd. "And as always, I'm gonna keep smiling, but don't get upset if today I cry just a little." The young man pushed aside a final tear. "May the three of you rest in peace."

The gang was gathering their collective things, getting ready for their departure. It had been several hours since the funeral, and Thomas was saying goodbye one last time. There had been no body, but this place had brought finality. The site would serve as his father's final resting place. It seemed to make sense to Thomas.

The young man rejoined the group. He passed Ziza as he bowed to one of the trees. "Thomas, I would like you to meet Takagi Katsuo. He was my Augmentor."

"Pleasure to meet you." Thomas bowed.

"The pleasure is all mine, Thomas Scargen." The tree bowed. "We thank you for today, and for helping Itsuki."

"If it weren't for Itsuki, none of us would be here. Do you know where he is? I wanted to say thanks." The massive tree pointed over the young man's head.

"He is over there talking to Daiki." Thomas followed the barked finger. He saw the boy talking to his father. The young man made his way over to the two.

When he got closer, he noticed that a small branch had started to grow to replace the one that that Arkmalis had removed. *This place is not normal*, Thomas reminded himself. He made his way over to the father and son. "Hey, Itsuki. I'm sorry if I'm interrupting, but I just wanted to say thanks."

"You are not interrupting, Thomas. My son was just saying how much he admires you, and I would have to agree. It is we who owe you thanks," said Itsuki's father.

"Thank you for your kindness, Mr. Katsuo," said Thomas. "I'm just gonna borrow your son for a couple minutes."

"We were just finishing. *Musuko*," said Daiki Katsuo as he bowed to his son.

"*Otōsan*," said Itsuki, returning the gesture. "I feel blessed that we had this time together, but I think we both know it is almost at an end. It was an honor to fight with you on this day."

"And I with you, Itsuki. You have my blessing. Go in peace." They bowed, and then Thomas bowed to Itsuki's father.

Thomas walked away with his Augmentor. "What about Tollin Grimm? He knows where you are now. That makes you a target. You should leave this place and come with us."

"That was a foregone conclusion. I have packed everything I need in this sack." Itsuki lifted a neatly wrapped pack that he had been holding.

"But what if he comes back and destroys this place?"

"The Scythe found him, Thomas. Like the Gauntlet, the Scythe has great power." Itsuki threw his pack into the storage container on Bartleby. "I assure you he has no idea where this place is located, and even if he figures it out, this knowledge will do him little good."

"How can you be so sure?"

"Like I said, Thomas, this place is not like other places. It exists only momentarily in a given location."

"What do you mean?"

"It shifts."

"Like Sirati?"

"What is a Sirati?"

"Where we're going—at least for a while. The place is also never in one place for too long."

"It must have been created by the Gauntlet," said Itsuki. "This place was also forged from the Gauntlet's power millennia ago. The shifting is part of the Temple's design to make sure people like Grimm could never impede the augmentation process, which is now complete."

"Until the next stone is found you mean, right?"

"No, Thomas. That part of my job is done."

"What do you mean *done*? We are just starting. If I'm ever going to beat Grimm, I'm gonna need as many of those stones as I can find. You saw him. His power was ridiculous."

"You will have a different Augmentor for the next stone."

"What?"

"Yes, one stone per Augmentor. It's the first rule. I'm afraid the next will be someone new, and there is no way to determine who he or she may be."

"Another precaution?"

"Precisely."

"Oh . . . then why are you coming with us? I assumed it was to further augment the Gauntlet. I mean you are obviously welcome to, but I just figured that you have accomplished your life's mission, maybe it's time for a rest."

"There's no time for rest, and as for me, I've just begun my life-long mission. You're going to need help. That much has been established. It is now my task as First Augmentor to protect the Bearer and serve him."

"Another rule?"

"Number twenty-seven—my personal favorite. Besides, I can help locate the next stone."

"I guess that means your mother is coming as well?"

"Yeah . . . well . . ."

"I heard that . . . what would you do without me?" Moriko hovered towards them with Itsuki's swords in her arms—the two wisps danced around her. "You would leave without your swords. That is for sure." Moriko turned and folded her arms, grumbling to herself as she levitated in front of her son. He took *Onikira* and his other swords out of his mother's arms.

"*Okaasan* . . . I don't know how to say this, but . . . I'm going with Thomas." The apparition turned to face her boy.

"I know, honey. I'm going with you."

"What I mean to say is . . . I'm going with Thomas alone." The Augmentor looked away from his mother.

"You must not joke that way with your mother, sweetheart. Why would you say that? I am coming with you, and that is final."

"I think we both know that's not possible or wise. This place gives you strength."

"What are you talking about, dear?"

"It's time, *Okaasan*. I am ready. You have done a great job raising me, and it's time for you to move on."

"But—" She began to cry. The flames ceased dancing. Itsuki grabbed her hand in his. Thomas felt instant jealousy. He would have given anything to have had that moment with his dad.

"It will be all right, Mom. Thomas will take care of me." Moriko glanced at the young man. "He will keep me safe." Her tears intensified. "This is what I was meant to do. This is my destiny. Father is waiting for you." Her head lowered, and she sniffed trying to stop the emotional assault. She looked over at her husband and smiled as water droplets fell down her transparent cheeks.

"I know, Itsuki . . . it is just that . . . I am not ready." Itsuki pulled her close and hugged her. "I do not know what I am going to do without you."

"I love you, *Okaasan*. Without you I would have never gotten here. It's time for you to go to Father. It's time for your happy ending." She pulled away from her son and wiped her tears away.

"You are ready, my son," said Moriko as she bowed. She floated over to Thomas as the blue wisps orbited around him. "Take care of him, Bearer."

"I will, Mrs. Katsuo, and I won't forget what you said to me." She hugged the young man and hovered back to Itsuki.

"*Sayonara*, Itsuki. You have made us so proud." The blue flares came back to her. "I will do as you say. I will go to your father, but I leave you my *hitodama*." The two flames moved quickly to Itsuki. "They now serve you." She bent over and kissed him on the top of his head. "I love you, Itsuki."

"I love you too. You honor me with your gift I . . . I will . . . miss you." He leaned over and kissed her cheek and hugged her. "*Sayonara, Okaasan.*" She backed away and bowed, gliding backward—still facing her son. The wisps remained with Itsuki. When Moriko was halfway between her son and her husband, she turned and moved swiftly to Daiki Katsuo. Their hands met each other, and he pulled her close. They kissed as she hugged his trunk. The roots of the tree slowly replanted themselves into the soil. Moriko Katsuo slowly vanished. The trees were still again. The *sakura* once again rested. A wind blew slowly around the tree as the forest swayed. Cherry blossoms fell to the ground. Thomas and Itsuki looked out across the battlefield. The trees had all rerooted. The cooled lava rocks now joined the landscape. The smell of heated sap dominated the air. The two warriors were awestruck with the impromptu splendor of the scene as the blue wisps buzzed around them.

"I'm going to really miss this place."

"You could always stay."

"That is not an option. I am First Augmentor—and besides, I have a feeling we will be coming back here. This Temple has many more secrets to share."

"And who knows when we might need a tree army again?" Thomas winked at Itsuki. The two laughed.

The dragons were packed and ready. Malcolm held his brother in his arms. LINC was stored on Bartleby. It had been a tough day, but he knew more of these were coming. Ziza gingerly walked over to them with his staff.

"You ready to go home?" asked Ziza as he approached. Thomas looked at the old man and realized that Sirati was his new home.

"Yes, I am."

54

all good things

"I was naive going into the fight, Thomas," said Merelda Scargen to her gauntletless son. They were both in her library inside the Gauntlet. He was seated in the middle of the room. His mother sat across from him. The young Ziza quietly paced behind them.

"In what way?" asked Thomas.

"I thought I could defeat Tollin Grimm, but as the battle continued, I become conscious of the fact that I didn't have the power. I realized I had to do something, and then it came to me like a voice in my head. Although I could not destroy Grimm, I could seal him in one of the stones, but I knew it would take all of my power. The only thing I could think of was you and your father. This gave me the strength to do what I did. I remember sealing him in the brown stone. Something inside of me insisted on using the brown one. The rock turned and twisted and changed color. Grimm's cell turned black.

"I made sure I marked the rock with a warning, and then I sent the stone to Egypt. With my last bit of energy, I buried the dark stone as deep as possible, covering the jeweled cell in all of the sands of Egypt."

"So that was you. I didn't know whether to believe Grimm." He looked at his mother. "What happened after that?"

"The last thing I remember is lying in Ziza's arms, smiling. You were safe, as far as I knew, and then I awoke inside the Gauntlet."

"I'm sorry it took so long for me to visit, but I was out of it for a few weeks. Apparently expending all that power affects your body or something. Long story short, I've been rehabbing, but it gave me time to work on controlling the Gauntlet more. I am finally getting the whole shifting-the-stone thing down," said Thomas as he looked down at his naked right arm. He felt awkward without the Gauntlet on. It was a part of him now.

"It took me a while to perfect that myself," said Merelda Scargen. She smiled at Thomas the way only a mother can. "So what did you want to talk to me about? I have a few things to discuss with you as well."

"I need to go first."

"Okay . . . what's on your mind?"

"It's about Dad."

"Did you find him? Why didn't you tell me sooner? I—"

"No, Mom." Thomas did not know how to say it, so he just did. "He was murdered by Tollin Grimm." She was silent. He knew the pain he felt, but could not imagine what she was going through. "I just thought I should be the one to tell you." She was quiet for some time, but then she began to talk between the tears.

"He was such a great husband. He would do anything for me, and he loved you so much, Thomas. Did he ever tell you about our first Christmas together as a family?"

"He tried not to talk about you much. It hurt too much I think. He never stopped loving you."

"I never stopped loving him. He was so selfless and caring." She wiped the tears from her eyes and continued. "We had gotten a tree two days after Thanksgiving. I loved our Christmases together, and this was going to be our first with you. We went to the local Tool Shed and picked out a beautiful Balsam Fir. It was six feet tall, the perfect size for our humble apartment. I loved it so much. Your father wasn't as enthusiastic. He had said, 'You buy screws and paint at Tool Shed, not Christmas trees.' But I wanted the tree, and your father could never say no to me.

"It made me so happy to have such a magnificent tree for our first family Christmas, but with one week to go before Christmas, our once beautiful tree had gone floppy." She giggled. "It was a sight to behold, Thomas. Its branches were curling under. They were holding the ornaments hostage and didn't want to let go. Needles were everywhere and had to be vacuumed daily." She laughed through her tears. "Your father tried to convince me that it was all right, but the tree was dead. Your father knew it, and I knew it. I had told myself that Christmas would still be just as good without a perfect tree, but who was I kidding. Three days before Christmas, I broke down. I told Carl that I was sad about the tree and that I couldn't bear to think of your first Christmas memory being of this scary, twisted tree. I cried. He held me in his arms and didn't say a word. Not once did he say *I told you so* . . . not once. I fell asleep hugging him that night.

"I had taken you with me the next day to go to Bulk Mart to get some last minute things, and quite frankly, being near that tree was depressing me. We were only gone for three hours, but when I returned home, I opened the door, and there it was. Where the dead, droopy, dry Tool Shed tree had stood now rose a perfect, brand new Douglas Fir, completely decorated. Your father had gone to a local farm and picked it out. He had set it up shortly after we had left and then took the time to place all the decorations where we had placed them on the original. Each light strand was carefully positioned. Each ball and ornament meticulously hung. I felt so spoiled at the time, and, for the first time in my adulthood, it felt like Christmas again. I felt like I did when I was a kid. If I had ever had doubts about this man before, they were destroyed right there and then. I kept that memory to myself. I use it whenever I feel hopeless or sad. The memory of that tree always brings me back. I had experienced real love, and not everyone gets that—and I did love him, Thomas. I still love him." She trailed off and began to cry again. The two were quiet. Thomas hugged her tightly. She pulled away from her son. "And now he's gone, and it's my fault." She said the words with a blank look on her face. "Whether he realized it or not makes little difference. He must have sensed part of me in the black stone."

"What are you saying?"

"To trap Grimm, I had to give a part of myself. It was the only way to seal the stone."

"Aren't you being a little hard on your self? I mean you did save the world. If it weren't for you, who knows what Grimm would've done."

"I appreciate that." Tears snuck out of the corners of her eyes. "I loved him, Thomas. The biggest injustice I ever did was not telling him that before I left. He deserved more. He deserved the truth."

"If there's something I have learned in the last few weeks, it's that if you truly love someone, even death sometimes isn't enough to keep two people apart. Dad loved you every second of his short life. I know that. He would be so happy that I got to meet you."

"Thank you, Thomas. It means a lot to hear that. I know this couldn't have been easy." He looked at her and smiled; he did not know what else to do.

"They promoted me, by the way." Thomas wanted to change the subject.

"Really? That's faster than me. Congratulations. My son, the Mage Warrior. Well done, Thomas."

"Thanks, Mom. Itsuki and I are going to be leaving soon to start looking for the next stone."

"That brings me to what I had to talk to you about." She cleared her throat. "My power that I was blessed with when living was the ability to see things before they happen. What I mean to say is, I could tell what was going to happen to someone by touching something that belongs to that person."

"Narsh."

"Yes, it is. Sometimes it's in a few hours, sometimes it's a few days, but in one instance, it was years."

"You saw something that was going to happen years from now?"

"No, Thomas. I saw something years ago that has yet to happen." She reached out and grabbed his hand. "I have seen you fighting Grimm all by yourself, and while I do not know the outcome, it didn't look good for you." This scared him. A tingle of fear shot up his spine.

"Why didn't it look good for me?" He needed to know.

"Well, in the premonition . . . you're not wearing the Gauntlet." He was stunned.

How could this be? I would never give up the Gauntlet.

"But the future is always changing. This was the premonition that sent me away. I thought if I could just stop him before you faced him—I was wrong. I didn't change anything."

"You don't know that. I will train nonstop if that's what it takes to stop that madman. My future has not been written yet. If anyone can help me beat Grimm, it's Ziza and you."

"Thanks," said the younger Ziza. Thomas had forgotten he was in the room. "I appreciate the trust you have in my future self."

"It was earned. I will be ready next time we face off."

"There is one last thing, Thomas."

"What?"

"It's about the Scythe. The weapon is as old as the Gauntlet. Some say older. It was a weapon originally created to help. It was taken and twisted into its current state, and Tollin Grimm made it his own. If you haven't figured it out yet, the shaft is made of dragon bone."

"The hardest substance known to man." The young man looked down and then at his mother. "That's how he opened the teleportal."

"Yes, Thomas. You must be careful with that Scythe. Opening teleportals is only a small part of that twisted weapon's capabilities. There is dreadful magic surrounding it, and when coupled with the new black stone, it is even more dangerous. The Scythe tears the soul from the flesh, and the stone collects this life force and gives its holder strength. It's what Grimm will use to regain his power. It might have seemed unstable in Arkmalis's hands, but that weapon wasn't made for the General." She moved closer to her son. "I fear Grimm will be unhappy about this loss, and he won't wait long to retaliate."

"Then I better get back to my training." He stood up and walked over to his mom and hugged her.

"I will never leave you again, my son." They said nothing to each other, but continued their embrace. Words had no place. After a couple of minutes, he disappeared from the scene and found himself lying down in a hammock. Itsuki was next to him.

"How was your nap?" asked Itsuki. The pair of blue wisps hovered above his shoulders.

"Eventful," said the young Mage Warrior. Itsuki looked confused by his response, but shook it off quickly. Thomas sat up, and, to his surprise, the rest of his friends surrounded him.

"So what are all you doin here?" asked Thomas. "I thought this was gonna be more of an intimate affair."

"I don't think anyone wanted to miss this," said Itsuki. "And I might have said something."

"What are you doing here, Fargus? You're supposed to be working on LINC."

"He's gonna be aw'right, Thomas. Quite frankly it's all I've been doin since we got back. I'm going a bit mad to be honest. I want to give 'im a shield. I don't fink your dad could've known duh types of attacks 'ee'd be facing, or 'ee'd a done it 'imself, wouldn't 'ee? I just needed a break an that. At duh end uv duh day, dis seemed like just as good a place as any." He went straight back to whistling to himself.

"I actually came to say goodbye, Thomas," said Bartleby. "I gotta go back and make sure everyfing is in order back 'ome. Plus, I miss Webster. Fargus also needs some parts to put 'umpty Dumpty back togevver again." Thomas winced like he was punched in the stomach. "Oh . . . sorry, Thomas. I didn't mean anyfing by—"

"I know, Bart." The twins walked over to Thomas.

"I wasn't gonna miss dis, Tommy," said Malcolm as he lit a cigarette.

"I must admit, I am a bit curious myself." Anson stood next to his vampiric sibling. He looked as good as new. "We know what we are, but know not what we may be."

"Thank you for everything, Anson." The wolfman nodded. Wiyaloo was now next in line, and Yareli was at his side.

"We just wanted to say . . . well I just wanted to say . . . thank you for saving my life yet again."

"I'm getting good at it," said the young man. She smiled and kissed him on the cheek.

"Good luck, Thomas." Yareli backed away with the others as they all moved over to the side of the clearing. *I gotta have that talk soon*, thought Thomas as he moved to the edge of the isolated canyon. It was at least a fifty-foot drop. Thomas waited on its precipice with Itsuki, looking down on this evening's obstacle. The blue *hitodama* whizzed around the two of them.

"Okay, he's not that strong," said Itsuki.

Thomas's lip pursed and his left eyebrow cocked.

"Okay, so he's the strongest Mage any of us knows. Just remember what I told you. Focus on the stone inside the Gauntlet. It must be engaged before you can use its power."

"And what exactly is its power again? Most of the battle is still a blur."

"It increases your speed in all facets, from perception to physical movement."

"So I can sort of slow down time in my head?"

"Something like that."

"I'm still nervous."

"You are a Mage Warrior now, Thomas. *Nervous* is not in your vocabulary."

"I'm gonna trust you on that one. Wish me luck."

"I believe it was your President Jefferson who said it best. 'I am a great believer in luck, and I find the harder I work, the more I have of it.' "

"Don't start with the quotes. It's hard enough with Billy Shakespeare over there." Itsuki stopped and bowed to Thomas.

"*Gokouun o inorimasu*," said Itsuki. "Good luck, Thomas." The two wisps stopped and hovered on either side of the Augmentor.

Thomas leapt off of the edge, down into the open clearing. The sun hung low in the evening sky. Ziza stood with his jeweled staff in the center of the clearing. Next to him stood Emfalmay. Thomas walked towards the elderly man as the wind smacked against the young man's ears.

"Take it easy on him," said Emfalmay.

"I will," said Thomas.

"I wasn't talking to you." The Lion patted Thomas on the shoulder as he walked away. "Good luck."

"Thanks a lot." Thomas turned towards Ziza. There was a calm silence shared between the two men. The young man disturbed the quiet. "Can you answer me one question?"

"Certainly, Thomas," said Ziza smiling.

"Well, Itsuki said it was damn near impossible to find the Temple because it shifts. So I was just wondering . . . how did you find me?"

"I started to get worried after the seventy-two hours had passed, and I had tried to reach each of you, but you must have been at the Temple by then because I could not establish communication. I had partially deciphered the stone's message and wanted to inform you of its implications."

"What did it say?"

"I thought it would be simple—at first, because of their similarity to the Ancient language, but there was something vastly different with these markings. There was a darkness to them." The old man paused. "It was a warning. The word PRISON was all I could decrypt, but it was enough. Your mother must have been trying to warn whoever found the stone. I could not believe it at first, but it all began to make sense. The Gauntlet must have reverted back to an extremely prehistoric form of communication. The marks on the dark stone were part of that forgotten language. It will take some time and research for me to decipher all of the symbols, but this could help us discover more about the Gauntlet and its origins."

"That doesn't explain how you knew where I was."

"Do not forget, Thomas. I too was once one with the Gauntlet." The High Mancer paced to his left. "I can sense its energy signature anywhere on the planet, although its anything but easy. It took a great deal of concentration to find you, but once the battle between you and Arkmalis began, anyone with such powers could sense what was going on." Ziza looked back at Thomas. "I must admit, I was not sure you could take him."

"To be honest, neither was I." The two laughed aloud. "Well shall we get this started?"

"Ah . . . always in a rush." He gingerly paced. "My boy, you are quite powerful. There is no denying that. You more than proved yourself against Arkmalis. And you also have proved you have control, but there is something that you do not have and that is technique. I was foolish to not immediately start training you myself, but there was no way to predict Grimm's interference." The old man looked down at the staff and placed both hands on it. "I am going to show you how to fight, Thomas, but first I'm going to need to assess your skill level."

"So we're gonna fight." Thomas gulped.

"You think you are ready?"

"Can one ever be ready to fight a five-hundred-year-old wizard?" The two exchanged glances. "I'm as ready as I'm gonna get." The young man's eyes began to burn with energy.

"I could start out slowly, Thomas, if you'd like." Ziza knelt down into an attack stance and pointed his staff at the young man. The stone on the top of the staff radiated green. His pupils did the same.

"That won't be necessary, and besides . . . " Thomas kicked his right leg back and twisted his hips. He slowly pulled the stone glove back. The rock palm began to glow the familiar blue tint. "I don't know if this is such a good idea for someone your age. What if you throw out your hip or something?" Thomas looked at the old man and smiled.

"I believe there is something to be said about experience, my boy." Ziza's staff blurred in the direction of Thomas as the young man's gauntleted hand pushed forward into the night air.

"Haaaaaaaaaaaaaaaaaaaaaaaaaaaaa!"

dramatis personae

the shadow of the gauntlet

sigmund jacobs	an archeologist
dr. carl scargen	a robotic engineer
thomas scargen	a chronic slacker
LINC	an artif
stella	a cat
yareli chula	a Spirit Summoner
wiyaloo	a Spirit Ghost Warrior
bartleby draige	a teleport dragon
captain marcus slade	Captain of the Aringi Riders
gibgot	a lava troll guard
fronic	a lava troll guard
corbin	an imp servant
evangeline the second	an Aringi Rider
dalco jakobsen	an Aringi Rider
general grayden arkmalis	General of the Grimm Legions
franklin hawthorne	a robotic engineer
ELAIN	a holographic interface
fargus hexelby	a gremlin technic
webster	a dragon's dog
orac	a Seer
lenore bugden	a gremlin
ronald hosselfot	a tech dealer
girard lesinge	a tech dealer
thatcher wikkaden	a Hunter
pekora	a Hunter
okland	a Hunter
nicolas gorter	a Re-psyche

acknowledgments

the shadow of the gauntlet

I would like to thank. . .

My Kickstarter backers—for making this possible
My first readers: Johnny "Oz" King, Gerry Burke, Jake Jacobson, Bryan Gulla, Nina Giacobbe, Cory Sweeney, Danny Edelman, Jeff Moore, Sean Guinan, Margaret Harris, and Jo & Marlin Corn—for your kind and extremely helpful feedback
Matthew Glazar—for being the first kid to discover the Gauntlet
Matt Suydam—for being a daily sounding board
My parents—for letting me be weird
Mrs. Hughes & Mr. Barbetta—for showing me the power of words
Caitie Caroleo—for being there for my wife
Matt Errico—for believing
Richard & Alexandra Sumner—for getting my back
Brett Gormley—for listening to my crazy nonsense for decades
Stu & Dawn Moriens—for everything you two have done for us
Mason Caracciolo—for geeking out with his little brother
William Shakespeare—for your words and wit and for Anson
Shanna Compton—for making my vision a beautifully typeset reality
Joe Hansche—for being tremendously particular
Christine—for constantly loving, editing, and being there for me
Stella—for being the perfect little monster and the best writing buddy anyone could've asked for. You will be forever in our hearts.

Casey Caracciolo has been creating fantastical worlds and characters since he was a child growing up in Bensalem, Pennsylvania. His active imagination coupled with his thirst for dynamic storytelling drove Caracciolo over the years to become a lover of all things geek. This love found a purpose in the fall of 2007, when Caracciolo began developing the concept for the Scargen series. In this series, Caracciolo wanted to create a world that seamlessly blended magic and technology. This futuristic world serves as the

photo by Dallas Gutauckis

backdrop for the coming-of-age adventures of Thomas Scargen.

Casey has spent the last six years working on *The Shadow of the Gauntlet*, the first installment of the Scargen series. *The Shadow of the Gauntlet* is Casey's first novel and was published in 2013 by Roundstone Publishing. He is currently working on *The Dragon Within*, the second book in the Scargen series.

When not writing, Casey is a bartender at Triumph Brewing Company in New Hope, Pennsylvania. He lives in Lambertville, New Jersey, with his wife, Christine, and their cat, Stella.

To learn more about Casey or the Scargen universe, visit:

scargen.com